ANOTHER LIFE

This Large Print Book carries the
Seal of Approval of N.A.V.H.

A BURKE NOVEL

ANOTHER LIFE

ANDREW VACHSS

THORNDIKE PRESS
A part of Gale, Cengage Learning

GALE
CENGAGE Learning

Detroit • New York • San Francisco • New Haven, Conn • Waterville, Maine • London

GALE
CENGAGE Learning

Copyright © 2008 by Andrew Vachss.
Thorndike Press, a part of Gale, Cengage Learning.

Thorndike Press® Large Print Core.
The text of this Large Print edition is unabridged.
Other aspects of the book may vary from the original edition.
Set in 16 pt. Plantin.
Printed on permanent paper.

LIBRARY OF CONGRESS CATALOGING-IN-PUBLICATION DATA

Vachss, Andrew H.
   Another life : a Burke novel / by Andrew Vachss.
     p. cm. — (Thorndike Press large print core)
   ISBN-13: 978-1-4104-1382-6 (alk. paper)
   ISBN-10: 1-4104-1382-9 (alk. paper)
   1. Burke (Fictitious character)—Fiction. 2. Private
investigators—New York (State)—New York—Fiction. 3. Saudi
Arabians—United States—Fiction. 4. Child molesters—Fiction.
5. Children—Crimes against—Fiction. 6. Kidnapping—Fiction. 7.
Terrorists—Fiction. 8. New York (N.Y.)—Fiction. 9. Large type
books. I. Title.
PS3572.A33A755 2009
813'.54—dc22   2008048154

Published in 2009 by arrangement with Pantheon Books, a division of
Random House, Inc.

Printed in the United States of America
1 2 3 4 5 6 7 13 12 11 10 09

for Pam

Revenge is like any other religion: There's always a lot more preaching than there is practicing. And most of that preaching is about what *not* to practice.

"Vengeance is mine" translates to: "It's not *yours*." The karma-peddlers will tell you how doing nothing is doing the right thing, reciting, "What goes around comes around" in that heavy-gravity tone reserved for the kind of ancient wisdom you always find in comic books.

Every TV "counselor," every self-help expert, every latte-slurping guru . . . they all chant some version of the same mantra: "Revenge never solves anything."

Their favorite psalm is Forgiveness. And

their hymn books are always open to the same page.

Get it? When you crawl away, you're not being a punk; you're just letting the cosmos handle your business. Whoever hurt you, they'll get theirs, don't worry. Just have a little faith.

Down here, we see it different. We don't count on karma. But you can count on this: hurt one of us, we're *all* coming for you.

A low-level maggot once got a little taste of power and overdosed on it. He murdered a thirteen-year-old girl after three privileged little weasels who had started the fun ran to him for help.

The boys hadn't *meant* to kill her; they were good kids who just got a little carried away. All they wanted was to gang-rape the little cock-teaser, take some pictures . . . teach her what it cost to humiliate people of their status. But when the girl suddenly stopped moving, their freakish plan tumbled out of control.

Terrified, they offered the maggot anything he wanted if he'd dump the body for them.

But when he arrived at the abandoned house where they'd left the girl, he discovered she wasn't actually dead — passed out from the pain, but still breathing, leaking blood. He touched her throat, found a good, strong pulse. If he'd taken her to the ER, she would have made it.

Instead, he went to work on her. His kind of work.

That little girl lasted a few more minutes. Alive in terror and praying for death.

More than thirty years later, the maggot and the three grownup weasels were blown away. They went out together — never saw it coming.

We got paid to do that.

Now *we're* paying.

The sniper who had pinned my father to the ground as we were making our getaway is gone, too. An on-target warhead from an RPG had turned the stone-shielded corner he'd been firing from into an incinerator big enough for him and the rest of the hired guns up there with him.

So many died that day. Every time my heart pumps, regret pulses through my bloodstream.

That's the worst thing about killing certain humans: you can only do it once.

"What more can we do, mahn? My father is somewhere between this world and the next. He must stay — his *body* must stay — with those people until he comes back to us. If he were only in a real hospital . . ."

"We've been through this," I told Clarence. "A thousand times, ever since it happened. You think we can, what, call a city ambulance? The Prof's prints would fall like a cinderblock on an egg. They'd handcuff him to the bed and turn the whole place into a goddamn PBA convention."

"I could —"

"You can't do *anything!*" I snapped at him, as sharply as his father would have.

"When *you* were shot —"

"Your father — *my* father, too, remember? — *he* made the call then. And he made the right one. This one isn't the same; the minute we unhook the Prof from those machines, he's done. This call was on me to make, and I made it. Now we have to play it out."

"If any of those doctors —"

Max pulled at the sleeve of Clarence's jacket, the same dove-gray cashmere he'd been wearing the night we dropped the Prof off — now it was almost black, darkened with fear. When Clarence looked up, the mute Mongolian made the universal gesture of pointing his finger like a pistol and dropping his thumb like a hammer. Then tapped his temple, and made a facial expression that spoke louder than words.

"You think those medical boys don't fucking *know* that?" I echoed. "They're not worried about some malpractice claim. They're running an outlaw operation, and they get paid a fortune to take care of people from our world. That's what we're paying so much for: not just the care, the risk — they're putting a lot more than their licenses on the line, understand? That's why you never threaten people like them — they've heard it all before. It won't make them work harder. But it might scare them into doing something stupid."

"But . . . for what they are charging, even with all the money we took from that last . . . thing, we will run out by —"

"I know," I said soothingly. "But don't worry about it, Clarence. We found a new way to keep earning."

"Nobody told me —"

"You had no role to play in this one, son," I said, channeling the Prof. "Not up till now, anyway."

"Listen to me, sweetheart." Michelle spoke just above a whisper, her voice the same mystery-blend as her perfume. "Trust me, the word's out: the Prof's in the consultant business now. Any serious thief playing for a retirement score would want the

Master to check over the plans, make sure there's no flaw. But they wouldn't expect a face-to-face. So the Prof's got a front man for that. Get it?"

"Yes," the Islander said, looking over at me and nodding. "But how is that going to bring in the kind of money we — ?"

"It already is," I cut him off. "Got more business than we can handle. We're even ready to have you start working backup, too. If you want."

Clarence opened his mouth to say something, but Max just shook his head.

Mama crossed the distance from her register at the front to my booth in the back. Looked us all over. Held Clarence with her eyes. Said, "Movie business very good. Those kind of people, spend money like drunks."

Clarence opened his mouth again, but this time it was Michelle who shut him up. "We've got a doctor too, baby. A *script* doctor. Best in the business. The only one who gets his quote *and* a percentage of the gross. Let's you and me go over there and sit down, okay? Buy your baby sister a drink, and I'll explain it all to you."

The apartment was spacious by New York standards. Three bedrooms, two baths. And on a decent West Side block, too.

But this was no luxury co-op. No awning over the front door. No doorman, never mind a concierge. No central air. The elevator only went down — *all* the way down. From a uniformed operator, to push-your-own-damn-buttons, to permanent "Out of Service."

Even the super was part-time. His one qualification was that he'd *done* time, and his real job was handling complaints with a "you don't want to go too far with this" look.

Thirty-six units, but only five of them still occupied. The building owner was warehousing the rest, playing stare-down with the remaining owners. No real-estate broker had any of the empty units listed.

Some of the holdouts had been stupid enough to try bribing the super. He introduced them to the Sucker Two-Step. Step one, he takes your money. Step two comes when you run into him again — a blank look, like he's never seen you before.

When it comes to bribery, citizens are out of their league. Even in this everything-for-sale pesthole of a city, you can't run to the cops when the guy you greased doesn't do what you paid him for — that would be like a loan shark suing you for missing a payment.

We paid the super for access to the apartment. Not a bribe: payment for a service. He didn't try his look on us — it's our kind he learned it from. He wasn't a genius, but he was smart enough not to confuse us with citizens.

The cell phone in the right-hand pocket of my jacket vibrated. My clients were on their way up . . . up the stairs. I nodded to Max. He opened the door just as they were about to push the disconnected buzzer.

The doctor was in.

There were three of them. Nice business suits, nothing too flashy. I knew the headman by rep only. He may have looked like a pita pocket overstuffed with suet, but if crime was a dance, he had the moves of a tango star.

The other two could have been his partners. Or crew members, or undercover cops. The way we had it set up, it didn't make any difference. Any tape they walked away with would be about as useful as a Vietnam body count.

My worktable was a rough-hewn slab of wood with fold-up legs. I gestured for them to sit wherever they wanted. Canvas director's chairs were the only option.

Nobody offered to shake hands. As I leaned back, Michelle swiveled over. All they saw was a blonde in a red latex derma-sheath skirt and a padded bra threatening a stretchy top — if they even looked high enough up to see the blonde part. She held out a tray of plain glass ashtrays. The guy to the left of the headman took one, placed it carefully in front of him.

Michelle snake-hipped her way out of the room, making it clear that they'd already experienced the full extent of our hospitality. No minibar in this hotel, and the only room service you could order was already *in* the room.

The headman opened a document case, took out some paper and a chrome pen. He cleared his throat, said:

"Now, the way we've got this scripted, the wealthy guy's seen all the movies, so he wouldn't rely on any motion-sensor system. He thinks you can blow talcum powder into the room, make all the laser beams show up." His smile was room-temperature.

I consulted the graph-paper pad in front of me. It was covered in tiny, autistic symbols. "So he's afraid some gymnast in a leotard —"

"You got it," the raisin-eyed pile of dough

15

seated across from me agreed. "We're looking for *realism* here. Remember, this is an
indie production; we don't have a few extra
million to waste on special effects. So —
what the guy in *our* script does, he keeps
the stuff in a bunker."

"You mean like one of those old-time
bomb shelters, or just a safe buried in the
ground?"

"Totally fucking nuclear," the blob said,
catching a confirmatory nod from the non-
smoker to his right — a solidly built guy in
his forties who was either too image-
conscious to be saying, "Yeah, boss," in
front of strangers, or an undercover still
feeling his way. It had been that guy's call
to Mama's that set this ride in motion, but
he wasn't the one with the gas money.

"You have him *living* in there?" I asked the
boss. "Inside the bunker, I mean?"

"Nah. But he *could,* is the point."

"You're saying, in this script, the way it's
set up, all he has to do is make it inside the
bunker before the take-away guys get to
him, right? Then he could just kick back in
the La-Z-Boy, toss some porno into his
DVD player, and sip fine wine until the cops
show up?"

"Not cops," the blob said, with an absolute
sureness that meant whatever they intended

to snatch was something the victim couldn't report to his insurance company. Straight out of the pro thief's bible: the best thing to steal is stolen property.

"Cops, *guaranteed*," I contradicted him. "Sure, a guy with whatever this one's got stashed away isn't going to give the Law a chance to see it for themselves. So he's going to have all kinds of communication equipment in there . . . probably an underground cable to an Internet connection that you'd have to dig up the whole backyard to find. All he needs to do is go online, click a mouse, and in comes the cavalry. His *own* cavalry."

"Not a chance," the headman dismissed my concerns. "Look, unless whatever this guy's got stashed — that doesn't matter, we can write it in later — actually gets taken, there's no movie. We *start* from there, which means he never makes it into the bunker."

"Get real," I shot back. "You're trying to tell me, the kind of neighborhood where you have this one set, people hear an explosion big enough to blast open that bunker, they're *not* going to be hitting nine-one-one like an old lady in Atlantic City jacking the lever on the slots?"

All three of them nodded without exchanging looks. None of them spoke.

"Bottom line: you need to flip this whole script," I told them. "When you show the heist team planning the job, they have to be figuring on two things: one, the guy with the stash never makes it into his bunker, and, two, *they* do. This isn't some safe you'd be cracking, or even a bank vault. Not only would you need a lot more than a few vials of nitro, you'd have to be working outdoors, with no cover. One nosy neighbor and you never even get a chance to blast your way in. And, like I said, even if you could, the place would be surrounded by the time you walked out."

"Well, what, then?" the blob asked. He wasn't agitated or annoyed, just expecting to get what he'd paid for. All thieves at his level were practicing Utilitarians: if you had skills they wanted, they had the price . . . and the patience. To this guy, everything was job-dependent. For some scores, a molecular biologist would be hired help. For this one, he needed a script doctor who wasn't going to go running to the Guild demanding screen credit.

Life's a gamble; all that ever changes is the odds. But in my world, there's no track take-out on the betting pool, and no IRS waiting at the finish line if your horse comes in.

And men like the blob sitting across from me only make one of two bets: fold, or all-in.

"So he doesn't *live* in the bunker?" I asked, giving him the choice.

The blob went all-in. "He's crazy, but not that kind of crazy."

"So it's all down to timing, then."

He made an "I'm listening" gesture.

The guy to his left reached into his jacket. I couldn't see behind him, but I knew a red laser-dot had just blossomed on the back of his neck. Clarence. Positioned around the corner — triangle-braced, a silenced 9mm in his hands. At that distance he could center-punch a microbe.

The guy came out with a single cigarette, lit up, carefully blew the smoke away from me.

My turn. "So the tension-point is, the thieves have got to get to this guy *before* he gets to the bunker. Agreed?"

"Okay, but we're showing him like one of those nigger bosses. Not here, I mean, like in Africa. Never goes anywhere without a fucking army around him. Not bodyguards, guys who hold rank."

"Drives an armored car?" I asked, wishing these guys would remember to stay in character, but not all that disappointed. To

19

be disappointed, first you have to be surprised.

"*Gets* driven," the headman said. "There's companies who'll make one for you. Any specs you want: bulletproof glass, armored sides, blast-plate underneath, all that. You end up with a four-ton Caddy or whatever, but, for driving around the city, who cares? But if you blow up the car with him in it, you might never get inside that bunker. That ruins everything. The plot, I mean."

I closed my eyes for a minute, as if I was working through the script again. Scribbled a few more symbols on my pad.

"What do we know about them?" I asked.

"Who?"

"The ones who go everywhere with the general."

"How's that important?" the blob asked, leaning forward with his voice, the way his body would have if it could.

"Well, this isn't a blank-page script you're consulting me on. My job is just fixing the ending. If you want me to figure out how to make it work, I have to know what I'm working *with*."

He glanced at the man to his left. Said: "Let's say maybe we could show the audience some of their private lives, if we had to."

I grudgingly gave him a little credit for at least *trying* to stay in character, said, "You'd have to get in pretty deep to make that work."

"Girlfriend-on-the-side, you're thinking?"

"No," I dismissed that nonsense. "Good enough excuse if you need a sex scene, but it won't work for getting to whatever's inside that bunker. What we need is their *personalities*. How they got to be where they are. You're not talking about hired help here. From the way you've got it scripted, these are guys he came up with."

"From the sandbox."

"And this guy, he's not a family man."

"Only thing this guy knows about guineas is that they do nice tile work," the blob said, grinning. The man on his right tightened his face. Just a touch, but more than I needed to make the diagnosis.

"So the people around this guy, *close* to him, there has to be a way they got there," I said. "I mean, none of *them* are on top. You said your man was the ace, right? So the guys under him, how did *those* cards get dealt?"

The blob's face flexed enough to show me he was on the same page.

"We're not looking for a bent guy we can turn. The way in is to find one who wants to *be* the ace, understand?" I asked, making sure.

"How — ?"

"Parallelism," I said, letting my Hollywood expertise show. "We could split the screen: One side, we show a little military coup, like the one they had in Fiji. On the other side, it's the same thing, only it's happening to *your* guy. Nobody's dressed in uniforms, but we get the same result . . . total take-over."

"But *our* guy, he can't be killed," the blob said. "Just because a man's close to the king don't mean he's got the keys to the castle. *Keys,* get it?"

I twisted my lips to certify the blob's cleverness. After all, he was the wordsmith; I was just the man he was hiring to consult on a script-fix project.

"Then it comes down to surveillance," I said. "Plenty of ways to show that, but it could cost a lot of screen time. Better to add a reach-out."

"Reach-out means sell-out?"

"More than that," I told the blob. "The character you're looking for, money won't work. What he wants is to *be* the man, not work for him, okay? And when the target's in his own car, surrounded by his own boys, that's when he's most vulnerable."

"You're losing me."

"The plot hinges on what the target keeps in that bunker of his, right?"

"Right."

"And he built it to be blast-proof?"

The blob nodded.

"He's the only one who knows how to open it?"

Another nod.

"Okay, then. You have to get to him before he gets inside. That's the plot-point, like you said — everything works off that. Either this guy's got some kind of disguised door-opener that's always with him, or there's some other way in, like a touchpad code number. Either way, he has to be *made* to give it up, and that could take some time."

Another nod.

"Okay, picture this: Four men in the car. One's the boss, the *only* one with the key. We want one of the others, the one who needs to *be* the boss. Find him; make the deal. And then it comes down to this: four get in, two get out."

"Does it have to be the *driver* who turns?"

"It can be anyone you want," I said. "Hell, it's a movie, not real life, so what does it matter? The guy who thinks he's going to end up being the boss, nobody's going to pat *him* down, right? And we know the *boss* won't be doing the driving.

"Your guy makes his move while they're still parked. Remember, those armored cars, they've got blacked-out windows and tons of baffling; he wouldn't even need a silencer.

"Two quick pops, and the four is down to two. Then the shooter taps his cell phone, and your people move in. One of *your* guys gets in behind the wheel, then both cars take off.

"Once the patsy hands over the boss — the *ex*-boss now, he thinks — you can write your own ending."

It took them only a couple of minutes to get out of the building, but it took us the rest of the afternoon to move the table and chairs down to the basement, scour the apartment, and give the whole area a final visual sweep.

If anyone ever came back there, the only difference between it and the other warehoused units would be that the one we'd used would be CSI-clean.

Not all the scripts were for major productions.

One group was very interested in a plot where the bad guys get a service tech to swap out the hard drive in one of those gigantic pay-to-use photocopy machines you can find in any of those joints that offer copying, fax, printing, and anything else a hustler with a cell phone needs to set up his "office."

In my revised screenplay, the new hard drive looks exactly like the one that came with the machine, but this one has a little USB port — just plug in a programmed memory stick and wait for it to fill up. Most of what you siphon out is useless, but it's like panning for gold — all you need is one big nugget, and they have search programs for that.

Always amazes me how people think they're being "anonymous" by using a public library or an Internet café. Keep clearing that cache, suckers; *that'll* fucking do it. Clowns who sign up for some free service that "anonymizes" their e-mails never stop to think that while they're flaming each other in newsgroups, somebody else is collecting all their *actual* addresses . . . IPs and all.

You can usually turn stupidity into money, but any good 419 man knows it takes more than stupidity alone to sell the heavier schemes. That recipe always needs at least a pinch of greed to make it palatable enough to swallow.

Nigeria originated this con — "419" is a section of their criminal law — so they get scam-trademark status, like "Ponzi scheme." The mark gets an overseas e-mail from someone who has managed to "divert" a certain sum of money — twenty million or so — by depositing it in a Swiss bank. But this person has a problem, which is why he's contacting you. A source, who cannot be named, has vouched for you as a person of discretion, honesty, and intelligence.

The current fave is Nepal. Now the source can vouch for your deep concern for human rights, too.

Of course, this person can't transfer that kind of money to *his* bank account; that's where you come in. All you have to do is open a Swiss account of your own — detailed instructions included. Soon as you do that, the money he "diverted" gets transferred to you. After a suitable waiting period, you send it back to the thief. Of course, there would be a commission involved for your trouble — say, 10 percent? All you have to do is open that account, wait a little bit . . . and *presto!* you're a couple of million to the good.

That's where your honesty comes in. Your new pal is counting on you to come through, do the right thing, take care of him. After all, you've been vouched for, so he knows you won't just keep the whole twenty mil for yourself, the way some crooks would.

Costs nine grand to open your own Swiss account. Should be more, of course, but everyone knows you've got to stay under ten on wire transfers, and the last thing anyone wants is the government — any government — poking its nose into *this* one, right, pal? What could be simpler?

You couldn't be, sucker. Open that Swiss account, send the password, and your nine grand is vacuumed out in seconds. The stupider — or greedier — you are, the longer it takes you to wake up and smell the scam.

Ah, it's not that bad. You get to go on TV and tell the world how you were "victimized." And how you're just telling your story because you want to protect others who might fall into the same insidious trap.

Uh-huh.

The Internet didn't create kiddie porn, but it sure made selling it easier. Spam-and-scam artists don't even have to spend money on postage or faxes anymore. But they still need a database to work from.

So help yourself to another "free" e-mail address. Post your contact information on your "personal" Web site. Add your kid's photo to your blog. Then call me a cold-hearted bastard when I don't give a damn about you being "cyber-stalked."

"My father is one of Jah's Men," Clarence said. "Jah's protection is on him, always."

Michelle shot him a look. She held it only a nanosecond before shifting it to me, but she was way too slow — Clarence could beat a scorpion to the draw.

"No, no, little sister," he told her, not offended. "You think I mean those boys who wear their dreads and beads, smoke the ganja, listen to reggae? No. I am not speaking of some club you can join, like being a Rasta-man. Jah's Men are *chosen*."

"The Prof always said he had the call —"

"You see, then?"

"You can be called *home,* too, son," I said, not pulling the punch.

"He is not going," the young man said, his voice so heavy with his own helplessness that the words fell of their own weight.

Max held his hands apart. Glanced from one to the other. Bowed slightly.

"If he goes, it would be his choice," I translated.

"My father would never surrender."

"Couldn't spell the word," I agreed. "But I want to ask you a question, Clarence. And

I want you to *listen,* okay?"

He nodded, brotherhood overpowering resentment.

"If you had the choice of living so that you had no control over what you do, a brain inside a body, but no power over that body, would you choose that life? Would you want someone to feed you, change your diaper — ?"

"I would never allow —"

"I know you'd do it for him, Clarence. He knows, too. You think he wants to put you in that position? You want that to be his last thought? The last thing he sees? You want to take that from him? This is your *father!* Show some respect."

The young man broke, sobs razoring his heart. Michelle moved close to him, just barely touching physically, but still holding him.

"John Henry never dies on his knees, I reminded my little brother."

Silence dropped like a shroud, transporting us all back to how the Prof had ended up caught between worlds.

Clarence blasted the Roadrunner down the narrow corridor like he was running for pinks. I spotted a black blotch against the wall just ahead, screamed: "Stop!"

The four-piston calipers locked like a heavy anchor in hot tar. I was out the door while it was still skidding, hit the ground rolling.

"Prof!" I screamed. The little man was lying with his back to the wall. I couldn't see anything but blood where his right thigh should have been.

I knelt next to him as Clarence charged toward us, holding his pistol like a voodoo fetish against the descending panic.

"Get that ride outta here, quick!" the Prof gasped. "Too big a target."

"Prof —"

"I was inside, 'cross the way," the little man wheezed out. He twisted his head toward a closed-down factory building. "I was on full ghost, but the motherfuckers peeped me anyway — must have had an electronic eye somewhere. I thought I'd got away clean, but they got a rifleman on the top floor. Left corner window."

Pain flashed across his face. "Ten, twelve more of them up there with him, too. Full gear. Probably be coming down this way any second." A warrior's grin drove the pain from his eyes. "That is, if they got the balls — I fed 'em some lead before I fled. Now go!"

"We will not —"

"You hush, boy!" the Prof snapped at Clarence. "I'm all done, son. But I can buy you enough time to get gone."

"Father . . ."

The Prof's eyelids fluttered. My turn: "Get the car around that corner, where that sniper can't see it," I ordered Clarence. "Pop the trunk. I've got something in there for him."

The Prof's eyes snapped back into life. A bubble of blood was in his mouth from where he'd bitten into his lip to revive himself. "Do like you told, boy!" he barked, his hard voice too full of love to be disobeyed.

A piece of the wall flew off just above us. I hadn't heard the shot — the shooter must be using a suppressor.

"Cocksucker ain't hardly no Wesley," the little man sneered. "I been laying here like a paper target, and he already missed me twice."

I leaned close, needing to catch every word, but desperate to get to my car.

"Honor thy father," he whispered. "Call my name, son. My true name. Call it! Call it *loud,* so those whores know who's gonna be barring the door."

"John Henry!" I screamed with everything I had in me.

The war cry pulled the Prof back from the brink. I could see a golden blaze flare in his all-seeing brown eyes.

"Fetch me my hammer, son!" the little man

commanded. "Time to drive some steel for real."

I was frozen — trapped between the two most compelling forces of my life.

"Get gone, Schoolboy," he assured me. "I'll be waiting when you show up. Me and that hound of yours."

I kissed him. Another shot splattered concrete dust over us both. I pulled a fistful of double-zero shells from the Prof's side pocket, lined them up on his right side. Found his sawed-off 12-gauge a few feet away, placed it reverently in his right hand. Then I ran for the corner.

The Roadrunner's trunk was open, but Clarence wasn't in the car. He was down on one knee, pistol out, a rabid wolf on a gossamer leash.

I grabbed the RPG out of the trunk, shouldered it, shouted, "Get behind the fucking wheel!" . . . and ran back the way I'd come.

The Prof was still down, but his sawed-off was up and ready for business. The concrete around his leg was a spreading red stain.

He never saw me as I dropped to one knee, sighted, and let loose at the sniper's roost, screaming, *"Die!"* inside my heart, like I'd been doing since I was a kid. I could actually feel my hate raging inside that whistling warhead, deadlier than the shaped charge it carried.

■ ■ ■ ■

In some professions, plastic surgery is a business expense. I remember a woman whose husband's cash had greased the skids for her political career. She finally overdosed on her own press releases and decided her act could play even better in a bigger room. Desperate to stay telegenic, she'd had so many facelifts that her eyes became the side-glancing goggles of natural-born prey.

The only difference between her and the "dancers" who buy spine-herniating implants is the price they pay to stay on the stage.

On my side of the law, you don't use plastic surgery to steal; you use it so you can *keep* stealing.

So when I didn't recognize the face of the slender, colorless man who showed up for the script consult, I didn't have an anxiety attack.

The guy who had called to hire my services was an established pro, but violence wasn't in his repertoire. I'd never known his name, and a new face might have been a smart investment, considering he was a specialized-target art thief who never varied his MO.

He put in years of research on Nazi-looted canvases. Not the ones in museums or sitting in Swiss bank vaults; the ones kept, very discreetly, in trophy rooms.

The paintings aren't the trophies; the power to acquire them is. And such power must be displayed.

This guy had everything he needed to get himself invited to some of those displays: that unbeatable combo of contacts, connections, and cash.

He wasn't one of those hit-or-miss thieves who have their bondsman's name memorized. No, this guy was so slick you'd have a better chance of picking up a drop of mercury with a pair of Teflon toothpicks. Plenty of high-skill operators could brag they'd never been arrested; this guy had never been *suspected.*

He could only make a move every few years, and his expenses were high, but he never let ego interfere with his pursuit of perfection. For him, paying for a script consultation was nothing more than checking the "extra insurance" box on a rental car.

But as soon as the man sitting across from me put his hands on the table, I knew he wasn't the art thief. It was the webbed fingers that tipped me. And I knew the tip was deliberate.

After the first time we'd met, a few life-times ago, I'd done some research. "Simple syndactyly" is what doctors call his condition. "Simple" means only the flesh is joined, not the bone; the attachment only goes as far as the first set of knuckles.

The condition is congenital — you're born with it — and easily correctable. Best if the surgery is performed during infancy or as soon as possible afterwards, but it can be done at any age, and it's about as low on the risk scale as any flesh-cutting could be.

No question that the man across from me — Pryce was the name I knew him by — could afford the best. But he liked his little jokes. I figure that's where he picked his name from, too.

Why he changed his face so many times but always left his physical ID in place was something it might take an army of therapists to unravel.

I smiled to myself at the thought: the only way Pryce would ever go near a mind-man would be to hire him to probe into someone else. A surgeon's scalpel can only open your flesh, not your secrets.

I didn't know what Pryce wanted, but having the art-thief specialist make the call was his way of telling me he knew what I was doing for a living these days. Getting a man to make a phone call isn't hard if you can get him killed just by making one yourself. Pryce was a certified no-limit man. Everyone in my world knew the only thing he *wouldn't* do was bluff.

The first time we'd met, he told me he'd planted an informant inside one of those "leaderless cells" that were all the rage in the White Night underground after Oklahoma City. The "agent" he was running had an infant son, but his wife had fled with the baby. She was somewhere inside a safe house, one run by a network Pryce had never penetrated.

I'd known about Pryce for a long time before that meeting. *Of* him, anyway. He was some kind of psycho-patriot, a man who drew his own maps. But he was a purist in his own way: whatever he worked for wasn't people, it was some . . . concept in his deranged mind. Administrations changed; Pryce didn't.

The cell where his informant was planted was planning some major act of terrorism, details not yet known. One problem: the informant was demanding possession of his son as payment for staying on the job.

I had a problem, too, but picking a winner wouldn't fix it. I needed to hit the exacta: a walk-away for my brother Hercules, who'd finally managed to bulldoze his fool self into an escape-proof box, *and* a disappearance for the same baby Pryce wanted to hand over to his informant.

We made a trade.

That was then. Now he was sitting across from me again. Just a couple of old buddies, playing five-card stud. The minute he let me recognize him, we were down to his last draw, but that didn't matter — it was his hole card I had to pay to see. So I kept playing . . . playing like he was there for the "script consult" the art thief had called about.

"The way to make this work is change the house to a custom-built one," I said, tapping my pad.

"What good does that — ?"

"The guy you're looking for would be a subcontractor. The electrician, specifically. Anything he installs, he knows how to make it malfunction. Just a little twist on the standard route. The pro burglar looks for the guy who reads the gas meter, the maid, anyone who has regular inside access. What he ends up with is the whole schematic: floor plans, security systems, like that.

"That's fine for cash or jewels, but not for what your script calls for. No maid ever gets near your target's trophy room; the meter reader probably doesn't even know it exists. The architect would know there's space there, but not what it's used for. When it comes to lighting, air quality, temperature, stuff like that, the electrician's the one you want."

"But wouldn't the cops immediately suspect him?" Pryce said, still playing the role.

"If anyone reported the theft, they might."

He nodded.

"Okay," I went on. "So the way the script starts, the star's just a regular B and E man. Top-quality, but no specialist. One night, he gets inside a house. The camera shows him looking around for the goods. Then he stumbles across the trophy room.

"Soon as he sees it, he knows there's *something* special kept in there. All this money spent just to build a setup like that, whatever's inside has to be worth serious bucks.

"Immediately, he knows he's out of his league. So he slips out without taking anything. Then he starts poking around — you can have him doing it on the Net; there's Web sites that list the stuff, with images and everything. Makes a nice visual, too. *That's* when your guy has this . . . what did you call it again?"

"Epiphany," the man across from me repeated.

"Right. So he finds that electrician. Pays him a fat wad of cash to *cause* the system to malfunction — that can be done over the line, no need to go anywhere near the house. Naturally, the trophy-collector calls the same guy who installed the system to come in and fix it. And while this electrician's doing that, earning triple-time plus a bonus, he plants a locator."

"A what?"

"You can program a device no bigger than this," I said, holding up a nickel-sized disk — same circumference, but much thinner — "so that it alerts at the presence of . . . hell, anything." This was like showing a surgeon what a scalpel looks like, but Pryce went along with the gag.

"Like canvas," he said, as if he'd just caught wise.

"Exactly. It's a transmitter. You download all the info, check off the *known* missing works, and one of them will match."

"That's brilliant," he said. "You should have been a screenwriter."

"And you should have just called."

Pryce shook his head. He opened his palm, the webbed fingers on snare-drummer's wrists underscoring that he hadn't tried to trick me. "I don't like phones. Besides, it's been a long time."

"Not long enough."

"Just in time, actually," he said, turning over his hole card: "A private hospital. Top of the line. Best doctors on the planet. And you can visit. All of you. In the state he's in, he hears your voices, it could make a difference. *All* the difference."

I didn't pretend I didn't know what he was talking about, but I sat back as if I was stunned, using the time to think of a way to get him to up the payoff. Because with what he was offering, he had to want something way off the charts in return.

"Herk and Vyra are doing fine," Pryce said, lighting a clove cigarette as he stepped inside my thoughts.

I made a "So what?" gesture with my shoulders. Vyra had been a lot of different things before she met Hercules, including a rich man's wife. When Herk disappeared, so had she.

"They wanted to get married," Pryce said, the expression on his face just short of rolling his eyes at the strangeness of some people. "New York has archaic laws for contested divorces. Adultery counts, and so does abandonment, but that's what *she* did, not him. The husband didn't want to let her

40

go. Not even when she offered to sign away everything, including the joint account and the house."

I shrugged.

"We could erase Hercules — right back to the cradle. But Vyra had no record to clean, and a name change would make any marriage to Herk void *ab initio.* That means —"

"That you speak Latin, or hang around too many lawyers."

"You want to know what happened or not?"

"I don't even know who you're babbling about," I said. Pryce's native tongue was Oblique, so maybe he was reminding me of the deal that put Herk inside the same cell where Pryce was running an informant . . . and the insurance policy I'd added. Not double indemnity, double-barreled. The policy turned Pryce's new man into his *only* man . . . and showed him who he'd really signed up with at the same time.

I played the old tape in my mind, knowing Pryce was doing the same.

The white Taurus was parked on the street. No other car was close, but the block wasn't deserted: People walking around, maybe from the change-of-shift at some of the nearby factories, maybe locals. Cars crawled by, too.

I pulled in behind, leaving myself room enough to drive away without backing up first. "Let's do it," I said to Herk.

Pryce must have been watching — the back doors of the sedan popped open as we walked toward it. We climbed in, Herk behind Pryce, me behind Lothar. Pryce turned to look at me. Lothar stared straight ahead, as if the windshield held vital secrets.

"All right, let's hear this big emergency of yours," Pryce half-sighed.

"I want Herk to get his immunity now," I told him. "Before this goes another step."

"That wasn't the —"

"That's the deal *now*," I said. "I've got a lawyer in place. You say when, he'll come downtown, you'll put the whole thing together. Probably take less than an hour."

"You can't expect to have that sort of payment in front," Pryce said, annoyed at my mulishness. "You know better than that. Everybody will get taken care of at the same time. As we *agreed*."

"Me, I think Lothar's already been taken care of."

"That's different," Pryce lied, switching to the flat officialese they teach you in FBI school. "Lothar is an undercover operative of the United States government."

"So's Herk, now."

42

"But my . . . employers don't *need* him," Pryce said, in the patient voice you use on a slow student. "They don't even know he exists yet."

"How do I know you're going to come through?"

"I've done everything I promised so far, haven't I? You're just going to have to trust me."

I sat there quietly as a woman trundled past, pulling one of those little grocery carts behind her. Then I took out a thick tube of baffled steel, said, "Lothar?" When he turned sideways to listen, I put a slug in his temple.

It didn't make much noise, even in the closed car.

"You got it wrong," I told Pryce, as Lothar slumped over. "You're going to have to trust *me.*"

Lothar's head lolled forward, his body held in place by the seatbelt. I grabbed a handful of his hair and pulled him back so it looked like he was just sitting there. There was no blood, just a round little black dot on his temple — a reverse birthmark. Some of the powder had been removed from the cartridge to make it subsonic; the slug was still somewhere in Lothar's diseased brain.

"You —"

Pryce cut himself off, out of words.

I wasn't. "Now we're gonna find out," I told him, watching his hands in case he moved wrong. If it came to that, Herk would have to snap his neck from behind — the piece I'd used couldn't be reloaded.

"Look," I said, my voice as calm as a Zen rock garden, "Lothar was stalking his wife. That's a fact, well-documented. There's even an Order of Protection; you know that, too. Now, *here's* what happened:

"Lothar was spotted breaking into his wife's house. She isn't there anymore, but he couldn't have known that. Lothar had all his freak-tools with him: handcuffs, duct tape. . . . He was going to kill his wife and kidnap the baby. But first he was going to teach that race-traitor bitch a lesson.

"Nine-one-one goes off. Luckily, a sector car's only a few blocks from the house. Soon as the cops roll up, Lothar knows he's done. Decides to shoot it out. Gunfire's exchanged.

"The result of that is sitting right next to you. Just add a few more rounds to the body. Use different guns — that way, more hero cops can get their medals. And be sure to blow away a chunk of his head.

"*That's* the story that needs to get in the news. The others in the cell will find out what happened, probably on TV. It won't surprise them, either. They all knew Lothar was a sex-

44

torture freak — look how they found him in the first place. And he never stopped ranting about what he wanted to do to his wife.

"Get it? That leaves Herk. *He's* your inside man now. Your *only* one. And he needs that immunity. Or the faucet gets turned off."

"You're insane," Pryce said, not turning around.

The street was quiet.

"People could argue about that, maybe," I told him. "But nobody's gonna argue about Lothar being dead."

"You expect me to drive around with a dead body and —"

"I don't care what you do. It's time to prove up now," I finished. "If you're the real thing, you can make it happen. And if you're not, it's all over, anyway.

"You got no more cards to play, Pryce. You thought you knew me. Now you do. You take down the safe house, you dime out Vyra to her husband, you turn Porkpie's testimony loose on Hercules — *any* of that, you're finished, pal. I don't care what you put in the street, you'll never find all of us, because you don't *know* all of us. But one of us will sure as hell find you."

"Get out of the car," he said in a tight, controlled voice. "Get out now. I'll call you."

We watched the white Taurus drive away.

Smooth and steady.

I crossed the bridge into Manhattan. Pulled up to a deli on Delancey. A Latino in an old army field jacket was leaning against the wall, just out of the rain. He walked over to my Plymouth.

Herk rolled down his window. The guy stuck his head inside, nodded at me. He went into the deli, came back with a paper bag full of sandwiches and a couple of bottles of apple juice.

I glove-handed him the wiped-down steel tube and a packet of five C-notes. He pocketed both and walked off.

Back in the car, Herk turned to me. "Burke, I'm with you, no matter what, you know that. I don't gotta understand why you did all that, but —"

"You know what happens when a raccoon gets his leg caught in one of those steel traps, brother? You know what he's got to do, he wants to live?"

"Bite the leg off," the big man said. He probably couldn't spell "education," but he had a Ph.D. in Survival.

"Yeah. There's two kinds of raccoons get caught in those traps. The ones with balls enough to do what they gotta do. And dead ones. A bitch raccoon gets in heat, she wants a stud that's gonna give her the strongest babies, understand? You know what she looks for? Not the biggest raccoon. Not the prettiest one, either. A smart bitch, she looks for one with three legs."

"I get it, Burke. But we got a problem. I think, anyway."

"What?"

"There's a meeting. Tonight."

"Damn! Why didn't you — ?"

"I forgot," the dumbfuck giant said glumly. "Until just now. I'm sorry."

"Jesus, Herk. Even if Pryce goes for it, he can't make it happen right now. He's gonna need a day or so, minimum. The best we can hope for is the newspaper story. I thought we'd get to stand by and watch: Pryce makes it happen, *then* I believe he can do the immunity thing, see? That's when I was going to have this lawyer I hired go in and tighten that up for you. But if you go to that meeting and Lothar isn't there . . ."

"He's not *supposed* to be there, right?"

"Huh?"

"I mean, he's supposed to be out stalking his wife, right? And if Pryce comes through, he gets smoked doing it. No way I could know about that. None of us could. Why shouldn't I just roll on into the meeting? It ain't like me and Lothar was supposed to be cut-buddies anyway."

47

"Herk, that's if Pryce goes along," I said, thinking maybe the big man wasn't half the dummy we all took him for. Not anymore, anyway. "That's *if* he can do it, even if he *wants* to. That's if he hasn't already decided to cut his losses and take down the whole fucking crew. If you knew about the meeting tonight, Lothar did, too. So he probably told Pryce."

"What else *can* I do, brother?"

"You could jet," I told him.

"I was gonna do that, what'd you take Lothar off the count for? I ain't *that* stupid. I know what you was talking about. It was Lothar who got cut down, but me, *I'm* the one on three legs. So I'm hobbling, okay. But, fuck it, I'm hobbling *in.*"

We touched fists. I hoped it wasn't for the last time.

The way it turned out, Pryce did his part. And Herk went on to do his. The night the cell's plan was supposed to go down, a lot of men ended up dead on lower Broadway, but Federal Plaza stayed up. That was years before 9/11, but so was the first attempt to blow up the World Trade Center. The government's always listening *in,* but it never learns to listen *good.*

Pryce wasn't an outlaw like us. There was

always work the government needed done, so unemployment wasn't one of his worries. No surprise he'd been plugged into the White Night underground. He had informants all over the country, on both sides of the Walls. Some people thought he was a myth; others thought he was a magician. That's the rep you earn when you always find the tools you need to do a job. Any job.

Pryce wasn't some fantasy-world "spook." He knew survival wasn't about staying in the shadows; it was about never casting one.

"Maybe you're more interested in current events?" he said.

I shrugged again. I didn't know what he was going to say, but I knew it wouldn't be a threat. Pryce had already seen for himself how far I'd go if anyone threatened my family. Seen a piece of it, anyway.

"The Prof needs his right leg amputated," he said, like a mechanic saying you needed a valve job. "It should have been done a while ago. They've been keeping him in a comatose state so they can use an air tourniquet on the femoral artery, but he can't stay like that for much longer. Not only don't they have the facilities to do a perfect cut-and-reattach, they don't have a prosthesis-maker, a rehab facility, or a —"

I held up my hand, meaning, "Enough!"

That didn't stop him from talking, or even modulate his tone.

"They're afraid," he said, in that same mechanic's-report voice. "Everyone on your side of the fence knows the deal with that place they run. They don't report gunshot wounds, and they fix whatever they can — bullet extractions, stitching, just about any kind of patch-up work. They've got all the antibiotics, and they can even handle trans-fusions. . . ."

He paused, waiting for me to be impressed that I'd recently learned that one way to pay for blood is to replenish the supply. When I didn't react, he rolled right on: "But they don't have a cath lab or a —"

I raised my eyebrows. All the communication he was going to get, until he got to what *he* wanted.

He moved his head just enough to show me that he wasn't trying to outwait me, then spread his hand on the table between us. "Their thinking is this: If they cut, and the old man dies, they're sure you'd send them along to keep him company. And if they *don't* cut, and he never comes out of that coma, they're convinced they'll all end up in one."

I just watched him.

"It may surprise you," he said, with just

the barest trace element of sarcasm in his metallic voice, "but there seem to be a number of people there who believe if anything happened to that old man you might just lose it and turn their whole operation into a slaughterhouse."

"So . . . ?" I said, knowing there had to be more.

"So they made a phone call," Pryce said. "But what they had to say wasn't news to . . . us."

The heat from where Clarence was stationed was starting to peel the paint off the wall behind me.

"We have the whole thing on video," he said, more like a prosecutor than a mechanic now. "I didn't know you had access to that level of ordnance. That sniper you blew up — he was ours. In fact, the whole team up there was. We had our own operation in place, took years to set up. We had no idea you were going to make a move on our targets."

I speak Pryce's language, so the translation was instantaneous: "ordnance" meant the RPG I'd shoulder-fired at the sniper's roost; "ours" meant someone paid by the same agency that paid him.

I knew Pryce wasn't there about payback; he doesn't get emotional over chess pieces.

The sniper who had tried for the Prof was a paid assassin. Didn't know who he was aiming at, didn't care. Nothing personal. Not for him, anyway.

But Pryce hadn't stopped by to shoot the breeze with an old friend, either. Pryce didn't have friends.

"Let me guess," I said, contempt making a crop-duster's pass over my voice. "Homeland Security, right?"

"And you don't care about that?" he shot back. "No, that's right. You're not a patriot, you're a borderlord, aren't you? You should read some of Marc MacYoung's work. Very enlightening."

I gave him a blank look.

"Don't cross *your* lines, and the rest of the world can blow itself up, far as you're concerned," he decoded for me.

"And your point is . . . what? I'm not a terrorist; I'm a thief, remember?" I half-answered, sidestepping around that video. I believed Pryce had it, sure, but I also knew he wouldn't turn it over to the Law. Why bother? You lose one shooter, you just hire another.

"Just say what you want," I told him. No point pretending I had any negotiating room; if I turned down any chance to save the Prof, Clarence would have shot *me*.

"There's more than that on offer," Pryce said, as if I hadn't spoken. "I can do magic tricks, too. Like make prints disappear."

"From?"

"Everywhere they're logged. Local, state, federal, international. On all of you. Every single one."

"Why? You gonna make us all legit so your bosses can make us pay income tax?"

"*You* already do," he said, flexing again. " 'Scott Thomas' does, anyway. And 'Juan Rodriguez' did before him. I hit the right switch and you won't need to fly under the radar anymore. You know you could never get far enough under so I couldn't find you, anyway."

"Some doors swing both ways," I bluffed.

"Listen," he said, a thin vein of urgency in his toneless voice. "We've got a narrow window. Every election, the system changes."

"Politicians —"

"Not *that* system," he said dismissively. "Not the future, the past. Right this minute, we have *total* access, but that's not for long. There's two ways to alter existing info: delete it, or overwrite it. Our way, Burke *stays* dead. Scott Thomas lives. Or anyone else you pick. Backdated IRS, everything. But it all has to happen *quick,* understand?"

"If you say so," I said.

"Flower has a wonderful future," he snapped out, as precisely deadly as a balisong artist.

I slipped the thrust, said: "They're both W-2s. Her father works in a restaurant; her mother is a social worker. Max's prints are in the system, but only for arrests, no convictions. And Flower's on scholarship, anyway. *Merit* scholarship."

"The —"

"Save it," I cut him short. "What's with all this paper promising? The Prof hasn't worked for years. Neither has Michelle. And if the *federales* could have touched Mama, they would have done it a century ago. How do I know you're not just trolling, trying to find out who else is with us? I already said I'd do whatever you want done. I could be out there doing *that,* instead of sitting here listening to you talk about stuff I don't give a fuck about. And you know what my word is worth; you've cashed that IOU before."

"He's already in transit."

"The Prof?"

He glanced at his watch. "Another two hours, he'll be inside one of the finest facilities in the country. In a sealed-off wing. Same level of care they'd give the President if he caught a bullet."

I could feel the temperature in the room drop. Clarence wasn't angry anymore — he was merging with his weapon, controlling his body with his mind so he could take his shot between heartbeats. Waiting only for me to signal whether I preferred Pryce disabled or dead.

"And that's the card you're holding?" I said, my voice very measured, hands not moving. "You've got the Prof. And he's not in Walter Reed."

"I don't work like that," Pryce said. "And you know it. I'm just explaining why you should sit and listen. Nothing *you* want is being held up."

He was telling the truth. "Go," I said, putting both hands flat on the table.

Clarence stepped into the room. I shot him a look. Pryce intercepted it, said, "Don't blame the young man. And don't think he's just told me something I didn't know."

"My father —"

"Is getting the best care there *is*," Pryce told Clarence. Not the way a salesman makes a pitch; the way a scientist states a fact. He wasn't being reassuring, just reading a chart.

"Whatever Burke says he will do, I —"

"Yes. I know."

Clarence looked at me, eyes glistening.

I ignored him. "You going to get to it now?" I said to Pryce.

"Terry?"

"What about him?"

"*He's* the one who needs my magic tricks."

I waited, thanking Satan that Michelle wasn't there that day. If she ever heard her child's name come out of this man's mouth, even Max couldn't have stopped her.

"Terry's a piece of paper," Pryce said. "A lot of pieces of paper, every single one of them a three-dollar bill. And they're all stacked like dominos on an earthquake fault line. One little tremor and . . ."

"Too late. He's already in —"

"College? I know. But that was an easy enough slide. He might even go all the way through grad school without a ripple. Of course, he'd be the first person to have his tuition paid in cash. Cash *over* the table, that is," he said, nasty-chuckling at the idea that his last paymaster had gotten into Yale on his SAT scores.

Dealing with Pryce was like juggling spun-glass balls, each one filled with sulfuric acid. I knew he had a calling of his own. Whatever that was, it was strong enough to make him overcome his loathing for whoever paid him.

"You think we can't put together a legit

checking account?" I said, tossing chum into the water.

"Here's what you *can't* do," he said, showing his quads to my full house as he ticked off the poison-tipped arrows on his webbed fingers. "You can't come up with an *authentic* marriage license for Michelle and the Mole. And even if you could, you could never create a birth certificate for any child born of *that* marriage. You can't —"

"What's 'real'?" I shot back. "The morons you work for had as much chance of finding 'weapons of mass destruction' in Iraq as I would of catching the Colombian drug lords who murdered O.J.'s wife."

"Terry's going to be famous, Burke," he said, utterly self-possessed. "That young man's IQ is immeasurable. His science teacher is *afraid* of him. There's no limit to what he could achieve. And you, you want to keep him out of anything that wouldn't survive a deep-background check? I can change all that. I can let him live in the light. *Blazing* light. I can make it all go away: where he came from, how he ended up where he is, all that."

"DNA."

"I can fix that, too, if I move *now*. But I see what you mean. Who knows how long any one of us is going to be around? It's easier if I paper it so he was adopted. At *birth.* His biological mother died during childbirth, father unknown. For at least a few more months, I've got the key to the Records Room. Write your own story; I can turn it into non-fiction."

"Maybe," I conceded. "But why *would* you?"

"Why would you care?"

"Because I know you, Pryce. And I know there has to be a reason for you to be sweetening a deal I already took. There's a piece missing, somewhere. And it's not some green card," I said, glancing at Clarence.

He nodded a silent agreement, then said: "It's not a piece that's missing; it's a person."

"So call out the —"

"And get what? A 'profile'?" He dry-laughed. "I'm already dealing with cops who'd Taser a drunk lying in a puddle of water, and I don't have time for them to grow a brain. This is *tight.* Most of the sand's already out of the hourglass."

"No 'national security' pitch this time, huh?"

"I'm a freelancer," he said tonelessly. Underground-speak for "unattached." Pryce would take money from anywhere, but he

58

wouldn't take orders from anyone.

I shook my head. Not refusing, showing I was confused.

"Your old friend Morales died a hero," Pryce said, almost formally. "Charged the Towers while they were still coming down. He's not talking — not that he ever would. But that plant of his didn't make you disappear, just moved you to the 'missing and presumed' category. There's no wants or warrants; you're not on parole. But your past is on paper. Which means your future . . ."

"I'm living on my residuals."

He put a disgusted expression on his reconstructed face, but his eyes never changed. If you shine a bright light into a bayou at night, you see a bunch of paired orange dots out there. Alligators have reflectors in the back of their eyes, so they can pick up even the tiniest flicker of movement. Part of their predator's arsenal. Even if Pryce lost those webbed fingers, I'd always recognize him. He came on like he was money-only, but I knew that was just a piece of the truth. A long time ago, Wolfe had shown me the other side of the two-headed coin Pryce was always flipping.

"They're so lucky," Wolfe said, looking out at a

tanker going up the Hudson.

"People with jobs?"

"No." She laughed. "People who get to be on the water all the time."

"You like that stuff?"

"I love it," she said quietly. "If I had my way, I think I'd live on a boat."

"Like a cruise ship?"

"No, a sailboat. A nice three-master that I could sail with a small crew."

"*You* could sail it?"

"Sure." She grinned. "I captained a ship from Bermuda all the way back to Cape Cod once."

"By yourself?"

"There were other people on board, but I was in charge."

"Where'd you learn to do that?"

"I was a Sea Scout."

"A what?"

"A Sea Scout. Like a Girl Scout, only we went out on boats instead of camping."

"I'd be scared to death," I told her. "The water . . ."

"You don't know how to swim?"

"No. I mean, I guess I wouldn't sink — we used to dive off piers when I was a kid. But it's so, I don't know . . . I mean, you don't know what's down there."

"There's worse things on land," she said.

I knew she was right, but it didn't comfort

me. Once, when I was small, I went down to the river to see what I could hustle up. It was night — I always felt safer at night. A boat was there. Not a big one, some kind of sport-fishing rig. They had a shark up on a hoist. It was twitching wildly, like it was going to break loose. The men were laughing, drunk, celebrating their conquest. I looked out at the black water. I thought about more sharks being down there. Men hunt them for fun. I wondered if the sharks knew.

"Sure," I said, getting back to it. "This Pryce, is he one of them?"

"Those worse things? I've run across his trail a few times over the years, but I only met him face-to-face once. He said he was with Justice, but when I tried a trace, it got lost in the maze they call 'cooperation.' By the time I finally found someone who'd talk to me, Pryce was gone again.

"That's the way he works. Tells people he's with the Company sometimes. Or DEA, ATF, you name it. And by the time anyone can actually check, he's moved on again."

"Transferred, maybe?"

"Not a chance. I think he's sanctioned, but he's on permanent-disavowal status."

"What the hell is that?"

"Pretty much what it sounds like," she said, combing both hands through her thick mane of dark hair as a river breeze came up. "He does contract work, but never on the books."

"Hard work?"

"I don't think so. He's an information guy, not hands-on. What he is, I think, is kind of a super bounty hunter. A bounty spotter, if there's any such thing. I never heard of him making a collar, or doing any wet stuff. He only works the edges. But he's not just a tracker; he manipulates situations, makes things happen. Like I said, he's self-employed. So he doesn't have to play by anyone's rules."

"Could he get favors done?"

"From the feds? I'm sure. At least he could from whatever agency he's bird-dogging for at the time."

"And he doesn't play for headlines?"

"I remember one thing he said to me. 'I never take credit. Only cash.' I think that about sums him up."

"You had a beef with him?"

"Not at all. He was very polite, very respect-ful. Said he knew about a pedophile ring. A new twist: online molestation, in real time."

"What!?"

"One of the pedo-skells would get the little girl — they only used girls in this one — in his studio. Then he'd set up the cameras, notify the others, and flash her image over their modems. They could tell him what they wanted him to do to the little girl, and they could all watch as he did it."

"And Pryce knew this how, exactly?"

"He didn't say. But I got the impression that he had reached one of them. Had him in his pocket."

"Was he trying to make a deal, have this one guy roll over on the rest in exchange for a walk-away?"

"No, it wasn't anything like that. He doesn't work for defense attorneys. As near as I could tell, he was willing to let the guy who tipped him go down with the rest."

"So what was the problem?"

"Pryce wanted to get paid. He didn't want a favor; he wanted cash."

"How much?"

"He never said. But he made it clear we were talking six figures."

"And you wouldn't go for it?"

"I couldn't. We don't have a budget for anything like that, and neither does NYPD. Nobody ever posts a reward until there's a victim, right?"

"And nobody knew — ?"

"This was the first *I'd* even heard of any such thing, and I wasn't even sure I believed him when he told me. I tried to put on some pressure. Told him if he didn't turn over the information, not only was that one little girl going to continue to be gang-raped over the Internet, there had to be others, too."

"And . . . ?"

"Didn't faze him. In fact, he said that should make his info worth more. I even tried threatening him with obstruction. He just stood up, gave me this weird smile, and disappeared. Nobody remembered seeing him leave; the security cams didn't pick up his image. I never saw him again."

"So what they were doing to that girl, it just . . . kept going?"

"Actually, no. A week later, there was a huge bust. Federal. The FBI vamped down on the whole operation, took it all in one fell swoop. A beautiful case; even the first freak to roll pulled serious time. And the Bureau got major press, from the Director on down."

"You think Pryce sold it to the Gee?"

"There's no way to know. I asked a friend over there how they got word, and he said all he knew was that it came from a CI."

"Pryce, you don't think he was the confidential informant?"

"No. But he could have been running him, whoever he was. Or maybe there was no CI, just a bogus setup so they could get a search warrant. They knew what they'd find when they did. *That's* the kind of thing Pryce gets paid for."

"You got anything else on him?"

"No. But I know he's out there. If I hear anything, I'll call you."

"You think I'm trying to scare you, Burke? After all the extras I just put on the table?"

"No," I admitted. Pryce already had more than enough to bury me in the basement of some no-name prison if he ever wanted to go that way. I'd hovered outside the grasp of the law for years, but I knew the truth — my freedom was nothing but a tethered kite. "Anyway, you've already got the Prof."

"Saving his life, not holding him as a hostage," he responded tranquilly.

I sat there. I kept my face blank, but my mind was in warp drive. Risk-gain. Threat assessment. And all of that meant nothing, because I knew Pryce was telling the truth. Once he'd taken the Prof in his hands, he'd given himself lots of choices. All the extras he put on the table had to be there for a reason, but whatever it was, it didn't matter.

"Tell me what you want," I surrendered.

That finally tripped his "on" switch. "You know who Prince Fazid el Kandal is?" he asked.

"No."

"He's a direct descendant of Abd al-Aziz."

"No kidding?"

"A Saudi," he continued, unruffled. "In 1902, Abd al-Aziz bin Abd al-Rahman al-Saud captured Riyadh, and spent the next three decades trying to conquer the Arabian Peninsula. One of his sons rules the country even today."

"Awesome."

He ignored me. "Saudi Arabia is governed by the Basic Law, which stipulates that the throne shall always remain in the hands of the kingdom's founder."

"Ah. So this guy's in line for —"

"The Saudis don't grow anything," he cut me off. I was there to listen, not figure things out — Pryce had already done that for me. "And they don't *make* anything. Most of their land is uninhabited. Their government makes North Korea look like the Berkeley city council. None of that matters to us. Tonga, Burma, Zimbabwe . . . 'Democracy' is whatever we *say* it is. And oil is what we need.

"The Congo is lousy with untapped oil reserves. All of central Africa is, actually. But getting to it, that's another story. Even close to the coast, there's all kinds of interference: kidnappings, pipeline bombings, sabotage. Some of that's just banditry, extortion masquerading as revolution. But some of it seems to be your old pals at work."

"You lost me," I said, knowing he'd done the opposite.

"Nigeria's a military dictatorship, playing itself off as a democracy. That's not a new script: the Brits colonize a country, and the minute they grant 'independence,' it goes up in flames.

"You remember?" he said in his ice-cored voice, twisting his lips just enough to tell me that he had *that* in his files, too. "The 'rebels' were Igbos and Yorubas. The 'government' was Hausa. Tribalism? Muslims versus Christians? Same difference. The breakaway group claimed some of the Niger Delta area for their own. They named it the Republic of Biafra before they were exterminated like termites in a Hollywood mansion. Nobody called it genocide, because . . ."

"There was oil under that ground, and only niggers were standing on it, anyway."

"Yes," he said, the way a teacher congratulates a slow student who *finally* solved the equation on the blackboard.

"So what's with the history lesson? The Saudis don't have a rebel movement to deal with. Any group who even *looks* like trouble, they just pay them to attack somewhere else. That's why they financed 9/11."

"Thanks for the insight," Pryce said, drier than dead cactus. "Try and pay attention, all right? We can't *rely* on the Saudis. If the pressure gets too strong, they'll fold. We don't need to develop new allies; we need to develop new sources for oil."

"So I'll drive a Prius, okay? Can you wrap this the fuck up? I know I've got work to do, and I'd like to know what it is."

But Pryce's river kept on rolling. "In Africa, all the natives are good for is grunt work, like diamond mining. For large-scale oil extraction, you need geologists, drilling experts, rig constructors, pipeline designers, CAD-CAM experts. . . . Understand? For that level of expertise, you need outsiders, and you need them to do more than just pay a visit, they have to *live* there."

"Good luck with that one," I said. "I don't care who's on the throne, warlords still rule the interior. You think that little sprinkling of blue helmets can keep anyone safe in the Congo? They've probably *sold* more weapons than they ever fired."

Pryce shrugged that off, as excitable as a mortician. "That's just a military problem — clear-cutting could get it solved in a few weeks."

"Then what's *your* problem?" I asked him, still just a raft drifting down on Pryce's river.

"What did you think all this 'cure for malaria' press-release slop was really about? Unless there's a way to vaccinate against it, we can't get personnel to remain there for the length of time we'd need. No amount of firepower will take out those damn mosquitoes. Malaria kills millions of Africans every year, but not half as many as it would if the indigenous people hadn't developed *some* genetic resistance over the centuries.

"That's why blacks get sickle-cell and other races don't. You want non-native experts to *live* there, you have to guarantee them more than protection from the warlords. Human-borne disease isn't a problem: we can fly in whores every week, certified clean. But those miserable little bugs . . ."

"So the people who are putting up all that money are just . . . ?"

"Businessmen," Pryce finished my sentence. "This is about money. Period, end of sentence. And they get a triple-return on their investment, too."

I looked a question at him.

He held up a hand. Went back to his trick of ticking off points on his webbed fingers. "One, there's all that recognition as saviors of humanity: prizes, great press, tax

69

breaks . . . maybe even a goodwill barrier against hackers. Two, there's the oil. Three, the drug companies get to experiment on humans."

I remembered that one — it was the Mole's theory of where HIV had actually been developed: in Haitian prisons, when Papa Doc was in charge. "No lab rats, no FDA, no . . ."

"Exactly. You could test *anything* on those sorry bastards. Africans don't trust us. Why should they? Nigeria may be the richest country on the whole continent, but it has the highest rate of polio in the world. In South Africa, they think they can prevent AIDS with a good hot shower and lots of soap. Once we get deep enough into the Congo, all we have to do is pay off the warlords, and they'll round up the cattle for us to brand."

"To do real research, you have to keep records. . . ."

"So? Even the Nazis kept records."

"That got some of them hung."

"You really believe *that* was the reason?" he said, shaking his head. "Hitler knew what was coming, so he hid in his bunker until he could make his hands stop trembling long enough to take the easy way out. All that 'evidence' was just a sales pitch, and

Americans lapped it up with a spoon. I don't mean there *wasn't* hard evidence — those 'Holocaust deniers' are nothing but Nazis in suits. But the government had to keep the public's eyes on the right spectacle. To this day, the average American doesn't even know there were Japanese war-crimes trials, too.

"Think about that, just for a second," he continued, in a suddenly professorial tone. " 'When his master dies, the true samurai performs ritual seppuku.' What a crock. Those banzai pilots weren't volunteers. And *their* master — the Emperor — wasn't dead. No, he was safe inside his palace as those kids took off in their balsawood bombs. They weren't following some ancient code of honor; they'd been ordered to their deaths. And the man who gave those orders? Hirohito himself never even went on trial.

"It was all symbolism. Pure Kabuki. If 'just following orders' was no defense to war crimes, how come only a few dozen Nazis had to pay the bill for killing so many millions? And how come the ones with skills we could use got a pass, so they could come over here and help us build our weapons? You know, the ones we'd need to deal with our 'allies' down the road."

He tilted his head, inviting a challenge.

Waited a beat, long enough to make sure I wasn't going to say anything. Then he leaned closer, letting a lower harmonic into his voice. "This is supposed to be *your* city, Burke. Take a look around, why don't you? Got any idea how many foster kids end up taking part in experimental drug trials?"

I shook my head "no," but Pryce got the message: I didn't know the number, but whatever it was, it wouldn't surprise me.

"Besides," Pryce said, his voice somewhere between bored and bitter, "it's not like the people living in that jungle have street addresses; you just tag-and-release. Their average life expectancy is about fifteen years anyway. This way, you could end up with the oil *and* a cure for cancer at the same time. Here, researchers can't even use stem cells. Over there, they can use humans. It's perfect."

Something lurked just beneath the way he said that last bit. Made me think about how he always made sure I could see his fingers. As though he was clinging to them as . . . what?

But now wasn't the time to think that through; what I needed was to get him back on track, close the deal, and protect my father. So all I said was "Okay. You tell me what you want; I do it, period. For that, I get the Prof and Terry . . . and that other stuff you mentioned. Done?"

He nodded.

"What if I can't pull off . . . whatever you want?"

"You still get everything I promised. But you have to go at it with everything you've —"

"This is a blood contract," I cut him off. "I'll do it, or I'll die trying." I gave him a few seconds to scan me, opening myself up to whatever truth-detecting skills he thought he had. "Deal?"

He held out his webbed right hand. I grasped it. Tight, like it was the Prof's only chance to live.

He opened with: "A missing kid."

"You want to me find — ?"

"Prince Fazid el Kandal wants you to find. Not you personally — he doesn't know you exist, and he never will. He wants his son, Amir Aziz Ghazi, returned. And our . . . government wants his wish granted."

"Runaway?" I asked. No idle question: runaways may end up on the Most Wanted lists, but most of them start out on the Unwanted one.

"The boy is two years and seven months old," he said, cutting out my next hundred questions.

"Snatched?"

"Four days ago. No ransom demand, despite the well-known fact that the father has unlimited assets."

"So did Lindbergh."

"Meaning what? Lindbergh never got his kid back."

"Not alive, he didn't. But they executed a patsy to make it all come out even."

"This isn't about covering up a crime," Pryce said, "or finding someone to pin it on. If it was, we'd hardly need *you.* There's a whole . . . department in place for that sort of work, and they're very good at it."

"Why me, then? You've got access to far more resources than I could ever —"

"Because, whoever took the baby, we think he's one of yours."

"I know you must mean something by that, but I don't like riddles. Just get to it, okay?"

"Not one of your *people,*" he said, as all-in-a-day's-work as a doctor signing a fake Medicaid claim. "One of . . . those you hate. The kind you used to hunt. One of your sworn enemies. By tribe, not name. Whoever took the child, he's somewhere in a world that nobody knows better than you do."

"And *you* know this because . . . ?"

"We have a deal?"

"You want me to just keep *saying* that, or you want me to get to work?"

"We need you, Father. Please come back to us," Clarence whispered urgently, as if the presence of all the gleaming, pristine machinery had put the steel back in his voice.

"He is trying," a white-uniformed nurse said. She was a slender woman with an achingly beautiful café-au-lait complexion, and midnight hair so lustrous it would make a raven jealous. The pain she saw every day had turned her exquisite dark eyes into occupied territory. Any other time, any other place, Clarence would have been siren-called.

But he didn't even look up. "Father," he prayed. Very softly, holding the Prof's hand.

We never left the Prof's side, handling it in shifts. Except for Clarence, who always seemed to be there.

Michelle spoke, Max touched, the Mole hovered.

We expected Gateman to show. But when we saw Terry pushing his wheelchair, Michelle threw the Mole a look that would have made Godzilla flinch.

The Mole didn't even blink. Neither did the kid.

Mama came, too. Seeing her outside her restaurant was like running across a polar bear sunbathing in Tucson. The nurse looked at the soup she brought, opened her mouth to say something, scanned the black-ice eyes in Mama's ceramic face, and let it go.

Clarence finally passed out. The nurse, Taralyn, told us they knew it was going to happen, and they were ready for it. No shortage of "special beds" in *this* hospital.

I wasn't there as much as the others. I was working. Paying the hospital bill.

"Under the Basic Law, all human actions are on a continuum: obligatory, meritorious, permissible, reprehensible, or forbidden."

"Spare me," I told Pryce.

"You think Shari'a is —"

"A fraud? No more than any other god-control crap. The *rules* are fine. But any fucking pervert can 'interpret' them, like that 'God Hates Fags!' tribe of degenerates in Kansas. And everyone knows rules don't apply to bosses, anyway."

"Everybody?" he half-scoffed.

"Everybody who's not a serious candidate

for a CAT scan," I said, slamming back his lob, but working extra hard on using a mild tone. Non-believers can still be fanatics, and evangelical atheists can be dangerous. "You think the high-school football players who kneel in the locker room before a game don't know that the guys on the other side are doing the same thing? What, they think God has a point spread? The Sunnis and the Shiites who slaughter each other both swear they're serving Allah. Enough, already."

Pryce didn't move.

"It doesn't matter what oath you take, who you pray to or swear behind: the bosses are always the bosses," I said. "Like that *omertà* handjob the movie boys love so much — you ever met a don you *couldn't* turn?"

"Gotti —"

"— was dimed out by his personal hit man. Gotti was the top of the pyramid, so what did he have to trade? You know how it works: you have to rat *up,* not down. He'd reached jurors before; maybe he just liked the odds. Or maybe he already knew he had cancer, and wanted to take his rep along for the ride.

"Besides, it's not like he had a choice. Any soft-sentence deal prosecutors make, they have to sell it to the media first. That's what counts. That's *all* that counts. You think New Yorkers would have gone for the sweetheart package they put together for the 'Preppy Killer' if the DA's Office hadn't talked the victim's *mother* into holding press conferences supporting it?"

"So you think — ?"

I made a chopping motion with my hand, telling him I was done talking. I'd let myself slip, temporarily forgetting how information was plutonium in Pryce's hands. He'd rather pick a brain like mine than the lock at Fort Knox.

"This isn't about me," I said. "How about we stop this debate-society routine and get to the part that is."

His blue-for-today eyes held my one good one for a long second. Then he moved his head in a barely perceptible nod, released a shallow breath, and then laid it out.

"Prince Fazid el Kandal's car was found at approximately 3:05 a.m., near an abandoned pier off the Hudson, south of Canal. He was slumped in the front seat, immobilized. The vehicle was his personal car: a bespoke Rolls, rebodied as a 'shooting brake.' You know what that is?"

"Brit-speak for 'station wagon.' "

"Close enough. This one had a lot of

custom work, including a column shift, a fold-down padded panel between the front buckets, and a permanent slot for a baby seat, centered in the back. That seat was for his son. The Prince was in the habit of taking the child out in that car during the evening, just the two of them."

"Not even a — ?"

"The windows were prescription glass; you'd need an astigmatism to see inside, especially at night."

"But he still got nailed?"

"This wasn't an assassination," Pryce said. "In fact, whoever's responsible went to a lot of trouble *not* to go that way. It's easy enough to detonate any car if you have the right equipment. Or a tank, for that matter. But what this team wanted was *inside* the vehicle, so it had to be a surgical extraction, not a scorched-earth blast."

I waited, listening to a faint echo of admiration in his voice for whoever had put such a complex operation together.

"The Prince had been chemically restrained; some sort of full-body paralytic. Whoever hit him with it knew exactly what they were doing."

"You talking about how they hit him, or the dose?"

"What does that matter?"

"If you want to get a specific result with a drug, you need to know a lot more than chemistry."

"Such as?"

"Weight, blood-alcohol level —"

"He's a Saudi. They don't drink."

"And they never have diabetes? Or bum tickers? Epilepsy? See where I'm going?"

Pryce blinked his eyes. Once, like a camera shutter. "According to the Prince, he was swarmed by a group of men who sprayed some kind of mist in his face. And before you ask, they were all masked, gloved, wearing generic clothing. They never spoke. The Prince was just waking up when a sector car spotted his vehicle.

"Now, this is important: the Prince had *not* been reported missing. The cops were not responding to a BOLO of any kind, just drawn to the sight of such a car in such a place.

"Actually, the Prince was lucky that night. When the uniforms opened his vehicle, he was still wearing all his jewelry. In that neighborhood, if the cops hadn't gotten there first, he would have been picked clean."

"In that 'neighborhood,' they would have harvested his fucking organs."

Pryce shrugged. I didn't waste any focus

trying to interpret what that meant.

"The baby was taken. That was all I got from him."

"And you think someone took all those risks, spent all that money . . . just to get their hands on a kid?"

"No ransom demand," Pryce repeated. "You tell me."

"How could it *not* be some kind of political thing?" I said. "One baby's the same as another to traffickers. Value varies, but the kid you're describing, he'd be too old and too dark-skinned to be worth much."

"Too *old?* He was only —"

"Worth maybe one percent of a blond-and-blue, doll-faced white baby girl. The kind of money it would have cost to put together an operation like you described, it had to be that *particular* kid they wanted. So how could it be anything *but* political?"

"Watch" was all he said, reaching for a thin black box on his desk. His eyes directed mine toward a flat-screen TV.

"Car tricks are always scary." I put the age of the woman on the screen at anywhere from sixteen to thirty — impossible to tell more because of the slightly out-of-focus image and hazy lighting. I figured the tape had been diffused to produce the copy

81

Pryce was showing me, so I didn't put much stock in the voice being her own, either.

She looked like an upscale streetwalker: a lush packaging of illusion and delusion, from the plastic breasts to the expensive wig to her pass-a-polygraph belief that what she did was all about "love." Half reclining in a stark white padded chair, she recited her lines: "All G.K.'s ladies stroll, but he won't let us do business outdoors. He's got a deal with a *very* fine place — private parking around the back, no register, satin sheets, fresh flowers . . . everything.

"G.K. says a john isn't buying sex; he's buying an experience. You don't buy *us,* you buy our time. We're actresses, not hookers. That's why G.K.'s the king of —"

Something out of camera range induced her to cut out the infomercial and get back to what she was being paid for *this* time: a quick round of Truth or Dare. And Dare wasn't an option.

"Look," she said, haughtily, "you want a quick blowjob while you're sitting behind the wheel of your hoopty, you drive on over to Skankville. G.K. says I'm double-fine enough to work outcall, but we all live by his Three Commandments: no credit cards, no paper trails, and no partners. Some other girls use the Internet, but even that's a —"

Whoever cut her off the first time did it again.

"Okay," she said, after a little pause . . . long enough for her complexion to get closer to the color of the chair. "One time, a cop got me in his car. He told me I could either take a ride around the corner and do him for free, or take a ride downtown. My choice: front seat or back. I told him I'd take the back," she said, pride swelling her fake chest. "I carry a panic button, and I knew G.K. would have a lawyer — a *real* lawyer — waiting for me at arraignment.

"Besides, G.K. says, you give it away to a cop even once, he keeps coming back for more. You call his bluff, he *might* bring you in, but most of the time it's not a collar he's trolling for.

"And G.K. was *right.* The cop went into this rap about working for Internal Affairs, just 'testing' me, some line of bullshit like that. Whatever, I was done for the night. That's another of G.K.'s rules: any cop contact means your shift is over. And he knows I'd never lie to him."

The interrogator, whoever he or she was, had the good sense or natural instinct to stay quiet. Let the whore keep rolling, even if that meant listening to her explain why she could have been a grand-an-hour out-

83

call star.

"So I was on my way to get a cab," she said, "but when I saw *that* car, I knew it was something supernova. Maybe a pro baller, maybe an actor, maybe even an out-of-town player, trying to pull me. That happens *all* the time," she boasted, "but my man knows he doesn't have to worry. He's got my heart.

"I remember thinking to myself, no way the Law's got a ride like that. I mean, it wasn't flash, it was just . . . *better,* you know what I'm saying? *Way* past anything I ever saw in my life. I know a Rolls when I see one — who doesn't? — but to go *custom* on one? No way. That's not bling; that is *class.*"

That last word almost made her come. For real, for once.

"The window slides down and I get over there *quick,* before one of those other . . . But that wouldn't have mattered; it was *me* he wanted. 'Mink,' he said, soon as I get close. So I knew he'd been scouting me, using my name like that," she said, still excited about winning the pageant.

She tossed her store-bought dark-streaked mane of cornsilk hair, said, "A thousand, cash. In my hand. *Before* he so much as touched me. I hadn't even gotten in the car! Anyway, we end up under the FDR. Dark, but not scary. Plenty of people close by there. Always is.

"That front seat was *big*. Then he said I could have another thousand if I did exactly what he told me to do.

"The man was way cool, how he put it. No bargaining, no games. If I didn't want the extra thou, I could leave right then. Just open the door and step out. *With* the money he'd already given me."

She looked over at whoever was on the other side of the thick slab of matte-black material that formed some kind of table between them.

"Naturally, I went for it. He gave me orders. Nothing special; nothing I hadn't heard before. He didn't hit me, or make me call him 'master' or any of that scene, but he was very, very precise: get on all fours, unzip him, pull up my skirt. . . .

"When it was over, he said — God, I swear I will never forget this — he said, 'You see? A whore will always do as she is told. You pay; she obeys. Whatever you want. Anytime you want. However you want. You *want,* the whore *does.* That is the world.'

"At first, I thought he was talking to himself — some of them do that, especially afterwards — but I . . . couldn't help myself, I guess. I looked where *he* was looking. Into the back seat. And that's when I saw it."

Silence.

"A *baby!* Strapped into one of those little seats. I couldn't even tell if the kid understood a word, or what he might have seen, but it scared me worse than the time a trick made me suck off his gun. He put the barrel right in my mouth and made me slobber it good. When he cocked it, I . . ."

Maybe the interrogator made some gesture; I couldn't tell. But this time, it didn't slow the flow:

"That psycho with the gun, he was doing himself at the same time, with his hand. He spermed all over the dash when I . . ."

Silence from the interrogator. Same result:

"That time — with the gun, I mean — I just kind of staggered out of the car," the hooker said. "I remember throwing up. I remember pulling off my panties and throwing them away. Then I washed myself with every towelette I had on me. I couldn't stop shaking. I could smell myself.

"But *this,* this was a million times worse. I can't explain it, but . . . seeing that baby, thinking about it *watching,* I just . . ."

Silence.

"Then the guy in the Rolls told me to get out. He didn't call me dirty names like some of them do when they're done. He was very calm. But I'll never forget those words. 'I

86

have no more use for you, hole.'

"He said 'hole,' not 'whore.' I could hear it. He made *sure* I heard it. I *still* hear it. He said, 'When you close the door behind you, it is as if I have flushed the toilet.' And then he said: 'You see?' He was talking to the *baby*."

By then, her hands were shaking too violently to pull a cigarette out of her pack. A hand reached into the frame, holding one out to her, already lit. A web-fingered hand.

The hooker took a long, deep drag. Closed her eyes. Said: "Please don't make me talk about this anymore. You promised me, if I told you everything, you'd take care of —"

"That's already been done," Pryce's undisguised voice said.

"That's it?" I asked him. Knowing it wasn't.

"Three more. Cross-confirmed."

"And you think this one is mine because . . . ?"

"You're the pattern-master," he said. "The feds have a billion bucks' worth of computers, but they're working with ten cents' worth of data. They've got a lot of different names for what they do, but it all comes down to the same thing: Guessing for Dollars. That's fine for proposal writing, but, in your world, it's what suckers do with bookies. People come to you for only one reason: because you *know*."

I stopped fencing, asked: "You have a chronology?"

"The one you saw was the third of the four. But we assume many others had preceded her."

"Yeah," I agreed. "Way too stylized. You think he was going to keep escalating?"

Pryce shrugged; guessing wasn't his game, either.

"But there's at least one you know about that you don't have on tape."

"Why do you say that?"

"Because she's not talking," I said, not guessing. "Was she paid off or . . . ?"

"The other."

"Got a body?"

He shook his head "no."

"But enough of a spoor so that you know it was him, right?"

"Yes," he agreed.

"And any evidence that *did* exist, your guy has the scratch to have it erased."

"Given the known data, such a scenario meets the criteria for both validity and reliability," he acknowledged. "But on paper, it *didn't* happen."

"This prince of yours, he knows about your 'data'?" I asked.

Pryce gave me a blank look. He wasn't confused; he was drawing a line.

Being me, I stepped over it. "A working girl's gone. One you *don't* have on tape, but you're sure your guy had . . . contact with her, right? That means some pimp never got his merchandise back."

"How do you know she wasn't just some — ?"

"How about we stop, okay? No way we're talking about some underage runaway scooped off the street. You already said your guy was riding an escalator, and you don't find girls who turn edge-tricks down on the sidewalk. You want one of those, that's the penthouse — reservations-only territory."

"You're the expert; you tell me."

"Okay. Those girls never work blind. They don't go out every night, or even every week. Takes time for the marks to heal. Surgical repairs take even longer. So every rental brings mammoth money, but there's a long turnaround time between them. A manager loses a girl like that, costs him a *lot* of cash, at both ends."

He looked a question at me.

"Front-end investment. You have to set up contact points for clients to find you. Web sites are for dominas, not subs . . . at least not the kind that can command major bucks for a single session. You need all kinds of screening mechanisms to protect your merchandise. *Serious* security. You need a way to wash the cash. Accountants. Lawyers. Offshore men. All that money is spent to *make* money. An investment, understand?"

"So, if a trick *does* go too far, it's the perfect blackmail scenario — is that what you're saying? Because his identity would already have been verified, and —"

"Not this time," I said, catching the wisp of surprise that flickered over his face. "In fact, your guy isn't blackmail material at all. He's got money, all right, but it's so fucking *much* money that threatening him could get you very dead."

He nodded at the back-alley logic: Anyone who did the kind of research you need to work a stable of edge-girls would know that some tricks are too high up to touch. That kind, they have a stable of their own — assassins with diplomatic immunity.

When I was sure he was with me, I asked: "So why not spend some of that money in front, eliminate all the back-and-forth?"

"I don't under —"

"There's places in L.A. where you can rent a Bentley, but that's all about front. The rental places might call you 'sir'; they might ass-kiss like a doorman at a Beverly

Hills hotel . . . but they *know.* It's in their eyes. They've got your number. If you were the real thing, why would you be renting?"

"You mean — ?"

I shrugged. "I don't know this 'missing' girl. So I don't know who was running her. But I know their kind. And if the price was right . . ."

"Are you saying — ?"

"Your record's stuck in the same groove. You know as well as me that humans get sold all the time. They're just a commodity, like wheat, or pork bellies. What lawyers call 'fungible' goods; one grain of wheat's the same as another. But *some* humans are unique property.

"Even for sex, there's a general market price, but it still varies, depending on the person *and* the packaging. A lap dance in a backstreet dive in Queens won't cost you anything close to the same thing in some upscale Manhattan joint.

"Girls who turn lump tricks get used up quick. The harder and longer they get used, the less they're worth. Baby-sellers know how quick the price drops for used goods — you think pimps are any different?"

Now it was his turn to shrug. "I told you, this isn't about money. Or law enforcement. This is very, very simple: the client wants

91

his baby returned to him. We want to satisfy the client. That's the place where you come in. The *only* place."

I caught his meaning, and the warning it was wrapped in: If their precious prince had bought himself a human sacrifice, that wasn't their problem. And I better not make it mine.

"What's all this about 'patterns,' then?" I asked him. "What do you need me for?"

"Without the baby, the client appears to have stopped his . . . nocturnal activities."

"So?"

"So we don't believe we've come close to interviewing all the other women he may have . . . used. But we don't know any places to look for them that we haven't tried."

"You think maybe one of the pain-for-pay girls set him up?"

"How would we know?" Pryce said, reasonably. "We found some of them by going back down the money trail. But that's such a murky world that there *must* be others. And we were told there are women who do . . . this kind of thing for their own reasons. Not prostitutes, women who actually seek out such encounters."

"Sure," I said, putting a "who doesn't know that?" look behind it.

"As I said, that world presents a rare barrier for us. Money will provide access, but not to the . . . depth we require, especially in the time allotted."

I got it then.

The woman who opened the door for me was wearing a maid's outfit. A costume, not a uniform — she wasn't dressed for housework.

"Hi, Rejji," I said.

"It *is* you," the fantasy-dressed brunette squealed. "Those 'security' cameras — you can never be sure."

"Shut up, you stupid little bitch," a tall blonde whose severe black dress did nothing to de-emphasize her outrageous breasts snapped. She gave the maid a mild slap and pointed toward a corner of the living room. "*I* was sure, or he never would have gotten past that simpering little 'concierge' downstairs."

As the brunette stood in the corner, hands clasped obediently behind her back, the blonde smiled at me. "You finally decide to come out of the closet yourself, Burke? Good timing. Rejji was due for a punishment tonight anyway."

"When I do, you'll be the first to know, Cyn," I told her, playing off her long-standing joke — if that's what it was — that

I was hiding my true nature from myself.

"You're *so* lucky," she hissed at the brunette, who shivered her bottom in mock terror.

"Cyn . . ."

"Yeah, I know. Business. Sit down over there and tell us what you want."

When I was done talking, Cyn said, "I don't think you're looking for a risk-taker." She glanced over at Rejji, who was sitting next to her on the loveseat. They were holding hands.

"That's right," Rejji said. "It's all about the lines."

I looked from one to the other, waiting for them to decide who should lay it out for me. On their Web site, Rejji spent a lot of time being "disciplined" by Cyn; that's what their customers paid for. Cyn owned Rejji. They lived in a world you could look in on, provided your debit card had enough for the ticket. But all that would let you see was a small slice of the globe — like the tiny little tattoo on Rejji's right hip, or the dog collar she wore on special occasions. The rest of it — the never-for-sale part — was that they loved each other. I didn't know what they did when they were off camera; I didn't know where the acting started or stopped. But I knew the love was unscripted.

Our accounts had been squared years ago; I was there to put myself back in their debt. There was never a question in my mind that they'd tell me whatever they knew. And not because the pendulum is always swinging, they might need me again someday. That's the way it is in Pryce's world, but even he knew he couldn't buy his way into this one.

"You know how it works," Cyn began. "We don't do stills — just our video library and some real-time. Pre-pays only. The client sends in the scene he wants, and we play it for him. We've got a lot of stuff stored. Usually, we can just click-click and they're 'watching' what they asked for. Sometimes, over a thousand of them at the same time — like an afternoon matinee. Subscribers get a discount, and we pay a lot of money for the encryption."

"They're not all men," Rejji put in, and caught a look from Cyn. "Well, they're *not,*" she said, pouting. "One woman, she always asks for —"

"He's not here about that," Cyn said, more sharply than before. She turned to me, said, "Everyone in our business has a 'line,' okay? A client asks for . . . well, it doesn't matter, just something you don't want to do. So you say no. Sometimes, that's it. Sometimes, they offer you more money. After all, we do it *for* money, so, the way people like them think . . ."

"I get it."

"With me and Rejji, regulars know better — you don't even *ask*. And for newbies, it's right on our site: Just click the 'Don't Even Go There!' banner and you get an 'Out of Bounds' list. Ignore that even *once,* you're barred for life. But some stuff, well, it's marginal, and we have to make a judgment call."

I made a "like what?" gesture.

"Lots of clients want to see naughty-schoolgirl stuff. That's okay, but if the dialogue goes wrong . . ."

"I know!" Rejji said. "Like that foul —"

"Shhh," Cyn said, patting the other girl's thigh tenderly. "He wanted Rejji to be a *little* schoolgirl," she explained. "I mean, she's never going to look like some ten-year-old, not built the way she is, but this client wanted her to *talk* like one. And I wasn't supposed to be the headmistress of her school; I was supposed to be her nanny."

"I know you didn't just let that one —"

"If you've got more than a screen name — like say a credit card — it's amazing what kind of information the feds can come up with," Cyn said, solemnly. "Apparently, enough for a search warrant."

I bowed slightly, said: "Beautiful. But I need to go darker than that one."

They exchanged looks.

"You're looking for a kid?" Rejji finally asked. "An *actual* kid?"

"It's not that simple," I told her. "Yeah, I'm looking. But not for pictures. Not for scenes. Not even for buyers. I'm following a trail. Starts with a guy who works the strolls. He's not the kind of wannabe dom you run across in your business; he's only interested in piece-of-meat merchandise."

"Use and abuse?" Cyn asked.

"His use *is* abuse. But all we've got documented is verbal. He doesn't need to role-play; he *is* what he wants to be. He pays; the girl does what she's told. Every time he does his thing, he's making a point."

"Not fooling himself?" Cyn asked, making sure.

"Not even close. This isn't the kind of guy who pays to spank a girl while she calls him her boss, or her 'master,' or whatever gets him off. The one I want, he's right out front. With him, it wouldn't be 'You're a bad girl,' it would be 'I pay you cash; you bend over and take it.' No scenes, just payment for services."

"That's asking a lot," Rejji said. "Most pro subs like it at some level. I mean, they may not like the *client,* but they get off on the scenes themselves. Spanking, that's the comfort-zone end. But some of those girls, they're pretty close to the other edge — RL."

I raised my eyebrows.

"Real Life," she said. "Even if they're being pimped, their boyfriends — or their girlfriends — have to be into the scene themselves. One girl we know, she broke up with the guy she was living with because he wouldn't choke her. In her mind, that was supposed to be their special thing. She'd let a trick flog her for money, but asphyx sex, that's not for strangers. You've got to *trust* to play that way."

"Maybe. But anytime you let a stranger tie you up . . ."

"That's right," Rejji said. "That game, it's *all* risk. If you're going to trick, you never know. Not everyone follows the script. You remember Olivia?"

"Mistress Greta," Cyn added, as if that would clear things up for me.

I shook my head.

"She did the whole Nazi thing," Rejji explained. "You know: blond wig, black uniform, high leather boots, German accent." She stifled a yawn with a very lady-like patting of her lips. "Had herself a complete dungeon setup, very expensive. Regular clientele, too. Like making an appointment for a facial."

"And?" I asked, ignoring her word games.

"And she's dead. Somebody — probably more than one — put her through hell before they finished her off."

"You heard this?"

"We *saw* it," Cyn told me. "On the Internet. Somebody posted the video, and made sure it got around. The URL's gone now, but we figure it's been downloaded plenty of times. Not even illegal to possess it; they only showed her taking it, not the finale. That makes it art. Probably could have sent it in to apply for an NEA grant."

"No strangers; no exceptions," Rejji said, schoolgirl-proud that she'd memorized the material.

"No *contact.*" Cyn pulled the leash even tighter. "We deal with strangers all the time, but never in the flesh. Rejji and I, we make little movies. We do it all: casting, directing, set design, lighting, sound. Now if *you* want to be the screenwriter *and* you've got the money to finance the production, we'll consider it. But, no matter what, you never, ever get to meet the actors."

"That's *your* rule. But it's not the — ?"

"Of course not," Cyn said. "There's . . . levels in this business, same as any other. Standards, too."

"You mean, like, security systems?"

"No," she said, crisply. "I mean what I said: *standards.* Wait. . . ."

She walked out of the room. As soon as she was gone, Rejji leaned over and licked my mouth.

Cyn came back in, looked at Rejji, said, "Your cheeks are red, bitch," causing a deeper blush. "I'll help you with that later." Then she turned to me, said, "Even the phone-sex operations — and, trust me, you wouldn't want to meet some of the girls *they* use — have guidelines. The classier ones, anyway." She handed me a piece of paper, neatly typed:

The following scenarios are STRICTLY
   FORBIDDEN:
Violence or use of weapons
Rape fantasy
Beast work
Incest
Red or brown showers
Amputation or mutilation

"See what I mean?" she said as I glanced

100

over the list. "That particular service is Gold Card or better. A girl gets caught breaking any of these rules, she's gone, no matter what kind of earner she is. And a supervisor spot-checks every call."

"I get it."

"We don't," she said, a faint aura of accusation in her voice. "We know you're hunting." She turned to the still-blushing Rejji, said, "What? You think Burke came over here to play with you, brat?" She turned back to me. "What's your problem? You don't think you can trust us, why come at all?"

"You know better than that," I told her. "I'm just feeling my way through this. I didn't come to ask you for something; I came over to learn."

"And did you?"

"I might have."

"Which means . . . ?"

"If you know a girl who fits a certain profile, I'd like to hear about it."

"You said that funny," Cyn said, tilting her head. My fault: sometimes I forget that her IQ is as outrageous as her chest.

"Hard-core sub," I got specific. "Professional. No boundaries. The kind who'd let a trick do anything to her, even with a kid in the room —"

"Ugh!" Rejji.

"Shut up!" from Cyn, who was listening intently.

"— and might have access to people who could put together a snatch of that same kid."

"Like a mobbed-up boyfriend?"

"Heavier than that," I told them, measuring my words. "I'm talking about a girl with a client list that could include the kind of guy who could put together a military-type operation. A man willing to gamble big bucks, if he can play for much bigger ones."

"So she'd have to be in on it herself," Rejji said.

"At first," Cyn said, "but maybe not in on anything, anymore."

I nodded. You can recycle the script, but the ending never changes.

"Same number?" was all she asked.

"Why didn't you just level with them?" Michelle asked, later that night. "Rejji and Cyn are —"

"Leveling with them means telling them the truth. And I don't *know* the truth, girl."

"You think that baby *wasn't* snatched because a professional sub wanted to make some money?" my little sister said, her voice a blended sourmash of anger and disgust.

"Please!"

I knew better than to say anything.

"This rich freak pays whores, and has his kid watch the action, right?" my sister said. "Who knows why *he* does it, but we know why *they* do. So maybe one of them has a pimp, or maybe her trick book's full of big-bucks clients. Either way, somebody smelled a big payday, and called in the troops. What's so . . . ?"

"Girls with that level of client don't go dropping names, sis. They may know things, but they know what it costs to *say* things, too."

"And you think, just because they're into pain, you couldn't *make* them talk?"

I ignored her sarcasm, said: "Whoever put together that snatch team was top-drawer, with a lot of experience. Maybe armored cars, maybe banks . . . I don't know. But it had to be the kind of man who would be very touchy about who he'd work with."

"Meaning?"

"Meaning you can forget about torture — a pro won't deal with anyone into that. Nothing to do with morals; you just never work with guys who're bent, because they bend too easy themselves. Plus, we're look-ing for a heister; no way blackmail's his regular business."

"Maybe surveillance is his business, mahn. That would mean he already *has* a team. And a team is what it would take to clamp a twenty-four/seven on an address, never mind a moving target."

"Sure" — I nodded at Clarence — "unless that custom Rolls was GPS'ed. Pryce thinks he's looking in the right places, but he can't get in deep enough; that's why he came to me. For *us,* the key isn't the baby, it's the ransom."

"But there's *been* no —"

"That's just it, girl," I told Michelle. "If anyone had contacted that scumbag, he would have forked over whatever they asked for. For him to go to the government, and for *them* to reach out for Pryce, this can't be anything money could fix.

"Remember, no contact's been made. None. This sheikh had to be way past desperate to go to the feds, because now his hobby's not on the down-low anymore. That kind of info is unbelievable leverage; he has to want that baby *bad* to put his own head on the chopping block."

"So the feds know there's a missing baby, and Cyn and Rejji *don't?*" Michelle said, glaring at me.

"Step back, okay? Sure, I told them that much. But in their minds I'm working for the parents. What's the point of telling them anything else?"

"You don't actually know. Not for sure. And that baby *was* —"

"No, honey," I told her. "This was no damn kidnapping. Unless you can show me how this whole thing adds up to money — *major* money — I think this little prince of theirs is reading it right. There's something else in play here."

The *a cappella* voice was as pure as pain, called up from a place that only a child who lost his father to a soulless assassin can know.

Don't need no silver spade
To dig my grave

Don't need nobody cryin'

I'm ready to pay for the sins I made
And I don't need no preacher's lyin'

Just put me down
In that cold, hard ground

And tell Mamma I died tryin'

I knew the song; the Prof once told me

he'd learned it as a boy coming up in Louisiana. One of those sly "spirituals" that mocked the opiate the slavemasters were feeding their captives. That was when "Prof" was short for "Prophet," not "Professor." Depending on where you stood, he could still be either one.

Clarence's voice was low, but it carried like an ICBM. He stood on the outdoor terrace, one floor below where the hospital was cradling his father. He was on his feet, both hands gripping the railing. Standing like the Prof did when he was preaching to his congregation, back when we were Inside:

"The Lord don't want you on your knees, brothers. The bars only keep us in; *they can't keep us* down. *We don't gotta be in* their *house; we can be in* God's *house . . . if we make it so.*

"You know how it go: Twelve jurors, one judge, half a chance. We all here because we got convicted. So we all convicts by law. I say convicts! *Convicts, not inmates! An inmate is an animal in a cage. A convict is a man of conviction! And a man stands up for his convictions, am I right? Now stand up with me, brothers. Stand up right now! Being a convict ain't about color; it's about being a man. So stand up* together. *Show those*

punks in the gun towers what men *look like!*
Now give that *an amen!"*

I'd gone looking for Clarence; I knew he had to be somewhere close by. But when I found him, he was looking, too.

I vaporized; it hadn't been me Clarence had gone looking for.

"I only do restraint." The woman was past full bloom, but still ripe, even with the Shirley Temple curls and raccoon eyeliner. "And only here, in my own place."

"But when you're restrained . . ."

"It just *looks* like I am," she told me, very matter-of-factly.

"I understand. But when you *look* like you are, the clients, they like to talk?"

"Some do," she said, as if stating the obvious. "Some like to listen."

"The talkers, some of them, they can get . . ."

"What are you, anyway?" she said, fitting a cigarette into an ivory holder. "Cyn told me you were a real heavy."

"So I'm not supposed to have manners? Not supposed to show some respect?"

"I'm not used to it," she said, warily.

"Meaning you don't trust it? Or that you think Cyn made a mistake?"

"If a guy who I expect to pay me to put

107

on a dog collar so he can walk me on a leash and make me say I'm a filthy bitch cunt shows up with roses one day, that would spook me."

"I'm not that guy. You've never seen me before; you'll never see me again. And, so far, I'm not paying you, either."

"Cyn said you would."

"Oh, *now* her word's good, huh? She negotiate a price, too?"

"She . . . she said, if I had information, you'd pay for it."

"That's what I've been trying to find out, if you have that information. That's why I asked you about guys who like to talk."

"I don't get it."

"You don't need to. Here's what I'm looking for, okay? A regular. Ties you up, whatever. But this one, when he's finished, he always tells you you're nothing but a hole."

"A . . . ?"

" 'Hole.' Like in the ground. That's the word I'm looking for. That specific word."

She gave me a look I couldn't decipher. "I *did* have a guy once who —"

"Was he alone?"

"Alone? Who else would be there? I don't do sets."

"He'd have a baby with him. A little baby. Maybe in a stroller."

"And I'd let him do me in front of a *baby?* What the fuck kind of woman do you think I am?"

As I stepped across the threshold to the Prof's room, I saw the nurse leaning over the armchair where Clarence had fallen asleep during his vigil. She shook the exhausted young man gently, said, "He is here now."

"My father . . ." Clarence was half dazed, half on fire.

"Go look," she said, flashing teeth whiter than heat.

"Son?"

"It's —" both Clarence and I said as one, the "me" that would have ended the sentence never reaching our lips.

"How long?" the Prof whispered.

"Few weeks," I said.

"I got called over to the other side," the old man said, more strength in each successive syllable, "but I wouldn't take the ride."

"They never built the joint that could hold you, Prof."

"I remember . . . some of it. Caught a round. Went down. Thought I had my . . ."

His voice trailed off.

Clarence was slumped on the floor, shaking like a man with ague. His face was wet, but he didn't make a sound. Not out loud, anyway. It was up to me, then.

"They never came, Prof," I said, talking out of the side of my mouth, like he'd first taught me on the yard. "Soon as they saw you holding your hammer, they ran like rabbits. By the time we got the rescue wagon over to you, the whole street was empty."

"For true?"

"John Henry *barred* that door," I said, bending close to kiss his cheek.

"He's back to himself," Michelle was telling Clarence, much later. "He lost a few pints of blood, honey. But not a single brain cell."

"Thank you," he said. We didn't know who he was talking to. Didn't ask.

"You know that gorgeous nurse, Taralyn?" Michelle asked him.

"The Island girl?"

"No, the space alien," she snapped. "Couldn't you even bother to learn her name, you pig?"

"I was not —"

"I'm so sure. Well, anyway, *Taralyn* was there when I showed up a few hours ago. Just in time, I might add. The Prof was asking her how'd she gotten to be a nurse, with that disease she got. Taralyn thought he was still brain-fogged — I could see it on her face — but she got over that idea quick enough when that old rogue told her she needed to gain some weight if she wanted to haul the freight."

"My father only meant —"

"Oh, for Hera's sake!" Michelle exploded on the young man. "You think *I* need a translator? Besides, he was talking about you."

"Me? I do not —"

"That old devil was telling her what *you* like. Bragging on you like you were a combination of Billy Dee and Denzel, only with Einstein's mind, Trump's money, and . . . well, he just went *on*.

" 'Time I had me some grandbabies to play with,' " she growled, imitating the Prof's tone to perfection. " 'But my boy ain't looking for no toy.' He was just . . . impossible! Told her she had the hips for it — can you *imagine?* — but, no matter what she had in her hope chest, she needed some more in her trunk.

"I swear, Miss Taralyn couldn't make up her mind between slapping him and kissing him. 'That old man is *bold*,' she says to me later. I told her, 'Wait 'til you get to know his son.' "

If you think a black man can't blush, one

111

look at Clarence would fix that.

"He does not yet know?" he asked Michelle. Anything to get her off the scent.

"About the leg? No, baby. Taralyn said she would tell him if we wanted. But she thought we'd —"

"I'll do —"

Clarence and I, again speaking as one. But we both knew that one was mine.

"I'm a star," the slim young woman with vaguely Oriental eyes and short, dark hair told me. "Spanking videos — well, DVDs, really — earn a ranking, just like in any entertainment industry."

"I heard that," I lied. Thinking she wore her hair short so she could put on whatever wig the role required, keeping Rejji's words in mind:

"She goes by Barbi. How yesterday can you get? Barbi Lacoste. It's a pun, get it? You know what makes her such a 'star'? You can find a nice round butt anywhere. But she's got real pale skin, so the buyers don't just see her get spanked, they see the results — makes it more real. And some want serious *bruising for their money.*

"This one, I heard she can work all day! *You know what that means? She'd have to take . . . God, I don't know,* hours *of it. And she doesn't*

*need a whole lot of downtime, either, the way
some do. I heard she gets a shot of novocaine
in each cheek before —"*

*"You're so jealous," Cyn interrupted, laugh-
ing.*

*"Of that trash?" Rejji fired back. She turned
away from Cyn, said: "Look, Burke, I know
her kind. Maybe she loves it, maybe not. But
you pay her enough, she could learn to love
something else."*

So I didn't word-play with this Barbi.
"You know who I am?"

"I *heard* of you, that's all."

"Then you know what I do. This isn't
personal. I want something. If you've got it,
I'll pay you for it. Either way, you'll never
see me again."

She lit another cigarette, fumbling a little
with an intricate gold lighter.

I sat there radiating no-threat, misting it
like soft fog over her fear.

"I don't smoke much — except when I'm
a naughty girl sneaking a smoke. On camera, you know? But I . . . want to think about
this."

"I'm not coming back."

"You already said that."

"I did, but I don't think you were listening. So let's try it this way: if you want to
get paid, it's now or never."

"You're afraid I'll make a phone call, huh?"

"No," I said, just above a whisper. "You're afraid *I* will."

"How did you find me?" she asked, snubbing out her cigarette.

"Like you said, you're famous."

"Yeah?"

"Yeah. You're a for-real sub. When *you* get to pick your partner, you wouldn't even think about cash. But when you don't . . ."

"You're quick."

"I can be."

"Do I do anything for you?"

"Not yet," I said, fanning a sheaf of centuries.

"You didn't answer my question."

"You're quick, too."

"Sometimes, I think better after —"

"This isn't about thinking, Barbi. It's about talking. Or not. You call it."

That got me a through-the-eyelashes look. When I didn't react, she said, "What do you want? And how much is it worth?"

"A private client. The more little-girl you get, the better he likes it. Drops hints that what he wants is the real thing. Maybe even comes right out and says it."

"A little girl? You mean, not playing: a *real*

little girl?"

"Babies. He'd want to know if you knew someone who could connect him. Maybe he's a black-market adoption guy, maybe —"

"I've got a whole lot of them who want to spank naughty little girls. But it's *me* they come to. *I'm* the little girl. I'm like an actress: you want a strict librarian, you want a brat, I've got the outfits *and* the attitude. None of that's really about pain. You want to know what pain is, try getting yourself a Brazilian. So, yeah, I've got the costumes. And the lollipops. But Little Lolita would be too old for the guy *you* want, right?"

"Right. I'm not looking for a client of yours — I want someone you would have turned down. A buyer, not a renter. Maybe even someone looking for a regular supply."

She blew a smoke ring expertly. Waited a beat. Said: "How about one who brings his own?"

"Baby?" I asked casually, controlling my voice.

"No. She's maybe, I don't know, five, six years old, like that. I mean, she's his own kid, right? So if he wants her punished for doing something wrong . . ."

"He pays you . . . ?"

"To spank the little snot, that's right," she

said, daring me to say anything. "Kink is kink. I don't judge."

"Me, either," I lied, thinking how Rejji had nailed this one cold. "And he does sound like he could be the right guy."

"He pays real good."

"Me, too."

"*He* pays regular."

"I get it. But *he's* not the man I want, just one who might give me a lead in the right direction. So you're not going to lose a client, see?"

"How high will you go?" she said, flipsiding the question I'd never ask her.

"I don't bargain. You want *me* to name a price, then you either take it or you pass. Or *you* can pick the number, and I get to do the same."

"I like it better when the man's in charge," she said, twisting her lips just in case I missed the point.

"Five large. Cash. Here. In your hand. Now."

"He pays —"

"*I'm* paying five large."

She sat there, pouting. I stood up.

"Okay," she said.

"She travels for this one," I told Clarence, signing the same to Max. "Her client only

116

gets his kid every other weekend. Visitation. It's in the divorce decree."

"House or apartment?" Clarence asked.

"House. Nassau County," I told him.

"One of those tacky developments?"

"No, girl," I answered Michelle. "He's got himself a serious piece of ground. An acre plus, easy."

Max made the sign for a dog snapping its jaws.

"No," I answered.

"Does he have any other protection, mahn?"

"The usual," I told Clarence. "But all electronic, nothing live."

"Burke, she's not going to see — ?"

"No, honey," I promised Michelle. "The whore told me how it goes. How it always goes. She drives to his house after dark. They sit in the living room, sip some wine, discuss what the little girl's done *this* time. The scene is like they're married, and the whore handles the discipline in the family. Meantime, the little girl's in her own room, way in the back. Waiting for him to call her."

Michelle's eyes went arctic.

"But this time, he's not going to call her," I went on. "It'll take a while, but, sooner or later . . ."

"The little girl comes out . . . and finds

117

the bodies."

I nodded.

"I do not like that," Clarence said.

"*She* will," Michelle told him. "Trust me on that one, honey."

I swept the room, holding all their eyes, one by one. This was family business, and we don't do "consensus" crap. Why vote when there's only one candidate?

"There's not going to be a sound," I said. "The little girl, at first, she'll creep down the hall, sneak a look. Probably think they just fell asleep. She'll go back to her room; I can't see her trying to wake them up. But next morning, when her father's supposed to be bringing her back . . ."

"That's when she'll call the cops. Like her mother should have," Michelle snarled.

"Mother?" I said. "Mom gets ten large a month. 'Child support.' You think she *doesn't* know?"

"There are all kinds of whores, little sister," Clarence said, gravely. Michelle was turning tricks before he'd been born, but she just nodded.

"A pro hit," was all she said. "A double, in fact. Who're the cops going to look at first?"

Max made a dismissive gesture.

"That's right," I agreed. "The wife wasn't

118

in on it, probably has the kind of alibi too good to plan. But the life-insurance guys are going to take a *hard* look at her. And they've got enough muscle to make even the Nassau County cops work for that insane money they get paid."

Max nodded.

I unzipped an airline bag. It was stuffed with cash. All I'd told Pryce was that the spank-whore was endangering the ongoing investigation; he wasn't the kind of employer who asked for expense-account receipts.

"Things just don't seem the same." Paul Butterfield, moaning his bluesboy anthem out of the sound system the Mole had wired for me. "Born in Chicago." Before my time. Gone before mine, too.

The blues aren't about color, they're about truth. Fuck those self-proclaimed purists who insist only genuine black males — preferably Delta-born ex-cons dying of TB — qualify. Probably the same twits who used to sport "Honkies for Huey" buttons and delude themselves how they were getting *down* with the "brothers." Today, they "keep it real" with gangsta-rap CDs that scream "nigger" louder than the KKK.

Naturally, they make an exception for Eric Clapton, which double-proves how weak they are. Clapton's fingers never danced like Mike Bloomfield's, and his voice doesn't belong in the same juke as Charlie Musselwhite's . . . but they probably never heard of either one.

I tried the TV. Watched some "sports journalists" sit around and blather about "team chemistry." Funny how they never say a word about the team chemist.

I remembered back when they blamed steroids for some pro wrestler killing his wife and young son, then hanging himself. "Why all this focus on baseball?" one of them demanded, righteously indignant. "How come they don't do drug testing in pro wrestling?"

The intellectual on the panel explained that drug testing wasn't a congressional priority because pro wrestling wasn't a sport, it was entertainment. Steroids were wrong, of course, but it's not as if you needed a competitive edge in a staged event.

The others nodded at this trenchant analysis, proving doping *is* allowed in the broadcast industry. Sure, nobody cares about steroid use in pro wrestling, but that isn't because it's not a "real" sport — it's because you can't *bet* on it. Who do you think cares more about an "undetected competitive edge" — protectors of the purity of the game, or the gambling industry? Just look at how hard they slammed that pro-basketball ref who admitted taking money to fix games. Those lobbyists really earn their money.

I chewed a few burnt almonds to get the sickening taste out of my mouth, hit the mute, and opened the paper. Some wet-brain on the city council announced he was sponsoring legislation to ban pit bulls. It's not that he wasn't an animal-lover — he had a bichon frise, didn't he? — it's just that he felt a moral obligation to protect citizens from those "genetically vicious" creatures. Guess he'd know about genetics, since his only qualification for public office was that his father had held the seat before him.

But the moron made me realize something: I'd waited long enough.

"I want to buy her."

"I ain't in that business, *ese.*"

"I know," I told the man who owned the two-pump gas station where I keep my Plymouth stashed, inside the same chain-link cage that protected trespassers from the pits who lived back there. Jester had built them a dog condo big enough for a family of six. Probably put in central air, too. "But, come on, bro, you went out and got a mate for that dragon of yours. They got together, she had a litter, and you kept one of them. So you must've done *something* with the others, yeah?"

"Never sold one," he said, as flexible as a suicide bomber. Jester was a businessman whose business you didn't want to know. Even if you missed the message of PELI-GRO'S AUTOMOTIVE sloppily spray-painted over the never-opened garage slots, the OUT OF GAS sign permanently fixed to the pumps was clear enough.

"I know that," I assured him. "And I know they never went near a scratch-line, either. I was here when those punks tried to get you to put your big guy back into the same game you pulled him out of, remember?"

He nodded. Crossed his arms. The python-tattooed biceps said he wasn't willing to concede he couldn't have handled all three of them by himself, but the nod granted that me slipping out from under the Plymouth and showing them I carried a snake of my own — a four-inch Colt King Cobra .357 — had changed the odds.

"I've been coming here for years, right? You think I'd ever — ?"

"No, no, *ese*. I know you don't even be *thinking* that. This on me, not you. When they was pups, I could find them homes with righteous folk, okay? But the little one, she been here too long. I call her Rosita, 'cause she's so pretty, but I never talk to her, you know? Not to her mother, either. That one's *muy loco;* a stone *cocodrilo.* You try and take her baby, she maybe take a piece of you, *comprende?*"

"I've been teaching the little one to trust me, Jester. For a long time now. I'll risk it."

"You sure, *amigo?* You know her father. Nova, he was a murder machine when I took him away from those *maricóns* who put him in the pits. Only got him a girlfriend because I thought it would calm him down a little. But the bitch I found, she turned out to be even meaner than him. Got those *bruja* eyes, you know? Any baby *those* two make, got to be hellfire in a fur coat."

"I'll risk it," I said again. "How much for — ?"

"Why you talk to me like that, *hermano?* Remember the first time you come around, ask me about storing your ride? I tell you, got to make some calls first?"

"I remember."

"Took a while, do that. What you think I am?"

I made a confused face, not knowing where he was going. Vacant lots don't scare me, but landmines do.

"I mean, you know I'm not no citizen," he explained.

"Me, either," I stalled.

"But you *look* like one, *ese*. Come on, you make me for, what, Mexican, maybe?"

"No."

He narrowed his eyes. "I'm *some* kind of spic, *sí?*"

"Okay, I get it." I looked him over carefully, said: "But not Cubano, not Puerto Rican. No way you're D.R., either."

"You pretty good, man. Got any more?"

"I can cross off Brazil."

"That was an easy one. You don't know no Portuguese, huh?"

"Escudo."

"Bueno!" He chuckled. Jester was a good eight inches shorter than me. Maybe a hundred pounds heavier, with less fat on him than a runway model on the snort-a-line diet.

"I know you've been locked up," I said, deliberately looking at the prison-issue tattoo that gave him the name I called him by. "But not on this side of the border."

He shrugged.

"And I don't see any MS-13 ink. Which means you're older than you look, because you've been across a long time."

"Pablito said you was a detective."

Now it was my turn to give him a look. Not many could call Dr. Pablo Cintrone "Pablito." You don't claim kinship with Una Gente Libre unless you're for real . . . or don't like oxygen.

Back in the day, UGL didn't operate like most so-called underground groups. No letters to the newspapers, no phone calls to the media, no bombs in public places. They had been credit-blamed for a number of outright assassinations over the years — a mixed bag of sweatshop owners, slum landlords, dope dealers, and some apparently honest citizens — but they never counted coup.

The word would go on the street that UGL wanted someone — and that someone would disappear. Dead or fled . . . without a body, you could never be sure.

The Puerto Rican *independistas* had been quiet for years, working a different angle from decades ago, when they were all about urban warfare and the FALN was the most feared of all the guerrilla groups.

Pablo and I go back a long time, to years before he became *el jefe* of the UGL. When he'd first introduced me to some of the fighters, he'd been careful to call me *"amigo mio,"* not *"amigo nuestro."* We don't exchange Christmas cards, but I was there the night his daughter was born, and I was there when one of his enemies had gone in the other direction.

His daughter's grown now. But all the years haven't widened the gap; if either of us reached, he'd still be able to touch the other.

"You the only gringo El Cañonero ever did a job for." Jester half-smiled, flashing his badge.

El Cañonero had been the second-most-feared sniper in the city. Never missed, never captured. He's been out of action for years. Like the Prof always says, "If there's a reason, there's a season." With UGL walking the slower road, switching from revolution to infiltration, El Cañonero was a hibernating bear. But spring always comes.

If Jester could even *find* Pablo, never mind get the UGL boss to vouch for me personally, his own roots went deep.

"Guatemala?" I guessed.

"I got this when I was thirteen," he said, flexing so the jester tattoo popped. "You know what it means?"

"Respect."

"*Sí*. Only one way to get that. I was born strong, and I learned to take a beating real young. Nothing special about that, not where I come from. They had some very bad *hombres* in that joint, but none of them laughed at the car batteries those cocksuckers used.

"That's how I got my name. I think it made me crazy, the pain. I don't remember actually laughing, but that's what they said I was doing when the *puercas* threw me back into the cage, after they finished their fun.

"In that cage, I had special respect. The old man who put this mark on me, he'd been locked down all his life, never to leave. He was the one who taught me. When I learned enough, I hired out.

" 'Your name can fly right over these walls,' he told me. And it worked just like the old man said it would: One of the *narco-reyes* bought me a pardon. I was supposed to go work for him, pay off what it cost him."

"Yeah, I know. A labor bond. They heard about how you handled enforcer work, so . . ."

"You got it."

"That old man, he named you right. The joke was on them, huh?"

"Three of them were there, all in white. They told me what I was supposed to do. Very simple. They bought me, so they owned me. They saw a big, stupid dog. Me, all I saw was three chicken necks. Snapped like dead twigs.

"After that, I found the people the old man had told me about, and they got me across. Pablo, he was waiting, just like the old man promised."

"You ever get enough cash together to spring him?" I asked, knowing that would have been Jester's first move.

"More than enough," he said. "Took a few months, but then I made the call. That's when I found out he was dead. They killed him the day after I made my move. The powder men marched right into the prison, took the old man out of his cell, and dragged him into the yard. They held him down on a block and sawed off his head. Slow, so everyone watching would see what it cost to fuck with them."

"Evil fucking —"

"That didn't buy them respect, bro; it cost them. The guy who told me about it said the old man's head kept rolling around the yard for a long time. Said his face was grinning like a cat in cream. Talk about the last laugh, huh?"

"Madre Dios!"

Jester laughed out loud. "You sad, Burke," he said, using my name for the first time. "Pablito always said you speak Spanish like you dance."

"I can't —" I said. Then I started laughing, too.

I used my key on the three-pound padlock, opened the chain-link, and stepped into their territory, a gallon thermos of Mama's beef-in-oyster-sauce in one hand.

The big stud strutted out, eyeballing me same as always. His world was like his little girl's coat: black and white. Either he recognized me, or I was a dead man.

Nova was a special brand of warlord: he *expected* tribute, but trying to bribe him would be suicide.

I poured out the contents of the thermos on the marble slab I'd installed over the concrete for just that purpose. Nova walked over, followed closely by his mate . . . and that orca-spotted little female I'd been courting so long.

While the others tore into Mama's cooking, she slipped behind me and deftly snatched the solid cube of filet she knew would be waiting, just for her. "That's my good little girl," I said.

Then I squatted down and patted her. A real one this time, not just a quick touch of her head, like I'd been doing. I even scratched her behind one ear, just to make sure.

This time, she didn't trot away.

"You want to come home with me?"

She sat, eyes shifting from my face to her father and mother.

"It's time," I told them.

The stud just watched. The mother looked at me. Into me.

Judge and jury, side-by-side. The only role still up for grabs was executioner.

I waited for the verdict.

Counted to fifteen in my head.

Then I started up the Plymouth. Let it reach operating temperature, the way I always do. I'd been keeping the passenger-side door open while I warmed up the engine for months now, getting them all used to the sight.

Usually, they all went right back into their dog condo as soon as I started up. This time, none of them moved.

The temp gauge said the Roadrunner's engine was ready. I took one more look. Nova was nowhere to be seen. But his killer-witch wife was still there, standing next to her last child.

I opened the passenger door, patted the seat, said, "Come on, sweetheart."

The dog I knew I was finally ready for

jumped in next to me. I reached across her, closed the door. Her mother's body was a statue, but her eyes crackled with death-threats.

I drove out slowly. Stopped. Went back, locked the gate behind me. And took my puppy home.

"She's a *beauty,* boss!"

"She sure is, Gate," I told the man in the wheelchair who slipped his hand back from under his guayabera shirt when he saw me come in the front door of the flophouse he "managed" from behind a thick wooden plank.

"Yours?"

"I hope so, brother. You know what they say."

"Time will tell," the shooter replied, confirming the only test a born convict recognizes.

If being carried up a few flights of filthy stairs bothered her, she didn't let on. I opened the door to my place, put her down, said, "It's yours, if you want it, Rosie."

That's when I realized I'd named her.

Training a dog isn't any more complicated than immediately rewarding them anytime they do something you want them to learn. Every time they do it, you add praise and a command, so they make the connection. Eventually they don't need the treats anymore. But that's just the mechanics of training, not the heart.

Rosie was a young dog, not a puppy. I'd never had a semi-grown one before, but I knew this much: if she was ever going to be really, truly mine, I had to be hers first.

She spent hours inspecting the place. I encouraged her verbally, but I didn't try teaching her anything. That night, I made her a bed out of thick blankets, right across from my cot.

When I opened my eyes the next morning, she was curled up next to me.

Some wino on a lower floor started screaming. Rosie jumped down and charged the front door, snarling, wagging her tail happily at the prospect of battle.

Defending her home.

When I had to, I used to be able to leave my Pansy alone for days; I rigged it so she could get food and water by herself. But I'd raised Pansy from a pup, and she knew I'd *always* come back, so I never worried about her getting all anxious while I was gone. Neos aren't exactly Jack Russells, anyway.

132

For the next couple of days, I took Rosie everywhere I went, but I didn't want her to think that's how it was always going to be. So I started leaving her. The first time, it was only ten minutes. The second I walked back in, she started spinning in place with excitement, then rushed me so hard she almost took me down.

Gradually, I increased the time between returns. "I'll *always* be back for you, Rosie," I told her, every single time.

Gateman was crazy about her, so I started leaving her with him, too.

"Watch this, boss!" he practically shouted when I came in late one night. Rosie had run over to me, and I was patting her and telling her what a perfect, beautiful girl she was, when Gateman yelled out: "Rosie, sit!"

And she did.

"Yeah!" Gateman cheered. "Come and get it, girl!"

She gave me a look, then trotted over and took whatever Gateman slipped her, swallowed it in one gulp.

"I never had a dog," the wheelchair-bound shooter said. "I know she ain't mine" — catching a look from me — "but I'm part of her family, right?"

"True blood," I notarized. Then I glanced behind the counter, saw the trailer-hitch

133

eye-bolt screwed into the floor, attached to a length of heavy chain.

"Got to have it, boss," he explained. "This little girl sees anybody coming through that door, she just *goes*. No yap-yap bullshit for her; she's a natural."

He didn't have to add "killer."

"I know it, Gate. But, look, that means, if any of our crew shows up and she's up there with me —"

"I call up and warn you, bro. She's gonna be one of us, but we go step by step, am I right?"

I tapped fists with him. When I said, "Home," Rosie charged up the stairs like a Great White who just heard a surfer convention was in town.

"Rose is such a beautiful name," Michelle said, stroking my dog's triangular head. "Why do you have to call her Rosie? That's a washerwoman's name. Not fit for a princess, is it?" she asked the pit.

"When you train a dog, you need a two-syllable name," I told Michelle. "It's all about getting them to focus, lock in on whatever you're saying, pay attention."

"Oh, for the love of —"

"I know what I'm doing, honey."

"Yes, you *are* quite the expert when it

comes to females."

"Give it up," I told my sister. "You're not winning this one."

"Men are like that," she said to my dog. "Aren't they, *Rose?*"

Only a certified imbecile licenses a pit bull these days. They've got that "born bad" tag on them so deep that lawmakers all over are trying to make them illegal. They're even a "banned breed" in some countries, and the disease is spreading. Pits can't hire lobbyists, so nobody's running around screaming about their right to own one, even if they can be dangerous in the wrong hands. I mean, it's not as if they were something sacred . . . like guns.

You know how those gangsta-boy punks "train" their dogs to fight? They feed them gunpowder. Ulcerates the lining of their stomachs until they're in so much pain all the time that it turns them vicious. I guess that doesn't qualify as irony — not cute enough for the bloggers, and too nasty for the poets.

I couldn't wait for Michael Vick to find Jesus, snatch himself some forgiveness, and go back to pro football. I could watch every game, hoping he'd get his spine snapped. Then they could just push his wheelchair into a swimming pool, and throw in a plugged-in space heater. Hey, if he can't breed, what good is he, right?

Still, I wasn't going to let Rosie walk around without tags and give some cop an excuse, so I did the good-citizen thing. The clerk didn't even blink when I put down "Taurus Uniqua" as her breed. I wrote "Rose" for her name.

You pay the money, you get a dog license, no questions asked. But if you want AKC credentials, you have to paper the provenance. Otherwise, you can't enter one of their oh-so-special shows.

The Nazis would have loved the spectacles those "dog lovers" put on: the winner is the one who comes closest to the physical-perfection template. Blue blood, blue ribbon, big bucks. That's why some breeders "cull" their litters. Can't have below-standard pups running around; those defective genes could pollute the perfection pool. A German shepherd with a spotted coat — now, *that's* a sin against nature.

I had Rosie microchipped, too. Things happen. If she was running loose, a Good Samaritan might get her to a shelter. The phone would ring at Mama's, and one of us would go get her.

Plus, I didn't want some Animal Control

idiot stopping Gateman's wheelchair for walking Rosie without tags. I consider it my civic duty to prevent violence.

"They had to take the leg, Prof," I said. Straight out, the way I knew he'd want it.

"Kind of suspected so," the old man said. "That skinny little nurse, Taralyn, I could see it in her eyes."

"Prof . . ."

"What's wrong with you, Schoolboy? I didn't lose nothing I'm gonna need. I look like fucking Bojangles to you?"

"You look like you always do," I told my father. "Sound the same, too."

He looked around for a long few seconds. Said, "This setup, it's not no charity ward. Am I right?"

"Yeah."

"What'd you do, son? Sell your soul to the Devil?"

"Not my soul," I told my father.

Then I told him the rest.

The papers quoted the cops as saying they had a "person of interest" in the double homicide that had been dominating the headlines. The crime was perfect fodder for tabloid slop, with a little TV-cop talk sprinkled in. Both victims had been shot in the back of the head — "execution-style," of course — so the "Mansion Murders" must have been the work of a "professional."

"The kid's in temporary foster care," Terry said, looking up from his laptop screen.

"That didn't take long."

"Come on, Burke. My part shouldn't even count as an exploit, not with all the social engineering you did first."

It was good to know I still had the phone skills — scamming the names of a random group of CPS caseworkers had been easier than bribing a congressman.

Terry's first trick — accessing public records to get the vitals on each one — had hit pay dirt. "They let them use anything they want for a password," he explained, shaking his head in disgust. "They don't even require alpha-numerics, just has to be six characters or more. Pathetic. Most people, they just put in their own name or birthday. Hit it on the third try."

I patted the kid — I was going to have to stop calling him that, even in my mind — on the shoulder.

"Nice work, T. Probably means the little girl told the cops what that woman they found next to her father was really there for. And you *know* the cops looked at the father's computer. It was a crime scene, right? No warrant required. Maybe the whore's prints were already in the system, too.

"The media's gonna be all over this, so there's no way CPS gets to look the other way . . . not with people looking at *them.* Guaranteed they'll be asking that 'mother' some questions."

"I've got some questions I'd like to ask her."

"Leave that to the insurance investigators, T. Those cold-blooded bastards will be looking for as much ammo as they can stockpile. See, here's a trifecta you can bet the farm on: the mother files a claim on the father's big-bucks life insurance; the company denies it, and she sues."

"She is just as guilty as —"

"More," I said to Clarence, who had been standing quietly, watching the computer screen. "But that's the kind of 'trafficking' that they don't do TV specials about." I was thinking of Beryl, the little girl I'd "saved" so many years ago. Thinking about what she'd become — even psychopaths will tell you the truth if they want to.

And how *very* much Beryl had wanted to.

"You didn't ping me to make a progress

report," Pryce said. "And you didn't need a meeting to get more money. So you must want something done."

"A meeting. But not with you."

"Who, then?"

"This 'prince' of yours."

"Look, Burke, this isn't a man you can just —"

"I'll play by whatever rules you lay down. But if you want a win, I've got to get in the game. People always know more than they think they know, only that never comes out unless you ask the right questions. If this guy really wants the baby as bad as he —"

"What are you trying to say?"

"Trying? I already said it."

Pryce looked at me, no expression in his inky eyes. An apex predator isn't programmed for deep analysis. On *this* island, Pryce was a Komodo dragon — every living thing was his potential prey. He wasn't trying to read me; he was reading the menu.

"There's a lot of talk about you," he finally said. "A man could get a headache, reading through all of the files."

"Is that right?"

"Yes," he said, almost sorrowfully. "The problem is, one piece of intel contradicts the other."

"That's because it's not 'intelligence,' it's

politics. Like a Supreme Court judge: He doesn't give a fuck about the law; he just knows what *he* wants. So he orders his clerks to go find enough bricks to build his 'opinion' with. Like that 'partial birth abortion' pile of crap they came up with."

"You think everyone's bent, don't you?" Pryce said. Not being sarcastic, looking for that straight-from-the-source "intel" that he'd spent his life collecting. And using.

"No," I told him. Not just because it was the truth, but because I don't like pigeon-holes any more than I like prison cells. "And I don't think 'every man has his price,' either. No pun intended."

"But the law itself — ?"

"Bent? It's downright twisted," I cut him off. "All the way from the root to the branches to the dirty blossoms with that foul smell. In this city, the lower-court judges are 'merit appointments' . . . meaning the mayor gets to pick whoever he wants. The higher levels, you have to run for election . . . meaning the party bosses get to pick whoever *they* want. Nothing to do with politics, right? Or money? Take it all the way to the top, it doesn't change. Ask George Bush how this Miers broad got herself qualified to be nominated for the Supreme Court.

"What's with the innocent act, all of a sudden? You actually think any of those judges *don't* have a personal position on abortion? Or capital punishment? Or gay rights? No matter what they say, they know their real job is to make the Constitution dance to the tune of whoever appointed them, okay?

"Come on, tell me I'm wrong. Tell me they *don't* come in with their own agendas, and twist their rulings to fit. What else are you selling today? Lobbyists got that rich by playing the horses? Congressmen made their fortune in the real-estate market? Jesus."

Pryce just did his thing: watched, and listened.

And, despite knowing I should have shut up minutes ago, I hammered on, hating myself for falling under his spell. "Maybe you're even one of those mopes who thinks jury nullification is some kind of 'black protest' thing? Better not ask the jury on the Emmett Till case. How come 'states' rights' was good enough when they had to justify segregation, but it went down the tubes when medical marijuana showed up? How come kids who've been abused get actual lawyers in some states, but others only give them a warm, caring amateur who has to kiss the judge's ass if she wants to be allowed in the courtroom at all?"

"Just Us," Pryce said.

"Spare me the Paris Hilton stories, pal. A guy like you, you'll never get it. Sure, that's how cons spell 'justice,' but that's not like saying you're innocent; it's saying you didn't have enough coin to buy a walk-away. You rolled the dice and crapped out, that's all. You don't sit around and wait for things to *be* fair; you just learn to never *fight* fair."

He looked at me for what I guess he thought was a long time. Then he said: "I mentioned intel for a reason, Burke — I'm not the only one with access to it."

"Meaning, this prince guy has got friends who can pull files?"

"And that's just what he *will* do, on anyone he meets with."

"Including you?" I asked, guessing that it was one of the no-budget-line government departments that had contacted Pryce, not the Prince himself.

"That part's no problem," he said dismissively. "I'm on the books. You're not."

"So put me on them. Pick a name, make up a background — you know, whatever they do for you, every time they send you out."

"You're not listening," he said. "There is

no *Central* Intelligence Agency." Pryce would know — he spent his life sliding through government walls like cigarette smoke through a window screen. "The Sheikh might have access to more than one source. Especially from the international desks."

"So?"

He leaned back, a boxer dropping his shoulder to launch a hook. "Does the '4 Commando' unit ring a bell with you?"

"Huh?" I slipped the shot, throwing back the look of honest confusion I'd been perfecting in police interrogations since I was a kid.

"Mad Mike Hoare's crew," he went on, unruffled. "In Katanga, it was the '5 Commando.' After that, he disappeared for a little while. Resurfaced in Biafra sometime in '67 or so. Rumor has it that it was his team who escorted Ojukwu out of the kill zone, once it became obvious that Nigeria was going to wipe out the rebels."

"Never met him." The truth. "Never even heard of him." A deliberately transparent lie.

"You *do* understand that you're still listed as a war criminal by the Nigerians?"

"What's a 'war criminal'?" I said . . . a more polite form of "I don't give a fuck."

"Good question," he answered, surprising me. "Everybody knows about the Geneva Convention. Because it was supposed to establish rules for armed combat between nations, it was assumed the combatants would be *members* of those nations. Of course, that never was the truth, but it wasn't until the late Seventies that anyone admitted it. Then the Convention was amended — called 'Protocols Additional' — to cover hired guns.

"Boiled down to the essentials, the Protocols say that mercenaries aren't soldiers, they're common criminals. If captured, they're not entitled to POW status. They can't be repatriated to their home country, because their home country isn't at war with the country they were fighting in. Ask Simon Mann.

"So, what they get is a trial," he said, parboiling the last word in a thick soup of sarcasm. "If the court finds the combatant to be a mercenary, they can do whatever they want to him."

"Even if — ?"

"A few years after Vietnam, some 'guerrillas' in Angola were put on trial right after they were captured. About a dozen in all. Three British nationals were sentenced to death. One American, too."

"Sentenced?"

"They were executed about two weeks later. Firing squad. The rest of them got the kind of prison sentences nobody expected them to survive."

"I'm guessing there was no U.S. Embassy there."

"What if there was? America never signed that protocol. Why should we? America never uses mercs, it only sends 'military advisors.' If a private citizen commits a crime in a foreign country, he's on his own."

"Fuck you *and* your Protocols, Pryce. Isn't there one about not using child soldiers, too? For my money, we should tell the UN to find a new place to live, turn the whole building into condos."

"I was just giving you some info I thought you might —"

"What, *use?* This 'war criminal' crap, it's just another way of saying that a tourist visa to Nigeria would only buy me a one-way trip. Is that supposed to be news?"

"I thought you might be interested in knowing the Nigerian government has a long memory."

"Which government would that be? The guys who won that last 'election'?"

"Don't be deliberately stupid, Burke. The Prince is a Muslim. And Muslims rule most of Nigeria, no matter who's supposedly in charge. Shari'a is the only law in the parts of the country they control, which is most of the land."

"So?"

"So *they* have a list of every mercenary who served in the Biafran conflict."

I made a "so what?" gesture.

"That's right," he agreed. "All they have is the name you were using at the time. No photographs, no fingerprints. But they *do* have access to an individual who says he can identify all his . . . former comrades."

"I bet they do. The mercs who fought there were a real mixed bag. Some were just nigger-killers, some thought they were fighting Communism. But most of them were strictly about the cash. Not just the salary, the 'finders-keepers' booty. A diamond's not a rare stamp or a painting. It doesn't have a history that can be traced. Fits in your pocket, too.

"So, yeah, I'm sure they got one of them to point out anyone he'd ever seen in-country: Peace Corps volunteers, before they had to flee. Red Cross workers, before one of their supply planes was shot down. Even the priests who never left São Tomé — that was the staging area, wall-to-wall with mercs coming and going."

"Is that where you flew in from?"

"Is this where I'm supposed to tell you if your guess is right?"

"I don't guess," Pryce said. "And I'm not dumb enough to buy what I already own. Those Canadian pilots are incredible, aren't they?"

"I thought the Count was Swedish," I said, acting as if he was talking about the mad-with-courage Quixote who built the "Biafran Air Force" out of spare parts, instead of the no-nerves pilots who flew ancient Connies over the war zone through the black night, diving down to a dirt runway lit only by flares, as casually as if they were dropping off a truckload of Budweiser behind a 7-Eleven.

"You were lucky," he said, giving up.

"I was stupid," I told him. "A stupid kid who thought he was going to be a hero. But if *you* don't know what I was doing there, I'd be real surprised. And if you think I'd ever so much as set foot on that *continent* again, you should change therapists."

He gave me a look that could mean anything.

"You think Katanga isn't *still* a butcher shop?" I said, deliberately referencing where he'd started this game. He was an opponent I couldn't KO, maybe, but I could take whatever he threw. For as many rounds as he wanted to go.

"I understand," he said, calmly. "But the Prince could still have sources we don't know about."

"What he doesn't have is a photograph," I said, confidently. "And even if he did, it wouldn't resemble what you're looking at now. There's no risk."

"What would I tell him?" Pryce asked, throwing in the towel.

"Why tell him anything? I'm a man you hired. I don't need a name for that. He wouldn't expect me to give him one."

"You don't want to give him anything else, either," Pryce warned.

"You don't seriously think I'm walking into some *embassy*, do you?" I half-laughed. "Here's how it goes. I pick the spot. I don't search him; he doesn't search me. He can bring anyone he wants, but the only DNA left behind at the scene is going to be his."

"He'll never —"

"This one's nonnegotiable," I told the shape-shifter. "He doesn't like it, fuck him. At least you'll find out how bad he really wants that baby back."

"The Devil don't need to breed to sow his seed."

"So *having* the baby —"

"— wasn't enough. You can't be born with what that scumbag was teaching his child. He loses the kid, he loses all the work he put into him."

"So you think — ?"

"That the baby's seen a whole lot more than Pryce's people found out about? Sure! That wasn't no single meal the freak was feeding him, Schoolboy; it was that little child's *diet,* hear me?"

"Yeah, Prof," I said to the old man in the hospital bed. And I did. That's why ethnic cleansers use rape as a weapon of war. Any baby born from those rapes will be doomed, rejected as impure by his own people, a living symbol of their enemy's triumph . . . if it's allowed to live at all. What better place to leave your mark than inside your enemy?

Genocidal rapists always claim a holy reason for what *want* they do.

Only one thing is true about Truth: when everybody claims to be telling it, some of them have to be lying.

Years ago, I'd watched Wolfe throw a brick through that plate-glass window. A man and a woman — citizen's words, not mine — had been convicted of slow-killing a little baby. At the trial, the Medical Examiner testified that the exact cause of death couldn't be determined. Too many possibilities: complications from the violent sodomy, food-deprivation, traumatic shock . . . All he could say for sure was that the death was a homicide.

Wolfe stood up at the sentencing hearing, wearing her trademark black-and-white colors, gray gunfighter's eyes locked on the slab-faced political appointee who got to make the final call. I can still hear every word:

"Your Honor, as you know, the law provides for Victim Impact Statements, so the victim's loved ones have an opportunity to tell the Court how the offender's crime affected their own lives. All this *Court needs to know about* this *case is that there isn't a single human being on this planet who could make such a statement."*

The judge listened to the mother's lawyer claim she was a battered woman, totally under the control of her sadistic monster of a husband. He listened to the father's lawyer say how the mother had taken her frustration at her husband's repeated affairs — "for which he takes full responsibility, Your Honor" — out on the helpless child.

Then he maxed them both. Whether it was the truth of the torture chamber that had been the child's life, or the truth of Wolfe's clear threat to answer the media's questions the wrong way, nobody knows.

The mother would be out by now, released while she was young enough to have a couple more babies and score a Welfare check to hand over to her new "man."

The father had been on Rikers, waiting for his transfer Upstate, when someone slid a concrete-honed sliver of steel deep into his kidney, then snapped off the taped handle. When the guards couldn't wake him up the next morning, they rolled him onto a gurney.

Nobody claimed the body.

I didn't like working so close to the Mole's junkyard, but it was the only place where we could have built the set in privacy before the opening curtain.

Identical black Mercedes sedans formed a circle around the aluminum Quonset hut like an army laying siege to a flimsy fort. A dozen men positioned themselves, weapons starkly outlined against the Hunts Point prairie twilight.

Two men entered the hut, immediately stepping to opposite sides in a gears-meshing move they must have practiced a thousand times. Each held a shoulder-strapped machine pistol in one hand and a portable spotlight in the other. One swept up, the other down.

All they saw was a dirt floor, a bare aluminum ceiling, and a man sitting on an old padded secretary's chair with a hollow orange crate to his right, topped with a blue glass ashtray. The man's face was covered with a black mesh mask, slit at the mouth. Pale-yellow glasses covered his eyes and distorted the shape of his face. A dull-gray sweatshirt hung loosely over his upper body.

They could also see the back of a brand-new black leather armchair, with its own orange crate and ashtray.

The man they saw was smoking. A red scar was visible on the back of his hand.

One of them said something in Arabic into a hand-held. About a minute later, the door opened again, and another man made an entrance. He lacked the centered balance of the first two, but moved with the confidant grace of an Invulnerable.

"The hardest thing to disguise is the voice," the Mole had told me. *"It is fortunate that your teeth . . ."*

It was a while before he said, "There! Now concentrate on moving your lips as little as possible. Let your voice come through the new upper bridge. Do not speak from your stomach or your chest; use only your throat.

Shallow breaths. Are you ready to practice?"

When I nodded, he flipped some switches, adjusted the microphones, and watched his meters until he was satisfied.

The special man took the leather armchair, reached into a jacket that cost enough to buy a hundred human lives in his home country, removed a single dark-papered cigarette from a slim, dull-colored metal case, and fired it up with a lighter so small it looked as if flame had materialized in his hand. He took a connoisseur's sip of his smoke, leaned back, and regarded me silently.

"When I grant an audience, I expect to see the face of the man who sits across from me," he said, after he realized I wasn't going to speak until he did.

If I'd been one of those Chandler-clone private eyes, it would have been time for a wisecrack about burqas. But I don't walk the mean streets, I live below them. I'm not an ex-cop with friends on the force; I'm an ex-con who knows the cops for what they are. I'm not a war hero; I'm a man for hire. So I just said, "This is what you agreed to with my boss."

"When a man takes my money . . ."

This glossy, silk-wrapped thing was cruder than the stuff they pumped from the ground he owned, about as subtle as a Tijuana sausage show. Whoever was paying me, he could pay more — gee, never heard *that* one before.

"I'm on salary," I told him, listening to the reedy voice of a man I wouldn't have recognized myself. "I just do what I'm told."

That he recognized. An almost effeminate gesture with the fingers of his right hand dismissed the two professionals who had cleared the path for him. They barely disturbed the air as they left, but I knew I had been photographed somehow.

"I need to get the facts straight," I told him, no authority in my voice, just a man explaining his assignment.

"I have already —"

"This is my specialty," I interrupted. "Some of those who do . . . what was done in your case, have what we call a 'signature.' A highly stylized way of doing things, as distinctive as a fingerprint. This is even more prevalent for teams. Everything you told my employers was recorded, of course. But that was an account, not an —"

"I do not submit to interrogations," he said, in the tone of a man who was making it clear he was used to *ordering* them.

"I was going to say 'interactive conversation,' " I told him.

"I have a title," he reminded me.

"I understand. I even understand what that means to the people I work for. I already told you what I do. No disrespect intended, but I can't do my work if I have to keep remembering titles; it breaks the rhythm, and I might miss something. Something important."

"Then perhaps your employers can provide someone with a better sense of his place."

"I'm sure they could. I'm sure they would do whatever you asked them to."

"Including disclosing your identity." He smiled.

I lit a fresh cigarette, as if his devastating riposte had shaken my confidence. "That's up to them," I admitted.

"I have come this far, you may as well go ahead and ask your questions," he said, satisfied that things were finally as they were meant to be.

"You were parked overlooking the Hudson River?"

"Yes," he replied, annoyed at having to repeat the memorized lie so many times.

"Approximately two-thirty in the morning?"

"Yes."

"Your vehicle was a . . ."

"Rolls-Royce. A 100EX drophead."

That model was supposed to be a "concept" car, not available to the public. But it wouldn't surprise me if this human pile of privilege had one of his own, sitting in a private garage. But you'd never find the custom Rolls he used to train his baby there. It wouldn't be in any police crime lab, either.

"Your son —"

"The Prince."

"— was in the front seat with you?"

"Next to me. In his own seat. He is still too young to sit quietly by himself."

"And the top was down?"

"Yes. The sun rises in the east, as Allah intended. We were facing west, because I was teaching him to anticipate its emergence."

"No other cars pulled in? After you did, I mean."

"None."

"And then?"

"Then!? From nowhere they appeared. I was turned to my right, speaking to my son, when I sensed some kind of movement behind me. Suddenly there was a sharp pain somewhere here" — touching the back of his neck — "and the next thing I remember, two police officers were talking to me."

"By then, you were in a different car, in a different place?"

"Yes. That car was mine as well. Another Rolls, but with custom coachwork."

"Do you have any idea how — ?"

"I ended up in the other car? The keys were in my pocket, and the other car was parked within eyeshot, in front of a ship-builder's facility. I had arranged all this the day before. The drophead has a panel to cover the area into which the top is lowered. The panel itself is teakwood — as on a yacht — so it requires regular maintenance. I was planning to exchange the cars when the facility opened, and drive the one in which I was later found back to my residence."

"So you think the kidnappers changed cars because the one you were originally in would be so visible?"

"The drophead is a sort of iridescent blue, while the other is plain black, very low-key. How else to explain such conduct? Obviously, these were no common thieves. My wristwatch alone would have brought —"

"And by moving you all the way downtown to where they did, they bought themselves some time before you'd be discovered."

"I am certain that is also true."

"So two teams . . ." I trailed off my voice, letting him hear my thoughts. "One to take the baby away; another to transport your other car, with you in it."

"It seems so," he said, not really interested. I'd already shown myself stupid enough to buy his story, so how useful could I be?

"Do you remember — ?"

"I have already —"

"— anything you *haven't* been asked about," I went on, as if he hadn't spoken. "Like, for example, a strange smell?"

"A . . . smell?"

"Whoever took you out had to be very close to do it. That's what anesthesia is: it doesn't 'put you to sleep,' it knocks you unconscious. No puncture mark was found, so they probably used a nerve block. And your nostrils and upper lip showed slight chloroform burns."

"I never smelled any —"

"Not chloroform; you would have already been out by then. I mean just *before* there was any physical contact. There had to be a gap there, if only for a split second. It would take a minimum of two men to do what I just described, and —"

"Alcohol!"

"Alcohol as in — ?"

"Liquor," he said, nodding slowly to himself, as if absorbing a revelation. "Liquor is forbidden among our people. I can instantly detect its presence, just as a non-smoker can discern if another person uses tobacco, even if they are not doing so at the time they meet."

"Was it overpowering, or just a — ?"

"Not drunk," he said, thoughtfully. "But it was a man who *does* drink. It wasn't his breath, it was his body. Do you follow what I am — ?"

"Yes," I encouraged him. "Liquor remains in the liver for a long time. That's why you see alcoholics dying from cirrhosis even years after they quit drinking."

"Nobody asked me that question," the Prince said. He lit another smoke, slightly less ceremoniously this time. "Do you have others?"

"Did anyone know your plans for the day your son was taken? Or for the night before?"

"My . . . plans?" he said, as if the very concept was beyond comprehension. Nobody had ever taught him that haughtiness is a lousy disguise for anxiety. "I had no 'plans.' I told you, I only wanted my —"

"Ah. Excuse my poor phrasing," I assured

him, indicating I wasn't suspicious, just ignorant. "I meant your *schedule.* A person of your position, there would be a secretary, perhaps more than one? A personal assistant? A *chargé d'affaires?* And there are always security considerations as well, isn't that so?"

"In some situations, certainly," he said, choosing to respond only to my last question. "But I have no need to travel about with bodyguards all the time."

Not unless you go back where you came from, I thought. But I wasn't going to let him divert the probe so easily: "Still, the staff . . ."

"I have no need of —"

"With all respect, *someone* would have to keep track of your appointments, make reservations —"

"If you mean at restaurants and the like, I require no reservations. My appearance is sufficient."

Real good at talking about what you don't *need, aren't you?* I thought. "But there are so many trivial matters. . . ."

He demonstrated his understanding of both royal privilege and triviality by not deigning to respond. I'd seen that move, too.

"Your clothes?" I tried another tack.

"My personal tailor sees to that. He comes to my residence whenever he is summoned."

"Jewelry?"

"I do not go 'shopping,' as you Americans seem so addicted to. That is women's work, shopping. When one of the designers I have deemed acceptable has something to show me, he will call and seek an audience."

Call who, *you dumb fuck?* I kept that one to myself, and switched angles. "Doctors . . . ?"

"This is quite annoying," he reminded me. "Apparently, you do not understand. Those who serve me always *come* to me. Doctors, lawyers, financial managers . . ."

My turn to remind *him.* "Somebody knew where you were going to be that night. This was no random attack. They had to have *some* advance notice in order to get both of those teams in place."

Sometimes you have to tighten a soft interrogation, pressurize the situation. But you still have to color inside the lines, keep the subject thinking you believe his story as long as possible.

"Nobody knew," he said, firmly. No problem believing *that* part: no way he told some secretary every time he went out to find another way to show his son that all women were holes.

"That leaves only one possibility," I mused out loud.

"Which is?" he asked. He spoke casually, but his body posture was too rigid to carry it off.

"Surveillance."

"That cannot be done," he said, with a sureness I knew he couldn't possibly feel, even if his eyes weren't already clouding with doubt.

I was inside before he realized there'd been an opening. "An operation such as you described is very expensive," I said. "And very risky. Whoever pulled it off had only one objective: the baby. *Your* baby. That leaves only three possibilities. Ransom —"

"There has been no request for money. If there had been, I would already —"

"Then two more. Does the baby have an unusual blood type?"

"He is the direct linear descendant of —"

"Not that kind of blood. A rare type that could make a certain transfusion work. Or a bone-marrow donation. Or even a transplant."

"They would harvest *my* — !"

"I don't know. I can only work with what we *do* know. Your baby was taken for a reason. If we can find the reason, we can find the baby. That's why I'm here."

He made a visible effort to calm himself. I would have helped him with his breathing if I didn't know that it wasn't the thought of someone chopping his baby up for parts that was making that vein throb in his temple; it was the personal affront. That baby was *his* property.

It took a long minute before he could calm himself enough to talk. But by then, he had recaptured the imperiousness of a ruler instructing a slow-witted servant:

"The child's blood type is O-positive. He has been examined since birth — *before* birth — by the finest physicians in the world. Not a trace of unusual . . . *anything* has ever been detected. He is an exceptionally intelligent child, very handsome — all have remarked upon this. But to even suggest he has some rare genetic trait is insane. All such information would have been presented to me long ago."

Yeah. And all you Nazis know what to do with defectives, don't you? I thought. I knew no member of the Royal House of Saud was going to have a Down-syndrome kid. Not for long, anyway.

"A ransom demand could still come," I said out loud. "But it's been a while. Holding on to a baby is tricky business. For all the kidnappers know, the child could have a serious allergy. A medication he has to take. A special diet. It's a long list, and every hour increases the risk. *Their* risk. And there's one thing we know for sure. . . ."

He raised his royal eyebrows.

"The baby *must* be kept alive. If they want to sell him back to you, they have to show the goods."

"But no one has even —"

"If they wanted him dead, why not do it right there?" I countered. "You, too, for that matter."

"You said three," he said, wanting to get away from all these frightening speculations and return to where he was comfortable.

"I did. So . . . do you have any enemies?" I asked, blindsiding a man who couldn't even see what was sitting across from him.

Minutes passed. The Prince smoked another cigarette, shifted in his chair, play-acting a man thinking through a complex problem.

I acted like a man wearing a toe-tag.

"The Jews would never do this," he finally said.

"I'm not following —"

"The Zionists. They are rabid dogs, a blight on Allah's earth. But they are clever, too; it is in their blood as deeply as their greed. They have many friends in this country, I know. But those are political friends, and such friends cannot be purchased for a lump sum, as one would buy a car. No, that sort of friendship must be fed, as a plant is watered. Otherwise . . ."

His voice trailed off as he looked at me, making sure I understood the insights he was sharing. A nod was all I needed to turn the faucet on again.

"The Jews murder Palestinian children in their beds, but American politicians can still take their money without fear of criticism. They will call anything the Israelis do 'self-defense,' or an 'accident,' or whatever they need to. No one will challenge them.

"Yours is a bizarre country. Those Christian leaders who admitted that the destruction of your World Trade Center was proof of their *own* God's anger at the moral degradation of America? They, too, hate the Jews. Yet they love Israel," he said, curling his lips.

I said nothing, just tilted my head to show I was listening.

"The Jews are too sly to kidnap the child of a man whose only crime is to love and serve Allah. That would show this country their true nature, and your politicians could no longer support them in safety," he finished his sermon. Then leaned back, leaving his irrefutable logic on the table.

I nodded, still looking for a way in. "I was asking about a *personal* —"

"Your politicians may be reviled, but the average American is a 'believer' of some sort — he does not understand the need for realism in life. Your former president, the one before that simpleminded tool, now *he* was a master at mixing politics and realism."

"Clinton? He was a fool. If he hadn't —"

"Meaningless," the Sheikh scoffed. "Clinton did what any man of power would do. He understood that all the self-righteous hysteria would pass. As it did. You do not appreciate the finesse of a man who could pardon a Jewish thief like Marc Rich, while refusing to release a Zionist patriot like Jonathan Pollard."

I didn't say anything. Clinton *had* been slick at dispensing that special brand of compassionate largesse. Like when he commuted the sentence of Mel Reynolds, a Chicago pol who used an intern for sex.

Don't go for the cheap joke: Reynolds's intern wasn't a mistress or a wannabe wife, she was an underage girl. And then there was that solicitation to get her to pose for porn, too. While Reynolds was doing time on that charge, a federal indictment dropped on him, for all kinds of political corruption.

That was the sentence Clinton cut, so Reynolds could serve the rest of his time in a halfway house. Working for Jesse Jackson.

You know what they call a Chicago politician who lives on his salary? Unfit for office.

The Sheikh took my blanked-out face for skepticism, and answered the question I hadn't been planning to ask. "A man of higher intelligence is capable of recognizing the commitment of his enemies. Pollard was a Zionist fanatic, but his acts were in service to his filthy people, not for personal profit. That is the difference between a soldier and a mercenary. Both fight, but one for a cause, the other for cash.

"A man clever enough to balance the interests of others is simultaneously serving his own. Clinton was a friend to our people, as was Bush. A wise man understands that different tools may be used for the same purpose, if employed skillfully."

"*Personal* enemies," I repeated, kicking myself for having given him an excuse to continue his pompous little *Realpolitik* lecture. Another Machiavelli disciple who didn't know his idol had spent his last years on earth rotting in a dungeon. But I knew better than to derail an interrogation by arguing, so I stayed subdued and patient:

168

"Someone who hates you enough to want to do whatever would hurt you the deepest way possible. Not some petty grudge, a blood-and-bone hatred. And it would have to be someone with significant resources, too."

Another couple of minutes of silence. His thinking was transparent: in his mind, most of his subjects might fit the first criterion, but none could fit the second.

"There is no one like that," he finally said.

"There's a clock on this one, and it's ticking way down," Pryce said. He was seated across from me in my booth at Mama's, sipping "house soup" that might have cyanide as its secret ingredient, nervous as a wolverine watching a squirrel.

"Clock? Well, I'm ready to punch mine," I told him. "Go home for the day, or *call* it a day, whichever you want."

"Why did you go so . . . extreme?" he asked, ignoring my offers.

"This sheikh of yours, the way his mind works, I'm sitting there, disguised in the darkness, because I'm someone he might see again one day."

"You mean when that van he had stashed a few miles away returned to the place where you set up the meet . . ."

"That 'van' was a rolling lab. As soon as his little caravan passed by, it was going to move in. No way humans occupy space without leaving some kind of trace evidence. I wasn't even wearing gloves."

"Wouldn't a simple fire have worked as well? That explosion sent the whole building into orbit."

"A fire big enough to cleanse that Quonset hut would bring all kinds of attention."

"And an explosion *wouldn't?*"

"Nope. That's the badlands out there. Right on the frontier; a known trading post for *contrabandistas,* especially those who deal in weapons. Somebody test-firing product before they buy, that's just business-as-usual. Boom! So what? But arson, now, *that's* suspicious. Better the whole thing just disappears."

He took another sip of his soup.

"Besides," I said, "doing it the way we did sends your pal a message he needed to hear."

He shifted posture to ask the unspoken question.

I shifted mine, to say I wasn't going to answer.

"You wanted him to *know* you expected him to return and vacuum the place for some clue to your identity," he finally said.

"And that you were the type of individual who doesn't take those chances?"

I nodded, thinking of the scar decal now gone from my hand.

"What if some of his people had been — ?"

"They wouldn't send anyone in right away; no way for them to know when I'd vacate the premises," I explained. "Anyway, they couldn't possibly get the van there in under ten minutes. The place was a hole in the ground thirty seconds after I left."

I didn't bother telling Pryce that a few dead prince-protectors would bother me about as much as canceling reruns of *The Brady Bunch*.

"So . . . nothing?"

"He didn't tell any lies you didn't already know," I confirmed.

"How about some truth?" he asked, still politely sipping his soup. I was having some, too, only mine was in one of the BARNARD mugs Mama used for family. Pretty generous of her to buy us each one of those mugs, considering she'd been slicing a piece off every score "for baby's college" from the moment Max's woman, Immaculata, had announced she was pregnant.

Flower came from inside Immaculata's body; Michelle had taken Terry's shivering little body into her arms and never let him go. That happened in the backseat of my car, as I was driving away from what I'd left of the pus-sack who'd been renting the kid out.

Came *from,* came *to* — no difference. They're both ours. Our blood.

How *you* look at it doesn't matter to us. Citizens think a trial verdict depends on the evidence; *we* know all that counts is who's on the jury. Some of you get to visit our world, but none of you really sees it. Some of you try too hard, stick your nose in too deep. Then you don't get to leave.

"He doesn't have a clue," I told Pryce. "And not just because he's a forty-watt bulb who thinks he's a chandelier. But he's not lying when he says he wants the baby back — whoever has that kid could be a billionaire tomorrow."

"And you still don't think it was a job?"

"A job? Sure. Contracted out, too. But that kind of work has rules — you never work where you live."

"So . . . not Americans?"

"It doesn't matter where they were born. I'm saying, if this was an orchestrated snatch, you're dealing with top-tier players. Internationalists. The kind of globalized organization that could make a hundred mil wire-transfer disappear in seconds, and turn the cash into precious metals before the commodities market closes that day."

"High-stakes gamblers, then?"

"No," I said. He was grasping, without a straw in sight.

"No? Think of the *investment* involved in a project like this. Surveillance isn't just manpower; it's equipment. Expensive equipment. Some information can't be gathered; it has to be bought. Then there's the cost of transporting a baby out of the —"

"That's not gambling," I cut him off. "If this was done by the kind of organization you're talking about, they wouldn't extend their risk by holding on to the kid. Which means they were hired guns, not working for themselves."

"We've reached out —"

"And *struck* out, or you wouldn't have come near me. And *I'm* telling you: there is no way this was a kidnap scheme."

Pryce nodded. "It wasn't any of the contract organizations we know about."

"And the reason you know that is because they know *you*, see? That means they know you've not only got the cash to pay them, you've also got ways to make *them* pay if they don't take it."

He nodded again.

"There isn't a baby on this planet that's worth what this whole deal had to cost. The kind of freaks you think *could* have done it — the reason you came to talk to me in the first place — there's even less chance this was their work."

"Because you asked around or . . . ?"

"I did ask around. But I'm saying it because somebody wanted that *particular* kid. *Only* that kid. The baby-snatchers you're thinking of, they're opportunity-players. Sure, their sensors are always out, and they've got trip wires strung all around. A kid steps into the wrong spot, he's gone.

"And, yeah, sometimes they work in pairs. *Pairs,* not teams. But telling a kid walking home from school that you've got a puppy in the back of your van isn't exactly 'professionalism.' This was a coordinated operation, tightly planned. Different men, different specialties. *Very* specific orders. And lots of rehearsal time."

He opened his lizard-slit of a mouth. I held up my hand to stop him. "Yeah, some-times you get a freak who fixates, death-grips on his obsession. Maybe some child star, maybe some kid who got his picture in the papers. Doesn't matter how it happens, but the freak just knows they're *meant* to be together.

"Those kind, some of them stalk, some of them shoot, some of them snatch. And nothing is ever going to change their minds. Not restraining orders, not prison time, not fucking 'counseling.' Once the wires get twisted in their heads that tight, the only way to untangle them is with a .45-caliber lobotomy.

"But, remember, that's always about a 'relationship,' okay? That holds true even if the relationship has to be with a corpse. Ask that smirking little slime they exported from Thailand after he convinced a pack of dimwits that he was on the scene when Jon-Benet Ramsey was killed. Now he's on permanent 'pervert interview' status, guaranteed to perform his little 'Maybe I know something, but I'm not telling' act on camera at a moment's notice. The only reason he can't get the book-and-movie deal he's been chasing is that he'd have to actually *prove* it. The '*if* I did it' trick only works if everyone already believes you did.

"Anyway, the 'relationship' freaks never want an infant; they need a kid old enough to 'love' them, okay?

"The kind who *do* want babies — that's another tribe entirely. Disturbos who've been padding their stomachs for months, telling everyone they're pregnant. Or baby-

175

rapers who need fresh meat; peddlers who have a pre-sold market for the product . . .

"That last kind, they buy wholesale and sell retail. Some sell to the 'collector' kiddie-porn filmmakers who never recycle their product, just the evidence of what was done to it. Some sell to yuppies who don't want to wait for an adoption agency . . . although the Estonians and the Chinese have just about killed *that* market."

"I didn't know you liked puns," he said, telling me he knew that even a too-damaged-to-sell baby could have some perfectly useful organs. The Chinese rulers know the value of things: adults are good for slave labor, the used-up ones can be parted out, and the babies can be sold intact.

They know the price of remembering things, too. Like the Rape of Nanking. You can't sell product if you alienate your market, so they put their scientific geniuses to work and found a way to get tigers to breed in captivity. Now they sell the newly manufactured tigers. Not the animals themselves, the surgically dissected remains. There's a huge demand for every single part of a tiger, from the teeth to the testicles.

In Japan.

The Chinese press releases say they're

breeding tigers as an anti-poaching measure. Buy *that,* chump. And why not? If they can hand out Olympic gold medals in Tiananmen Square, what's next? A Nobel Peace Prize for torture?

But you only talk about things like that when you're with your own kind. Pryce was a diamondback who'd evolved enough to grow a silencer where the rattle should be. So all I said out loud was:

"*None* of that was in play when that baby was taken. Whether you call it high-stakes gambling or risk-gain investing, it still doesn't add up, not the way I see it. Somebody's got their own in this."

"*Now* you see why I came to you?" Pryce said. I didn't think he was talking about Mama's soup.

Pryce wasn't handicapped by ego or image — his idea of a profile was not to have one. Never uses a passport, just morphs his way across borders, takes what he needs, and atomizes. He might leave all kinds of carnage behind him, but he'd never leave tracks.

An aikido master once told me that the ability to generate force, no matter how powerful, was a second-tier skill. *Redirecting* force, that was the ultimate. Creation always yields to control.

Max can feather-brush a nerve juncture and put you down, temporary or permanent. His target's vulnerabilities stand out for him like candle points in a crypt. Pryce was a grandmaster, too, only his discipline was information. He knew how to get it; he knew how to use it. He could make it reproduce, pay dividends, blow up networks — whatever he needed done.

Control.

Pryce frightened me, but he never used that fear *on* me — he'd seen for himself how I react when I get *too* scared.

And there's another reason why Pryce never played that card.

Wesley.

Hovering somewhere.

Maybe.

Frightening Wesley wasn't possible. The human-skinned demons who assembled him from spare parts of terror-traumatized babies left fear out of their creation. They ended up with a thing fueled by a chemical coldness not found in nature.

"Motherfucker's got more blood on his hands than the Red Cross," the Prof had said about Wesley once. "But not a drop of it in his veins. Dracula got his fangs into *that* boy, he'd die of starvation."

Pryce never lied to himself. He knew no man can stop the rain. All you can do is seek shelter, wait it out, and hope your supplies last. Pryce was a lot of things, but he was no gambler. My hole card wasn't Wesley; it was Pryce not knowing . . . not for sure.

"If he's really gone, you'd never say, would you?" he'd asked me once, aura on 360 alert, every sensing mechanism open. Knowing I wouldn't answer; watching for a tell.

He never saw it. How could he? Pryce was an info-master, but I knew one piece of hard data his computer couldn't process: Ghosts are real. And some of them are close by.

When I talked to Wesley, he answered me.

Maybe I was just hearing things in my head. Maybe Wesley only lived there now. But just because you couldn't touch Wesley didn't mean he couldn't reach out and touch you.

Pryce could never really know. And that scared *him*.

"So. All this work to set up the meet, it was for nothing?" he asked, between sips of his soup.

"I got what I came for."

"Which was — ?"

"He *doesn't* know who took the baby. And

he's not lying when he says it."

"Because . . . ?"

"Because I know," I told Pryce. I could have told him *how* I knew, but you don't lend a gun to a man who might test-fire it into the back of your head.

It was as simple as this: The Sheikh had never developed liar's skills. He had no reason to learn them, and no one to practice them on. Why lie when anything you say *becomes* the truth?

"Spell it out," Pryce said, giving up.

"There's places I could look. A lot of ex–military guys sell what they know. Or *say* they know, anyway — most of the jerkoffs who pay a fortune to take some 'combat skills' course couldn't tell a Ranger from a Rambo. But whoever pulled this one off was a team that had been trained *as* a team. Mission-specific."

"What he said to you about Pollard . . . ?"

"Yeah, the Israelis could have done it. They've got all the tools, and they've had cells working this city since forever. But this one has a reverse signature on it."

"I'm not a cryptographer."

"Missing pieces. You may not know who did the job, but you know who *didn't,* see?"

"See what? You haven't shown me anything."

"No? Tell me, does this sheikh of yours have the juice to change Saudi policy? I mean at some mega-level, like, I don't know, getting their king to condemn Iran for denying the Holocaust?"

"No." Pryce's answer was so devoid of expression that I knew he'd already asked the same question — in a lot of places — and always gotten the same answer.

"Then the Israelis wouldn't spend any Mossad coin on him; he'd be a lousy investment."

"You said *pieces.* As in plural."

"Sure. You tell *me* how whoever put this together picked the target?"

"I'm not sure I —"

"Why *this* prince? Aldo Moro–type political kidnapping is always about prisoner swaps, and the Saudis don't *take* prisoners. Plus, we already know it can't be money. Your guy would pay, no question. But nobody's asked."

"And you already said it couldn't be one of those . . . psychosexually motivated individuals."

"A fucking *team* of them? Not a chance. That second missing piece splits into two more. Two questions, that is. Who paid for this job? And why?"

"Whoever planned this had to know of

the target's . . . proclivities," Pryce said, touching his no-fingerprint thumb to his plastic chin in a thinker's pose.

"Right. And wherever they got *that* info from is the same place they got the money to do it," I told him.

He held his pose. When he figured I'd had enough time to believe he'd been pondering a decision, he said, "Have you got places you could still look? Other places?"

"Sure, but —"

"Money isn't the issue," Pryce stopped me. "But time, *that* is. And we don't have much more of it."

It took me over twelve hours to find Lune. I wasn't going back to his — I don't have a name for it: village? compound? halfway house? — ever again. His border control had too many checkpoints, and too many radioactive maniacs manning them.

When we were still kids, Wesley and me broke out of one of those jungle-law joints they built to warehouse write-offs like us. We took Lune along. He wouldn't have lasted an hour in there without us, and you never leave a partner behind.

Me and Wesley knew where we were going, and what we'd have to do once we got there. Lune couldn't walk that road, so he went off on his own.

I didn't think he could survive the outside world. Lune had been institutionalized all his life, but not for crime. Once you got labeled "incorrigible," you went into the same garbage can as criminals like us. They called it a "training school." And I guess it was.

Somehow, Lune found his own world. That was a lifetime ago, but I knew he'd still take my back. And what I needed was the one thing he did better than anyone on earth.

So I went to one of those "electronics" stores that clog the West Side with re-branded crap only a tourist would buy, paid a guy who looked like he was auditioning for a part in a hidden-camera documentary two grand in cash for an IBM laptop. He must have left his receipt pad the same place I'd left my faith.

The Mole reconfigured the torn-out pay phone in the South Bronx as Clarence lounged against the metal pole, one hand inside his dull-khaki coat. The islander had changed his outfit but not his nature. Clarence was known as a cobra with 9mm fangs, but that was playing him cheap. Cobras aren't as quick, and their bites aren't always fatal.

I plugged in the modem, booted up, hit a memorized URL, waited. Eventually, a box with a giant "?" appeared in the center of my screen, with white space underneath. I typed in my question. Got back "Parameters?" and typed some more.

"Wait," the screen read.

Ten minutes passed.

"No," came up on the screen. "More details?"

I typed in: "No. Thank you, brother," unplugged, and handed everything to the Mole. He got into Clarence's beloved '67 Rover 2000TC, resplendent in its new coat of understated BRG, and they went off together. I got into my rusted-out Roadrunner, and went back to where I belonged.

Wesley once told me that he never took a contract that called for anything but the killing itself. "The more time you spend with the body, the bigger the risk," the iceman said. "Let them take out their own garbage."

The swampland around JFK used to be a no-tombstone cemetery, but it's been mostly filled in — covered over with strip joints and high-turnover motels. Once the feds caught wise that the entire airport was a mob paradise, things started to change. Throw Homeland Security into the mix, and that territory isn't used so much anymore.

The whole borough of Queens is a crime pendulum. The DA's Office there boasted the city's first "Special Victims Bureau." But that was nothing but a political showcase for a hand-picked star. There's no "stats" in celebrity journalism, so the pill got swallowed whole. When the head of that bureau decided to run for national office, all the coverage was about her "99-percent indictment rate." Not a word about trials.

Then Wolfe took over, and the axis shifted. The "fondling" that once got you probation and counseling suddenly got you felony time. A lot of defense lawyers who'd been working that territory for years figured the new deal was a pose. After all, who actually *tries* those kinds of cases? Kids? Everyone knows they're unreliable witnesses, what with implanted memories and all. Street whores? The mentally ill? Retardates? Women married to the alleged perpetrators? Come *on!*

But Wolfe opened her own graveyard, and kept it well stocked. While other sex crimes prosecutors were racking up perfect conviction rates by cherry-picking the slam-dunks, she was taking on all comers . . . even those "bad victim" cases that were routinely dealt away — or thrown away — in other offices.

The pendulum swung, and the freaks dropped Queens from the list of their favorite places to work. Sex-crime rates plunged.

Then a new DA took over, and immediately proved he was worthy of his appointment by obeying orders. His first move was to fire Wolfe.

That was like telling the vampires that Buffy just left town.

I prowled through war-zone streets where the only light was the occasional flare of a crack pipe, found the address I was looking for, and pulled the Roadrunner into the spot I'd been promised would be waiting behind the boarded-up house.

The back door opened just as I rolled up. I stepped into a single large room, dimly lit, lined with benches and cots. A scrawny black woman in a cheap electric-blue dress gave me a dull look before she took her hit, slamming a spike full of short-term escape into a vein almost as collapsed as her hopes.

I took the stairs. Exchanged looks with the thug at the top. He stepped aside, and I entered Quayshon's office.

"I heard Bones was putting together a string. Talking a serious six figures *each.*"

186

"Meaning you passed?" I said to the red-haired, blue-eyed, mahogany-colored man seated across from me.

"Bones a *hard* man, bro. The way I figure, that number he quoted is righteous, but, me, I don't need *that* big a funeral."

I thought that one through. Bones was about a hundred years old. Born a bluesman. Got his name because he played the kind of joints where you had to bring it *vicious* just to get the audience to stop their knife fights long enough to listen. The man had done time in places that most people wouldn't even believe had existed in the twentieth century.

Bones had been free just long enough to figure out that they don't give Social Security checks to men who never paid taxes, so what would be an all-or-nothing bet for most people was a can't-lose proposition for him. Bones had been blues-shouting, "I don't mind dying!" all his life, and he was a man who lived his lyrics.

But here was Quayshon, saying the whole thing sounded crazy to him. And Quayshon was such an outrageous madman that he usually won the arguments he had with the voices in his head.

When I walked into his room, the Prof was

watching one of those "You are *not* the father!" shows.

I sat down next to him. On the screen, some hideous mass of female flesh dressed sexily enough to induce projectile vomiting was pointing at a photo of a shaved-head, dull-eyed exemplar of inbreeding. The sub-simian's picture was TV-positioned next to one of a round-headed baby, and the XX chromosome was screaming out the resemblances. The XY's riposte was that the kid didn't look like any of his *other* babies, so it couldn't be his.

"My baby's even got a tiny [bleep], just like his daddy's," the mother shouted out her memorized line.

The host — a smarmy sleazeball who made Jerry Springer look like Charlie Rose — put on a piously disapproving face.

The accused father grinned, proving that "white supremacy" would never make it as a toothpaste slogan.

"Makes a man sick, Schoolboy," the Prof said.

"What?" I asked him. What I *didn't* ask was why he was watching the show in the first place.

"Bitch hits you that low, you got to crack *back,* Jack! But that lame-ass just sits there

188

grinning. It's like watching a lump taking a dump."

"It's TV, Prof."

"Boy, what you think I'm talking about, going upside her head? You know I don't play that. But that punk makes me ashamed to be a man. Come on, now! Bitch says your cock ain't man-size, you supposed to say: 'The tunnel's wide enough, *any* train look small comin' through it.' I mean, this is *tragic.* Don't people know how to play the dozens anymore?"

"Not at your level, Prof."

"Hey, I ain't saying they got to be good; I'm just saying they got to return fire, okay? Punks be throwing stones when they need to be *growing* some. You stand there and just take that kind of down, you know it's just gonna keep comin' around."

"Amen."

"How'd it get this bad, son? We down to where calling some motherfuckers 'motherfucker' ain't even insulting them?"

"It's always been there," I said. "Just wasn't on TV before."

"Lord Jesus. That baby they screamin' about? Kid's got as much chance in life as a cross at a Klan convention." The old man closed his eyes, as if to banish the images twisting in his head. When they snapped open, he was back. "Ah, fuck all that," he said. "What happened with that perfect score you heard about?"

The Prof listened to my account, nodding slowly. When I finished, he said, "Anytime you see a red-haired, blue-eyed nigger, you know you lookin' at a born life-taker. That don't necessarily mean he got to be spongy under the skull, but Quayshon, he's the total package. That boy ain't nowhere *close* to right. Probably been off the rails since his mama gave him that weirdass name. Hear me? Quayshon tells you some scheme is insane, you listening to a man who *knows*."

I just nodded, the way you do when there's no reason to say anything.

"Tell you something else about Quay. The man is one serious schnorrer. Crazy as he is, motherfucker would still rather pick up gonorrhea than a check."

"Yeah," I agreed. From experience. Then I got back to business: "It wasn't any White Night crew, Prof. They don't have that level of discipline, for one. And they may call the Arabs 'sand niggers,' but they love anyone who thinks Jews need exterminating — a lot of them sent congrats on 9/11. This was way too professional. Some of the Valhalla boys may be ready to pick up the gun, but most of them just put up Web sites."

The Prof looked down the hall, using the periscope-style tube the Mole had made for him. Satisfied, he turned back to me, lowering his voice:

"When I was a boy, they had some *creatures* down in Louisiana. You serious about finding you a mojo hand, that's where you got to go. Zombies walk those swamps, boy. But even *they* walk light around those witchy old women. They can work roots, kill you from the inside out, you fool enough to cross them.

"Got some animals you wouldn't believe, too. About a million years old, but still playing the same tricks. You know why, son?"

"Because they still work?"

"You listen good, Schoolboy."

"I still am."

He shifted position in the bed-chair they had just installed. "You know what an alligator snapping turtle is?"

"I can guess."

"Nah. You can't add words like numbers, boy. Alligator snapping turtle don't mean alligator plus snapping turtle. I'm talking about a *demon*. Seen 'em this big," he said, gesturing with his hands held about three feet apart. "Fucking dinosaurs, they are. Got tails with big spikes, heads like a chunk of rock with little red eyes. I saw one crack a broomstick in his jaws like it was a wooden match.

"Now, listen: They ain't fast. Can't hardly move on dry ground, and can't swim for shit, either. You know how they get their food?"

I made a face to tell him I couldn't imagine.

"The food comes to *them,*" he said, twisting his lips to show his own teeth. "They dive down *way* deep, bury themselves in that black mud so they look like part of it. Lie there all day with their mouths open. Inside those mouths, they got these . . . tongues, I guess they are. Anyway, they're all pink and wiggly. Look like big fat worms, or maybe even little fish.

"Those boys are *gravely* patient. Never make a move. Sooner or later, something down there sees what looks like a meal, goes for it, and . . . *snap!*"

I closed my eyes, seeing it. Said, "So, if I backtrack . . ."

"Now you tuned in, Jim. You go looking for whoever snatched that baby, all you gonna do is spook anyone who's listening to the drums. You always going to be too late to catch *that* freight."

"But if I put word out that I want the

same kind of job *done . . .*"

"*That's* how you run, son!" the old man said, extending his clenched fist for me to tap. "Remember, now: we in the market for a fur coat, but it don't have to be no mink, you with me?"

"I want a *particular* baby taken, but not an Arab one. I'll pay what it costs, and there can't be any killing — I just want the kid."

"Not *you,* you. That pile ain't your style, and anyone checking your pedigree gonna get in the wind. This is for a *client,* okay? You just the man putting it together . . . finding the man what he wants."

"But that wouldn't fit, unless . . ."

"Bring it," my father encouraged me. Like he had from the day he claimed that title.

I let myself become the beast. "Kid's being abused by his mother's new boyfriend," I said, forging the hook. Then I baited it with: "Father's got a ton of cash, but he spent too much of it on hookers, so Mom got custody. She picked a new guy right off the Sex Offender Registry — that's the one thing that Megan's Law bullshit's good for, freakish broads who want to hook up with a degenerate — and the father's desperate enough to do *anything* to make it stop. So he asks around, hears about me. . . ."

The old man put his hands together as if

praying. Opened them to form a "V." Waited a beat, then snapped them shut.

Violence is total commitment. Middle ground is a myth. Equivocation is quicksand. Where I live, selling wolf tickets buys you a one-way ride. Could be now, could be next year, but every hand gets called.

I remembered the Prof talking to me on the yard, back when I was still a stupid kid: "The biggest lie in the whole dictionary is 'foolproof,' Schoolboy. Ain't no such animal, 'cause a fool is guaranteed to *act* the fool. You got to survive *before* you thrive. Only sure way to win a gunfight is, don't show up for it."

And Wesley's mantra: "They're easier when they're sleeping," whispered to me one night in the dorm. Both of us were children then, but only one of us was a kid.

What kept me alive was that I was always smart enough to listen.

I still am. So I put out the bait, and waited for the line to quiver in my hand.

The whisper-stream is never calm below the surface. Sifting truth from its depths isn't an exact science, but you know it's down there somewhere, buried among the lies, rumors, and myths. I'd worked for years to keep my "dead and gone" label certified. It was Burke's "brother" — me, and my new face — who had been running the family business since I'd slipped away.

The old Burke they all knew would have solved my made-up client's problem with a double-tap for the boyfriend and the mother. But that Burke had vanished years ago, when I'd gone "missing and presumed."

I'd been born a suspect. I guess I died one, too.

The cop who'd made that possible was still around, but he'd never be questioned — he was part of the micro-glassed air that had once been the World Trade Center. Pryce always played it as if he knew the whole story, but he was really just working me: testing, probing, looking for a weak spot, as opportunistic as an infection. But I never gave him an opening. Pryce was like the malaria I still carried — it was in me forever, a permanent standoff: I couldn't make it leave, but it couldn't stop me from staying.

No matter how the people who live below the underground figured it, *any* version of the Burke they knew would never pass up the chance to make a pile of cash and take out a couple of baby-rapers at the same time. Some people were confused about my motivations, but nobody doubted my hate. If certain humans crossed my path, they were done. Pay me enough, and I'd go out and cross theirs.

So the whisper-stream's Help Wanted board got a new entry. Some might wonder why our crew would subcontract work we could do in-house, but most would just put it down to me not being willing to risk those of us still left.

The first-responders were what I expected: wannabes, with no track record, the kind who used to put ads in *Soldier of Fortune*. They always exposed themselves quicker than a subway flasher.

The next wave wanted the kind of info a pro wouldn't need . . . or even want to know. Too many idiots are using cable broadband for serious business. There's a reason they call that a "shared pipe," and the FBI wasn't just monitoring the traffic, it was contributing some of its own. "Sex slavery" may be what got the trash-TV shows excited, but "domestic terrorism" rang the White House bell even louder than the one in their private chapel.

Next up, the usual dumbfucks demanding moral assurances. Meaning: make sure they didn't blow a book-and-movie deal. "Rescuing" a kid — perfect. But abduction-for-dollars — now, that isn't network material. Not even cable.

A few teams phrased their inquiries as double-edged as daggers. Very "define the mission" military, with just enough cred slipped in so I could find out if they were solid . . . provided I knew where to look.

Nice. Only none of them had any Stateside work on their résumés. Some countries sell citizenships like any other product, and they issue passports, too. Those deals always include no jobs on U.S. soil. They never spell it out, but it's as clear as the image in a sniper's scope. Foreign aid is America's biggest weapon, and any country that'll sell you a passport will sell *you* even quicker, if Big Daddy says the word.

Nobody had used the snatch job on the Sheikh's baby as a prove-in credential. I hadn't expected to get *that* lucky, but I had been hoping for some vague references to having done similar work.

I got a few nibbles, but none close enough for me to snap the jaws.

"This one is all wrong," I told Rosie. She was curled up on a nest she'd made out of the rug Mama had sent over as a greeting gift for the new pup. "Persian," she said, tossing it to me like it was a used rag.

The pit's ears went flat against her skull. She hadn't learned to speak my language completely yet, but I knew hers. I walked over, patted her, told her she was a perfect little beauty, and scratched behind her left ear.

She watched as I positioned the circle of mirror-polished stainless steel with a red dot painted in its precise center.

I sat lotus across from the transporter, got my breathing right, and fell into the red dot.

"Pryce is lying, or he's being lied to," I told Max and Clarence much later that night. Like always, I was speaking aloud and signing, too. Max reads lips perfectly, especially mine, but I always used the silent language we'd taught each other anyway, so the others could learn it from me.

"No way the team that pulled off that snatch was doing it cold," I said. "That's the kind of thing you rehearse, over and over, until you can do it blindfolded. Like dry runs for a getaway man, or field-stripping a rifle in the dark."

Max made a saluting gesture.

"Yeah. There's military in this somewhere, past or present. And this was no snap decision; they had the mission way in advance."

"And the equipment," Clarence said. "Scopes, mics — maybe even a tap. Also vehicles, a stash house . . ."

"Uh-huh. And the manpower, too. This operation was running around the clock *long* before they made their move. That means they had people on the street, people who could blend right in."

"This is not a city of just one color, mahn."

Max nodded agreement, spreading his arms wide for emphasis.

I sat quietly for a few seconds. "One theory fits, but it's got a real flaw in it . . . a deep crack in the foundation."

Both men looked at me, waiting.

"It smells like G-men," I said. "Hell, it *reeks* of them. But if the FBI was running the show, why bring Pryce in on it? He's too dangerous to play those kinds of games with."

Max tapped his heart, tilting his head to mean he was asking, not telling.

"Pryce? He's got *some* kind of access, that's right," I said, remembering how quickly he was able to put a team in place outside Federal Plaza, remembering how only one of the RAHOWA boys survived — the one that turned canary on the spot. Highspeed interrogation is easy when you can show one captive the price of a wrong answer by killing another one.

That had closed the books on our deal. Herk got to walk away. All the way into another life. But it wasn't as simple as a man keeping his word. "Pryce takes government money, sure," I told them. "But no way he takes orders. If the government hired him, the government wants the kid back. Why? That I don't know. The only thing I'm sure of is this: the G-men might pay him, but they can't play him."

"Outlaw agents, then? High-rankers who know they will not survive for long after the new boss takes over?"

I considered Clarence's hypothesis. "Can't rule it out," I said, after a minute. "You could be right. But there's an even better candidate. The Agency's been in a turf war over this whole Stateside terrorism thing. They didn't win any points for getting suckered on the intel about Iraq, and they keep pointing fingers at the FBI over 9/11."

"CIA, you're saying, mahn?"

"Why not? What if they pull the snatch themselves, and *keep* it to themselves? They don't even trust each other, so whoever's paying Pryce wouldn't have to be in on it. And if they end up making the Sheikh twist in the wind before they rescue his kid, maybe that convinces the White House to extend their territory to inside our borders. That's what they've always wanted. When Hoover was alive, no chance. Now . . ."

"But that would be —"

"What, illegal?" I half-snorted. "It's not like any of them gives a rat's ass what the law says. Or Congress, for that matter. You think politicians who take habeas corpus out of the Constitution would draw the line at letting the CIA work local? If the Agency even bothered to tell them, that is."

"So we have no chance, then, mahn?"

"Not if that's what's going on, no. But that would mean someone sent Pryce on a wild-goose chase, and *that's* the part I don't buy — they'd be trying to douse a fire with gasoline. If I'm wrong, we're fucked anyway. But let's say I'm not. Then there's another path we could still take."

Neither of them moved, so I answered their unasked question, signing to Max as I did: "We just ask Pryce."

Waiting for him to call me with a time and place, I patted the couch for Rosie to take a nap with me.

I don't know if she dreamed. I know I did. I call it a dream, but it was just a memory, replayed so vividly that I was transported back to a lifetime ago.

The old man next to me on the bench was too clean to be a bum. He was dressed like a dockworker who knew he'd never be picked at the shape-up, but still doggedly showed every morning.

Big, heavy-boned, with thick, gray-streaked brown hair. His eyes were the color of soot; hands callused on the palms, scarred on the backs.

"When clowns say 'anarchy,' they mean a riot," he was telling me. "You know, like a 'state of anarchy'? But anarchy isn't a condition, it's a philosophy. Anarchists don't want a lawless state; they want a state governed by the natural order of humanity. Breaking down the government isn't enough. In fact, it's a mistake, because fear is all it takes for fascism to emerge. People want order restored so desperately, they don't think about what that's going to cost them later. Or who's financing it."

"I thought anarchists threw bombs," I said.

"Some people hang a black man from a tree, then go right to church."

"So it's all a lie?" I asked, ready to believe *that.*

"Nothing's *all* a lie." The old man drew in a deep breath, expanding his chest like he was going to shout, but he never raised his voice. "Anarchism is anti-authority, not pro-violence. Anarchism is the enemy of exploitation, in any form. It's not about blowing things up for the sake of destruction; it's about razing a foul structure, so you can build a better one. Collectively."

"That sounds like —"

The old man knew the joint I'd just been released from had no shortage of explain-it-all philosophers, and he sensed which one I'd been about to quote. "Anarchism is *not* Marxism, young man. The 'dictatorship of the proletariat' is *still* a dictatorship. We broke with that crowd a long time ago."

I knew the old man was IWW. Maybe one of the last. I knew they were stand-up guys. Even high-status cons talked about them with respect. That was about all I knew, but more than enough to make me listen.

"No government doesn't mean no law," he said. "While you were locked up, you ever read any Proudhon?"

"Never heard of him."

"I figured," he said. Not surprised, resigned. "But I know you heard the story about the guy who wouldn't let the government pick the time for him to die. The guy who made a bomb out of match heads packed into a hollow leg of his bunk, lay down next to the radiator, and blew himself up right on Death Row, just a few hours before they were going to execute him?"

"Sure!" Cons treasure that story the way career soldiers do Medal of Honor winners.

"But you think it's a folk legend, am I right? You know, like how the guy they gunned down in Chicago wasn't really Dillinger?"

"I . . ."

"It's no bullshit, son," he said. Not persuading, just laying it out for me. "Louis Lingg was the man's name. And he wasn't some crazy 'anarchist,' he was one of us."

"Us?"

"A syndicalist," he said, proudly. "The government always tried to make us out to be all the same, but the Wobblies weren't fighting to take over the country; we were fighting for social justice. *Years* before the unions rotted from the top down, we were out there, organizing the workers.

"Yeah, some of us used dynamite instead of pamphlets — like the McNamara brothers when they blew up the L.A. Times Building. But those men weren't after anything but justice. They *believed*. And if that whore Darrow hadn't sold them out —"

"*Clarence* Darrow?"

"You heard me," he said, still not raising his voice. "The newspapers were all killing us.

204

Look how they lied about Haymarket Square — maybe that's why our biggest force is still in Chicago.

"But how they *really* nailed us was to make out like we were against the war. World War I, I'm talking about. They said we were anti-American, agents of the enemy. Sedition! Treason! Vigilante mobs attacked us everywhere . . . and the cops helped them do it."

I offered my pack of cigarettes to the old man. He took one, lit up. So did I.

He exhaled like a sigh of relief. "Centralia, Washington. November 11, 1919. That's when they lynched Wesley Everest. They had him locked up for organizing, which they called spreading sedition. Now, Wesley wasn't some theoretician; he was a combat veteran. So when they came for him, he didn't go quiet. There was a big shoot-out, but they finally wounded him bad enough so they could drag him to jail.

"Then the *guards* handed him over to a lynch mob. Those dirty cowards castrated Wesley before they strung him up, then they used his body for target practice. People cheering, taking pictures. Real patriots, they were. The coroner wrote it up as a suicide. Where were the 'reporters' then, huh?"

"I never —"

"— thought that happened to *white* men,

right? Yeah, well, it did. But even that couldn't stop us. It was the damn Commies who got *that* job done."

"But I thought —"

"Emma Goldman — you ever heard of her?" He didn't even wait for me to confirm what he suspected, just rolled on as if I'd admitted I hadn't. "She supported the Bolsheviks. But the minute they took over, they kicked her out of Russia, so she came over here. Even did time on Welfare Island for campaigning against the First World War.

"That's when it started to all go wrong for us. See, the IWW led the world in anti-fascism. Wesley Everest, he *served* in that war, because it was the right thing to do. We were the first to fight for equal pay for equal work; that's not the same as goddamn Communism, and it never was. So we blazed that trail, but what are we now?"

"I don't know. I just heard you —"

"I know," the old man said, not bothering to hide his sadness anymore. "Look, I just gave you enough information so you could do some work, maybe even discover you haven't been spending this afternoon talking to a crazy old man. Then, when you see I wasn't lying, maybe you'll pay attention to the one thing I have that's actually worth something to you."

"I will," I said, knowing it was a promise I

was making.

"Always stand your ground," the old man told me then. "Yeah, you know that. *Think* you do, anyway. But standing your ground means not just picking the right ground to stand, it's making sure you've got the right people to stand it *with*.

"There's where we went wrong. And, by the end, we had more martyrs than we had movement."

I never saw him again.

Never forgot him, either.

I woke up realizing that, even way back then, I was always paying attention. Listening to anyone who I thought might have answers for questions no kid should ever have to ask.

I was trying to find the path. Not to some Taoist ideal, to someplace where I could belong. The path that would prove my father — the State — was wrong. *They* thought I belonged in some kind of cage. As I got older, they kept changing the names of the cages, but they never changed their mind.

Every time I got back on the streets, I knew prison was somewhere down the road, a cheap motel with a bright, blinking VA-CANCY sign. Even stronger than the hate in my heart was my need to believe prison was a stop on my journey, not the final destination.

Belonging to a street gang wasn't what I was looking for. I'd been there, and I knew. A gang is something you belong *to,* not *with.*

It was a long time before I figured out the only place you ever truly belong is the place you make for yourself.

You can't buy it; you have to build it. "Blood in, blood out" — that's just another pair of handcuffs. Tattoos don't make you anyone's "brother."

I was searching for something . . . anything . . . to explain why I'd been picked for the diet of blood, terror, and pain I was raised on.

Back when I was still a gang kid, I thought prison was where true men of honor were formed: a test you had to pass, with self-respect the top grade. I finally learned that was a lie, but I learned it *in* prison. From my true father.

"You *can't* do your own time in here, Youngblood," he broke it down for me. "You try, you die. This school only got two rules. You volunteer for lockup, or you walk the yard."

I didn't say anything. I was there to listen. And we were standing on the yard.

"Yeah," he said, as if I'd answered a question correctly. "Okay, boy, here's the slant on the plant: you don't diss, you never kiss, but if your name *still* gets called, make sure you don't miss."

I nodded, still too awed to speak. The Prof was a legend Inside. And he had picked *me* to school.

"Only thing that's true is what you *do*" is what he taught.

I live that. That's how I found the one place I rightfully belong. My heart and my life. *Your* life doesn't mean any more to me than I ever meant to any of you. Trespassers should bring their own body bags.

The one-use-only, cloned-chip cell buzzed.

"Location Four," Pryce said. "Plus two."

I checked my watch: 11:00 p.m. Plenty of time. I threw in a stack of bootlegged CDs and listened to Stevie Ray Vaughan destroy a stereotype with "The Sky Is Crying." I went out of the door on Bobby Bland's "I've Got to Know."

"You want company, boss? Ain't nobody going to check in this late, especially in this weather."

"No thanks, Gate. But I'd appreciate it if you'd —"

By then, Rosie had already vaulted into his lap.

■ ■ ■ ■

Pryce didn't like public places. Liked them even less after dark. I reversed the Plymouth into the open bay of a Brooklyn factory slated for the wrecking ball. I wasn't surprised when the accordion door descended in front of my windshield, sliding on soundless runners.

He climbed into the front seat of the Roadrunner, making the capture a two-way street. Pryce wasn't into ceremony or bravado; he was the kind of man who keeps his copyrights up to date.

"You have something?" he opened.

"Just a suspicion."

"Go."

"Cui bono?"

"I didn't know you studied Latin in prison. But I *do* know you didn't call another meet just to tell me this wasn't a ransom snatch *again.*"

"No, I didn't. I think you knew that even before you called *me.* But I also think you hired me to find porterhouse in a fish store."

"English, okay?"

"Not a ransom, so has to be a freak. Maybe a sex freak, maybe a Master Race freak. Or one with dual membership. That's your math, right? So your next play is, ask the man who knows them."

"And?"

"Sometimes, you can bond a man to you with gratitude. Especially if you do something for him money can't buy. You know all that; you *did* all that. Only the tree you planted sprouted a lot of branches."

He made some faint gesture with his right hand.

"Someone wants something from your sheikh," I told him. "Not money. Something he *could* get done, but nothing you could *make* him do . . . unless he was bonded to you, too."

"Maybe," he conceded.

"You'd think he could just have another baby. Ten more, if he wanted."

"Agreed."

"And that . . . training he was doing — he *liked* doing it. Right also?" I pressed.

"Yes," Pryce said. You had to be listening real close to catch the slight change in his breathing. I always listen real close.

"The baby gets his value because he's a direct descendant of the OG himself. That's what your boy told me," I said.

"It's true."

"But that bloodline runs through the father, not the mother."

211

"So you're saying the baby isn't irreplaceable. Unless . . ."

"He can't make another one."

"But he *could,*" Pryce said, sticking a pin into that balloon. "There was no fertility clinic involved in the birth of this one. No embryo implant, no special . . ."

"And if the *mother* was shipped home, tried for infanticide, and found guilty, what then?"

"Tried?" Pryce snorted.

"Exactly. So the Sheikh starts over. No shortage of choices. Maybe even covers his bets, since he needs a son if he wants the kid to stay in the running for the throne."

"Yes. So?"

"So it *still* wouldn't be the same for him. He had *years* invested into training his successor. Starting over, that would be tricky. Especially with what he has to figure you found out about him by now. But if *this* baby was recovered somehow, and handed back to him — maybe with a hint that it cost a few lives to pull it off — then he might . . . *might* be grateful."

"A man like —"

"I know. Anything he gets, he believes he's entitled to. Probably doesn't even know what gratitude feels like. But whoever returns that baby gets two cards, not one.

One might pile up some gratitude, but that's no ace of trumps. The other is: the Sheikh *has* to be thinking, 'Maybe the people who returned the baby to me are the same ones who took him.' Which means —"

"— they could do it again."

"Anytime they wanted," I said, using language the Sheikh himself would understand.

Pryce went so still that his pulse rate probably couldn't be detected.

Time passed.

"You think the Prince went to the wrong people for help, before he came to us?" he finally said.

"Could be."

He studied me for a long minute. "He did," the shape-shifter admitted. "But *they* didn't. Never mind the theorizing, okay? Just keep doing your work. I've got some of my own to do now."

He handed me a gym bag.

"There's enough in there for whatever you could possibly need, next two, three weeks. Don't reach out for me. Every contact you have is already erased. When I'm ready, I'll find you."

"Good enough," I agreed. "But what if I find the kid myself, looking where *you* told me to? I've got to have some way to —"

"Tell the guy who manages that flophouse you live in to wear a bright-red jacket next time he walks the dog."

"He's in a —"

"I know. He won't have to go far; a couple of blocks'll be enough."

"Got a camera on me, have you?"

"Better," he said. Then he slipped out of the Roadrunner and back into the darkness.

The garage door rolled up. I rolled out.

It took the Mole a round-the-clock session with his machines before he finally announced: "Not in here."

He might have completed the sweep-job quicker if Michelle hadn't shown up. The Mole just tuned her out, leaving the harder work to me.

"Pryce is watching us, honey," I told her. "We have to know where he's watching from."

"How do you know that he's not just — ?"

"Pryce doesn't work that way. Besides, he'd have to *see* the signal we agreed on for it to do him any good."

"Okay, so he's got a way to watch the street. Why would he want to plant anything inside your place, too?"

"I don't know. Truth is, I don't think he

could. But information is his god, and he never misses a service."

I turned to Max. He'd spent the night crawling the rooftops. Nothing.

"What's that leave," I asked my family, "a fucking satellite?"

Either Terry didn't get my sarcasm, or he shared his father's respect for my techno-knowledge. "That could be it" was all he said.

The Mole nodded. "The mechanisms are already in place. What he would need is a private channel. There is only one way Gate-man could exit —"

"Two," I reminded him.

The Mole shrugged. "If Pryce already has images — and he must — he could load the channel with recognition software. It would alert only if its pre-sets were triggered."

"He gets a picture of Gateman," Terry explained. "He gets one of Rosie. He makes a series of digital files. He knows the height of the dog, and the height of the wheels on Gateman's chair. When both show up at the same time, all he'd need was a color-code activator."

"I hope that's exactly what he's got," I told them all.

"What?" Michelle wasped out at me.

"If Pryce has what it takes to get that private channel you're talking about, he's also got enough to find out if the CIA took the baby. And one thing we know for sure: the FBI's been fighting to keep the CIA out of Stateside work. Maybe they've succeeded, maybe not.

"So they can argue over who gets to cover what ground, but there's no argument about who covers the skies. That probably means the CIA's in this. But it *also* means they didn't take the kid, and they don't know who did."

"What does that make us?" Michelle said.

"Even, honey," I told her. "Dead even."

When Clarence showed up carrying a slim black aluminum attaché case, wearing a perfectly fitted midnight-blue suit instead of his usual peacock regalia, I knew he'd consulted Michelle. Diagnosis confirmed by the bouquet of deep-purple orchids he presented to Taralyn, with a courtly bow and a simple, "This is a poor way to show my gratitude and my admiration. I hope someday you will permit me to do better."

At least *somebody's* plans were working out.

The Prof shooed them both away, glanced around the spacious room, made a "come on with it" gesture to me.

"I can't make it add up," I told him. "There's a piece of this, a percentage of that, but nothing I can build anything with."

"Even if —"

"Yeah. Even if I figure they're *all* lying, it doesn't get me anywhere. I know some people lie just to be lying — maybe they can't help themselves, maybe they get off doing it, who knows? But there's truth *somewhere* in all this. The baby *did* get snatched. That Sheikh *does* want him back. And Pryce for *damn* sure wants the Sheikh to get what the Sheikh wants."

"What you saying, boy? You can't go until you know?"

"Maybe that's right, Prof. But I know this much already: that asshole had never even *considered* the possibility of his kid being snatched."

"He told you that?"

"Yeah," I said, not bothering to explain that I didn't need words to ask a freak a question, or use my ears to get an answer. "This one thinks he's untouchable . . . and he probably is, as far as the Law is concerned. But this game of his was strictly private, and he wouldn't want some tabloid putting him on the front page, so he knew he was in a risk zone every time he went out on one of his training exercises. Training the baby, I mean."

The Prof nodded at the indisputable truth of life at street level. Every hooker who steps into a stranger's car knows she may be getting ready to turn the Death Trick. But the john never thinks that the whore climbing into his front seat could be wiggling her hips like that alligator snapping turtle's tongue. She could have a pistol in her purse and Aileen Wuornos on her mind, seeing everything in trauma-vision.

"Yeah, he stinks of entitlement," I said. "You can smell it on him. But he's not retarded. Or nuts. If he thought bullets would bounce off him, why have bodyguards at all?"

"So . . . ?"

"So . . . so it's like, to him, exactly what he says on the tape. Women are holes. Plenty of men think that's all they're good for, but how many think that's all they *are?* A hole's not dangerous, unless you step into one . . . and that he'd never do. So he's in total control. That's why the conversation through the window first. That's his screening interview. He thought he had it all covered.

"Kidnap his son? Outdoors? In the middle of New York City? That'd never cross his mind. He's no military guy, but he's got a stalker's mind. He knows you have to plan things. And who'd plan *that?*

"The capper is, even after it happens, he's *still* not really believing it. Who would plan such a thing, pull it off, and *not* be doing it for money? That's the ultimate mind-fuck for him, because it violates the one thing I *know* he believes in."

"And that ain't Allah, true enough. But . . . come on, son: they jumped him, then they just dumped him. Like they didn't —"

"— care if he lived or died, I know. Where's the money in that? Fuck, if some skells *had* come along and cut his throat to make sure he wouldn't wake up while they were helping themselves to his jewelry, where would ransom money even *come* from?

"That's how I know there's no way he staged it himself, just to watch the White House kiss his royal ass. He was *seriously* out of it when the cops found him. He just got lucky that he woke up and started pulling strings, before someone came along and cut his."

The Prof closed his eyes. Not from being tired. I'd watched him do the same thing a million times, closing his eyes to see deeper. Saying anything to him while he was work-

219

ing criminal algorithms in his head would be like pulling the plug on a running mainframe.

I sat there and waited. I'm good at it.

I hadn't looked at my watch, so I couldn't tell how much time passed before the Prof suddenly said, "Remember what I taught you, son: only a dope always stays inside the ropes."

Meaning: playing by the rules is playing the game of the guy who *made* the rules. Outlaws have rules, too. But they're *our* rules. Robbing a bank violates your laws. Ratting out a crime partner violates ours.

"I can't get past —"

"Yeah, you *can,* Schoolboy. A bigger punch don't mean the other guy's gonna eat your lunch." He tapped his temple. Brought his palms together in Max's gesture for "focus." "You remember that 'Rumble in the Jungle' bullshit? Soon as Foreman figured out the script, he up and quit."

"I remember."

"Break it down," the old man said.

I took that as a single question on a bigger test, said: "Yeah, Foreman quit all right, they just *called* it a KO. That second Duran-Leonard fight? *'No más'* didn't mean 'I quit,' it meant 'Fuck this!' Duran wasn't hurt, he was just disgusted. Once he realized he couldn't sucker Leonard into playing *'Quién es más macho?'* like he had the first time, Duran knew he didn't have a chance. So he just walked away.

"But Foreman didn't have that problem. He was an intimidator, a stone thug who could back up the look with the stones in his gloves. Sent Norton into cardiac arrest before their fight even started. But that was never his whole game. Guys he couldn't scare, like Frazier, he'd just pound on them until they *stayed* down. Not like Tyson. He never could beat a man who wasn't scared of him in front."

"That's what Holyfield knew, that secret," the Prof agreed. "Heart. You go against Tyson thinking survival, he tears you apart. But if you go in thinking destruction, Tyson don't know what to do. You didn't have to hit harder than he did, you just had to take what he threw and *keep* throwing back.

"That would never work with Big George. You remember Ron Lyle? How was *he* gonna be scared of any prizefight? You can't hold a shank in a boxing glove. And Lyle, he could put you to sleep with either hand. But he was a prison fighter — spent too much time with the weights, never got his head straight.

"Ron *drops* George a couple of times, but George, he just keeps getting up. It was a hell of a fight, but George finally put Lyle down for the count. You could outbox George — Jimmy Young showed that — but that's like dancing around a building: looks easy, but you better make sure the fucking thing don't fall on you."

"Prison fighters," I said, nodding. "Jumbo Cummings looked like he could knock out a buffalo, but . . . And remember that head case, Etienne?"

It wasn't really a question; I knew the Prof tracked anything that came out of his birthplace. Clifford "The Black Rhino" Etienne had proven he was the perfect parole candidate by winning the Louisiana prison boxing championship. Soon as he was cut loose, he turned pro, won a lot of fights, made some excellent money. His biggest score was the million-plus he got for lasting less than a minute with Tyson. Now he's back where he started, doing a telephone-number sentence for aiming a gun at the cops after a botched robbery.

"How'm I gonna forget that sorry-ass dope fiend?" the old man said. "Louisiana ain't never gonna change. Now, Leadbelly, he could sing his way out of the camps more than once, because a bluesman only gets better with age. Ain't no boxer who ever did that."

"No," I said, thinking of Ricky Womack, an undefeated heavyweight who turned pro young, did a long stretch Inside for a homicide, then went back to Detroit and climbed into the ring. He was forty by then, but he put together a few straight wins . . . and then he died. The coroner said it was suicide.

Bobby Halpern was even closer to home — did his time right here. Older than Womack when he finished his stretch, he was one of the first guys to lose to Trevor Berbick. Probably had no illusions about big money, but he could fight locally, make a few bucks on the side. Ten days after his last fight, person or persons unknown used him for target practice. Bobby survived, but his boxing career didn't.

I remembered how network TV covered the career of James Scott for years. A light-heavy contender, Scott was supposed to be the next great thing, so doing a life sentence for murder wasn't a problem — they just brought the cameras inside.

As soon as he dropped a couple of fights, they dropped the coverage, but the same deal still works, even today. When the women's junior-flyweight world title became vacant, the match to determine the championship was held inside a Thai prison. After the Thai won the fight, the government immediately announced she was going to be freed. After all, she could be stripped of her title if she didn't defend it within six months. Such injustice cannot be tolerated in a democracy, even one where making fun of the King is a double-digit crime.

"So — Ali, then?" the Prof came back to it, boring in, demanding more.

"I think, that first time, he *was* scared of Liston," I said. "But that didn't matter; Sonny did what the people who owned him told him to do.

"After a while, Ali wasn't scared of anyone. Somehow, he discovered he could take a shot to the head like nobody else. That was his secret weapon, and he used it too often. Look at him now.

"Foreman knew he couldn't scare Ali, but he figured he didn't need to — with what he was packing, it'd only be a matter of time. A few rounds later, Foreman found out the truth. Throwing bombs at Ali was like pounding on the heavy bag — it's a great workout, but sooner or later you're too gassed to throw another punch. When the other guy keeps taking your best shots and laughing them off, he takes your heart, too."

"That ain't the question," the old man said, shifting from Professor to Prophet. His eyes could slice diamonds.

"I don't under—"

"Try it this way," my father said. "Ali. What was that boy . . . a fool or a tool?"

"You mean the Muslim thing?"

"Damn! What we really talking about here? We got places to go, and not much time to get there. Come on, son. Use what you got. 'The Rumble in the Jungle,' they called it. You remember *which* jungle?"

"Zaire," I said, just starting to catch a glint . . . like the reflection off a straight razor in a dark alley.

"So Ali goes to fucking *Zaire* because he's all about liberating his people? *What* fucking people? 'Zaire' was just the name that baby-killing snake Mobutu slapped on the piece of the Congo he controlled. That butcher murdered more black folks in a day than the Klan did in a century.

"You know how many of his slaves — that's right, I know what the fucking word means — you know how many of them died to build the goddamn stadium they held that fight in?

"For years, that Mobutu motherfucker

was big-time pals with every president we had. Just like the Shah used to be. All he had to do was dance for his masters and they'd let him rule the other niggers. Same as they used to do with the convict bosses. Make those field hands *work* during the day, you could do whatever you wanted to them after dark.

"Mobutu, he was always a good nigger; always knew his place. *Hated* those fucking Commies. And that's all it took, back in those days."

The old man's voice never changed volume, but it penetrated like an icepick through cardboard.

"The whole business — you know, when the Supreme Court cut Ali loose — that was a whore's kiss. See, Ali, that's a *strong* black man. So him fighting in Zaire, that tells the world that Mobutu is one righteous dude."

"You're saying Elijah's boys had a deal with — ?"

"I'm saying all you got to do is add and subtract, Youngblood. Who was president when the Supreme Court all of a sudden reversed that bullshit case they held over Ali for all those years? Simple trade: Ali makes Zaire all about 'black liberation,' and Mobutu keeps the Commies from getting a foothold in the Congo. Fucking sweet, huh?

"And everybody kept up their end of the deal, right down the line. You know why we never made a move against all that killing in Rwanda? Because Mobutu wouldn't have liked that — he was fucking *backing* it."

The old man leaned back, closed his eyes. " 'African unity,' my black ass," he snapped. "You got to ask yourself: you think *Ali* picked Zaire? Was he too fucking stupid to know who Mobutu was? Or did he tank for the government, just like Sonny had tanked for him?"

"So why should I be trusting — ?"

"Now, *that's* my son," the old man said, approvingly. "About time you showed up. Sure, it's an old, cold trail. But you got to go back down that road. There's still freelance units working over there. Sure, most of them probably be dead, but it's the only place where you still carry that cred."

"Talk about long shots. . . ."

"What other shot we *got,* Schoolboy? That spook Pryce is good for the coin, and he won't ask questions. We're down to our last pass, and we got to be dead straight on the hard eight. If we want to know, we got to throw."

As Clarence re-entered his room, the Prof slipped into a backward segue so smooth it

227

took me a few seconds to catch up.

"Only difference between pro boxing and pro wrestling today is the costumes," he sneered.

"You're saying they're all fixed?" I played along.

"Why fix a fight when you own both of the fighters, Schoolboy? When I was a kid, they had these carnival fighters. Usually little guys, especially compared to some of those farm boys who'd step up and try them out. Fighters like that, they knew how to do their thing in a ring."

"Then why didn't they — ?"

"What? Sign up with some promoter? A carnival fighter, that was a *man*. A *free* man, get it? He might never get to wear no plastic belt, but he made a living with his skills. Fed his family, and didn't have to kiss ass to do it."

"I guess that's gone now," I said, more to keep the Prof rolling than anything else.

"That last part *never* be gone, son."

"I was talking about —"

"You think they don't have carnival fighters no more? Hah! You know better than that. You was *taught* better than that."

"You never said anything about —"

"Where's the truth?" the old man demanded. "Where you always go to look for it?"

"Ground up," Clarence and I answered as one.

The old man beamed. "Yeah, you my boys, all right. My own boys. Someday" — he paused to look directly at Clarence — "*your* boys gonna learn from you. The flame never goes out. Nothing changes; it just burns different. Truth stays truth. If it ain't a lie, it can't never die."

"So where are the carnival fighters?" I challenged him, knowing I'd lose, wanting his younger son to see that happen.

"You ever hear of Reggie Strickland?" the old man asked, a triumphant grin on his face.

"No. Who's —"

"Reggie is your modern-day carnival fighter, Schoolboy. You know how some clowns get a title shot after a dozen fights? That's not behind their skills, that's behind their management. You got more undefeated boxers out there now than there used to *be* boxers. How's a thing like that happen?"

"They put them in against stiffs."

"Sometimes," the old man conceded. "But how long can one of those tomato cans last, doing that? Reggie, he's been fighting more than twenty years. Over four *hundred* professional fights. Started out as a forty-pounder, and now he goes against middleweights, light-heavies, cruisers — anybody you *pay* him to fight, get it?"

"How could anyone have that many — ?"

"You know these nicknames some fighters got, make you think they got a gorilla for a father and a tiger for a mother? Not Reggie. He about *business,* okay? For what he does, you don't need no nickname, you need an alias. Way I hear it, he fights under half a dozen different names. There was even word going around that he fought on the same card twice in one night."

"Damn."

"That's right. Reggie, he's a professional record-builder. Your fighter needs a win, Reggie's your man. But you not asking the right question, boy. How's a man *stay* on the road, go wherever the bus stops, climb off, work a few rounds, get back on the bus . . . and keep doing it for so many years?"

"I . . . don't know," I said, honestly. "What's he do, flop in the first round every time?"

"Reggie?" The old man drew back his head, clearly insulted. "My man's *won* more fights than most fighters ever *have.* Even for those Mexican kids they let turn pro when they're only fifteen, fifty-, -sixty fights is a long career. Reggie's no tanker, he's a *boxer.* You put him in some four-rounder in your boy's hometown, you *gonna* get the decision. Build that record. But that's all you're gonna get. See, you can beat Reggie, but you not gonna *hurt* him.

"Man's got to be past forty, fighting kids half his age and twice his size, and they still can't do nothing with him. Reggie losing, I don't know, maybe three hundred fights, that's just like the carnival fighter who lets the farm boy fire those haymakers that never really land, see? He knows how to smother a man's punches, make sure the local wins the prize for lasting the whole round with the pro, sends the crowd home happy.

"It's not about Reggie being a tough guy. You know what happens when a fighter catches too many to the head. Sooner or later, it hurts you just to listen to him talk. Reggie, he got *skills.*"

"Has to have," I admitted.

"You just got to know where to look," our father admonished both his sons. "And keep looking until you find it."

"If it's there," I said.

"Only one way you get to say." The old man shifted his head to take us both into his thousand-fathom eyes. "You want to be sure there's no mouse in a house, you need to spend a few nights there yourself. And leave some cheese out, too."

Border-crossing isn't what it used to be. But Homeland Security never *was* what it was supposed to be.

All it took was a quick conversation over a sat-phone, ending with a PIN number that would disgorge bank-certified cash from a certain ATM. The one we used had security cameras that were easier to grease than a poultry inspector. Less than forty-eight hours after my call, I touched down in Geneva.

The hotel was still there. Same name, same spot. Only now it was part of an international chain. You never have to worry about some Historical Preservation Society interfering in a country where the most treasured tradition *is* treasure.

Looking around the lobby, I didn't see anything I remembered. But I wasn't looking for memories.

The last time I'd been there, it had been an all-cash experience. This time, my suite had been direct-billed to an import-export company. That company was as phony as my passport, but it was flush with some of the absolutely real money Pryce had handed over in that gym bag.

I wasn't worried about the hotel running any serious check on my personal paperwork, but I knew the credit card would have already been vetted like a candidate for bank president.

I was booked in for eight days. I had to move fast and walk slow. Like being back Inside.

Dinner didn't give me any hints. The only way to tell the wealthy vacationers from the arms dealers was the age gap between them and their female companions. And even *that* was a guess. All the servers were too young for me to even think about asking them my question.

Access to the hotel's personnel records was about as likely as the chef allowing me to take over the kitchen for the evening.

The concierge was everything you'd expect in such a joint — he knew all the answers, including the ones he couldn't give out.

In a spy novel, I'd charm some luscious chambermaid into bed. Her best pal would be a girl who worked in the pension department. A few hours of expertly inducing full-body orgasms, and I'd have all my answers.

Me, I went for a walk. At least the damn river still looked the same.

The little shop where I'd gone after I'd been taught to say, *"Avez-vous des livres anglais?"* was still there . . . but it wasn't a bookstore anymore.

The man who'd taught me that phrase was who I was looking for. Norbert had been a junior concierge when I'd come to this same hotel, eons ago. He was only a few years older than me, but a century ahead in experience.

I'm not sure what tipped him, but the possibilities were endless: my clothes weren't right; I couldn't speak French or German, never mind Russian or Chinese; I didn't know "steak tartare" meant raw meat. And the only time I'd seen the inside of a prep school had been during a burglary.

After I'd waited a couple of days, Norbert came over to where I was sitting in the lobby. I was smoking the last of the Dunhills I'd picked up in England, figuring they'd give me some class.

He asked me if he could be of any assistance, phrasing it so I'd know he wasn't putting me down. I told him I was just waiting for some friends — we'd all arranged to meet in Geneva before taking off to go skiing.

Norbert smiled thinly. Then he asked me if I had ever seen the Rhone at night. It was a unique spectacle, not something I'd want to miss. And there were benches just a short walk from the hotel's door.

He was there when I arrived. I'd seen plenty of men sitting on benches in my life, but this was the first time I saw one do it elegantly.

I knew I was in the kind of jungle where I couldn't tell the parrots from the piranhas, but something in Norbert pulled me hard, and I ended up telling him as much of the truth as I could.

"Biafra?" he said when I finished, making the word into a question.

"Yeah," I repeated.

"All those children."

I just waited for the rest.

"You are a very brave man" was what he said.

I didn't feel brave; I felt worthless. That's the core truth of why I had grabbed at the chance to be a hero, and get paid big money, too. I knew at least *some* of what the men in suits had told me was the truth. A whole nation *was* being exterminated while the world watched. So sad. Enough to make you change channels.

When the Nigerians got the money they needed from the countries that wanted their oil, they stepped up the slaughter. The generals bought a lot of new toys, from surplus fighter jets — and Egyptian pilots — to missiles, bombs, and river-killing poisons. By then, they had the Biafrans completely landlocked, like they were all trapped in the same cellar. The only exit led to a tornado of bullets and bombs . . . or they could just stay in there and starve to death, if they didn't suffocate first.

At first, the world got to see it happening. But after the Nigerians turned up the heat, the reports stopped coming. The journalists were the last to go — once all the communication links were cut, they couldn't file their stories. When the "war" turned into an extermination project, it stopped being televised. For the first time in history, a Red Cross plane was shot down.

The outcome was never in doubt, just the timetable. The only way to get food into what was left of Biafra was to fly unarmed cargo planes, taking off every night from São Tomé. If they got past the attacking jets, a radio signal would direct them to "Uli Airport," a dirt strip in the jungle lit only by flares. They had thirty seconds to get down before the flares went out. Then only a few minutes to unload and get back up — the flares always drew fire.

The world's heartstrings had almost

snapped from the earlier images, and money flowed in to anyone collecting it. Some of that actually got turned into food, but most of that food was rotting in warehouses. You couldn't get anything humans needed to survive past the blockade, only over it. And even the few planes that made it didn't have the cargo capacity to make any real difference.

So when men in suits approached a State-raised kid who'd just been released from his first adult prison sentence, I was so dumb and so desperate that I never questioned why they would pick someone like me for such an important mission.

All I could think of was, *When I come back, I'll be a different man.* In their eyes, and my own, too. I wouldn't be a kid who'd spent his life never being wanted by anyone except the police. I'd be the hero who helped save all those starving kids. And have some legit money in my pocket, too.

My assignment was to find an overland route into the landlocked area. The men in suits said they could convoy food and supplies through Cameroon — they called it an "open market" area, a place where cash solves all problems. The supplies themselves were stockpiled in Gabon, the next country over. That one was a "friendly," one of the

237

few countries that actually recognized Biafra.

The way they explained it to me, I was perfect for the job. They told me to picture Biafra as one of those juvie joints I'd grown up in. My job was to escape . . . and leave trail markers behind. All I had to do was get over the border into Cameroon. They told me what names to say as soon as I made it across.

Those convoys in Gabon were all ready to roll on through. They just needed to know a spot where it was safe to slip into Biafra.

And, me, I would have helped save all those babies.

Me.

When you've got no one to trust, you end up trusting anyone. If I'd been anything other than a born-to-lose kid with nothing in his future but more time behind bars, if I'd had anyone I could talk to, if I'd . . .

It doesn't matter now. I took the "assignment."

I must have believed what they told me. Or wanted to so badly that it didn't make a difference. Because, when I explained my "mission" to Norbert, his dry blue eyes teared up.

The very next morning, people came to visit me at the hotel. One of them brought a bunch of official-looking papers. "The Swiss love their documents," Norbert told me, tonelessly.

Next stop, Lisbon. More exchanges, and I was on my way to Angola.

After that, it got ugly. Biafra fell. Maybe a million dead. Later, I found out that the people who sent me actually got what *they* wanted. No surprise: they were used to getting what they paid for. Maybe that's how my name first surfaced in Pryce's parallel universe; I'll never know.

What I do know is that I never got to be a hero. I was just a thing they used. I guess those men in suits were my guidance counselors, because they sure picked my career for me.

I learned a lot during that career, most of it by watching. And listening. What I don't know would fill a galaxy. But what I do know, I know better than any of them.

Patience. Waiting. Being sure. Every time I'd been wrong about someone, I'd go back and figure out what I'd missed. One time, it took years. But I had plenty of time to think during that stretch.

Now I know. Humans who could flat-line a polygraph wouldn't get past the first round with me. All it takes is a few minutes of conversation, and I know you. Not because I have X-ray eyes. Not because I have powers. Because, whoever you are, I've met you before.

Baby-rapers don't "age out" the way armed robbers do. Deep truth doesn't change. If Norbert was still alive, he'd know how to find people who could put together an operation like snatching a baby from a sheikh.

And I knew, somehow, that if I asked him, he'd do it.

I wasted one more day of my second visit to Geneva before I accepted what I should have known from the opening bell. All I'd ever had was a puncher's chance, and I couldn't keep waiting for the other guy to come to me.

So I unpacked the stupid-expensive outfit Michelle had separately stored in my luggage, remembering her warning that it wouldn't "work" if I left out any single piece. Then I called, asked for the manager, and politely inquired if I might have a few moments of his time. His assistant asked if noon would be satisfactory.

I shaved, showered, and dressed. Then I sat in my corner and waited for the bell.

"I have not visited your hotel for a *long*

time," I told the short, round-faced Eurasian man. We were in the private sitting room reserved for consultations with guests — guests who had booked suites big enough to hold revival meetings.

He raised his perfectly sculpted eyebrows a quarter-millimeter.

"I was a guest in 1969," I said, smiling nostalgically. "A lifetime ago, it seems. I was a young man, doing what my parents thought of as the 'Grand Tour.' "

I didn't think the guest register from 1969 would be preserved on some damn computer he could instantly access, but I was prepared to explain the name change, if those eyebrows of his moved again.

"Anyway," I continued, "I really was very naïve, about so many things. And I believe I learned more during my stay here than I did from any educational institution, before or since."

"We are honored," he said. His body posture was expectant, not anxious.

"My father started a coin collection for me when I was born. Not simple currency like this," I said, placing a ten-coin clear plastic cylinder of Canadian Maple Leafs on the coffee table, a thick slab of pure-white marble with an orange sunburst inlaid in its center, "but true numismatic gems."

I put another cylinder on the table, un-screwed the top, dropped a coin into my hand, and hockey-pucked it across the marble with my finger. "Gold coins are quite good for some transactions, especially in places where the local currency is . . . unstable. But," I continued, taking out a third cylinder, "I was only looking for rari-ties, hoping to find something special to show my father when I returned."

"Ah," was all the manager said.

"One of your employees took me under his wing. He gave me a sense of confidence that I had never possessed before . . . and never lost since. As a result, I was able to make several purchases that truly impressed my father. I vowed that, one day, I would come back and express my appreciation per-sonally."

He tilted his head, waiting.

"But time seems to just slip away from you," I said, regretfully. "I was too busy *run-ning* things, making money I never needed in the first place. And . . . well, I never came back. I realize Norbert must be retired by now — I can't imagine him leaving; this hotel was his life — and I was hoping that you still had him on your books . . . a pen-sion recipient, perhaps?"

"You wish to contact a former employee

of ours?"

"I do."

"Switzerland is a country where we value confidentiality above all, Mr. Jackson."

"I understand that. In fact, I respect it deeply. I have had many good reasons to do so," I told him, implying that I had found my country's tax laws somewhat burdensome on occasion. "I would never expect you to divulge information. I merely, humbly, request that you transmit a message to Norbert. He, of course, could then decide —"

"The message?" the manager cut me off, politely.

"Just that the young man who was about to embark on a great journey in 1969 never forgot his kindness, and would greatly appreciate an opportunity to pay his respects."

The manager stood up. We shook hands. His hand came away as empty as it was when he opened it. You don't insult a man of his status with crass bribery. But I suspected that the three tubes of Canadian Maple Leafs I'd forgotten to take with me when I left the sitting room weren't going to be called to my attention.

The cream-colored envelope was slipped under my door at just past two in the morning. I let it stay there, untouched. If a second message was going to come, better to let the deliveryman believe I was fast asleep.

The gift I'd bought for my wife was in my hand, ready for work. Wüsthof cutlery is made in Germany, but some of the best Swiss shops carry it. I'd told the obsequious salesman that I wouldn't dare return home without a proper present, and my wife already had more jewelry than a team of Clydesdales could haul.

He'd been puzzled by my lack of interest in having him mail the set directly to the States: "Those airport people, sir, they can be extremely . . ." I told him that I had quite a number of presents yet to purchase, and the hotel would handle the whole packing-and-shipping thing for me — no point in even gift-wrapping what I'd bought.

I waited until a little past seven in the morning before I used the point of the knife to pull the envelope all the way inside. I slipped on latex gloves before I opened it, working under the screen I'd made out of one of the shirts I'd packed. The cloth it was made from wouldn't breathe — if you actually put it on, you'd be sweating like a lobbyist under oath.

But there was no disposal-dust inside, just

a folded piece of hotel stationery. The note was handwritten, using a fountain pen in close-to-calligraphy formal script:

Ce soir, encore

N.

I was there early. The river was calm. I embraced it, merging its current with my own.

The man who approached was using some kind of walking stick, but his movements were straight-backed and dignified. His fair hair was thinner, stirred by the faint breeze.

"It's me, Norbert," I assured him, knowing my face wouldn't resemble the one he'd seen a lifetime ago.

He sat down next to me. Extended his hand. His grip was the measured strength of a man who knew he didn't have to prove anything.

"War wounds?" he said, looking at my face.

"Some," I answered, wondering how he could see so well in the night. "The rest is from the lousy repair job they did on them."

"I am grateful you returned," he said.

"From Biafra," he added, telling me two things: I'd never had the class or the decency to even drop him a note when I'd made it back. And I was there now only because I wanted something.

"You were nothing but good to me," I told him. "I won't insult you by claiming I showed up to apologize for never thanking you properly."

"Oh, you did that," he said, gravely. "Those . . . sources I introduced you to, they confirmed I had not misplaced my trust."

"How could they know I got out? I was on a —"

"Not that you got out," the elderly man said. "That you went *in.* I believed in your . . . quest then. What I . . . arranged, you know it was not for the money I was paid."

"I know."

"And now you are back."

"Yes."

"Tell me what you came for this time," Norbert said, cutting right to it. If Alzheimer's ever saw this man coming it was going to run for cover.

"When I first came here, I was a kid," I told him. "A stupid kid. You know what I wanted. What I . . . Ah, that doesn't matter.

Not now. When I finally got out, I actually went into that business. But in America, I was playing on a field I knew. And I managed to win a few."

He made a sound I couldn't interpret.

"I'm here because I'm trying to find a baby. A baby who was kidnapped."

"And you believe the baby is here?"

"No. Let me tell you how the baby was taken." I waited for his nod. Then gave him everything I had.

"Nobody I knew of . . . back then . . . would do such a thing," he said when I finished.

Meaning either they didn't have the ability to work Stateside, or they wouldn't touch that kind of work. I didn't ask him which — a man who believed a street kid when he said he was going to be a child-saving hero was entitled to believe some mercenaries had a moral code.

"It was a team," I said. "Not one of those regime-overthrowing specialist outfits, and not the kind of 'private contractors' who work in Iraq. This was a small, elite unit. So it wouldn't be incorporated, wouldn't have a Web site, and wouldn't take checks. I understand it couldn't be any of the people you used to . . . know about. But I thought you might be able to ask a few questions of old friends?"

"And you want?"

"The baby. *Only* the baby."

"There is a reward?"

"A huge one."

"For you?"

"Not a penny for me. Everything goes to whoever helps me get the baby back to his parents," I said. Telling the truth and lying at the same time, a skill I'd taken decades of practice to perfect.

"So many years, you still want to be a hero?" Norbert said, his smile a mixture of wonder and pity.

The next morning, Norbert introduced him as *"mon frère aîné."* To which the hard man seated to my right added only, "Alain."

He was at least eighty, thin as a tire iron. Blue-agate eyes, ramrod posture, and the kind of baldness that only a used-daily razor produces. Everything about him screamed Military. At his age, that would have put him in the middle of World War II.

I had been seated when they approached. It took Norbert's brother only a half-second to figure out that my right eye didn't work — I didn't think his choice of where to sit was an accident.

He ignored my offered handshake, locked

my good eye with his flat-screen blue ones. "You know La Légion Étrangère?"

"Rumors," I answered, my body language saying that I didn't put a lot of stock in them.

"Most are lies. The French, they are . . . how shall I say?" He made an eloquent gesture with his hands and shoulders, suggesting anything I wanted it to mean.

He snap-checked my face, saw I wasn't going to respond. Whether he read that as professionalism or respect, I couldn't know. What he said was:

"Their rules are as flexible as their historians. Loyalty is very important to the French. Loyalty to *them.* They see what they wish to see, so the concept of purchased loyalty does not strike them as illogical."

I glanced over at Norbert. His face was expressionless. I guess he figured I had grown up enough to know when to shut up.

"You are not looking for soldiers," the man who called himself Alain said. "Those you seek are not men who fight as brothers-in-arms. True warriors care nothing for some 'cause,' " he dry-spat, that last word so heavy with revulsion I was surprised it didn't shatter the stone floor when it fell from his mouth. "Warriors fight because war is their life. The flag under which they fight counts for nothing, the bond between them is everything."

We were at the outdoor café where Norbert had told me to be waiting. None of the other tables were occupied. No waitress approached. The place wouldn't open for business for another couple of hours. People occasionally passed on the sidewalk. Curiosity didn't seem to be a Swiss trait.

"Independent units still exist," the man of unrusted iron said. "They are much in demand, but the same . . . benefits are no longer available. Money, yes. But who wants to become a citizen of some filthy, savage country? Our breed . . . it is dying."

He moved his head just enough to indicate he was finished with preambles. "The training required for the operation you described to my brother" — nodding slightly across at Norbert — "would take considerable time and expertise, but there is no shortage of either. There are always men for hire. Some have no homeland to return to — ex-Stasi, perhaps. Some can never return home. Each would have his own reason; none would be asked.

"Some men who were once part of elite fighting forces from all the world's armies are well entrenched in the Congo. Some are employed by those who claim to be legitimate rulers. Others are search-and-destroy teams commissioned by those with a political interest in certain areas — the Sahel, for example.

"To train a team for what you describe requires a purpose-built unit. To capture is far more difficult than to kill. The usual procedure is to question the survivors, rather than isolate any particular one prior to the assault.

"Therefore, such a unit must be assembled like a fine chronograph. This requires considerable investment, because even the most brilliantly written play will fail if the actors are not sufficiently rehearsed. Sets must be created. Sometimes destroyed, rebuilt, and destroyed again. The director must be able to fine-tune, modify . . . *perfect* the production before it ever goes public.

"Military intelligence is a flexible concept. What works effectively in one climate will be useless in another — the Russian front in winter is not the jungles of Burma in the rainy season. In addition to everything else required, *absolute* secrecy must be maintained during preparation. Total isolation; no communication. There is only one place where operatives such as you described could be trained."

I waited, making sure he had nothing

more to say, before I asked, "Can you tell me — ?"

"I can theorize only," the man who called himself Alain said. "It would be a camp, but not a permanent one. I cannot tell you where it would be, exactly, but I know the borders within which it must . . . could *only* . . . exist."

"I heard there was an entire ex–SAS unit working in the —"

"No," he said, sharply. "I told you: there will always be men who cannot return. Once there was a place in the world even for them. A place where no judgments were made except those of the warrior. You are" — he scanned me as dispassionately as an MRI — *"nicht reinrassig,* yes? Perhaps *Zigeuner?"*

I shrugged. I didn't need a translator. He wanted to make sure I understood he knew I was no purebred.

"That would not matter to us," he told me, telling me my translation was all wrong. He wasn't being magnanimous or condescending when he ID'ed me as a man with Gypsy blood; he was just telling me how it was. Once. "A legionnaire is a fighting man," he said. "He who becomes one of us leaves *everything* behind: his politics, his religion, his family. The only blood that ever mattered to us was that of the enemy."

I nodded. Whether what he was saying was true or not didn't matter to me. But what he said next did.

"We were a fighting *force*, not hired killers paid to use machine guns against machetes. To *those* kind of people, bloodlines *would* matter. In fact, they would be *raison d'être*."

Robert Johnson stood at the Crossroads, but he didn't get to keep the fruits of his bargain long, I thought. *But you, you still have yours more than fifty years later, don't you? You made a deal with the devil to protect your baby brother. And when that devil died by his own cowardly hand, you made a deal with another, to keep yourself alive. You had nothing America wanted; all you knew was soldiering, not rocket science or nuclear fusion. But the French, they always had work that needed doing.*

I got it then: asking this man for anything more than he'd already told me would be like trying to sculpt marble with a butter knife.

Back in my room, I added it up. Norbert's brother hadn't been "theorizing"; he'd been giving me an expert's analysis. His credibility was his own past. This was a man who would stand in front of a firing squad and refuse the blindfold; he'd want the executioners to see a warrior's final contempt for murderers who called themselves "soldiers." His funeral shroud would be his own loyalty. Not loyalty to some "Fatherland." Not loyalty to an army, or a team of mercenaries. Loyalty to his blood-oath. I don't know who whispered "Protect your little brother" to him so many years ago. But I knew he had never wavered, no matter the cost.

So when he'd told me snatching the Sheikh's baby hadn't been the work of any mercenary unit, I believed him. When he told me where the team who had done the job must have been trained, I believed him.

I believed — because I knew what telling me had cost him.

"I am very grateful," I told Norbert that same night, looking at the river. It seemed to have grown blacker, less settled.

"Non pas rien."

"No," I said. "I know the value of things. What you did was . . . everything."

"How do you know Alain was . . . accurate?" He chose the last word delicately.

"I can't tell you. Not because I don't want to, because I don't know a way to say it that won't make me sound insane. I have . . . a gift."

"You trust this . . . gift, then?"

"Yes, my friend, I do." I handed him a slip of paper with the number that redirects to one of the pay phones right behind my booth at Mama's. "Please tell your brother that, should he ever require whatever assistance I might be able to provide, this will find me."

His unlined face flexed just enough to tell me he believed me. Believed *in* me. And in my gift.

"If they already moved him, he's out of reach," I told my family, Rosie curled at my side on the couch. "But if they're still here — in the city, I mean — we can find them. Maybe."

"Why not just tell this man Pryce?" Clarence asked. "Surely, he would have better resources . . . if what you were told is true."

"It was all true," I answered, thinking, *Even the things Alain never said in words.* "But the people who hired Pryce don't want theories, they want a baby."

"And the people who took him, what would *they* want?"

"I did have an idea, but I've let go of it, honey," I said to Michelle. "If the goal was to humiliate the Sheikh, there were better ways, especially with the kind of money they spent on this. What we know for sure is that they weren't out to cancel his ticket. He was there for the taking, and they passed."

Max rubbed his thumb against the first two fingers of his hand, the universal sign for money, shaking his head at the same time.

"This *can't* be about money," I agreed with my brother. "That would make it all some kind of stupid gamble, like Pryce first thought . . . and there's not a trace of stupid in any of this."

"That is the only theory which fits the known facts," the Mole said, firmly.

"Not a word on the Web," Terry added. "Nobody taking credit. There wasn't even much screening to do, because —"

"The newspapers don't have the story, so there is no way for the usual frauds to claim credit," Clarence finished for him.

Terry tapped some keys, said: "NYPD has it coded as a gunpoint robbery. Victim was a homeless man named Milton Johnson. Black. Age fifty-seven. Long sheet. In fact, he was arrested a couple of days later, whole list of petty misdemeanors. Died in custody before they could even transport him. Autopsy is mandatory in all such cases. Cause of death was multiple organ failure — he was a long-term drug-and-alcohol abuser."

How Pryce got *that* done, I don't know, but every paper door had already been sealed shut. Even one of the docket-divers looking for something to sell the tabloids wouldn't stumble over the Prince's name.

"It is time to visit my father," Clarence said, looking at his watch.

Max gestured drinking from an imaginary mug held in both hands, making it clear who *he* was going to consult.

The Mole, Michelle, and Terry took off to have dinner together. Ever since Pryce had delivered Terry's birth certificate, Michelle couldn't stop introducing him to everyone who crossed their path. She hadn't worked out the mechanics yet, so she alternated between pride and suspicion anytime someone told her she looked too young to be his mother.

"You think he got those looks from his *father?*" She'd viper-smile, inviting a look at the Mole's remarkable resemblance to a formless mass wearing Coke-bottle glasses and a stunned-ox expression. Michelle could do magic with clothes, but the Mole was immune — give him five minutes, and he could transform a four-grand suit into something you'd pass up in a Goodwill bin.

Terry suffered in silence. His father had

taught him a lot more than science.

On our way out, Gateman was already ordering a pizza. Apparently, Rosie loved hers with extra cheese. The minute I'd explained how chocolate was toxic to dogs, Gateman had tossed out his entire stash, Godiva and all.

When Clarence and I walked into the Prof's room, the bed was empty. Clarence gasped some wordless sound. I felt it in a place I thought had frozen over years ago.

"He's around somewhere," I told my younger brother as I walked him to the door. "Come on."

We found the Prof near the end of a long corridor. His right hand rested on some kind of thick metal pole that hit the floor on a triangle of rubber-capped legs, his left was around the tiny waist of a woman in a nurse's uniform. They were slowly covering ground.

"Taralyn," Clarence whispered, his voice a blend of different sighs.

"Recognized her from this angle, huh?" I said.

I didn't look at his face, but I felt like I was standing next to a sunlamp.

We caught up with them just as the Prof lowered himself, with a little help, onto a free-form couch positioned to provide a magnificent view of the city at night. They can do amazing things with one-way glass these days.

"You ever been in New Orleans?" he said, by way of greeting.

I knew he wasn't asking me.

"No, Father," Clarence answered.

"You know those dumbass hansom cabs they got in Central Park? The ones for tourists?"

"I have seen them," Clarence said, caution seeping into his voice.

"Burke here, he hates the whole idea. Hell of a way for a racehorse to spend his last days, right?"

"Any days at all," I agreed.

"Well, now, see, in New Orleans, they got the same thing. Only they don't use horses; they use mules. You know why?"

"I do not," Clarence said, being *very* careful now.

Taralyn sat next to the Prof, as composed as if she was in church. But her eyes never left Clarence's face as the Prof continued.

"Gets too hot, sometimes those Central Park horses just keel over in the street. Supposed to have all kinds of rules about it, but you know how this city is about keeping the rich folks happy. Now a *mule,* it gets too hot, he pulls a work stoppage. That's all there is. You can't beat 'em and you can't bribe 'em. Can't trick 'em, either. Now, what am I telling you, boy?"

"They should use mules here?" Clarence guessed.

"They shouldn't do that crap at all," the Prof told him, nodding at me. "But that ain't the point. What I'm telling you is, sometimes, people don't understand the difference between stubborn and smart."

"Ah."

"You take this little girl here," the Prof said, reaching for Taralyn's hand. The gesture looked so natural that it couldn't have been the first time. "Look like she couldn't lift a bag of groceries, but she strong as a damn mule, son. Twice as stubborn, too."

"Mr. Henry!" the café-au-lait beauty protested. "You know very well that physical rehabilitation is not magic. If I hear one more story about roots and mojos and —"

"Nothing but the truth, girl," the Prof shot back. "You think those boys running around here in their white coats, they know everything?"

"I do not. But I *do* know that you are to have exercise *every* day. Before the prosthe-

sis can be fitted properly, you must be in
—"

"*Now* you see?" the Prof said to Clarence.
"Son, please, I beg you. Distract this woman
long enough for your brother to get me back
to my room."

"Come on, old man," I said to the Prof,
extending my hand to help him up.

"It's like your long shot pays off, but when
you show up to collect, you find out the
bookie grabbed the first thing smoking,
Schoolboy. What that old guy told you, it
has to be right. Never fails: you strain out
the trash, whatever's left is pure cash. So,
yeah, we got the winning ticket. Only we
can't turn it in for the payoff."

"By me, we already did."

"You mean this joint? Go bring me my
sounds."

I carried the black Bose machine that
could handle six CDs over to his bed. Following his gestures, I popped the lid. The
CD inside was unlabeled. Watching the Prof
for hand-signaled instructions, I closed it
again. Immediately the LED glowed, as if
the CD inside was spinning. But no sound
came out of the speakers.

"That's the Mole-man's," the Prof said.
"He started to tell me how it works, but

Little Miss Michelle started in on him about shoes or something. All I know is, it throws off some kind of noise-canceling signal. When that CD's in, whatever ears they got on us ain't picking up nothing but a conversation between you and me. One we *had,* not the one we *having,* see?"

"They're bugging a recording?" I said, shaking my head in wonderment.

"Hope so," the Prof replied. "But, just in case, keep it all light salad, get me? Nice round olives, no pits."

I nodded. Said: "I've got no contacts I can trust overseas."

The Prof motioned me to lean in close, whispered so softly it was barely a breath.

I stepped back.

"That's the truth," I agreed. "But the only way I'm going to get to even *ask* is —"

"One call could do it all, son. But you down to your last dime, and even less time," he cautioned, just as Clarence walked in.

"Why'd you leave that little girl?" the Prof demanded.

"Father, she *works* here. She cannot just . . . go for a walk whenever she desires. This is her *job.*"

"Sit down, boy," the old man said, hardcore serious.

I took a seat, too, in case the Prof needed me. That *might happen,* I heard Michelle snicker, somewhere inside my head.

"The little girl ain't no crime-man's wife, Clarence. You understand what I'm telling you?"

"Father, I —"

"No way I'm leaving this junkyard of a planet without some grandchildren," the old man cut him off. "That ain't up for negotiation. *This* one," he said, nodding in my direction, "he disqualified himself from that job before you was even born."

I didn't know if the Prof was talking about my commitment to crime or my vasectomy, but I did know it didn't matter.

"Listen up, now," the old man said to Clarence. "You a natural stud — you my son, what else *could* you be? — but all you ever had so far was girlfriends. Burke, he had *women.* That Belle girl, Jesus rest her sweet soul, now, *she* was a crime-man's woman. Never a doubt, right down to the minute she cashed out."

My chest hurt from the memory. Belle. A rock-candy girl, born without choices or chances. The day her older sister told her she was also her mother, she told Belle to run for her life. Her mother-sister knew "Daddy" had decided Belle was grown enough to be next on his list. Belle was still scrambling through the swamp when she heard the gunshots that ended the life of the woman she had always called Sissy.

After that, she did whatever it took. Drove getaway cars for heist artists, took off her clothes on grungy stages for money. Always running from what was inside her.

We found each other in the dark. It was Belle who told me that most baby alligators never live past a few days. As soon as they're hatched, they charge for the water, but there's too many things blocking their path. Even the ones who make it, there's things waiting for them in the water, too. Very bad odds. The way Belle told it, the few gators who manage to grow big enough to be safe spend the rest of their lives getting even for their brothers and sisters who didn't.

It all ended the night I killed a man who was blocking our family's path to the water. The same night Belle went out in a blaze of police gunfire, drawing the cops away from me, the way her mother had drawn her father away from her. The father who had infected her with that "bad blood" she always believed she carried. Believed it so strong she would never carry a child of her own.

The Prof's voice took me right back to

when we'd settled that account, years before Clarence became part of us:

I was standing on the upper level of the Port Authority Bus Terminal, waiting in the night. Back to the wall, hands in the empty pockets of my grimy raincoat. Under the brim of a trash-bin fedora, my eyes swept the deck.

A tall, slim black youth wearing a blue silk T-shirt under a canary-yellow sport coat. Baggy pants with pegged cuffs that broke perfectly over creamy Italian shoes.

Today's pimp, waiting for the bus to spit out its cargo of runaways. He'd have a Maxima with tinted windows waiting in a nearby parking lot. Rap about how hard it was to get adjusted to the city, how he was the same way himself when he first hit town. Now he's a talent scout for an independent film producer. If the girl wanted, he'd let her stay at his place for a few days until she got herself together. Plenty of room there: projection TV, VCR, sweet stereo, too. Some fine liquor, even a little coke. High-style. "The way it's done, babe."

Another black guy, this one in his late thirties. Gold medallion worn beneath an unbuttoned red polyester shirt that would pass for silk in the underground lights. Knee-length black leather coat, player's hat with a tasteful red band. Fake gators on his feet.

Yesterday's pimp, waiting his turn. This one would have an old Caddy, promise to make the girl a star. The audition would be in a no-see hotel just down the street. One with metal coat hangers in a closet that would never hold clothes.

Once a wide-eyed runaway got off that bus, she could go easy or she could go hard. But she *was* going.

Two youngish white guys, talking low, getting their play together. Hoping the shipment of fresh new boys wouldn't be past their sell-by dates.

A blank-faced Spanish kid: black sweatshirt, hood pulled up tight around his head, felony-flyers on his feet. "Carry your bags, ma'am?"

A few citizens, waiting on relatives coming back from vacation, or a kid coming home from school. A bearded wino picking through the garbage, muttering.

The Greyhound's air brakes hissed as it pulled into the loading port.

Night bus from Starke, Florida. A twenty-four-hour ride, changing buses in Jacksonville. The round-trip ticket cost $244.

I know; I paid for it.

The man I was waiting for would have a letter in his pocket. A letter in a young girl's rounded handwriting. Blue ink on pink stationery.

Daddy I know it's been a long time but I didn't know where you was. I been working with some boys and I got myself arrested a couple years ago. One of the cops took my name and put it in one of their computers. He told me where you was but I didn't write for a while because I wanted to have something goot to tell you first. I'm sorry Sissy made me run away that time without even telling you goodbye like I wanted. I wrote to her but the letter came back. Do you know where she's at? I guess she got married or something. Anyway Daddy you will never believe it but I got a lot of money now. I'm real good at this business I'm in. I got a boyfriend too. I thought you could use a stake to get you started after you got out but I didn't want to mail cash to no prison. Wasn't that right? Anyway Daddy when you get ready to come out you write to me at this post office box I got now and I'll send you a ticket for you to come up here. It would be like a vacation or something. And I could give you all the money I saved up for you. I hope you're doing okay Daddy.

Love Belle

The slow stream of humans climbed down, most carrying plastic shopping bags, cartons tied together with string, shoulder-duffels. Not a lot of leather luggage rides the 'Hound.

He was one of the last off the bus. Tall, raw-boned man, small eyes under a shock of taffy-honey hair. Belle's eyes, Belle's hair. A battered carryall in one hand. The Spanish kid never gave him a second glance. A cop might have, but there weren't any around.

I felt a winter's knot tighten in my chest.

His eyes swept the depot like a prison searchlight.

I moved to him, taking my hands out of my pockets, showing them empty. He'd never seen me before, but he knew the look.

"You're from Belle?" he asked. A harsh voice, not softened by the cracker twang.

"Yeah. She sent me to bring you to her," I answered, turning my back on him so he could follow, keeping my hands in sight.

I ignored the escalator, took the stairs to the ground floor. Felt the man moving behind me. I knew Max was behind him; shadow-quiet, keeping the box tight.

My Plymouth was parked on a side street off Ninth Avenue. I opened the driver's door, climbed in, reached over, and unlocked his door. Giving him all the time in the world to bolt if he smelled something wrong.

But he climbed in next to me right away. Glanced behind him. All he could see was a pile of dirty blankets.

"No backseat in this wagon?"

"Sometimes I carry things."

He smiled, long yellow teeth catching the neon flash from a topless bar. "You work with Belle?"

"Sometimes."

"She's a good girl."

I didn't answer him, pointing the Plymouth to the West Side Highway. I lit a smoke, tossing the pack on the seat between us. He helped himself, firing a match off his thumbnail, leaning back like a man in charge.

I turned east across 125th, heading for the Triboro Bridge.

"Y'all got nothin' *but* niggers 'round here," he said, looking out his window.

"Yeah, they're everyplace."

"You ever do time with them?"

"All my life."

I tossed a token in the Exact Change basket on the bridge and headed for the Bronx. The Plymouth purred off the highway onto Bruckner Boulevard, finding its own way to Hunts Point.

He watched the streets pass, said: "Man, if it ain't niggers, it's spics. This here city's no place for a white man."

"You liked the joint better?"

His laugh was short and ugly.

I motored on, past blacked-out windows in abandoned buildings — dead eyes in a row of corpses. Turned off the main drag and headed toward the Meat Market. Whores working naked under clear plastic raincoats waved at the trucks as they passed by.

He just watched.

We crossed an empty prairie, tiny dots of light glowing where things that had been born human kept fires burning all night long.

I pulled up to the junkyard gate. Left him in the car while I reached my hand through a gap in the razor wire to open the lock.

We drove inside and stopped. I got out and relocked the gate. Then I climbed back inside, rolled down the window, and lit a smoke.

"What do we do now?" he asked.

"We wait."

The dogs came. A snarling pack, swarming around the car.

"Damn! Belle's *here?*"

"She's here," I told him. Pure truth.

The Mole lumbered through the pack, knocking the animals out of his way with his knees as he walked, the way he always does. He came up to my open window, peered past me at the man in the front seat.

"This is him?"

"Yeah."

The Mole clapped his hands together. Simba

came out of the blackness. A city wolf, boss of the pack. The beast stood on his hind legs, forepaws draped over my windowsill, looking at the man next to me. A low, thick sound came out, as if his throat was clogged with unswallowed blood.

"We walk from here," I told the man.

His eyes were ball bearings. "I ain't walkin' nowhere, boy. I don't like none a this."

"Too bad."

"Too bad for *you,* boy. You look real close, you'll see my hand ain't empty."

I didn't have to look close. I knew what he'd have carried in his satchel — Greyhound doesn't use metal detectors.

The dirty pile of blankets in the back of the Plymouth changed shape.

The man grunted as he felt the round steel holes against the back of his neck.

"Your hole card is a low card, motherfucker." The Prof's voice, big-chested powerful for such a tiny man. "I see your puny pistol and raise you one big-ass scattergun."

"Toss it on the seat," I told him. "Don't be stupid."

"Where's Belle?" he said, frightened now, evoking the name of his property like it was a prayer. "I came to see Belle."

"You'll see her. I promise."

His pistol made a soundless landing on the

front seat. The Mole walked around and opened the passenger door. The man got out, the Prof's shotgun right behind. I walked around to his side of the car. "Let's go see her," I said.

We walked through the junkyard until we came to a clearing.

"Have a seat," I told him, pointing toward a cut-down oil drum. Took a seat myself, lit another smoke.

He sat down, reaching out a large hand to snatch at the pack I tossed over to him out of the air. Good reflexes, lousy survival instincts.

"What now?" he asked.

"We wait," I said, again.

Terry entered the clearing. A slightly built little boy wearing a set of dirty coveralls. "That him?"

I nodded.

The kid lit a smoke for himself, watching the man. The dog pack watched, too. With the same eyes.

The Mole stumbled up next to me. The Prof by his side, holding his sawed-off like an artist with a paintbrush.

"Pansy!" I called. A Neapolitan mastiff lumbered out of the darkness, 160 pounds of muscle and bone. Her midnight fur gleamed blue in the faint light, baleful gray eyes pinning as she walked toward the tall man like a steamroller approaching freshly poured tar.

"Jump!" I snapped at her. Pansy hit the ground, her eyes still locked on her target.

I looked around one more time. All Belle's family was in that junkyard. All that was left, except for Michelle. And she'd already done her part: not just writing that letter — she'd been waiting in the shadows next to my Plymouth, in case the guy had spooked and made a run for it.

The Prof handed me a revolver. It warmed my hand.

I stood up.

"They got the death penalty in Florida?" I asked the man.

"You know they do," he said. No fear in his voice; he still thought he was being tested.

"They got it for incest?"

His eyes flickered as he realized he'd already been graded. "Where's Belle? Let me talk to her!" His voice was a feathery whine.

"Too late for that," I told him. "She's in the same ground you're standing on."

"I never did nothin' to you."

"Yeah, you did."

He tried a feeble stab: "I got people know where I am."

The Prof sneered, "Motherfucker, *you* don't even know where you are."

273

"You want the kid to see this?" I asked the Mole.

Light played on the thick lenses of the underground man's glasses. "He watched *her* die."

I cocked the revolver, wanting Belle's father to hear the sound.

He didn't panic, kept his voice low, trying to sound reasonable. "Look, if I owe, I can pay. I'm a man who pays his debts."

"You couldn't pay the interest on this one," I told him.

"Wait! I got money stashed. I can —"

"Save it for the Parole Board," I told him.

The hammer dropped. The man I had waited too long to kill jerked backwards off the oil drum. I fired twice more, watching his body shudder as each hollow point slug went home.

The Prof walked closer. His shotgun spoke. Both barrels.

I looked at the body of Belle's father for a long, dead minute.

We bowed our heads.

Pansy howled at the dark sky, grief and hate in the same voice.

The pack went silent, waiting for its meal.

I didn't feel a thing.

"Burke was born a criminal, and raised to be a better one . . . by me," the Prof told his other son. "I trained him to be a true thief instead of some hothead gunman. But *you,* you was raised up to be a gentleman. Your momma wouldn't have wanted to even *meet* some of those give-it-up sluts you always playing around with. But you ain't no baby anymore. You been a man a long time. When you and Taralyn get married, you *through* with what we do."

"But . . ."

"You could open a million oysters and never find you a perfect black pearl, boy," the Prof kept rolling. "Coming as close to crossing over as I did, it's like every inch of your body picks up signals, not just your eyes and ears. So I *know.*

"Listen now: That young woman will not tolerate you doing anything *but* right. She might — and I say *might,* can't never tell with those Island girls — let you slide on church, but you want to be her man, you got to do her right. Take care of her, understand? You got to bring home the bacon without no faking."

"I do not know how to —"

"You putting up the gun, son," our father told him. Not asking, telling. "This job we got now, we all gonna finish it. Our family always pays its debts. But when this one's done, you done, too. That Taralyn, she stand behind you if you gotta mop floors. But one wrong move, and she show you the door. I got her memorized, don't I, now?"

"Yes, sir."

"You ain't gonna mop no floors," the Prof assured him. "I got me some ideas, but they can wait. For now, only thing you got to play is *straight*. Working here, she got to know a lot more than how to do this rehab stuff. The way that girl's made, you can't keep her in the shade. She brings her own sunlight. Brings it *wherever* she walks. You want her to walk with you, you got to walk right. Be true with everything you do."

"Yes, Father."

"How many women you think you been with in your life? Pussy is pussy; pink don't think. Don't go to waste behind your taste, boy. Sex ain't love. Ask Little Richard; that boy knows what I'm talking about.

"A *real* man, he don't raise his son to follow in his footsteps; he raises him *up* so he can walk further down the road than he ever did himself, even if that means the father ends up walking alone for a while, understand? Now Burke is my true son, but he's only got but one path to walk. Not you. And now it's time for you to change yours."

"But what if — ?"

"Don't buy no ring without you talk to

276

your sister first," the old man said. "Men don't know 'bout that kinda stuff." Then he closed his eyes and drifted off.

When a man pays for sex, the price rises with his age. It can be anything from a lap-dance to a marriage, but it's still what the Prof always called it: cash-for-gash.

The older I get, the more I find myself back where I started. Every woman I've ever loved, they all left, one way or another. Some dead, all gone.

Maybe, one day . . .

But until love comes into my life again, I pay. I don't pay more; I just pay more often.

I still remember what my father told me the night before I wrapped up my last felony fall: *"Youngblood, listen good now. You walk out that door, I know pussy's first on your list. A man in this Life don't need no wife. But never forget: when you get with a whore,* never *look for more. Do that, you gonna get fucked in more ways than I could ever say."*

I never forgot. Whores sell things for money, and you could end up being one of those things. They may be sporting a beauti-fully stacked deck, but there's no ace of hearts in there.

I learned from Murphy men when I was still a kid. I learned the badger game later on. I never knock on a stranger's door.

The street can be an anonymous play, but the Monster is always loose out there, and I'm not just talking about AIDS.

I met one of those monsters once. A long time ago, when I was looking for someone. The car-trick hooker's name was JoJo, and thinking about her still scares me. I guess she's dead by now. I wonder how many she took first.

You can't call an escort service; you could be calling the cops. You can't make appointments; you never know what will be waiting. You can't deal with Web sites or setup services. Records can get seized. Or sold.

So I stick with women I know. None of them are working girls, but none of them work for a living. I don't make dates, and I never drop in unexpected. Not fair to them, too much risk for me.

I just call. Out of the blue. My blue.

If they're ready to go, right then — I make sure I'm close by when I call — the tiles fall and the mosaic forms. They come downstairs — they never live on the ground floor, not in *this* city — and wait on the corner.

If they get there quick enough, and if I don't pick up on any visual dissonance while I'm waiting, I go the next step.

I slide the window down, and say the right

words. I have to do that — if I tell them I'll be driving a white BMW, it'll be a red Chrysler that pulls to the curb. Those extra few seconds could make all the difference if the girl decided to make a call of her own.

If everything's clear, she gets in, we drive to a place she hasn't been before, and we play out our script. Different ones for different girls, but it's always some version of: I'm on the run from the law, an undercover FBI agent . . . anything that explains why it always has to be come-and-go.

Then I drop them off at the opposite end of the city from where they live, with enough "cab fare" to fly to Aruba.

Maybe some of them buy the story, most probably don't. But even if they tell, who*ever* they tell, nobody's going to wait outside their place for me to come back — you can't set your alarm clock to "random."

Saudi Arabia, that's our bosom buddy. So was Iran, once, remember? The shot-callers here have their own magic label-maker: Pinochet was a realist, Castro's a fascist, and Vietnam's a good export market.

Letting Idi Amin run a country was like making Ted Bundy warden of a women's prison. Idi Amin never sat in an electric chair, he sat on a throne. But once syphilis gets inside your brain, money can't get it out. His last years were spent in a castle, not a prison cell. A castle in Saudi Arabia.

Our government counts Uganda as a major ally in what they call a "troubled area." An area close to where Mobutu used to fill the same role.

I learned two things in my life. Everything's connected. And you never want to be the connection. You know how therapists do that word-association thing? Some people, you say "connection," first word that comes to their mind is "sever."

I remember the Prof chuckling out loud at the whole idea of arming America's friend-of-the-moment. "Fools think, just 'cause they can get a snake to dance, it won't bite 'em the second it gets the chance."

That's all about international alliances, not families. Still, I had to reassure Max a dozen times that Mama would *never* find out who was with us the night we checked out the Sheikh's fortress.

Our alliance with the third man on the roof started a few years ago, when I first came back home. We were almost down to our case money, so we started piling up cash any way we could.

Some people are fool enough to think that a shared profession makes them safe from their own kind, like the embezzler who blows his take on pump-and-dump penny stocks.

"A fool *is* money," the Prof always said.

That first job we'd done together was trickier than it looked. Disabling that traveling circus of "bounty hunters" was easy enough, but we'd been paid to handle it ghost-style — absolutely no-trace guaranteed. The targets had to wake up *permanently* discouraged, but without a clue how it had happened.

Nobody was worried about them running to the cops — bounty hunters aren't exactly an NYPD favorite.

Picking them out was embarrassingly easy. Four men, in two "unmarked" cars that were about as undercover as Britney Spears, never mind the stupid baseball caps the men wore, or the cage bars between the front and back seats.

It had taken us a couple of days to make sure they really *were* that lame, not just posing for some TV crew.

Once we locked on, Michelle slut-voiced an anonymous call to the bondsman. He'd figure it for the bail-jumper's wife. Her divorce lawyers would have told her she'd only get to keep what the government didn't take, and if her husband didn't show up for trial . . .

The professional man-hunters pressed buttons at random until someone buzzed them into the building. They exchanged knowing looks — yeah, people who live in slums really *are* idiots.

If they hadn't been such pitiful amateurs, they might have wondered why the light-bulbs were all burned out in the hallway where they positioned themselves on either side of the door, getting ready to kick it in.

I guess too much TV *can* rot your brain.

Being highly experienced in such matters, only three of them went to the bail-jumper's door. The other one waited out back in case the bad guy tried the fire escape, a Desert Eagle dangling from his hand. Good choice; that piece is heavy enough to practice curls with, and it's harder to conceal than a fluorescent brick. Naturally, the genius chose the all-chrome model — it picked up enough ambient light to sparkle in a coal bin.

That one was mine. Max and his friend took his partners.

Going in, we knew it was a three-man job, minimum. No matter how we disabled the bounty hunters, we'd need a driver to remove each of their cars, plus one more to follow them to the dump site and get us back to Manhattan.

The extra man Max brought in was a stranger to me. I didn't know his name, never saw him before that night. He was an older guy — I wouldn't even try to guess his age — wearing some kind of mottled-shadow bodysuit under a long, cowled coat, his hands hidden somewhere inside the sleeves. A night-merging hood covered his head. I deliberately didn't make eye contact with him, but I already knew the one part Mama couldn't *ever* know: he was Japanese.

And now the three of us were working together again. Standing on a rooftop on the East Side just before dawn, trying to see an answer.

The cowled man gestured to Max as if I wasn't present. He spread his arms, up-turned palms and a slight movement of his head indicating he had seen nothing that could keep him out of the building we had been scanning. He held up an admonishing finger, then mimed a man walking . . . walking slow. Shook his head.

Max tossed some invisible objects between his hands, like a juggler.

The black-cowled man placed his own

hands together, made a pillow of them, canted his head. Then he shook himself like a man coming out of a daze.

Max bowed, his eyes never leaving those of the ninja, who returned the bow to precisely the same depth. Maybe Max saw him disappear; I know I didn't.

The Prof's hospital room was the perfect place for us all to meet. "We've got a guy who can get in from the top, work his way downstairs, and open the side door for us," I laid it out. "But there'd be no way to cover up that the place had been visited. It's just too big, with too much staff. There'd be bodies all over the place. If they got put to sleep, they'd wake up. And if they didn't . . ."

"That ain't the half," the Prof said, almost condescendingly, taking the idea that a ninja might know more than he did about home invasion as a personal insult. "Even if Max's boy got himself an invisibility spell, what if the phone rings while he's doing the job? Or if they got something scheduled we don't know about, like one of those ambassador meetings? Take nothing more than some FedEx driver ringing the bell to send it all straight to hell. Come on!"

"Pryce —"

"Pryce *might,* is all you can say, son. I

taught you better than that; we don't go till we *know.* Pryce flops, we *all* drop."

"But it's the only thing we've come up with," I argued. "And even *that* window won't stay open long."

"It *is* logical," the Mole threw in, looking up briefly from examining the prosthetic they were fitting the Prof for, already thinking of ways to make it work better.

Michelle exchanged a look with Clarence, silently agreeing that, for the Mole, those three words were a damn filibuster.

"She never leaves?" Gateman asked. If hospital security had a problem with a man rolling his wheelchair onto the elevator with a reworked 9mm Kahr nestled near his colostomy bag and a pit bull in his lap, they must have kept it to themselves.

"Could be that way, Gate," I said. "She's not some rich man's playtoy; she's property. She's probably allowed out, but no way she'd ever be able to go alone."

"There still has to be . . ."

"Went over the options, Prof. She can't call a car service; they'd never let one past the gates. She can't even go for a walk around the grounds without 'protection.' Even if she could sneak into that underground garage, so what? It's against the law for women to drive where she comes from;

she probably doesn't even know how."

"That's a whole different set of —"

Whatever Michelle was going to say was chopped off by Taralyn's brisk entrance. She stood by, hands on hips, eye-dueling the Prof until the old man pushed himself out of bed, gripped the walker, and propelled himself out the door.

Taralyn whirled, her eyes hitting Clarence like a two-ton electromagnet on a pile of iron shavings. "I should walk with my father," he immediately said, and followed her down the corridor.

"I thought only a witch could cast a spell," Gateman said, grinning.

"You need to get out more," Michelle told him dryly.

"You want all this done because you've got an *idea?*"

"It's not an idea, it's a hypothesis," I told Pryce, echoing the Mole. "So it has to be tested."

"Has?"

"Or not," I conceded. "But I've checked every place I knew about, and a lot more I *found* out about. Nothing. Not even a tremble on the Web-lines. So it's either your scenario or it's mine."

I waited, but I could see he was waiting

on me. So I said: "Now, yours, I admit, it could have happened that way. I can even see how it might make sense to some sicko; power *always* makes sense to them. Rats are supposed to desert a sinking ship, but some rats are smart enough to know it's not the ship that's going down . . . only the captain.

"Thing is, I could never test any of that, but I know *you* could. In fact, I know you did," I gamble-guessed. "And if your theory had proven out, you wouldn't have even shown up for this meet."

Pryce steepled his fingers.

"What makes you think you could get her to — ?"

"I didn't say 'think,' I said 'might.' For all I know, she doesn't even speak English."

"Like a native." Pryce was old-school all the way — even liked his razors double-edged. "I'll have the rest for you in forty-eight."

I was on my way back home when my cell throbbed.

"What?" I answered.

"I fucked up, boss." Gateman's voice, street traffic in the background.

"I'm on my way."

I walked in the front door of the flophouse,

287

hands empty. If something wrong was waiting inside, Gateman would have tipped me when he'd called — we all know how to do that, even if we're talking with a gun at our heads.

He was behind the wooden plank, his semi-auto lying flat on the never-signed register book. Rosie ambled over to greet me. I saw she wasn't chained. Expecting company, then.

We all went into the back. The interrogation-room mirror behind the "desk" let us keep watch. As an extra precaution, we kept the glass dulled, even though the winos who flopped upstairs never seemed to want to look at themselves.

"I just blew it, boss. Straight up."

"Easy, Gate. Run it down."

"It was only a couple of hours ago," he said, glancing at the large-numeral atomic clock Terry had bought for him. Almost 3:00 a.m.

"I took Rosie for a walk," he continued. "I figured, past midnight, even those dipshits who like to play urban pioneer would be indoors, I'd have the streets to myself. So I'm a few blocks over — you know, where they're tearing down that old factory? All of a sudden, Rosie's hair goes up on the back of her neck. I know something must be just around the corner, but I don't get all hyped over it — any strong-arm guy working down here knows better than to fuck with me.

"Only it wasn't a mugger; it was this bunch of kids. All wearing the same gear, so I figure them for some kind of club. That's when I saw this huge pit one of them was holding. Heavy chain, spiked collar, you know the look — all that MTV crap.

"The kid's dog growls, and Rosie just *goes* for him. Boss, I ain't no weakling," he said, holding up a thick forearm heavily corded with muscle. "And I had my chair *locked,* too. But Rosie, she was *still* moving on them, dragging me like she was in a tractor-pull.

"I tell the kids, 'Get back!' But the one holding the dog, he screams, 'Get 'im, Tec!' Their dog starts his bounce. Cocky, like it was gonna be an easy piece of work for him. I didn't have no choice, boss; he was twice Rosie's size. I pulled my steel, told the punk, he drops that chain, his dog's a goner. Him fucking too.

"That stops 'em, but just for a second. One of them, he starts movie-talking. You know, 'I can't shoot *all* of them' bullshit. So I plugged him."

"Fuck."

"I know," he said, sorrowfully.

"Nobody went nine-one-one?"

"I didn't total the punk," Gateman said, sounding offended and defensive at the same time. "Just tore up his leg a little. They all took off then, dragging him behind. But how hard is it gonna be for them to find this place? All they gotta do is ask around about a man in a wheelchair. . . ."

I nodded.

"And you know how gang kids always go for payback, boss. Gas-in-glass, that'll be it."

I nodded again. Gateman might be wrong about the Molotov — although I didn't think he was — but it really didn't matter. *Any* comeback they made wouldn't be quiet. Win or lose, I was going to end up homeless.

"Wait here," I told him.

"Sure, I know who you talking about, bro. Call themselves Los Diablos," Jester said, grinning as only a man who'd seen the real thing could. "They got a little clubhouse in the basement of that building that's coming down, only a few blocks away. Didn't know they had themselves a bulldog, though."

"They called him 'Tec.' Probably short for 'Tec-9.' Either they weren't carrying when Gateman threw down on them, or they didn't have the stones to go for it."

290

"*Pendejos* flash steel when *we* show, it's *finito, ese.*"

"I wasn't asking —"

"That's *my* dog they got there," Jester said.

"We can't hurt them," I said to Clarence. "They've got to still be able to move when we're done. You sure you're okay with this?"

He fitted the silencer to his pistol, tested the trigger tension, nodded. I'd reached out for him before I'd left for Jester's. I knew I was doing wrong, bringing Clarence in. I knew what the Prof would say if he ever found out. Because if this gang wasn't going to listen, we were down to one option. That's why Jester had a pickup truck waiting, its bed lined with heavy black plastic sheeting.

Four-fifteen a.m.

I went in first, a pistol in each hand. The basement was a blotch of murky darkness. You could smell humans down there, hear the muzzled sounds of marijuana-and-wine sleep.

The big pit was good. He never barked, but I could hear him charging up the stairs. When he got close enough for me to be *sure,* I shot him in the chest. He stumbled, shook himself, and started to rise. I shot him with my other pistol, point-blank into his thick neck.

The pit tumbled backwards down the stairs, rousing the gang. By the time they staggered themselves awake, they were bracketed inside a death triangle.

I'd already pocketed the tranquilizer guns and switched to my .357. Jester had a double-barreled big-bore, cut down for close-up work; he held it in one hand as if it was weightless. Clarence played the laser-sight of his nine over each of them as I kicked the floodlight I'd placed behind me into haze-filtered life.

"You fucked with the wrong man," I said to the leader. I knew it had to be him — his eyes told me he'd already figured out what the silencer was for, but not his next move.

He played for time. "Look, man —"

"Do not say one damn word to me," I cut him off, careful not to call him names. If I wanted him to go along, I couldn't disrespect him in front of his boys. I was on a tightrope, and my balance had to be perfect: just a man doing a job, not someone with a personal stake in any of this.

"That man in the wheelchair, he has friends," I said, slow and clear. "A *lot* of friends. Our boss, he's one of those friends. So we got our orders. The boss said it was our call, but if anything, and I mean *any-thing*, happens to his friend, it comes back on us. You know what that means. That's why we're here. We have to take *something* back to our boss. We can take your word, or we can take your heads. Pick one."

The leader didn't hesitate. "The minute you leave, we count to a hundred and we leave, too," he said. His voice was steady; I could see why he was in charge. "We leave, and we don't come back. Never. Omar" — he tilted his head at one of the crew — "his baby momma's in the Ravenswood projects; she do whatever he tell her. We go there tonight, start looking for another spot to set up in the morning. It's easier to score over that side of the bridge, anyway. Look, on my life, we never cross your border again, okay?"

"You need to watch someone die, just to be sure we're not playing?" I asked him.

"No, man. Just say what —"

"What *you* said works. It's a good plan," I told him, letting him save face. "But, you understand, we gotta be sure. So we'll be outside. Somewhere in the dark. We can count to a hundred, too. All" — I looked around, counting — "five of you don't come out, anyone left behind is a corpse."

"Okay. Okay, sure," he said, holding up

his hands, palms facing me.

"There's three cars outside, too," I told him, holding up a cell phone. "You don't all stay together . . . *pop!*"

They didn't make a sound.

I pocketed the phone, pulled out two rubber-banded packets, and tossed them on the floor. "There's five hundred cash in there, plus a dozen MetroCards. You all *walk* over to the subway, even if you see a cab along the way.

"That one," I said, pointing at a kid with one leg wrapped in heavy rags, "he has to limp, too fucking bad. You leave him behind . . ."

The leader nodded. The kid Gateman had shot nodded harder.

"You stay together. You do *not* jump the turnstile. You do *not* get yourselves arrested this side of the bridge, not for *anything.* Got it? All right, there's just one more thing. . . ."

Backlit like we were, all they could see was the hardware.

"We need your pictures," I told them. "Polaroids. Just keep facing me. It's not gonna hurt; we wanted you dead, we would have done it already."

They all took the flash in the face without moving. One of them even turned sideways after the first shot.

"You know why we did that," I told the leader. "Our whole crew's gonna have copies by tomorrow morning. And don't even think about running your mouths, *ever.* We can find you on Rikers even easier than we did here."

Jester walked over to the tranq'ed-out pit, knelt, and scooped him up with one arm, keeping his shotgun trained on the gang. Then he hoisted the pit gently over his shoulder. One punk's mouth dropped open at the sight.

"Whose dog is he?" I asked.

"He mine," a dark-skinned kid in a red tank top said, probably thinking the money I'd tossed on the floor was some kind of payment.

Jester stepped forward and hooked him to the gut. The kid dropped, but he didn't pass out. The real pain wouldn't come for a while yet. Jester dropped to one knee, leaned in close. "I ever hear you got yourself another pit, you gonna die *real* slow." He stood up, kicked the kid in the ribs, and backed away to give us cover.

"You can take that one with you, too, or just leave him here," I told the leader. "But when you walk into an ER once you get across the border, you better tell a *real* good story."

"Drive-by," the leader said, smoothly. "We over near the Plaza, just chillin'. A bunch of white boys jump out of a Jeep, swing on us with baseball bats. Hector here gets hit in the stomach. We all running when we hear a shot, and Tony catches one in the leg."

If this was a crew that carried off its wounded, maybe their leader was the real deal. Or maybe he was just good at math — we weren't going to do *one* of them and let the rest just walk away.

I had counted up to ninety-one when all five stumbled out of the basement. One was limping, but still moving pretty good. The dark-skinned kid had both hands pressed to his stomach.

I was in the alley next to the flophouse, behind the wheel of my Plymouth. Gateman was inside, with Rosie. Clarence was behind the mirror.

The cellular throbbed against my chest.

"They walked a *long* way," Terry reported. "Sat together on the '1' Train until Forty-second, then they all got on the '7.' I didn't —"

"You went deeper than you needed to," I told him. "It's over now. Get gone."

Rosie watched with only mild interest as I used a small sledgehammer on the cell phone. Gateman said he'd take care of the disposal. Clarence went back to the hospital.

I returned the Plymouth, docked it, and then reported to Jester.

"I already got a spot for this one, *ese,*" he said, tilting his head toward the big pit, still unconscious, double-chained inside the cinderblock garage where Jester kept his office. Putting him out back would have been premeditated murder. "By tomorrow, he be in good hands."

I tapped my heart with my fist. Twice.

The next morning, I entered the hospital through the service entrance, held still for the retinal scan, then punched in the numbers that would match it.

Inside, I moved past a guard. His weapon was holstered, but his palm partially covered a big red button. He was holding it down the way you do a grenade after the pin's been pulled. Even if an intruder managed to slip past the scanners and put one between his eyes, his dead hand would still trigger the alarm. Instantly, the intruder would be caged. And whoever was watching the monitors would make sure the dozens of tiny jets implanted in the ceiling had gassed him into unconsciousness before signaling the capture team to move in.

The back way opened into an atrium that reached straight up to an all-glass ceiling. This was the break room for doctors and other high-ranking personnel, featuring a dozen different seating arrangements, a coffee urn that looked like it cost more than a Korean car, and a long table of fresh-baked pastries. Mini-trees in individual planters were scattered all around, each with its own auto-mist system. The floor was rubber-tiled; the walls were lined with glowing fiber-optic bands.

"Nothing but the best" was the message. One of them, anyway.

I had started over to the elevator when I noticed Taralyn, sitting by herself at a table in the corner. She smiled and waved. I knew it wasn't an invitation, just her natural Island politeness. I returned the courtesy and was about to move off when I spotted a medium-height white man strolling over toward her.

His suit coat was open, displaying a shoulder holster. Regulation haircut, gym-sculpted body. He moved with the flat-footed shuffle of a man who expected people to step aside.

Good luck with that, I thought to myself, figuring a woman like Taralyn must have years of experience repelling advances. But then I caught a glimpse of Clarence, his back to the scene, waiting patiently for an opening near the coffee urn, a cup and saucer in each hand.

I immediately flowed into a change of direction. Thunder was booming, and our house needed a lightning rod. I moved the way Max had taught me, covering the ground quickly without looking like I was in a hurry. I got there too late to hear whatever the bodybuilder had already said, but I heard Taralyn's response real clear: "No, thank you. I am waiting for someone."

The bodybuilder's hearing wasn't as good as mine. He picked up a metal chair with one finger, spun it expertly so it reversed, then straddled it and sat down across from Taralyn.

"Maybe I'll just wait with you," he said. His voice was too thin for his body — steroids will do that.

"Please —" Taralyn started to say. But by then I was in position behind him. I leaned forward and spoke in a barely audible voice, adding a tinge of anxiety to assure him that I was no kind of threat. "The young lady is waiting for her fiancé," I told the tough guy. "You see?"

He turned his head to look at me, not deigning to twist his whole body, letting his eyes send out the warning. Just in case I was too slow to understand, he popped the biceps of his suit jacket, adding an exclamation point to his unspoken threat.

"Yeah, I see. And I think I'll wait along with her," he said. "That all right with you, pal?"

"Not really," I said, apologetically, as I slid my right thumb and index finger deep into his wedged trapezius. I like bodybuilders; all that definition makes it easier to place the nerve blocks.

"This young lady's fiancé, he's one of those crazy-jealous guys," I said, very quietly. "You know the kind I mean, right? And he's over getting her some coffee, so this is kind of an awkward situation. How about if you and me find another spot?"

Despite the macho nonsense, this guy was the real thing — he had the kind of pain tolerance you don't get from lifting weights. "Sounds like a plan," he gritted out.

"Great!" I said, dropping my left hand inside his jacket, just above the hipbone. "Let's go."

He stood up, slipping out of the nerve block on his neck as he did. But there was nothing he could do about my left hand without taking all kinds of risks. That wouldn't stop him in the street, but in this place, the risk was much higher — I was an invited guest, and he didn't know who had issued the invitation.

We passed Clarence on his way back to Taralyn's table — I don't think he even noticed us.

When the elevator car arrived, I stepped inside, releasing the bodybuilder and turning to face him as I backed to the wall. I wasn't surprised when he followed.

"Who're you?" was all he said.

"Someone who just saved your life," I told him.

"Is that right?"

I didn't answer.

"How much longer?" I asked the Prof.

"Damned if I know, Schoolboy. I ain't in no hurry. Only help I could be to you on this job is what I'm already doing, anyway."

"It won't always —"

"Yeah, it'll be different," the old man said. "Different *way*, but the same play. Soon as I finish learning how to use that new leg, I'm out of here. You tuned in?"

"You'll be ready to go when you can *walk* out."

"That clue is true. Only a man who's been behind the wall can feel it all. Clarence, he thinks it's about medicine . . . not that he's paying attention to anything but that girl he gonna marry."

"He's asked her?"

"Remember what I told you when you knew you were going to the Double K that first time?" he asked. He was using prison-speak for Kangaroo Kourt, the "Disciplinary Committee" that got to decide if the ticket some hack wrote on you was valid. It always was; the only thing that mattered was what it was going to cost you.

"Even in the bing, the canaries still sing," I answered him.

A grin transformed the old man's face. "You don't forget *nothing,* do you, son? You get written up, you know you gonna get *some* time in the hole — ain't no fair allowed in jail. When we named them, we left off the last 'K,' but you know what they say."

"I'm —"

"Nigger ain't a color, boy. There always be a way for them to pick us out of a crowd. Hell, back then, if you shanked some motherfucker, they'd lock you down even if they knew you didn't have no choice. But at least they always kept it in the house. Today, they actually put your ass on *trial* for that. I mean, take you down to the same court that *sent* you down."

The old con shook his head in disgust.

"Making your time harder, okay. But giving you *more* time, that is seriously wrong."

"It's true," I said, remembering that first time I went before the Disciplinary Committee. The guy I'd stabbed had it coming, and the guards sitting there all knew it. So, okay, they had to give me some time in the hole, but that wasn't for what I'd done, it was for getting caught doing it.

"You know that three-strikes bullshit they got now?" the Prof said scornfully. "A small-timer with two falls on his sheet don't even *think* about that until it's all-or-nothing. Like that cop in California who got smoked 'cause the numbnuts who grabbed him and his partner figured they were headed for the gas chamber anyway.

"You put the death penalty on kidnapping, you *telling* the snatch-men not to leave no witnesses. That's why some useless junkie or a two-bit booster ends up blowing a cop away. He suddenly realizes he's going down for life-without even on a lightweight beef, so what the fuck? When you know you gonna die if you don't try, ain't but one thing to do."

"Hold court."

"Amen."

When I stepped off the elevator, the bodybuilder was waiting for me. I stood where I was, sensing the wall behind me, hoping he'd bull-rush, give me a chance to convert his energy to injury. But he closed the distance between us slowly, one near-tentative step at a time. I watched his eyes. Suddenly he stuck out his hand. Open.

I expected a bonecrusher move, so I just looked blank, giving him nothing.

"Look, buddy," he said, "that little . . . thing before. I already forgot it. I hope you have, too. I wasn't trying —"

"Do I know you?" I said. Not cold, quizzical.

He blinked rapidly a couple of times, twisted his lower lip, turned his back, and walked off. I watched him leave the building, wondering if he was pumped up enough to be waiting around outside.

That's when I glanced over at the table where Taralyn had been sitting. Pryce motioned me over.

"It's hard to find good help these days," he said, as I sat down across from him. "They can follow orders, but you have to use small words. Tell them to fill up the car, you have to make sure they understand the gas goes in the tank, not the backseat."

"Yeah. Why stay in the closet when it's got

a glass door?"

Pryce's eyes were veiled. "It's that obvious?"

"Where'd you find him, in a skinhead compound?"

"Close enough."

"So he's not on the books?"

"He thinks he is. But the kind of thinking *he* does . . ."

"You don't care who you use, do you?"

"What are you, one of those 'bushido' boys? You think killing a man with a sword is more honorable than shooting him in the back? Dead is dead. It's not the tool; it's the job. You use whatever works."

"Like me."

"Like you. Get over yourself, Burke. You think killing a few vermin makes you an avenging angel?"

"I'm only working for you because —"

"Did I *ask*? I made an offer; you accepted it. You're a contract man. How you get paid makes no more difference to you than how you get the job done makes to me."

"I'm *doing* what I was paid to do."

"I know you are. I'm the one who came to you. After no ransom demand came, I thought there must be another motive, and that you'd know how to find people with that kind of motivation."

"I still think I do. Only —"

"Only my original idea was no good. So why not just go through the motions? You already got what you wanted. All you promised was to look, and I know you've been doing that."

"Because you crossed the same trail?"

"No," he said. "Because I know you. No way you *don't* go all-out on this one. Because you know me, too."

"Fair enough," I said. Meaning his analysis, not our bargain. In our world, bargains don't have to be fair, they just have to be kept.

"So why are you *still* working? What's left to do, except for this crazy —"

"First of all, I'm *not* all done. I dropped a lot of rocks into a lot of different pools, and the circles are still radiating. I don't have high hopes, but I'm playing it out until you call me off. I already told you: I don't think this is a cold-trail case, I think it's a *no*-trail case."

"Yeah. I remember. Can you run that down for me, one more time?"

"Because . . . ?"

"Because, even though I think you're insane, I don't have anything else. And I *can* make what you want happen. But if I do that, I'll be playing for higher stakes than

I like. In fact, I don't like playing at all."

So I spent a couple of hours sitting in that atrium. Trying to convince the shape-shifter why he should step into the light long enough to cast a shadow.

Pryce wouldn't commit; said he had to think it over first. I didn't like that — the longer we waited, the worse the odds. I needed to find a way to hedge my bet.

There was only one other group that might have what I needed, but I couldn't find them on my own. And I knew what would happen if I tried.

"Let me just —"

"No," the Mole said.

"But you know what I'm trying to —"

"They don't trust you."

"Don't trust *me?* I did plenty of jobs with them, and never once —"

"You made *trades* with them," the underground man said. "And you kept your part of the bargain each time, that's true."

"So they know me, right?"

He gave me a look I couldn't decipher. Said, "What they know is what they know. What *I* know, that is different. They know what you did. They know what you do. I know *you.* They would not make such a distinction."

I closed my eyes for a minute. When I opened them, nothing had changed.

"Will you ask them *for* me, brother?"

He nodded.

Later that night, we met in his bunker. Terry and Michelle were outside, waiting their turn.

"They won't do it," the Mole said.

"Why not?" I asked him, half angry, half puzzled.

"If there was a single cockroach in your house, would you spend every penny you had on a platinum brick to crush it with?"

"Risk versus gain, then? No more than that?"

"No more than that," he affirmed.

"It was worth a shot," I told him, shrugging my shoulders to show what I thought my chances had been.

The Mole turned away. He got the joke, but he didn't think it was all that funny.

Mama pointed at the space behind my booth, held up three fingers. One of the four pay phones was ringing. I could never hear any difference between them, but she could.

I picked up the receiver, said, "What?"

"El Cañonero ha ido de nuevo a su hogar."

The line went dead.

■ ■ ■ ■

It didn't matter how I translated the message, it all came out the same. The UGL's sniper wasn't around. Maybe he'd gone *jibaro,* disappearing into the hills of Puerto Rico. Maybe he was in prison, or too deep underground to reach. But no maybe about one thing: he wasn't going to be doing any job for me.

Like with the Mole, even though I knew I didn't have a chance, I still had to ask. Sometimes you just have to spin the wheel, even if all the numbers but one are double-zeros.

"You can't go on the market for this one, son," the Prof had told me, and I didn't argue. Assassins can always be found, if you know where to look. Most don't, which is why fools who want their spouses removed generally end up hiring undercover cops. Makes for good TV, but not very good results.

I'd known that, just by asking, I was telling Pablo I couldn't call on Wesley. If the word got around that Burke was looking for a take-out artist, the whisper-stream would hum . . . and the cloak of protection my ghost brother had wrapped around me when he blew himself into mystery would disappear. Secrets are power, and trust is the path to them. But I never felt the slightest flicker of anxiety — if a man like Pablo would betray me, I was too wrong about the world to want to stay in it.

"I tried the Mole, but his people —"

"What's in it for them?" the Prof cut to the core. "Forget all that mad-scientist shit, Schoolboy. Two to the head, make him dead. Trick is, without . . . Wesley, we got to get close, and that's a high motherfucking wall to climb."

"If I can't *promise* to —"

"How many times you got to tell me the same thing, boy? You think I don't know when a lie won't fly? You get near enough to make that promise, you got to keep it."

"Who *is* that, mahn?" Clarence asked, transfixed by Dinah Washington's "Long John Blues" as it velveted out of the speakers in my workroom.

"That's Judy Henske's mother," I told him. "Listen to this." I pushed a button, and Magic Judy's "Oh, You Engineer" came driving through. "See?"

"I . . . I *do*. Yes. They both have voices you could hear in church, but they are so . . ."

"They're *women,* Clarence. Not half-dressed booty-shakers who think whining three octaves on the same syllable makes them divas. Torch singers know that the best sex is always in the promise. Not any promise they're making, the promise any man who wants to ride a champion filly like them has to *keep,* see?"

"I feel this. In my heart. Like our father says, you never lie to your prize."

"Taralyn?" I said, knowing Clarence wasn't making a social call.

"I know only one way to get money," he said, solemnly. "But . . . I have, I have *struggled* with this, Burke. I have studied on it, but I find . . . nothing. How I can prove I am the man for her? The true man?"

"You loved your mother?" Not questioning, opening a door.

"She was my heart," the once-lost boy said.

"What did she want for you?"

"Not what I became," he said sorrowfully, thinking of the teenager who had drifted the second his anchor had been pulled loose. "Not that."

"Are you a man of honor? Do you keep your word?"

"Burke —"

"Would you step between your family and death?"

He gave me one of those "are you insane?" looks.

"You honor your father? And your mother's memory?"

"Please. You do not —"

"Yeah, I do. It's *you* that doesn't, little brother. I'm going to tell you a truth now. Not just make a truthful statement, tell you a *truth.* You know the difference?"

"I do."

"Yeah, you do. Because you were taught, and you listened. Now listen one more time. Your father is my father. He pulled me to him as he pulled you. So hear me now: the Prof is in terrible pain. Not from bullets, from guilt."

"But he has done nothing but —"

"He loves you, Clarence. And he knows, deep in his heart, that you were never meant to be one of us."

"No! You are my —"

"Your family is always going to be your family. But *look* at us. Your sister, Michelle, can she step over some invisible line and turn into a citizen? Can Mama? Max? Me?

"When the Prof found me, I was so crazy with hate that all I wanted was to be Wesley. You never met him, but you know who he was. Who he is. And that's what *I* wanted to be.

"All I ever wanted in life was to never be afraid again. I still didn't wanted to be a good man; I wanted to be a good criminal. I didn't know the difference between earning respect and building a rep. I just wanted people to say: 'Don't fuck with Burke. You don't want to pay what that'll cost you.' See?

"The Prof pulled me off that path. We both love him the same, but I know him like you never could. One day, I don't know when it was, maybe just a short time ago, he started to count the days. He knows I'm going to carry on when he's gone. Remember, 'You carry my name; never bring me shame'? He expects that from you, too. But *not* the same way."

"I know," Clarence said, his love-torn eyes on my one good one, telling me he truly did. "My father wants me to be a man who can raise his grandchildren to be . . . ah, it does not matter. But not outlaws, as we are."

"Not *all* of us," I reminded him. "We taught Terry lots of different things, but we hope he never needs to use them. True?"

"It is," he admitted.

"Yet what have any of us taught Flower? For her, the sky is open. Anytime she walks out the door, her mother worries for her.

Immaculata is a mother, and a *true* mother always does this. But Immaculata, she worries about . . . things that might happen *to* her child, not anything her child might *do*."

"That is not me," the islander said, grimly. "When my father found me, I was already grown. He never forbid me to . . . live as the rest of us do."

"It wasn't the right time yet," I said.

"So what would my father fear for me *now?* Prison? How could I fear prison, when I have seen my father laugh at death itself? You were there, Burke. You saw it, too."

"He saw it coming, and he faced it, Clarence. But he didn't go looking for it."

"You are saying, now there is one thing my father *does* fear, yes?"

"Yes. Not for himself, for you."

"I know," Clarence said. "He didn't even have to say. And I know that Taralyn is for me, Burke. This was decided in a way I will never understand. Taralyn never knew her own father, just as I. But her mother, she never strayed from her duty. Her daughter is her life's work. If I am to be worthy of this, I must . . ."

His voice dissolved. I held my little brother against my chest as he sobbed out his mourning.

"We'll fix it," I promised him. "Your family will make it work."

"What do you want this for?"

"I ask you to do something for me, now I have to fucking *explain* it first?" I said to Terry, my voice harder than it should have been.

"It's . . . all over the map, Burke," he said, ignoring me, concentrating on the task. His father's son. "If I knew what you were looking for, I could narrow the search and —"

"I need all of this stuff first, kid. I have an . . . Ah, it's not even good enough to call it an idea, not yet. But it's not for me. It's not even for this . . . job we have. It's for Clarence."

"Why didn't you just say — ?"

"I didn't think I had to. But I guess you've got more of your mother in you than I thought."

"Fifty-fifty," the kid said, as focused on his work as a mongoose. "You know what that means?"

"Half of each?"

"No, Burke. It means I'm *theirs*. Nobody else's. *Everything* in me is from them. Not one hundred percent, *more*. I'm not a total; I'm a gestalt. And there's no room for anything else in that equation."

"I shouldn't have run my stupid mouth,"

I apologized.

"That's what Mom's always telling you," he said, chuckling to show I was forgiven.

New York's famous for its rats, but we've got the same vermin problem every other town has — the ones we voted into office.

The reason some of those imbeciles won't let you teach evolution in school is because they don't believe there's any such thing. Why should they? If evolution was real, how could they *stay* that stupid for so many generations?

I guess they figure God created fossils to throw heretics off the scent.

You want proof evolution is for real, don't waste your time with fossils; just check out the New York City rat. They started out as immigrants, stowaways in some ship's cargo hold. Only the survivors got to breed, and they've been improving with every new litter. Smarter, faster, stronger. Getting ready to rule. Manhattan wouldn't be the first island they took over.

That's where I got the idea for the mission I sent Terry on. Half of it, anyway.

"It's a shadow-stat," the kid told me, a couple of days later.

"Dumb it down, little bro," Gateman

begged him. Rosie sat up expectantly, like she understood every word, but she didn't fool me — Pansy used to do the same thing.

"You wanted to know how many cases of child abuse are never reported, right?"

I nodded, encouraging Terry to go on.

"That's what they call a pure unknown," he explained. "If you can find *one,* that means you're never sure you found them *all,* see?"

"Cocksucker finally beats his kid to death, *that's* when they find out he's been doing it for years?"

"Yes," Terry said to Gateman. "That's it, exactly. We know *some* cases of child abuse are never reported, but how many? That number could never be anything but a guess."

"Right. But how many crimes committed on kids by *strangers* aren't reported?" I asked.

"*Absolute* strangers?" the kid asked. "Not teachers, or coaches, or ministers, or —"

"Total strangers," I told him. "Mad-dog tree-jumpers, street snatchers, opportunity-grabbers."

"Like I said, you can't measure an unknown. But you can reason logically from known data, and come up with something pretty close." He tapped some keys, looked, tapped some more. "If . . . *if* any of the type of cases you described *wasn't* reported, that would be no more than a micro-percentage of the total."

"Sure! That's what blew the whole 'missing children' scam out of the fund-raising game. They got the grant money, all right. Only when the funders actually looked at the cases, they found out that almost all of them were some kind of custodial interference, not stranger abductions."

"But *some* of them had to be —"

"Yeah, Gate. And *those* still get maximum media. Nothing like a good old Amber Alert to grab the headlines, right? But how many times you see the parents go on TV and beg for whoever snatched their precious baby to return her . . . and, later, it turns out the kid's buried in their own backyard?"

"Somebody hurt *my* kid, I'd never call the cops," the wheelchair-bound shooter said.

"You might have to," I confronted him. "Sure, if you knew who did it, you could TCB yourself. But what if it was a wrong-place, wrong-time stranger-snatch? You'd have every lawman on the planet looking. Tell me I'm wrong."

"You're not," the old-school con admitted — it hurt him to even *think* about the prospect.

"Now, there's reasons why this fucking prince, or sheikh, or whatever he calls himself, there's reasons why he wouldn't go to NYPD. But he reported the kidnapping to *somebody*. Otherwise, the people who hired Pryce would never have known about it.

"And now that we know what he was doing with that kid, I buy his story. The part about how he got taken down, I mean, not the car-switch crap. If *he* wanted that baby dead, all he had to do was ship him home. And *no* way he lets himself be humiliated, or takes a chance on some stranger stumbling over him.

"So I *do* believe he was still coming out of whatever they spiked him with when he first told the story. Later, when he realized what kind of problems that might cause, he had the clout to make the report go away. NYPD brass probably got a *real* quick visit from some very heavy hitters. Word's out — any cop who runs his mouth about *this* one is a friendly-fire candidate."

"So that fucking little dirtbag, he *does* want the baby back?"

"Not a doubt in my mind," I answered Gateman.

"You know where the most expensive

house in this whole country is?" Terry piped up.

"What difference does that — ?"

"It's in Colorado," the kid said, unruffled. "Appraised at a hundred and forty-five *million* dollars. For a *house.* You know who owns it? Some former ambassador. Came here from Saudi Arabia."

"Okay . . ." I let the thought trail off, as close to impatient as I allow myself to become.

"I get it now," the kid said, proudly. "Why you wanted me to look that other stuff up."

"Do you?"

"Yeah," he said, speaking in a blend of his parents' voices. "For some people, a billion dollars is nothing. For others, a dime would be the world."

"That ain't news," Gateman said, kindly.

"It's not about the fact, but what you can *do* with the fact," Terry said. "You were right, Burke. This *is* the perfect way for Clarence to . . ."

He never said "live in the same world I'm going to" out loud, but my heart heard every word.

The restaurant was closed to customers. Nothing new: Mama still has the sign the last health inspector threatened to slap on the door if she didn't pay the "tax."

He was a real piece of work, that guy. Figured Mama claiming not to understand English was a ruse, so, when she wouldn't cough up, he came back and showed her he meant business.

It was only when he returned to pick up his loot that he learned she did, too. The restaurant hasn't been inspected since, but the CLOSED BY ORDER OF THE NEW YORK CITY BOARD OF HEALTH sign still goes up whenever it's needed.

The big round table in the corner usually had a plastic RESERVED sign on it, tastefully ornamented with dead flies. Today, it was covered in linen you could make a bridal gown from.

All of us were there except for the Prof. You don't bring a man to his own surprise party until you finish building the gift you're going to present him with.

"It's called 'micro-lending,' " I said to Clarence. "In some countries, you do it right, a man goes from watching his family starve to death to watching them grow up. Grow up into more than he ever dreamed they could."

"We're not talking about Welfare, honey," Michelle assured him, patting his hand. "This isn't charity; it's a bridge to another life. Nobody has to trade their dignity for food. No begging, no ass-kissing, no soup-kitchen religion."

"It ain't sharking, either," Gateman added. "Paying back a loan, that's nothing but showing the guy who fronted you the coin that he was right to trust you in the first place."

"I cannot just travel around the world looking for —"

"Come on, Clarence; you know what a *susu* is."

"That is different, mahn. A *susu* is no loan. All contribute, every month. Then, when your turn comes, you —"

"Every group that comes here has some kind of way to do that," I told him. "You think it's only people from the Islands? The Koreans do the same thing. So do the Greeks. It's not about where you come from; it's about *why* you came.

"I'm not talking about illegals in sweat-shops, working off their bonds; I'm talking about people who came here to *stay* here. What do they all want? Same thing anyone else wants: something of their own.

"So they work. You know what a Jamaican woman calls a man with two jobs?"

"Lazy," Clarence said, grinning.

"Yeah. Some people come here with skills

they never get to use; some people are born here, and they teach themselves. After a while, they got everything they need to make a go of working for *themselves,* except for . . ."

Max pulled a wad of cash out of somewhere, dropped it on the table between us.

"Right," I echoed. "But what're they going to do, get an SBA loan? Not for the kind of businesses I'm talking about."

"I thought you were —"

"Not crime," I cut him off. "Remember where you lived before you found the Prof? That neighborhood, I mean?"

"Of course, mahn."

"You always loved that Rover of yours, right? But when you needed work done on it, you never brought it to some certified mechanic in a fancy shop, did you? Even when you finally had the money to take it anywhere you wanted, you stayed close to home. How come? Because you knew guys who could make a dead car get up and walk, am I right? Word-of-mouth beats the Yellow Pages, every time."

"This is true, but —"

"That's the way it is, all over," I said. "Say you want some barbecue, okay? You know the best joint might not even have a sign on the door. Electricians, plumbers, carpenters . . . anything people need doing, there's somebody knows how to do it. Do it *good.* They make their living because word gets around. Yes?"

"Ah. Yes, we always have our own —"

"And what about the *craftsmen?*" I over-talked him. "There's men who can make miracles with their hands, build you a bookcase you could sell on Fifth Avenue for a fortune. But the only wood they'll ever touch is the broom they push in some warehouse. This city's full of silversmiths who scrub toilets. Women who could make you a copy of a designer gown from a damn *picture,* no pattern . . . and you'd never be able to tell it from the original. But the only sewing machine they'll ever see is in a sweatshop. You got gardeners who could grow lemon trees on concrete, but they'll never have any land to do it on. Right or wrong?"

"This is all truth. But how could I — ?"

"My girlfriend Alitha, she found herself a man with *substantial* assets," Michelle said, touching the islander's sleeve. "Now, she can get her hair done at one of those places that'll lick your feet while they paint your toenails. But she's still not letting anyone but Miss Jasmine touch *her* hair."

Clarence just looked puzzled.

"Alitha's a black girl," Michelle explained. "Where she's from, Miss Jasmine is famous. She doesn't have a shop; you have to sit in her kitchen while she works. But, like your father always says, when you want magic, you go wherever the magician is."

"Yes," Clarence said, gravely. "The man who works on my car — he is a genius. I would never think of allowing anyone else to touch my treasure. You are saying, if Miss Jasmine had her own shop . . ."

"Damn, kid. If you cleared leather as quick as you think, those fancy suits of yours would look like Swiss cheese by now," Gateman told him.

"Oh, stop that!" Michelle scolded. "Any kid can get all speedy; it takes a grown man to know when to take his time. Especially with something *real* important."

Gateman blushed at Michelle's triple-entendre. That's my baby sister. She gave up a lot of things when she chose the Mole, but making macramé out of men wasn't one of them.

She used to do surgery, too. I still remember her, back when we were runaway kids. A little tranny, way south of a hundred pounds, back against an alley wall, facing a quarter-ton rough-off artist. He had a bicycle chain; she had her straight razor.

"You hungry?" she hissed at him. "Come on, fatso! I got your diet, right here."

The tough guy hadn't seen me in the shadows — if he had moved on her, I'd have planted my switchblade deep into his liver by the second step. But Michelle was so raged-up she couldn't see anything but a pig who thought he could muscle her onto her knees. He wanted a quick piece, but Michelle wanted a piece of *him.*

I came back to business, said: "What did you think, our big plan was for you to be some *bodeguero?* You're not going to be building a little shop, Clarence; you're going to be building a network. Instead of collecting interest on the loans, you'll own a piece of every business you finance. A *little* piece, but there'll be a lot of those. You're going to have scouts all over the city. They know who to look for; the rest is up to you."

"Money-lending is a dirty business," the Mole said.

We all looked at him, waiting for more, as if we didn't know better.

"What Mole means is —" Michelle began, before a look from the father of her child made *her* blush.

"That is why I would not be lending, I would be investing, yes?" Clarence said, dubiously. "But there would have to be a *source* of the money I invest in any legitimate business. How would I explain — ?"

"For government, very easy." Mama spoke for the first time. "You own little building — maybe eight apartments. Plenty equity. Rents pay mortgage, leave plenty income. You use that money smart. Maybe buy special jade pieces. Some collectors, they pay big money. They tell government how much they pay. Tell insurance company even more."

"This is . . ." Clarence struggled for the words he needed. "But how could *I* do such things? Even if we could find this baby, Pryce would owe us nothing. What we are doing now, that is not earning; it is working off our own debt."

"You do what Burke tell you, build, how you say, 'network'? *Then* you have cash, yes?" Mama asked.

"But you have to *start* with cash, Mama. I cannot —"

"Cash goes in bank. Not like our bank, one of theirs. Pay taxes, everything."

Clarence nodded, but confusion was all over his face.

Mama tapped a long crimson fingernail against a glass to get our attention. "Americans always say stupid things like they saying smart things. 'Money not grow on trees.'

Then why money always have roots?"

"Yes, Mama," the young man said, choosing his words carefully. "But an apartment building, that cannot exist only on paper."

Mama smiled, said, "On *this* paper," and placed an official-looking document on the tablecloth in front of him.

Clarence picked it up, handed it to Michelle. She glanced at it, then passed it around the table. It was the deed to a building a few blocks from where we had gathered.

"Wedding present," Mama said.

Michelle started to cry. Clarence embraced her. Gratefully, so his own tears wouldn't show.

We all managed to look somewhere else.

But we all saw the same thing.

"How many of those do you have?" I asked Mama, after all the others had left.

"Buildings?" she asked, innocently sipping her soup.

"Cut it, Mama. I *read* that deed. It had Clarence's name on it."

"So?"

"So it had a *date,* too. On paper, he's been collecting rents, paying taxes, making repairs, the whole deal . . . for years. That's a CPA's work. Clarence never knew any of

328

this, which means there has to be a bank account in his name around somewhere, too."

"So?" she said, again.

"You have property for all of us, don't you?"

"Only for children."

"Children? That's not you, Mama. You don't mean children, do you? You mean *grandchildren,* right? How long has Flower owned a building?"

"Day born," she said, calmly, as if no other possibility could exist.

"Yeah. And Terry?"

"Day born," she repeated, patient with a slow learner like me. But I wasn't that slow: "born" for Terry meant the day he came to Michelle and the Mole.

"You never said a word. None of them know, do they?"

She gave me an "are you actually *that* stupid?" look that women have been giving men since Adam bit the apple.

"And their parents, they don't know, either?"

I got the same look.

"Because your *own* children — like me and Max — they can't own anything that has to be registered," I said, feeling it hit me then. Hit me deep. What could a man like me ever own? I don't even have a name. Neither does the Mole. Or Michelle.

It must have shown on my face. "You feel bad?" she asked.

"No, Mama."

"You think maybe I don't — ?"

"You insult me," I told her, just short of angry. Only her eyes stopped me from saying anything more. In all the years I'd known her, I'd never seen them go liquid before that moment.

An attack-trained dog isn't a "guard dog." Just about any dog will protect its own territory. If a puppy grows up associating you with its only source of food, if you're the one who plays with her, walks her, sleeps next to her, cuddles her . . . that'll usually do it. Depending on her personality, the dog might snap at anyone who gets too close to you, even a friend. But she's almost a sure bet to really rip anyone she thinks is hurting you.

Some bark at anyone who comes near your house, but that's a watchdog, not a protector. A burglar alarm might let you know someone's coming; it won't do anything to stop them.

A true attack dog is one who can do no-provocation work. You sit down across from some guy, patting your dog as you talk things over. The dog lies next to you, looks half asleep. No threat displays, no growling, no showing teeth. My Pansy looked so dumb and friendly that strangers would walk right up to her. And I'd let them. But if I said the right word, or made the right gesture, she'd turn a guy into scraps of flesh even if she'd just licked his hand.

When you think of an attack dog — a real one — think of a chainsaw covered in fur, with a remote-control on-off switch only one person can push.

A lot of trainers use agitators, usually drunks willing to dress up in protective gear and taunt a dog until it goes for them. You make sure the dog always "wins," build his confidence. Sounds good, but it's really sending all the wrong messages. You don't want your dog thinking that the smell of booze is a signal to hit. Or that biting a sleeve is how to bring a man down.

That kind of stuff is good enough for K-9s, but we're not cops. Where we live, we don't use dogs to run down escapees. And we don't deal with gunmen by telling them to fucking "Freeze!" either.

We trained Rosie using some of Max's advanced students; they had the speed and agility we needed. There's no scholarships

331

at Max's dojo. You pay your own way, *every* way.

We had to poison-proof her, too. That turned out to be one hell of a job; she was used to tearing into food without asking questions.

We couldn't train her out of her natural tendency to nail any stranger she decided was encroaching, so we taught her the signal for "friend," instead.

"I love this, boss. It's like learning all this new stuff and watching her have fun at the same time."

"She loves it, too, Gate. That's the trick to training any dog: make it fun. That's why we always keep the sessions short. Rosie pays attention because she *wants* to, not because we make her. That's why you always end a session with her getting it right, see?"

"Yeah! And she likes to just hang out, too, bro. I swear to God, that little girl sees something on TV she don't like, she lets me know."

"The only thing I'm worried about —"

"I got that covered, boss. Look what Terry hooked up for me."

The chain he had in place behind the counter was now attached to a padded circle of steel that was screwed into a concrete block about the size of a small sofa. Gateman called, and Rosie trotted over. She waited patiently as he hooked her up.

"She can't get past the desk now," Gateman told me. "Unless I press this little gadget." He held up a box the size of a cigarette pack, with a button that took up most of its surface. "Watch."

The steel-circle collar popped off, and Rosie was free.

"Got another of those buttons under the counter, one on the TV remote, another by the light switch. . . ."

"So anytime — ?"

"Oh, *hell* yes, bro. Look, we can't do this 'friend' thing with every rummy who staggers in here, right? The way it works now is, the door opens, Rosie *lunges,* but that chain holds her. We don't want her killing some wino, but it don't hurt that word gets around she might be behind the counter with me, either. And if I ever need her to really do some work, well . . ."

"It's perfect."

"It fucking *is,* boss. Terry even has it set so that the smoke alarm pops that collar off, too . . . just in case. Rosie, she's the most amazing thing I ever seen. Looks like such a pretty little pup you want to pick her up and give her a kiss. But she could be munching on your guts before you even knew what hit you."

"And some women got the nerve to think *they're* real bitches," I said.

We tapped fists, and Rosie followed me upstairs to our home.

I didn't use the red circle for this one. The answer wasn't buried that deep. I had it *somewhere,* if I could only . . .

"You have to let it just float over you," I told Rosie. "Like balloons drifting by. When you see the one you need, you reach up and grab it. But you can't be jumping around, understand? The balloons only float over you when the air is *very* still: you try chasing them, you *cause* the wind . . . and they sail away, out of your grasp."

I patted the couch. When Rosie jumped up and curled next to me, I went into the semi-trance I needed.

They always get the idea from somewhere floated by, but I never reached for it. I knew the taproot; knew I was looking for people who do things they've done before. Rapists rape; that's what rapists do. But the rapist who only targets blondes in red dresses and high heels is playing out some script. The general impulse is always there, but it takes a specific image to fire his synapses before he acts.

Porn can do that for some of them — narrow the general impulse into some specific imagery. Once that happens, it's *that* image they look for when they're hunting.

I never dealt with a sex-torture freak who didn't have a porn collection of some kind. Some even created their own.

The scrawny kid sported shoe-polish-black spiked hair with a green streak on one side, a leather vest, and subtle eyeliner. He was behind the counter inside the filthy-window storefront, thumbing through a manga porno-comic. He didn't know me, but when I walked into the computer-repair shop empty-handed, he knew I was a cash customer. And *I* knew there wouldn't be a security camera anywhere in the place.

He looked across at me, waiting.

"An armadillo walks into a disco," I said. "He sees the big mirrored ball, but it's too high for him to reach, so he walks out. Get it?"

"No. What's it supposed to mean?"

"Nothing," I told the Goth-geared slug.

"Huh?"

"Zen."

"Oh. Yeah, I get it."

"Nothing means something, because nothing means nothing. You with me?"

"Everything has a meaning," he said, nodding sagely.

"Yeah. But not the same meaning to everyone. Some people might even think there's enough work to keep a computer repair shop afloat, even though it's cheaper to buy a new one than get an old one fixed."

A fear-glint showed in his eyes. Too soon. I brought him back to where he'd feel like an insider, not a target:

"Some people, I tell them I got a friend's who's going to go all *Shaolin Cowboy* on their ass, they wouldn't even know what I was talking about."

"What friend — ?" he started to say, as Max materialized next to me.

"This is Max the Silent," I told him. "You see how he got his name? Now, I just let you in on a secret of mine, how about you let me in on one of yours?"

He was a lot smarter than he looked. Or played. "Kill the lights," he said. "That means we're not open." Then he led us into a back room, down the stairs, and into what looked like storage space.

As we watched, he showed us everything they had for sale, all the time repeating that he was only a clerk, a functionary who filled orders someone else gave him. "I don't even *look* at that stuff, man."

It took almost half an hour for me to accept that he didn't have any of the Sheikh's training program on a for-sale CD.

I didn't bother to tell him to keep our little discussion to himself.

I couldn't check out every porno shop in the city — that would take an army *and* a year. Besides, it's not like the dull-eyed piles of jaundiced flesh who sat next to the cash registers actually knew the contents of every DVD on the shelves — that's what the packaging is for.

The Internet would have them all, anyway. And if it was out there, Clarence would find it.

"You want me to search for *this?*"

"Yeah," I told him. "Remember what Terry taught you? The narrower the parameters, the easier the search. What could be narrower than these?"

"I will do it, mahn. But . . ."

He didn't have to say it aloud.

I didn't expect Clarence to come up with anything. Not because the "scene" I told him to search for would be too repulsive — I don't think that's actually possible, anymore — but because there'd be too small a market for it.

People think porn started with under-the-counter magazines, but it's been around ever since our species developed opposable thumbs. There's cave paintings of rape. And there was rape before there were paintings.

Jerkoff artists aren't the only market for pornography — politicians buy it too. The Meese Commission started a whole "porno turns men into rapists" industry. And now the hucksters who have the public believing kiddie porn started with the Internet are raking in federal grants to "find" it.

Always the same — you never know if they're stupid, crooked, or both.

When you want the purest information, you need the most neutral possible source. Finding one, that's the trick.

Especially today, when there's no such thing as actual "news," only press releases and "commentators" who go total Rashomon on every story until it all turns into white noise. If you get tired of blah-blah, you can always dial up some blog-blog. Fabricating stories is the new frontier of "freedom of the press." Anyone can play, and nobody pays . . . except the targets.

But if you actually *want* neutral, you go to

the total obsessives. They're so hyper-honed that there's no room for any agenda besides their own. But you have to hit that agenda on your first pass; their kind don't accept social calls — they wouldn't even get the concept.

"*Reform School Girl,*" I said into the phone. "By Felice Swados."

"Cover?" The other man's voice was just this side of uninterested.

"It's a photo, not a drawing. A weird size, too."

"Look for the year," he instructed.

"Nineteen forty-eight, it says."

"What else? It would be on the —"

"Diversity Romance Novel #1."

"Grade?" he said, now trying to sound calm.

"Your job, not mine."

"Agreed. But I need some indication of —"

"Looks like it was never read."

"Really?" The whole cellular network shuddered at the intensity of the obsessive's prayer-question. He'd gone from mildly bored to so deeply hooked that he even bypassed the bargaining ritual.

"I'm not asking you to take my word for it," I told him.

"Bagged and boarded?"

"Might have been. Not now."

"You haven't — ?"

"How else could I give you the info I just did? But I never touched it with my hands. Cotton gloves only."

"Listen," he said, in the same tone a bomb-diffusion expert uses when he has to guide a rookie over the phone. "I want you to open it. *Gently.* Just enough to read page numbers. Can you do that?"

"Sure."

"Is there a page three and four?"

"I . . . Yeah, there is."

"I have to see it."

He wasn't kidding about that — the cell phone in my hand was hot, like I'd been on the battery for hours.

"Name a —"

"Can you bring it over now?"

I pulled the Plymouth up to the gate and waited. There was a speaker with an inset communicator button standing on an aluminum pole, but I didn't bother touching it. I knew the security cameras were on me, so I just got out of the car and stood there in plain sight.

The gate swung open. I got back in my car and pulled up to the one-story warehouse. There were a couple of dozen parking slots marked in fresh yellow stripes, all unoccupied. I backed into one of them, plucked the silk-wrapped package carefully off the front seat, and walked up to the door.

The steel-ingot dead bolt retracted with a sound like someone had just jacked a spent round out of an elephant rifle. I turned the handle, stepped inside.

A big guy with all the movie-cued insignia — shaved head, forearms tattooed with Asian-looking symbols, wife-beater shirt — started to strike a pose. Then his remaining brain cells kicked in, and he remembered why his visual scan had been enough to get me through the gate. I'd been there before. With Max.

I knew what he was remembering. That first time, the poseur had pointed at Max, jerked his thumb, told me, "Just you, pal. Your friend waits outside."

"Save it for when you work the door at one of those velvet-rope clubs," I told him.

"You talk pretty tough for such a —"

He never saw Max move, but there's nothing like a locked-in choke to stifle a conversation.

Max was back standing next to me before the fool hit the floor. He wasn't unconscious — depriving *his* brain of oxygen wouldn't have any major effect — but he wasn't interested in getting up, either.

This time, I'd come alone. But the guard would have asked around. So he'd know Max hadn't been hired help; he was family. My family.

I walked past him like he was furniture, went through another door, and stepped into an open space about the size of an airplane hangar. A temperature-controlled, ionized-air, dust-free airplane hangar.

It looked like the world's biggest book-store. Aisle after aisle of modular shelving, all custom-made out of some space-age material, with adjustable slotting for each individual book. All paperbacks. I didn't know why the deranged human who had all this built wasn't interested in hardcovers, and I wasn't deranged enough to ask.

He stood up as I entered, walked over to where I was standing. A normal-looking guy, wearing a cleaned-and-pressed blue shirt with a button-down collar, no tie, sharply creased chinos, and a brown open-weave belt. The leather buckle matched the orthopedic loafers on his feet.

"Bring it over to the examination table" was all he said.

As I put down the package, he flicked a string of dangling baby-spots into life. I knew they each housed one of those "sunlight" bulbs; he could vary the lumination with a rheostat, and even adjust the distance from each bulb to the table.

I stepped away, letting him do his thing. He barely bothered with the magnifying glass, relying on his fingers and his nose.

"A true first," he finally pronounced.

"You're the master," I said.

"How much do you — ?"

I cut off his question by stepping away and starting to stroll the aisles. Everything was labeled, sub-labeled, cross-labeled, and color-coded . . . some in colors I never knew existed.

He followed, knowing I was going to ask him something. I never wondered if he ever thought about why I asked him questions. I knew he'd always answer, either because he knew that it was my price for something he needed worse than any junkie needs a fix, or maybe because he actually liked talking about his collection.

" 'Worm Noir'?" I asked, pointing at the slotted label above a whole aisle of books.

"That's a subset," he explained. " 'Noir' itself is a concept, not a genre. Similar to 'hard-boiled.' That's supposed to be a genre, too. Like, say, 'western' or 'romance.' But that's not correct; in fact, it causes overlapping," he said, clearly offended by the concept. "A 'western' could certainly be 'hard-boiled,' for example. And 'noir' could be anything from 'sci-fi' to 'true crime.' "

"Worm noir is about . . . worms?"

"No," he said, patiently. "It's a field unto itself. Some are pure pastiche, some grossly imitative to the point of plagiarism, but, in general, 'worm noir' is the kind of work that calls *itself* 'noir,' do you understand?"

"Because if it didn't . . . ?"

"It would be called what it is," he said. Not making a judgment, a scientist identifying a species. "Some form of simpleminded garbage, with various conventions splattered throughout. Impossible to characterize except *as* garbage . . . and *that* term is an adjective, not a classification."

He took a breath, made sure I was paying attention, then said: "To qualify, 'worm noir' must be part of the pantheon of the certifiably untalented. It has a certain . . . fraudulence about it, a distinctive odor. And all its authors seem to have followed the same path to publication."

"I'm not sure I —"

"How could a sheep walk the mean streets alone?" he said, as if dissecting an oxymoron. "What their herd produces is nothing but recycling." Out of anyone else's mouth, that would have been disdainful sarcasm, but his voice was as judgment-free as the Dewey Decimal System he had modified for his own purposes.

I kept strolling around, looking. He knew I was patient enough to keep this up all day. And I knew he wasn't.

"What are you looking for?" he finally blurted out.

"Porn," I told him. The most expensive record album ever sold had been the copy of John Lennon's *Double Fantasy* he'd autographed to Mark David Chapman. But if *this* guy had been into record albums, all he would have cared about was the condition; his obsession was collecting, not contents. So I wasn't surprised when he simply asked me, "Hard or soft?" like a salesman asking what size jacket I wore.

"Hard, I guess," I said, not really sure what he meant.

He led me over to a corner section. "Porn writing is how many fine authors began their careers . . . using pseudonyms, of course," he said, as if disclaiming any such association on their behalf. "But the market for it dried up decades ago."

"Yeah?"

"Oh, absolutely. I am referring to porn *qua* porn, not its gratuitous insertion into another genre. The entries from the Fifties and the Sixties never professed literary merit; they prided themselves on delivering a product. A conventional bookstore would not carry them, but there were stores which sold nothing but. And did quite well at it, too.

"Interestingly enough, while covers are usually the *sine qua non* of value to paperback collectors, the cover was rarely a factor to the original consumers of this material. For them, the value was all inside. They bought the books to *read* them," he said, as if that was a clear indication of mental illness.

I shifted to a respectful "I'm all ears" posture, said nothing.

"As I'm sure you can envision," he went on, permitting himself a delicate smile, "the Internet has utterly destroyed *that* market."

I had to shore up the levee quick; this guy could spill over at any second. "I understand," I said. "Now, some of the covers you showed me one time —"

"Those were *subtle* references," he corrected me. "Bondage covers, for example, were always presented as plot-relevant. Damsel-in-distress kind of thing. The pulps were actually more graphic in that area. The only pornography that still survives in current form is either 'literary' or visual. Some comic books, for example, are illustrating what it would be illegal to photograph."

He checked to see if I was still paying attention. Satisfied, he resumed the lecture: "The pornography in fiction today is always *called* something else. Like the plain brown wrapper they used to mail these in." His hand swept the shelves, leaving no doubt about what he was referring to.

I noticed his voice was devoid of disappointment. None of this mattered to him. He didn't want more product produced; his only need was to acquire all of it that existed.

I scanned the category labels. And the meticulously subdivided ones. No simple "Incest" here: "Daddy-Daughter" was positioned next to "Mother-Son," with "Father-Son" and "Mother-Daughter" ranked below.

Apparently, he didn't like "Kiddie Porn" as a category name, but he left the "Sibling," "Cousin," and "Uncle/Aunt" stuff on clearly separated shelving. He hadn't labeled any of it "Incest Between Consenting Adults," but his obsession demanded total obedience: every book *had* to be in its rightful place.

I moved past every fetish known to humanity, including some that required non-humans for completion, but nothing jumped out at me.

"If you could give me some idea . . ."

How he managed to actually *read* enough of all these books to set up his insanely complex system I'll never know, especially when he didn't like to physically touch any of the rarer ones, but I knew he never faked knowledge. So I said: "I'm looking for a plot where a guy has sex with women — not romantic sex; with prostitutes, or even rape — and brings his son along to watch, so he can teach the kid how to do it."

"We're in the wrong section," he said.

"Here," he pronounced, a couple of minutes later. The delay wasn't caused by the search; we'd had a lot of ground to cover to reach the area he wanted.

I took the paperback from him. Black cover framing a window, backlit, shades mostly drawn, but pulled up enough to show a man's hands, clasped at the wrist, holding some kind of small club. The man was already inside, waiting. I glanced at the title: *The Shoemaker.* Didn't ring any bells.

"Joseph Kallinger," the obsessive told me. "Serial sex-killer. Among other things. Check the author."

"Flora Rheta Schreiber?"

"Yes," he said, sounding vaguely disappointed. "She was the author of *Sybil*."

"So this Kallinger was a multiple?"

He made a gesture I couldn't translate. "I catalogue them as any library would. If the publisher calls it 'non-fiction,' then so be it. The operative word in 'true crime' is 'crime,' not 'true.' Some are later exposed as frauds — I have those separately shelved — some are merely suspected of falsification, but never conclusively proven. And others, of course, are actual journalistic accounts."

"Okay. But what's so special about this one?"

"Kallinger took his son along with him on many of his . . . crimes. Sex crimes."

I kept my voice calm, asked: "This paperback you're holding, it was a big hit?"

"I couldn't say. 'Best-seller' is a meaningless term. There is no way to know how many copies of *Pimp: The Story of My Life* by Iceberg Slim actually sold. It was perhaps *the* seminal outsider novel, and has never gone out of print. But why would the publisher, who, presumably, would owe a royalty on each sale, announce sales figures? I have several copies that don't even indicate which printing they were.

"This particular copy," he went on, opening *The Shoemaker* quickly, then handing it to me, "is a ninth printing. By the Eighties, that had no special meaning. The paperback market was believed to be skyrocketing, but it was actually peaking, nearing the top of a parabola. This one was no *Sybil,* that's for sure."

Meaning no movie, I guessed.

"Anything else?" I asked him.

"You've been looking in the wrong place all along," he said. "I don't mean for . . . whatever you're doing. I mean you're missing the intersection."

I looked confused. It wasn't an act.

"Why do you think I need multiple copies of some books?" he asked, going all Socratic on me.

"So you have extras to trade for stuff you want?"

"Of course," he said, the way you speak to anyone stating the blatantly obvious. "But there's a more important reason. Remember what I said about overlap? Here, look at this one," he said, handing me a pristine copy of *The Indiana Torture Slaying.*

I knew better than to remove the book from its protective housing, so I just scanned the cover. It showed a photo of a young girl next to one of a grown woman who looked evil enough for Leni Riefenstahl to worship in one of her "documentaries."

The subtitle was *Sylvia Likens' Ordeal and Death*. The cover promised all the sleazy details inside, including "sadism that shocked the nation."

"Published in 1966," he said.

"Written by John Dean," I read aloud. "Not the same — ?"

"No. In fact, the person who wrote this changed his name after Watergate."

"What am I missing?" I asked.

"The publisher," he said, pleased at my admission. "Bee-Line Books was, essentially, a porno house in that same era I showed you before. Notice the price?"

"Seventy-five cents."

"Yes. Now, let's go over here. . . ."

He found what he wanted in seconds. Handed it over. *Shipboard Stud* by David Key. The cover was about what you'd expect.

" 'David Key' was most likely a house name," he said. "But it was published around the same time, also by Bee-Line. Note the price."

"Ninety-five."

"Keep that in mind," he said, and took off again. He found the spot he wanted, pulled out a new-looking copy of *Doomsday Mission*. "This was by Harry Whittington, one of the all-time great paperback-original writers. See the price? Sixty cents. Year published? Nineteen sixty-seven. And look at this one: *Somebody's Done For,* the last book from the immortal David Goodis. Also 1967. And also sixty cents."

"So, back then, porn cost more than regular paperbacks?"

"Significantly. Don't think in terms of nickels and dimes; think of the *percentage* difference between sixty and ninety-five . . . and then multiply by, say, a few hundred thousand . . . per title! But let's go back to Bee-Line."

I followed behind him, thinking he must put in an easy ten miles a day.

When we returned to the "True Crime" section, he wordlessly handed me *The Coppolino Murder Trial* by Leonard Katz.

"Bee-Line," I said, to show I'd been paying attention. "Ninety-five cents."

"Nineteen sixty-seven," he replied. "Have you ever been inside one of their places?"

I knew who he was asking about . . . and I *had* been inside lots of "their" places. A furnished room, the basement of a tract house, a prison cell . . . I nodded my head "yes."

"What's on *their* shelves?"

I nodded again, thinking this was maybe the first time in his life that the obsessed man had ever asked a question about books that had nothing to do with collecting.

But that thought was replaced by what I'd just learned. Even if I got lucky and found the "why" of that sheikh's freakish home-schooling, it wouldn't get me any closer to the reason his student had been snatched. "I appreciate your time," I told the lunatic.

"As I appreciate you bringing me the book. What are you asking — ?"

"Token of respect," I said.

"Respect for . . . ?"

"What you taught me," I answered, watching for the tell.

While he was making up his mind about what to say, I had plenty of time to see the truth.

Driving back, my mind was recalibrating the pattern-recognition software that self-activates whenever I'm tracking. I could feel this new element downloading. The next time the cops were looking for a Green River Killer type — and I knew they would be, soon enough — they should be looking for books.

I'd been in a Wal-Mart once. I noticed they were real Christian-agenda about what books they allowed on their fiction shelves, but their "True Crime" section was exempt from that rule — sex-torture titles were the clear favorite.

Where's a serial killer going to shop for his tools? Some little hardware store that might remember a guy who keeps running out of duct tape? Or a big, anonymous joint with ever-changing personnel that sells everything from shampoo to dog food? Especially a store a lot more worried about the government finding out who its "subcontractor" hired to clean up after closing time than what its customers buy.

The national chains make sure every purchase goes into their computers. Collecting people's personal information is maybe the most lucrative business of all — ask Google. And I bet, if a certain government agency made the request, it might be allowed to run a scan for habitual purchasers of a certain kind of paperback. Especially if that same agency had enough juice to tell the Labor Department to look the other way.

There's one sure thing about serial killers — every one's a repeat customer.

Telling Pryce might get that info into the right hands. But Pryce was programmed for distrust. He could be dying of cancer, but if I offered him a no-charge cure, he'd spit out the pill.

■ ■ ■ ■

I hoped that book on Kallinger might show me a parallel, but it didn't come close. Yeah, he had brought his boy along with him, all right, but that kid was no baby; he was a teen. Kallinger himself had died a mystery. In prison.

I wasn't all that surprised. Facts don't change beliefs; facts get "interpreted" to fit those beliefs, and I'm not just talking about sadists who use "the Bible says" to justify everything from beating children to forcing them to "marry" men old enough to be their grandfathers. If you get to write the definitions, you control a lot more than the dictionary. You don't have to justify Iraq to people who believe "supporting our boys" means sending their parents condolence cards.

Hank Ballard was a bluesman in disguise. "Annie Had a Baby" was the truth. But his biggest hit was "The Twist." And he wasn't the singer.

Michelle once showed me something she'd printed off some Internet "encyclopedia." It was this heated discussion about whether some woman had been a warrior against sexual exploitation or a self-promoting fraud. One poster whose favorite word seemed to be "FemiNazi" said the woman's claim of having been raped *had* to be a lie, since she was a grossly obese, truly ugly-looking individual. My little sister was fuming. "Why doesn't someone tell that low-watt limp-dick about the Boston Strangler? That'd shut his nasty mouth," she hissed.

"No, it wouldn't, honey," I'd told her. "Sure, everyone 'knows' the Strangler targeted old ladies, but the whole DeSalvo story was hype. With all those rape-murders, the law had to come up with *something* or the press would keep crucifying them. So they got together and cooked up an everybody-wins scenario. DeSalvo wasn't the Strangler, but his 'confession' solved a lot of problems for a lot of people. Remember, he was never tried for any of *those* crimes — he was already going down for life on *other* stuff.

"But you're right; there's an entire porn industry based on 'preferences.' There's guys walking around who jerk off to photos of four-hundred-pound women. Or raped grandmothers. Never mind the double-amputee, or conjoined twins or . . . You know what I'm talking about.

"And anyone who's done time with them

knows there's power-freaks prowling every night. Drive one of them to the finest whorehouse in town, hand him a no-limit credit card, and he'd never go near the front door. He'd rather wait outside, in an alley.

"Humans like that aren't looking for stiletto heels and garter belts. *Pay* a bitch for some fake moans, where's the jolt in that? It's the 'fake' part that they can't stand. Turns them right off. But fear, now, that's *real*. Terror. Pain. Blood. Not what you buy, what you *take*.

"You can buy anything in this town. Anything at all. But once you pay for it, the costumes don't matter. You're not the dominator, you're the trick."

"I know, but —"

"See, they're *all* wrong on this one, baby girl," I told her, holding up the printout she'd handed me. "Both sides are just spouting the party line. Rape *is* about sex, but, for some, it's only the *taking* that makes it sexy. Get it? Once a belief system clamps down, it *stays* locked — reality never gets in the way."

I rubbed my temples, knowing I could never touch what really hurt. Michelle lit a smoke and sat back in her chair. She'd been with me too long to think I was done.

"A man gets arrested for sexual abuse of

his kid. If he's convicted, it 'proves' that kids never lie about things like that. To *one* side, that is. To the other, it 'proves' there's a witch-hunt going on, and the kid was 'alienated' into making up the story to please his mother. One side screams, 'False memories!'; the other screams, 'Believe the children!'

"So fuck the facts — no matter what they are, you can always make them fit. The truth *never* matters. Say that same guy is acquitted. Well, that 'proves' that some people are falsely accused . . . to *one* side. To the other, it 'proves' that people get away with child sexual abuse all the time."

"But not everyone —"

"You don't *need* everyone to win an election, sis. Hell, you don't even need a majority, not in this country. A true-belief system is the perfect sponge. It can absorb *anything,* but it never changes.

"It's an amazing thing to watch in action. Newt Gingrich campaigns to get Clinton impeached for having sex with a White House intern at the same time he's having sex with a congressional aide. So what? He's still a 'family values' guy, right? He divorced the wife he was cheating on and married the mistress, but that ungodly slime Clinton never divorced *his* wife to marry the intern.

See the difference?"

"No," my sister snapped at me. She sipped her tea, cigarette smoldering in the ashtray.

"You go in blank-slate, sweetheart. Patterns are good for narrowing things down, but that just takes you to where the real work starts. There's always a truth, no matter how deep it's buried. You start *believing* in things, you're screwed from the start."

"There's things I believe in," she said, quietly.

"Me, too, girl. But that's believing the truth we *found,* not what we were *told,* right?"

She leaned over and kissed the scar on my cheek.

"You think you really get it, don't you?" Cyn asked me.

I was half reclining in a body-molding sponge chair, watching her prance around in a black leather corset that had to have been put together by a structural engineer.

She was in full costume, right down to the six-inch heels and domino mask. She must have just finished a session with Rejji: live-feed, subscribers only. Not even close to illegal, but a lot more lucrative than either of them could make working straight jobs. Cyn had a master's in psychology; Rejji had graduated *magna* from Brandeis.

"I don't even get what you think *I* think I get."

Cyn reached up and took a long, thin metal rod down from a shelf. The rod had a tiny little circlet at its end. She tapped it into her black-gloved palm.

"We told you what we know," she said.

"And, the way you add it up, this guy hired props so he could teach his kid to be some kind of dom?" I asked her.

"He's no dom, not if he's paying for it."

Rejji giggled.

"Shut up, bitch!" Cyn said, without turning her head. "This isn't about his pathology, Burke. It's not about what he *is;* it's about what he can *do.*"

"Because he's got the cash to buy —"

"It's not for sale," Rejji said.

Cyn strode over to where Rejji was chained and slapped her, hard. Then she whirled and came back over to me.

"You know what this is?" Waving the metal rod in one hand.

"Not a clue."

Cyn snapped her fingers. "Come!" she commanded.

Rejji crawled over, still chained by one ankle.

"Remember Star?" Cyn demanded.

"Yes, Mistress."

"Tell Burke where she got her name."

Rejji looked up at Cyn. In response to a nod, she got up from being on all fours and knelt as if saying a prayer. "Star worked the Holy Coast for years," she said. "Not L.A., San Diego. Just far enough away, but close enough, get it?"

"No," I told her, truthfully.

"Her clients were all 'directors.' They got off on being obeyed. Star had her own rules. You could dress her up, spank her — with just about anything you wanted to use — but that was it. No blood, no handcuffs, and no sex, ever. She said it was the easiest gig she ever had. Maid, serving girl, geisha-type stuff."

"I don't get the last part."

"*That* was where the money was. She had to be . . . I guess 'worshipful' is the word I'd use. Tell the trick what a god he was, listen to him brag about how, when he said, 'Jump!' the biggest names in the industry jumped.

"Naturally, she'd jump, too. Fetch him whatever he wanted: a drink, a whip, it was all the same. Of course, she had to keep her clients separately catalogued, so she remembered what made each one such a big deal. That way, she could act like she was his little slave because she *wanted* to be.

"Money was never mentioned — that would have killed theimage. Not just because they could never see themselves as tricks; there was a lot more to it than that. To keep them coming back, she had to be a better actress than anyone they ever 'directed.'

"They couldn't even be her sugar daddies. It had to be like she'd pay *them*, if only she had the money. And the only reason she *didn't* have the money was because she couldn't hold a job and still be available twenty-four/seven for a visit from her master, could she?"

"She only had one at a time?"

"Jeez!" Rejji said, caustically. "There *was* no twenty-four/seven, Burke. Game, game, game. All of them had to make appointments, like any trick. Naturally, *they* didn't call them 'appointments,' they called them 'commands.' "

"She *was* a star."

"Sure was." Rejji smiled. "Only thing is, when you make a living pretending some sorry little loudmouth is your lord and master, you never get to be what *you* want."

"The money —"

"For some, that's right," Cyn said. "What

Rejji's telling you is the part you're missing."

I made an "explain it to me, then" gesture.

"If you're going to do men," Rejji went on, making a face to show that the very idea was distasteful, as if what had happened between us one night a few years ago . . . hadn't, "being a domina is the way to go. You wouldn't believe the captains of industry who can't wait to crawl down to some dungeon and be punished. See, that works for them — something about paying a woman so they can lick her boots balances out their world."

"They're still in control?"

"Of course. You know why?"

"Like you said, they pay —"

"No! Because they've got *choices*. They're not looking for a connection with another person; they're connecting with them*selves*. If one domina doesn't work out for them, they just find another. They know they're *playing* at being a slave, which means they can play anywhere they can pay. *That* fits."

"Don't they ever — I don't know, get . . . attached to one of the girls they pay?"

"They may like one better than another, but the only real attraction is to what they do. It's never more than that."

"How does this help me?"

"You know what this is?" Cyn asked me again, holding up the metal rod. "No? Well, this, *this* is the part you don't get."

I waited.

"A branding iron," she explained, handing it to me. The tiny circlet was some intertwined initials. "Rejji wants me to brand that perfect ass of hers. Been begging for it for years, haven't you, bitch?"

"Yes!" Rejji gasped, licking her lips.

Cyn never turned her head. "One time, I had just given this one a really serious whipping. Then I told her to get dressed and go out and buy me a nice hairbrush; I wanted her shopping while her ass was still on fire. The second I told her that, she came so hard she fainted. A few days later, she came back with this."

Cyn took the branding iron back from me. "I harnessed her up real tight, gagged her stupid mouth, and used a riding crop until she was *blistered.* Then I took out her gag and asked her, what did she want? When she begged for that branding iron, you know what I did?"

I waited.

"I gagged her again. Tight. Like I would if I thought she was going to scream. I let her wait a little . . . then I bent down and kissed her ass."

Rejji suddenly broke into tears.

Cyn ignored her, turned to me, said: "I told her that nobody tells me what to do with *my* property. If *I* wanted to brand her, I'd do it. *She* never gets to make that decision. *Any* decision. You let a sub tell you how *she* wants to be punished, who's really in charge? Get it now?"

"Maybe," I said, moving slowly, navigating without a map. "You're saying this guy, he wouldn't have stopped. If his baby hadn't been snatched, eventually he would have taught him how to . . ."

"Guaranteed," my consultant confirmed.

"But that would come later," I said, thinking of Kallinger, and how old his son had been when he took him along on his rampages. "After puberty. In the meantime, if he wanted to program the baby, the rougher he wanted to handle the merchandise, the more he'd have to pay to do it."

"Uh-huh."

"So it wouldn't be someone like this Star girl. He'd need . . ."

"For the extra-heavy stuff, you'd need a slave. I don't mean a captive. That happens, I know, but it's way too dangerous. This freak was building a dominator, not a murderer, and you can't let a captive go when you're done with her.

"Besides, even to a *little* kid, it would be obvious that the women were being forced. And he was teaching the baby that all it ever takes is money."

Cyn patted Rejji gently as she looked down at me, making sure I was still with her:

"You might find a woman who'd go along with damn near anything — you know, *Story of O*–type crap. But that kind needs a live-in, not an occasional visit."

"Like us," Rejji said, boldly. "You think, because I do whatever Mistress tells me, I've got nothing to say?"

"I don't know how it works," I told her, truthfully.

Rejji reached up and cupped one of Cyn's enormous breasts. "While you're telling him about branding irons, why don't you tell him about these?" she said, sounding about as submissive as a silverback.

Cyn took a seat on a padded ottoman. Crossed her long legs. Took off the domino mask. Said: "Rejji told me I've got two more years, max. Then, if I didn't have the surgery, she'd leave me."

I must have looked puzzled.

"You think these are store-bought?" Cyn said, bitterly. "No. They're all mine. And, believe it or not, all they ever did for me was get in the way. So the less seriously people took me, the more serious I got.

"I didn't bring Rejji out; she brought me. After we'd been together for a while, the orthopedist told us — we went together — that if I didn't have breast-reduction surgery I'd end up with curvature of the spine. But the minute I have the surgery, our business will take a real hit. We've got money put away, but not enough to maintain our lifestyle. We'd have to give up a lot of the things we've gotten used to."

I knew the "things" she was talking about: the designer dresses, the palatial two-floor apartment, the vacations, the gunmetal-gray Porsche with the Day-Glo orange bumper sticker:

YOU DECIDE IF I GET AN ABORTION? THEN *I* DECIDE IF YOU GET A VASECTOMY

"But we'd get to keep the only thing that counts," Rejji said, tenderly interrupting my inventory-taking. She turned to face me squarely: "*Exchange,* get it? Tonight, I'll be polishing those boots she's wearing. With my tongue. I give that to her, because I *want* to, and I want to because I love her. But I'd never give her the right to cripple herself."

367

"See why it could never fit?" Cyn said, recrossing her legs. "This . . . piece of filth who's training his baby, he has to show him money can make *any* woman do whatever he says — they're all 'holes,' right? So he'd need variety. A different one each time, I'm thinking."

"But there's a —"

"Limit? Please. There's more girls for rent than Hertz has cars. Some of them, they're not just commodities, they're consumables. You pay enough, you're not *expected* to return her when you're done."

"No good."

"Why?"

"Because his game is way more complicated than that, Cyn. He doesn't need to teach the baby that you can torture a woman for fun . . . or even kill her. Where he lives, you *can* do that, if you're royalty like him. What he's teaching the baby is that 'secret' all the freaks share: women *want* to be used."

Cyn nodded slowly. "So he'd have to rent," she said, thoughtfully. "And no spanking-for-sale stuff. He'd need merchandise he could return in *very* poor condition."

Rejji nodded her own agreement.

"That's got to be a small list," I said.

"Small enough," Cyn answered me, her mouth a hard, straight line. "We'll call you."

On the way back to my place, I saw a splash of graffiti. A lot of work had gone into this one. A huge section of the wall had been sprayed white; then the message was painted over it in spilled-blood red:

**BUSH WAS PRO-CHOICE
AND HE CHOSE WAR**

This was no teenage tagger's work; the message was stenciled, not freehand. I touched it lightly: the whole thing had been clear-coated with some kind of transparent material. That kind of operation takes teamwork and organization. I would have bet good money the same exact sign was popping up all over the country. Certain parts of it, anyway.

One of the first things I'd learned from Max was "hard to soft; soft to hard." Some men have concrete skulls, but no man's got a concrete liver. You don't "block" incoming; that's a good way to break whatever you block with. What you do is turn, deflect, absorb. The power of any strike is in where you place it.

Whatever "style" you call it, the foundation stone is always the same: balance disruption.

All that movie crap isn't just decaying people's brains, it's getting their bodies broken. They all know the screenplay answer to the "ancient master's" question: "Would you rather be an oak or a willow?" Me, I learned the real answer to that one in places where the grading wasn't "pass/fail," it was "live/die." That answer *is* a question: "Am I trying to withstand a hurricane, or fracture a skull?"

When you're up against humans whose moral compass is True South, the only rule is: Get it done. "Done," as in finished. Over. Ended. The only ceremony you care about is the autopsy.

In prison, "the enemy of my enemy is my friend" never stays permanent. It's a radioactive isotope, with a half-life that could turn out to be your own.

Too bad we don't send politicians to prison *before* they get elected, maybe they'd learn something. Instead, we get ideologues and morons — like there's a difference — who give major weapons and top-quality training to any government who's fighting our enemy *du jour.* Then, when our "friends" turn on us, the politicians point fingers at each other. If they'd pointed missiles in the first place, and aimed them at the right targets, we might actually have bought ourselves some safety. Maybe even some respect.

Cyn had told me she would be working a short list. While she did that, I worked on making my own list shorter, trying to narrow it down to that single thread I'd need to pull.

I turned on CNN to watch the scroll, the "mute" locked on so I didn't have to listen to the bobblehead dolls.

Turned out to be newsreel footage about a Russian journalist named Ivan Safronov who supposedly committed suicide — a step up from just gunning them down in the street like they'd done to Anna Politkovskaya when she'd dared to send dispatches from Chechnya.

I guess the point was how the same mask kept dropping everywhere. They showed Shinzo Abe putting his personal stamp on his tenure as Prime Minister of Japan by claiming that the "comfort women" forced into sex slavery to service soldiers during World War II were a myth. Oh, there may have been *some* women working in brothels, but the numbers were insanely exaggerated. Anyway, the ones who did that work were whores *before* they were chosen to "serve," so what was all the fuss about?

Maybe Iran will invite him to their next Holocaust Denial Conference. By then, they should be nuke-proof enough to do whatever they feel like.

The footage rolled on. A quarter-century ago, Denmark had set aside a squatter's roost for assorted anti-establishment types. Fit right in with the temper of the times then. Anarchists and artists from all over the world visited the huge building they called the Ungdomshuset. Some of them stayed, made it their home. But the Danish government sold the whole building to an evangelical Christian. Maybe they needed the money to do something about all the neo-Nazi biker gangs that had opened for business there.

Next, a Mississippi grand jury returning a "No True Bill" against Carole Bryant, the woman Emmett Till was supposed to have "wolf-whistled" in a little country store. Emmett Till was a black child. From Chicago. And he didn't know his place. Three strikes.

Bryant's husband and his race-protecting buddy had grabbed the boy one vile night, right in front of witnesses, took him away, and tortured him to death. After a Mississippi jury took an hour to hand down the mandatory acquittal, the killers took a reporter's money to brag about how they'd given the little nigger what he deserved. Years later, the same reporter tried the same trick with James Earl Ray . . . but all he got for his money that time was a useless stack of snide-smiled lies.

No question that Bryant and his partner had pulled up in a car that night. No question that it took the two of them to wrestle the kid into the death car, while someone *else* sat behind the wheel. Fifty years later, the FBI decided to check its files. They turned over the information they'd had all along to the local authorities, with the mild suggestion that they might want to look into Carole Bryant.

I thought about all the people who had been murdered in Mississippi to stop blacks from voting. And why the killers even bothered.

The cobbled-up documentary wasn't working for me — anger interferes with concentration. So I kept pressing buttons on the remote until I landed on a Road Runner cartoon.

"We *always* root for Wiley," I explained to Rosie, scratching her behind her right ear. "You know why? I'm going to tell you a secret, little girl. Wiley's not a coyote; he's actually a pit bull in disguise. You know how you can tell? Because, no matter what, he never quits. He's been trying to nail that lousy bird for a million years. Gotten himself blown up, dropped off cliffs, had boulders dropped on his head . . . but he keeps right on coming. Now, what's that *but* a pit bull?"

She made a chesty little noise.

"That's right," I told her. "And that's us, too."

When the cartoon was over, I pushed buttons until I found another of those *Law and Order* episodes where the DA gets the suspect to spill his guts by offering the ultimate prize: "We'll take the death penalty off the table."

"Now, *this* is what they call a sitcom," I explained to Rosie. "Even when there *was* a death penalty in New York, every working criminal knew it was a rubber check — only a Hoosier wouldn't spot it as worthless. They haven't executed anyone in this state since I was a kid. Even when a *prisoner* raped and killed a female guard, that didn't get it done. He's still waiting for the needle, and that was over twenty years ago."

Rosie snarled. I didn't know her well

enough to understand if she was showing contempt or disgust — takes time for partners to sense each other that deep.

I gave up on the tube, tapped the CD player, closed my eyes, and felt the blues mist over me.

Charles Brown, Chuck Willis, Jerry Butler, Chris Thomas King, Luther Alison, Freddie King, Junior Parker, James Cotton, Otis Spann, Dion, Dave Hole, Fats Domino, Solomon Burke, Bobby Bland, Dave Specter, Hank Williams, Delbert McClinton, Albert King, Lowell Fulson, Lightnin' Hopkins, when he was walking that road with Billy Bizor. Magic Judy, Marcia Ball, Etta James, Irma and Carla Thomas — not connected by DNA, by something deeper — Bonnie Raitt, Barbara Lynn, Dorothy Moore, Koko, Aretha — before she made a wrong turn and ended up lost in Motown . . .

As I came out of wherever I'd gone to, Johnny Ace was moaning "The Clock." He'd died young — gunshot wound to the head. The story was he'd been playing Russian Roulette. Some bought it. Some still don't.

I made a phone call.

"Where is the money in a whorehouse?" the black-coated man scoffed. He had a rabbinical face, with gentle, moist eyes. We'd done business before.

He took a deep hit off a hand-rolled cigarette that looked as crudely effective as an Uzi, said: "When a man goes to a whorehouse, he pays, he finishes, and he leaves. But a strip club, if everything is handled properly, instead of minutes, the man stays hours. And instead of taking a few dollars, you can bleed him white.

"Even those escort services, what is the ceiling — a couple of thousand, maybe, for all night? In a well-managed club, a man will spend many times that. He can buy magnums of champagne, glittery gifts for the girls, Cuban cigars . . . we have it all.

"We make that man a *king,* yes? He snaps his fingers, and a dozen gorgeous women are at his feet. They stroke him, put on shows for him, call him whatever he wants to be called. Any whore can spread her legs; our girls know how to *work* the mark. This is no easy task, and it takes more than beauty to be successful at it . . . but their rewards are spectacular.

"With a club, we can take credit cards. Corporate accounts. Men bring their friends for business lunches, gather their associates to celebrate a big deal they just closed. Girls for everyone, on the house!

"If they have the money, they can be tycoons, Mafia chieftains, movie producers . . . anything at all. When they enter our club, what they wish to be is what they *are*. The world becomes *their* world. Only a privileged few get a glimpse of paradise, but for those who do, it is more addictive than any drug.

"These are *gentlemen's* clubs," he said, his voice shifting toward a hint of what might happen to anyone who took his establishments for anything else. "No stuffing cash in G-strings, no ATM machines in the lobby, no blowjobs under the table. It is not sufficient that the women be beautiful; they must be cultured and refined as well. The furnishings must be correct. The lighting is *very* important. No blasting music, no . . . garishness of any kind. Ambience is critical. And security is discreet.

"We *create* all this magnificence. No matter what the outside world holds for him, once inside one of our clubs, the client is far more than a mere sultan; he becomes a god. What would *you* pay to be a god?"

I watched him puff on the coarse cigarette, keeping my body posture attentive to my role. Part of that role was not answering questions that weren't questions.

"In a whorehouse, the merchandise is

used. Used hard; used often. And what is used must, eventually, be used *up.* We rotate the girls among our clubs, keep them fresh, like flowers.

"Of course, we still have to accommodate the local police, but the expense is minor . . . especially compared to an actual bordello. *That* is why all the real competition is over territory. You can open a club anywhere, but the finest setup will not attract the clientele we require if it is located in some remote area. So . . ."

He never finished the last sentence, but the firebombing of a newly opened strip club on the West Side was still a hot story on the news. No suspects.

Time to show I'd been paying attention. "The blackmail risk is next-to-nothing, too," I said. "Every time a madam gets busted, she threatens to open her black book if they bring her to trial. But you show a tape of a guy walking into a strip club, it won't even cost him a divorce, much less a career."

"Uh . . . occasionally, an employee will overestimate the value of certain information," he said, opening his hands slightly. "No matter how well a casino screens its employees, there will always be some dealer who palms chips. Or cooperates with a team of signal-passers at the blackjack table. It *costs* money to prevent the *loss* of money. You see?"

"Yeah. In your business, blackmail threats are aimed at the customers, not the house, but protection is part of what your customers pay for. Same reason why a casino has to guarantee the games aren't fixed."

"Correct. And there is also what you people call an 'ancillary benefit.' The targets of such threats are generally not experienced in how to deal with them. So they turn to those who are."

I nodded.

"All they have to do is keep on paying," the black-coated man said. "For as long as their money lasts, the world is as they wish it to be. We create that world. And we *maintain* that world, as any blackmailers quickly discover. Although you claim otherwise, America has its own class system. Money. Whorehouses are for peasants. Our establishments, they are for royalty."

"I've been doing this all wrong," I told the Prof, the minute Clarence left us alone.

"Ain't the first time," he said.

They should have kept you on that morphine drip longer, old man, I thought.

"This was never about the fucking Prince"

379

was all I said aloud.

"Couldn't have been," the Prof agreed. "To groove that move, the snatch-men had to know the Sheikh was a freak. They wanted to shake him down, how hard could it be to find a whore who'll work with a camera in the room? And if they wanted to ice him, they coulda done *that* same time they took the kid."

"He's not shakedown material," I said, beginning to see . . . something. "How would that kind of tape be worth a dime to him? So he's teaching his kid that all women are sluts. Pigs, whores. *Things,* even. What'd he call them? 'Holes,' right? Who's *that* going to hurt his status with? The fucking Taliban? That's their national anthem. The State Department? Come on: they're *already* whores, and who knows that better than the Prince?"

"So it's the baby," my father said.

"It's the baby."

"That means one thing, Schoolboy. It ain't the whole deck we need to worry about, it's just that fifty-third card. 'Cause that one, it ain't no sleeve ace; it's a joker. And it's running wild."

I stayed with the Prof until Clarence finally came back. With Taralyn. As I walked out, the old man was explaining how Hillary and Obama had done their best to cancel each other out: "Couple of dumb-ass dogs — fighting over a Big Mac when there's a juicy T-bone a few feet away," he jeered. "Only thing that could have made it worse would have been one comes out with an endorsement from Satan, and the other comes out, period."

I'd already heard that speech: the Prof always worked himself up over how blacks and Latins cancel each other out in this city.

"Black folks finally get their chance here, what do they do with it?" he had ranted at me, years ago. "They pick a monkey too stupid to unpeel a banana. So busy taking care of his friends, he never takes care of business. Look at OTB. Got to be the biggest bookie operation of all time, and it ends up broke. You ever heard of a syndicate bookmaker *losing* money, son?"

"Long-term, I don't even see how it's possible," I co-signed. "And with OTB it's even worse. They get their own separate take-out on top of the track's, and every bettor has to front the cash, too."

"Yeah, well, it ain't all on Dinkins. Sure, he was the lame who wrecked the train, but he don't deserve all the blame. We finally get a chance to headline the show, and we

381

pick Stepin Fetchit to be the star?!

"And what's *he* do? Throws the whites into a panic. Voted Democrat all their lives, but when they see Dinkins giving away everything to the spooks, this Giuliani toad starts looking real good to them. By the time the fools in Queens and Brooklyn realize that 'their' man don't care about nothing but *his* people — not white people, *rich* people — it's too late.

"Then the Latinos say, okay, it's *our* turn now. And what do the blacks do? They just shuffle back on over to where the money is. Remember how it was Inside? Ain't no different out here."

He had it right. That's how we ended up with a white Republican mayor in a town where whites are a minority and Republicans barely exist.

Of course, the only reason the guy *became* a Republican is that the Democratic clubhouse wouldn't give him the nomination. With a few billion in spare change of his own, he didn't need financing, just a spot on the ballot. You can see his next move just as clear: he's going to bide his time until there's an opening, then pull a Perot.

I guess Clarence and Taralyn went on listening, maybe for different reasons. But the reason their hands stayed clasped was the same for both.

"Would they have it online?"

"The subway, for sure," Terry said. "The sewer system, I don't *think* so, but I can check."

"I don't need subway maps, kid. I can grab one at any station. What I need is *under* the underground. I know there's stations all over the city where no train ever stops. Some abandoned, some never put into service. Stations mean tunnels, and tunnels stay open even if no trains go through. It's one of *those* that we need."

"The sewer system *has* to be on the city's computers, so they could locate any problem immediately."

"But not on some Web site?"

"I don't think so. Especially now, with all the terrorism scares."

"I've got an address," I told him. "There's no subway stop close by, but we can walk there from one of the abandoned stations I already know about. It's the sidewalk that counts. They have to lay the concrete over *something,* right? I want to get as close to that sidewalk as I can. And that means we have to find the route from underneath, see?"

"I can try."

I handed him a briefcase. "There's a laptop in there. Brandname. All factory parts, but there's no record of it existing. No serial number, not even on the components. Supposed to be the latest thing going; just came off the assembly line last week."

"That's great if it gets seized, but the IP —"

"There's a building in Cleveland that's slated for demolition," I interrupted. "Somebody ran a T1 line into the basement. I'm not sure how they did it, but I think it was bridged from a downtown brokerage house. I don't want you on any security cameras, anywhere. So you and me, we're going to take a drive, okay?"

He nodded, waiting for the rest.

"We leave here about seven tonight, you're plugged in and running by three in the morning," I told him. "That gives you about two hours to crack into their system and grab what I need. In case that's not long enough, I'm bringing enough extra batteries to power that thing for a month. Gets too near daylight, I got a place we can stay, come back the next night. What do you say?"

"I've only got one class this afternoon," Terry answered, without looking up. "I'll be ready to go anytime after four. But we'll only get the one try, Burke. The second they detect an attempted intrusion, they'll lock it all down."

"Fair enough."

"Pick me up at school," he said. "I don't want to have to explain to —"

"Me, either," I assured him.

Anybody asked, I was taking my nephew on a road trip, a last bonding experience before he left home.

We didn't stop for food. Mama had us supplied with enough steel-canistered stuff to last a week. And the roadside darkness was all the restroom either of us needed.

I kept the Roadrunner at a steady nine-over all the way. Too much turnpike means too many troopers. But I did promise the kid we'd do something on the way back.

The key I'd paid a lot of money for let us in. And my blue-lensed LED Mini Mag found the promised T1 jack. While Terry was setting up, I made a seat for him out of some wood pilings. The windows were already boarded, but I draped a mesh shroud over Terry and the machine anyway.

"Jesus!" he said a few minutes later.

Then I heard the battery-powered printer go into action.

We left pieces of the computer and printer — *small* pieces, those things don't seem to handle claw-hammer blows real well — in a couple of dozen different places on the way back. The last traces went flying out the window somewhere past Youngstown.

The building itself was coming down on Monday. The printouts were in the trunk, in the hidden slot beneath the fuel cell.

"I can't believe it," Terry said. "The Department of Environmental Protection has got *everything* under the city mapped. See, it's the clearinghouse, so any other agency, or even a private contractor, can find what they —"

"What's so amazing?" I cut him off.

"What's amazing is, it's like they had *no* protection on it at all. I could have cracked in even without —"

"Safety first," I told him, as a Porsche blew by us like wind past a building.

The kid gave me a look. By the time we caught the Porsche, we were just a little over the century mark. I held the left lane until the other driver got insulted enough to try us. I dropped down a gear and let him stare at taillights until we disappeared.

"Holy —"

Before Terry could finish, I was already pulling over and killing the lights, waiting for the Porsche to fly past, chasing a ghost.

"Want to drive her?" I asked him.

"This would not be precise," the Mole said, studying the printouts.

"I know."

"No," the pudgy little man said, firmly. "You do not. This is a time-and-distance problem."

He drew a circle on a sheet of graph paper, then darkened the center boxes. "The object is in motion." He began to inch the point of a blue marker from an edge of the circle toward its center. "Speed can be estimated only imprecisely, at best. So, the more powerful we make *this*" — tapping the dark center boxes inside the circle — "the more certain of . . . success."

I just nodded, knowing what was coming, steeled for it.

"The closer to the center, the better. But we cannot control for closeness, so we must expand the center. That means anything with*in* that center will also be . . ."

"We can cut down those odds some, but it's still going to be a dice-roll," I admitted.

"Is there no other way?" he asked, clearly

pained by what my plan could cost.

That's when I told him the stake we were playing for.

"I . . . believe I understand," he said, minutes later. "But this is the quintessential chain-reaction formula: one faulty link and the whole thing fails. *One.*"

"We won't even *get* to this part unless everything else is already in motion, Mole."

"How will you ever — ?"

"I *have* to be right," I told my brother. "It's as simple as that. I have to be. If it happened any way except the way I believe it did, it's *already* over."

"But even if you *are* right, even if you could make it all work, there would be . . . consequences. The pursuit would be relentless."

"Mole, can I ask you something?"

He looked at me, as expressionlessly menacing as an Easter Island statue.

"If the Nazis had pulled it off, exterminated every Jew on earth, would they have stopped there?"

"No," he answered, giving away nothing.

"After the Gypsies, after the homosexuals, what then?"

"Anything not —"

"Come on, Mole. We're not doing politics

here. When someone gets called an 'anti-Semite,' that means — what? — he hates Jews, right?"

The underground man moved his head a fraction.

"But that's inaccurate, isn't it?" I said, deliberately using the language of science, not politics. "Aren't the Arabs also Semites? Aren't they as close to your biological brothers as anyone on earth?"

"In Europe —"

"Don't go there, brother. God couldn't have written the Bible, otherwise it would read the same in *every* language, never mind this Old and New Testament thing. Men created God, not the other way around. And where was the birthplace of that creation? The cradle of civilization itself? Come on! You know it wasn't Eden, so where was it? Where did we start? *All* of us, I mean."

"Evolution probably was occurring in different places simultaneously," he said, calmly. "There was no single starting point."

"I buy that. Okay. But tell me Jews and Arabs didn't spring from the same seed."

He went so still that I could only sense his presence. He was doing what he was best at. I was, too. Which is why I outwaited him.

"This is likely true," he finally conceded. "But, today —"

"I'm not running for boss of the fucking UN, Mole. I'm telling you why this could work."

"Because the pursuers would believe it was — ?"

"I don't know where they'd look," I told my brother. "But I know where *nobody* would be looking."

"My people didn't need no Einstein to discover infinity," the Prof said, his voice bitter enough to etch glass. "The trail never ends, 'cause there's nothing *at* the end. I can preach, I can teach, and I can reach. This is pure truth: the only place we go when we're gone is where we've already been."

"What we do here —"

"*That's* what stays behind, Schoolboy. The *only* thing. They used to tell us, You'll get pie in the sky when you die. And we believed it, 'cause it was the only way to make sense out of the life we had. But that pie was a lie, and some of us, we felt that like a fire inside us. A fire you have to *keep* inside, because you don't want it ever put out, and the whole world is nothing but steady rain.

"This fire, it burns so bright, it *makes* you see the light. The light you follow. I *know* some of us, we fed those slaveholders a whole lot of pie before *we* died. Look back with me," he said, closing his eyes. "You see it?"

"Yes." And I did.

"But I still believe," the old man said, fiercely. "Not in that hustler's handbook they preach from, but in the Word."

"I don't —"

"I believe in the truth," he said, reaching for my hand. He folded my hand into a fist. "You can't punch through the wall, son. Maybe you can't even make a little crack in it. But if you believe, you'll keep on hitting it until you can't hit no more, see? Then someone comes up behind you, hits that wall in the same spot. And someone else after that.

"And someday — not tomorrow, not next year, but some glorious day — that wall starts to look like a windshield that got hit by a rock. Spiderweb cracks all over it, and now you *know:* long as we keep punching, it's not gonna hold. *That's* the Word.

"You know why? I'm here to tell you. We on one side of that wall; they on the other. And you know what they doing over there? They ain't waiting on a fight; they getting ready to run. Motherfuckers are all froze up with fear, like a field mouse when a hawk's high in the sky. They know we coming. And we ain't taking prisoners."

"Amen."

"They got it all wrong, son. Money's the wall; blood's the punch. You got to pay the cost, all right. But not 'pay the cost to be the boss'; that rhyme is past its time. You pay the cost so *nobody* gets to be the boss. You tell the Mole to play his role. Tell him I'm going down the road with you. Right to the end."

I kissed his cheek. Thanking my father for backing my play this one last time.

"We're going to have it right here," Michelle told Clarence. The poor kid was trapped in my booth at Mama's, Michelle towering over him in her heels, hands on hips, bending forward to punch home every word.

I would have felt sorry for him, but I'd spent enough time with Taralyn to know he might as well get used it. I remember Clarence complaining to the Prof: "That girl, in a *second,* she can switch from cane sugar to what they use to cut it with," he said, lost in puzzlement and love. "I don't mean she's bossy. It's not like she nags or anything. No man could want a sweeter woman. But, mahn, when she plants her feet, you could not budge her with a bull-dozer."

"What other kinda woman you *want,* fool?" the Prof demanded. "Didn't I explain all that to you already? Her kind, they mate for life, understand? You play her wrong, she ain't gonna jump in your lunch, go all ghetto on your sorry ass. No. You do that, she gonna die inside.

"You *hear* me, boy? A woman like your Taralyn, even if you buy yourself twenty years Inside, you don't ever need to worry about Joe the Grinder comin' to call. She's gonna stand her ground, go every round. So if you ain't ready to go all the way, don't you even *try* and play, hear?"

"Yes, Father. I was not —"

"Don't be developing those habits, son."

"What do you mean?"

"You hear the Max-man talk about his woman?"

"Yes," Clarence said, putting his palm over his heart to imitate Max's gesture.

"That ain't talking *about* her, boy; that's talking about his feelings *for* her. You want to tell your buddies you love your woman, go on with it. But don't you *ever* complain, because you end up having to *explain.* Always gonna be some moke who don't get the joke, see?"

"Yes," Clarence said, nodding.

"A true-hearted woman like your Taralyn,

you can't buy her, you can't sell her, and you sure as hell can't *tell* her. You think she some no-pride bitch you can stay out all night on, buy her some jewelry and that'll make it right? No! You leave that kind of game to this one," he mocked, nodding in my direction.

"Yes, sir."

Poor bastard. And now he had to sit through Michelle "explaining" that the *only* place he could formally propose would be in a restaurant where ptomaine goes to die, the dirt is thicker than the carpet, and the vinyl had lost its virginity before he was born. "What were *you* going to do?" she mocked. "Take her out to eat, bury the ring in the dessert, some cheesy stunt like that?"

From the look on Clarence's face, apparently so. Me, I pretended I was somewhere else.

"We'll redecorate!" she said, half orgasmic at the very prospect. "You won't recognize the place, I swear."

"But this is not our —"

Mama strolled over from her perch by the cash register, tracking straight as a steel-hulled icebreaker.

"For one night," she said, closing the deal. "We get a car —" She cut herself off in mid-sentence, seeing Clarence start to open his mouth. "Not *your* car. Limousine. All special. Flowers, crystal. Make perfect."

"Mama, I so very deeply appreciate everything. But I would be . . . embarrassed, if I had to —"

"You think *we* be here?" Mama stared him down. "Sure, *someplace* here. But not in room. Waiters come, sure. Serve all special dishes. But not stay. You finish food, you signal, everybody disappear. Okay?"

"But the *minute* she accepts, then we can all — ?"

"Yes, little sister," he said to Michelle, grinning despite his anxiety.

Everyone was quiet, breathing in the moment.

"*After* we finish the job," I reminded them all, breaking the spell.

"We found six," Cyn said. "Certified."

"Okay, just give me the —"

"Already done," she said, looking over at Rejji as she spoke. "Three of them haven't had a customer in months. Two're still in the hospital; the other was just discharged. The only other one wouldn't go near an Arab; she only does Nordic."

I looked a question.

"Nazi torture chamber. The tricks play dress-up while they do her. There's two more we know of, but we couldn't reach them. One's been in Vegas for almost a year; the other one's not talking."

"Maybe if I offered her —"

"Too late for that," Rejji said, on the borderline between making a judgment and not giving a damn.

"You must find that child," Taralyn said. She was looking at me, but speaking to Clarence. "Your father has made remarkable progress, but he is going to need several more weeks of rehab and at least one more refitting before he can even *think* of —"

The Prof wasn't going to let anyone talk about him like he wasn't in the room. "Girl, I wanted to slide away, you think I'd tip the play?"

"Mr. Henry —"

" 'Sides, you think I'd ever put my own son under the gun?" the old man said, hitting her with a smile that made it impossible to disbelieve him.

If you didn't know him.

It took a while to get in touch with everyone, but we managed to get together just before midnight. I looked around the table, thinking how some of us were in each other's life from way back and some of us just knew each other's back-story. And how none of that made any difference now.

Michelle and me had been together since we were kids. Max hadn't been born deaf, and after so many years of keeping the vow he made never to speak while he was learning the death arts, he probably couldn't anymore. I'd been there when he'd told Mama how he lost his hearing. I knew why the Mole hated sunlight, but I was probably the only one.

The Prof had adopted Clarence as he had me, but before the young gunman ever spent any time behind the Walls. Terry knew his own truth, but he'd known his true family longer. His "childhood" had been a dirty little glass bead until Michelle used the telekinesis of love to roll a twenty-ton boulder over it.

Gateman had been in that wheelchair since he was a little boy. His father hadn't put him in there, but he liked dumping him out of it, especially when he came home drunk.

Nobody knew much of anything about Mama, but her name was no accident. Neither was Flower not being with us that night. She'd been kept out from the start. From *her* start.

"I can do it, boss," Gateman assured me.

"The whole block is shorter than a damn football field, and his place is just about in the middle. I can park myself at the corner. You know, the whole begging-bowl bit — nobody'll even look at my face. At that distance, I can put one in his eye socket without breaking a sweat. You know I can."

"Making the shot ain't the same as getting off the block," the Prof vetoed. He shifted in his chair, pillows bracing his stump.

We'd only gotten the Prof out after Clarence promised Taralyn we'd bring him back. He'd taken her hand and kissed it, said, "I swear on my love," and made her look into his eyes.

"I know it is true, then" was all she said.

"I done it before," Gateman told the Prof. "You know I have."

"Ain't no doubt you got the chops," the old man agreed. "But this ain't down where we live, Gate. This is rich man's country. People don't be going all Ray Charles when somebody gets himself popped off the count. Streets be *jammed,* too. Only way you get out is blast yourself a path. And you got too far to roll, bro."

"I'd only need to get as far as the van," Gateman insisted. "We done it before."

"Not in *that* neighborhood," I echoed the

Prof. "Those car chases through midtown, that's only in the movies. Nobody has to be chasing you; the regular traffic is a perfect roadblock. Remember, you're going *cross-town.* There isn't a getaway man alive who could make that run."

Michelle opened her cell phone, turned it so the screen was aimed at Gateman, said, "Gotcha!"

"Mom's right," Terry said. "Everybody walks around with one of those things. You could be on YouTube before you got ten blocks away."

That was true. Terry's words took me back to the freak who told me all about how he had invented "noir vérité" . . . just before he died. Now it was an epidemic, with "directors" posting their kitten-in-microwave masterpieces on video Web sites, to the delight of creepy-crawly fans all over the world.

One endlessly recycled fave was the prison surveillance tapes of Father John Geoghan being strangled in his cell. The notorious "pedophile priest" had been murdered nine years ago. But the guy accused of doing it demanded a showcase trial . . . which meant the tapes were part of the discovery evidence the prosecution had to turn over. How that tape got so popular on the Internet is less of a mystery than why so many people keep insisting there's no such thing as snuff films.

Gateman had picked up some of Rosie's habits; he wasn't going to drop the bite. "But what if I — ?"

"Listen, brother," I said. "I wouldn't care if we could blast him from a spaceship, we can't have it look like a shooter's work. We're building a skyscraper here. We leave out one lousy brick, the whole thing comes down."

"From what you say, there ain't but one way," the Prof said. Argument over.

"But . . ." Michelle started, then stopped herself. We all looked at her, waiting. "I know you can read, baby," she said to me. "But that doesn't mean you can write."

"I don't —"

"My girl's saying it like it is," the Prof backed her. "Just 'cause you a wizard at catching lies, that don't put you in the same class at *telling* them."

"Why would it be a lie?" I asked. Asked them all.

"You have always said —"

"I know, Mole. But how did *I* know?"

Maybe for the first time, Clarence explained something to his father . . . by saying something to me: "The Beryl woman.

Ever since her, you have been . . . different, mahn."

"Satchel Paige had it all wrong," I said, looking at the Prof. "You look back, maybe somebody *is* chasing you. But if you never look back, how can you know?"

"Ain't no way you could —"

"I know that door's closed," I said, admitting out loud that the truth of my childhood was beyond reach, forever. "And I'm not going back. Not even to find it, never mind open it. But what the Mole said was right: I always *thought* I knew. And now . . . now maybe I'm not so sure."

"*That's* the truth to tell, honey," Michelle said, reaching out to touch my hand.

"First study, *then* teach," Mama cautioned, pointing at her unreadable eyes.

"I will," I promised them all.

"You recognize my voice?"

"I might," the man at the other end of the line said, "but I couldn't put a name to it."

He wasn't being cagey, he was saying he'd never told anyone about me. Joel Dryslan, Ph.D., didn't get to be one of this country's elite forensic psychologists by reading books; he'd learned a lot of his craft the same place I learned mine. He was a prison shrink for years before he became Chief of

Forensic Services for the whole state. After a few years on that job, the climate in Albany caused him to call in sick. . . . He never came back to work.

"It's a permanent state of war in here," he told me once. "We can sometimes negotiate temporary peace treaties, but the one war we'll never win is Security versus Treatment. Some two-digit-IQ sadist can nullify any decision I make. And he'll do it just to show who's boss."

Today, Dryslan makes more in a few hours than he used to make in a month. He's for hire, but he's no whore. Pay him his price, and he'll take a look for you. But you can't tell him what to say after he does.

That means hiring him before the other side does isn't going to shield you, like with a lot of forensic "experts." You know the kind I mean: The defense hires them, they'll tell the jury the blood-spatter evidence proves the defendant's wife must have jumped from the balcony into the empty swimming pool. But if the prosecution is quicker to write the check, that same evidence will prove she was thrown to her death.

In some states, all you need to qualify as sane is to rote-repeat, "It is a sin to kill." A lifelong history of psychiatric hospitalizations, complex conversations with the voices in your head, being on enough meds to open your own pharmacy — so what? Just throw in the "confession," like the woman who told the cops she stuffed her baby in the oven "because Satan fears fire."

Then you bring in an expert guaranteed to label them all "sociopaths." Translation: they're not insane; they're evil. And perfect candidates for the death penalty.

Works the other way, too. You can buy an "expert" who'll tell an enthralled jury how a human who raped babies for fun and made videos of it for profit was psychiatrically overwhelmed. The poor soul was suffering from a witch's brew of personality disorders, depersonalization syndrome, and, of course, "pedophilia." A tormented creature like him should never be sent to prison; what he needed was a highly specialized, tightly structured, secure treatment program. In fact, having researched the matter thoroughly, the expert even knew the perfect place — it had all the latest "modalities," really tight security, and a recidivism rate lower than his morals.

The defense summation would pound all this home, reminding the jurors that this treatment program wouldn't cost the State a dime; the defendant's family stood ready to defray all costs . . . and compensate the victims, too. Now, wasn't that the best way to *really* protect society?

Dryslan's specialty was the effects of solitary confinement on mental health. He was enough of a realist to accept that some humans are too toxic to be at large, even inside a prison, but he'd been around cons long enough to understand that solitary confinement isn't always about protecting the other inmates.

I'd stumbled across him years ago, when I was hiding out in Oregon. I had to make money, so I took on some work. The trail I'd been following led to a teenage runaway trying to protect her younger sister. That teenager's best friend turned out to be Dryslan's daughter.

The two were so close, they'd called themselves the Crow Girls, after the Maida and Zia characters in the magical books of Charles de Lint that so many young searchers adored.

It ended like most of my work does. But not as ugly as what was going on before I stepped out of the night long enough to do the only *good* thing I'm good at.

This time, my call was to a 520 area code, not a 503 — it had only taken me a minute to locate Dryslan once the operator told me the first number I'd tried had been disconnected.

Another new experience for me: looking for someone who wasn't trying to hide.

"I need to talk to you," I said. "This has *nothing* to do with you or yours, past or present."

I could feel the change in him even as I spoke. Most people who cross paths with me share the same wish — that it never happens again.

"Professionally?" he asked.

"Yes."

"And it's not something you could do — ?"

"Face-to-face, Doc. But anything else you want, any other conditions: you say it, you got it."

The flight to Phoenix was a nice, smooth non-stop. I'd always thought of Phoenix as kind of a small town. Maybe it was, but the airport was humongous.

Walking out of baggage claim onto the sidewalk was like stepping out of a meat locker into the Sahara. An ancient, bleached-green BMW Z3 was just pulling up. I opened the door, climbed inside.

Dryslan looked the same: broad-chested, with a gentle smile and empathetic eyes.

His handshake conveyed just a hint of the wrestler he'd been in college.

"Ever been to Phoenix before?" he said, by way of greeting.

"Couple of times," I told him.

"Like it?"

"Long as you don't put the top down, I'll probably like it fine. How old is this crate, anyway?"

"You sound like the dealer every time I bring her in for service," Joel said, grinning, still in love with his toy.

And still driving with an urgency that was all about having fun, not being in a hurry.

"My office is in my house," he said, when we got on a main road.

"I've got a hotel room," I told him, handing him the paper with my reservation on it.

I'd met his kids. Jenn was a beautiful girl, but so unselfconscious about it that she never fell into the role. A brilliant student, with a deeply caring heart, following her father's path. His son, Mike, was tough enough to play rugby for entertainment, and walked around exuding a sincerity that even the best con man couldn't hope to copy. He was in a top MBA program, after working for two years to get real-world experience. I didn't care what business that kid ended up picking; I was ready to invest.

"Protective" doesn't get within a thousand miles of how Dryslan was about his family, so I knew what telling me his office was in his home meant. I admired the way he found to get that across without hurting my feelings.

That's why I'd come. About those.

Phoenix may have a world-class airport, but its idea of a high-end hotel came up a bit short. I only had a carry-on, and we were inside my "suite" in a few minutes.

Joel's presence immediately turned the place into his office. We each took an easy chair, nothing but artificially chilled air between us.

The shades were drawn. The only light was a floor lamp in one corner.

I talked and talked. Only realized I'd been at it for so long when I rotated my neck to crack the adhesions loose and got a glance at my watch.

I stopped then.

Joel was quiet for a little bit before: "How's that been working out for you?"

"Huh?"

"Your construct."

"Look, Doc —"

"You're not any kind of 'sociopath,'" he said. Not offering a diagnosis, stating a fact.

"Oh, you fit the DSM criteria: failure to conform to social norms, disregard for the rights of others, multiple arrests, deceitfulness, early-onset aggression, lack of remorse. But none of that is very persuasive. In fact, most of it's meaningless.

" 'Antisocial Personality Disorder' is what they call it now. The key word is 'personality.' And personality doesn't tell you much about anyone; only behavior does. A man's personality might be obnoxious, for example. But that wouldn't necessarily stop him from being honest.

"For a man like you, lying isn't a 'personality,' it's a tool. You use it for your work, but it's not who you are. Same thing with aggression. The only thing provable about you is a lifetime of criminal conduct. You want a diagnosis, try 'outlaw.' "

I looked at him, said nothing.

"Nothing complicated there," he went on. "Self-explanatory, really. You live outside the law. You support yourself by crime. You don't experience guilt as a normal person might. In fact, you find some forms of aggression to be fulfilling, at least temporarily so. You're filled with a rage that you . . . eventually . . . learned to control. Not because you wanted to be a better person; because you wanted to be a more skillful criminal."

"That still sounds like —"

"The entire concept of sociopathy is simply our profession's refusal to acknowledge that some people are actually evil. It's not a 'personality disorder' to be a thief . . . or even to feel no guilt about being one. Those 'criteria' I cited before? They could fit a not-too-bright thug, or a highly sophisticated predator. A chronic shoplifter, or a serial killer. 'Sociopath' is just a label . . . and it's so overbroad that it's lost all meaning.

"If we were to actually use the term diagnostically, we would say a sociopath is a person who lacks the fundamental human quality that prevents the entire species from reversing evolution. That quality is empathy. Not faking it, *feeling* it. No true sociopath is capable of caring what happens to anyone other than himself. He feels only his *own* pain. That's not you. It's never been you."

"I wanted to be —"

"No, you didn't," Joel said, cutting me off. "You *thought* you wanted to be. Right?"

"I just knew I didn't want to be —"

"Don't say 'afraid,' " he cautioned me. "Some people *do* lose the capacity to experience fear, but that's because they've gone numb. Permanently anaesthetized. *That's* what you wanted. What you thought you wanted. Not to feel. Not to feel *anything.*

"Everyone knows a kid's feelings can be hurt real easily — that's why emotional abuse probably causes more long-term damage than any other. But when you were a child, you didn't make those fine distinctions. You had it all figured out, didn't you? Feelings hurt. *All* feelings. *Any* feelings. To you, 'feelings' and 'hurt' meant the same thing.

"You told me once about a man named Wesley, your brother, you said. Actually, he was the outlaw ideal, wasn't he? Someone might be able to *kill* him, but no one could ever *hurt* him — isn't that what you told me?"

"It was true," I told him.

"No," he said, his voice bench-pressing the sadness off his chest, so the word came out like an expired breath. "If it was true, why did he ever protect you?"

"I never knew. He was just —"

Joel leaned forward, drawing me into the secret he was sharing. "I've met every kind of human horror you can imagine. I don't mean horrors done to humans; I mean humans who *were* horrors. Genuine psychopaths, if you like that label better. And you know the one thing they *always* had in common?"

I didn't answer.

"You thought 'child abuse,' didn't you?" he said. "But then you threw that out immediately, because you've known too many people who were abused as children who *didn't* carry it on. Yes?"

I nodded.

Dryslan's voice didn't change volume, but it dropped an octave. "A psychopath isn't a human being, he's a facsimile of one. He looks like us; he talks like us. Most of the time, he even acts like us. But he can never *be* one of us. He can do anything humans do except for one: he can't bond.

"This is what they all have in common, every single one: some variation of Attachment Disorder. They weren't *allowed* to bond during the time our species is designed to have that occur. It's simple; it's sad . . . and it's immutable. They never learned it when they should have — *could* have, in fact. But that's not a capacity you can develop if you start too late.

"That last part's only a guess, but it does seem axiomatic," he said, ruefully. "Why would a psychopath *want* to develop empathy? It would only weigh him down."

I closed my eyes, so that nothing I might

see in his face would get in the way of what I'd come to hear.

"At some level they understand they were cheated out of something so valuable they don't even know what to call it. They *all* know. Yeah, even the stupid ones. Forget that nonsense about them all being handsome, charming, and intelligent; that's just a made-for-TV movie."

"What if — ?"

"But they're only a tiny slice of the walking wounded," he rolled right on over what I was going to say. "All abused children keep searching. Some cut themselves, so they can feel *something*. Some find substitutes, even if they're only objects."

The paperback collector, flashed across the screen of my mind.

"Some convert abuse into proof of love," he said, never changing his tone. " 'If he didn't love me, he wouldn't beat me.' How many times have you heard that? But most of them, they just look for ways to stop the pain. Drugs, alcohol, a cult . . . Some actually *feel* the emptiness, as if it were a physical void inside themselves. It's a list without end . . . human searching."

"But *if* they're searching, they're not —"

"Yes!" he said, reaching out to smack my

upper arm, like I'd just scored. "What saved you?"

"My family," I answered, without a nano-second of pause or a microdot of doubt.

"You'd die for them?"

"Don't draw the line there," killing that cliché as quickly as I'd kill anyone who ever so much as . . .

"Where, then?"

"There *is* no line," I told him.

He didn't blink. And came right back with the foundational truth: "Of course there isn't. How could there be? Without them, there's no *you*."

I took it without a word, but he wasn't done:

"You developed your whole life story off a blank birth certificate. Told it to yourself until it became unshakable truth. Your reality. But it never got *all* the way inside, did it?"

"I don't under—"

"Your mother — the woman who gave birth to you — abandoned you. Didn't want you. And you didn't feel a thing, is that about right?"

"That's not —"

"The hate didn't come until later," he said, untapped power vibrating under the gentleness of his voice. "You said it was your mother, but it was the State who raised you. Every hideous thing ever done to you, the State did that. But no crying for Baby Boy Burke. That's for punks. Hate, that's a *man's* emotion. Who'd you learn that from, Wesley?"

"Wesley didn't hate anyone."

"Hate is a feeling," he said. "And, in your mind, Wesley didn't have any of those. But the truth is, that's not what you wanted to be. Not a hired killer, not the famous 'iceman' Wesley was.

"You didn't want to be afraid, I know. And you kept trying to find a way *there,* didn't you?"

"Yeah," I said, thinking of me as a gang kid. Flying between rooftops; kneeling with my head on the subway tracks, train coming, knowing I *was* going to be the last one to jump. Spinning the cylinder on a revolver with all but one chamber empty as the next kid waited his turn . . .

But Dryslan saw through that. "The one sure thing about dying is that it stops the pain. But stopping where the pain *came* from — that's where you needed your story."

"I'll never know if my . . ."

"Can't even say the word, can you?"

" 'Mother'? A mother is what you do, not

what you are."

"And yours, all *she* did was run."

"That's right."

"And maybe that's true," the doctor said. "But you don't know. You *couldn't* know. So you went with what worked. What got you numb."

"I . . ."

"Your family, I never met them. But I can tell you this: some of the strongest bonds are between those who never stopped searching until they found what they needed to make them human."

When I opened my eyes, he was saying, "If we get it in gear, we can still catch that return flight."

I took my seat, slipped on the noise-canceling headphones I always carry on planes to discourage anyone from talking to me, and closed my eyes again.

I'd gone to see Dryslan for the same reason a power-punching cruiserweight prepping for a title fight would make sure he had a top-class middleweight as one of his sparring partners. I couldn't let the decision go to the judges, and there was no rematch clause in the contract. So my job would be to cut down the ring.

If I could land one, I knew I could end it.

But to do that, I had to keep my moves razor-honed. Play the role, and play it perfect.

I couldn't think it; I had to *be* it.

As the plane touched down, so did I. I'd gone to Phoenix with questions, and I'd come back with answers.

Some answers.

But, like Dryslan had reminded me, there's some I'll never know.

"What difference would that make?"

"You already know," I told Pryce. "This has to be one-on-one."

"What if I could get you a simultaneous translator?" he countered. "Just like in the UN. You each put on headphones, it's like you're talking to each other in the same language."

"No."

"Because I told you she speaks English, or because you don't want me to have access to — ?"

"I've got no choice about that," I said, "so what's your problem? I need your people to make it happen. No matter how you get your part done, you're going to set up a way for you to listen in."

"Couldn't you — ?"

"No," I cut him off, trying to get past the

416

reflexive bargaining his kind always tries. "And I'm not putting any of my people in this, understand? Not to convince her, not to set up a meet, not to snatch her, not . . . *nothing.* That part's yours. We're not playing find-the-middle here. Say yes or say no."

"Why can't your — ?"

"I don't have a crystal ball. If she turns the wrong way, I have to be the only one she gets to turn *on.*"

He tried a bored-scornful face, watching mine. Finally said: "What makes you think she even *knows* anything? You think she hasn't already been debriefed?"

"I wouldn't be surprised if they went fucking total Guantánamo on her. But if I'm right, anything they did — anything they know *how* to do — they'd be wasting their time."

"But you, *you've* got some magic you think will work?"

"You think so, too," I slapped away his tsetse fly sarcasm. "If you didn't, you wouldn't be here."

He tapped his fingertips lightly on the countertop. "You know I work alone."

Nice try. "I know you don't have partners," I said. "That's not the same thing."

"What're the odds?"

"If I'm right, you're a mortal lock for hero

status. And whatever goes along with that."

"And if you're not?"

"Then the only way you stay out of a grave is to put me in one. And even if you managed that, you could end up in the plot next to me." I laid it out, straight. "If I can't pull this off, the best we can hope for is a lot of fires that have to be put out. And you'd better pray that the people who hired you think you're the only one with a big enough hose to do it."

"Sounds like a pass to me," he said, hedging.

"Is that right? I don't have to call to see your hand this time, Pryce. I know what you're holding — you've been drawing dead since the flop. So you can either try and double-talk your bosses, or you can open the door for me. There's no option three."

I watched his eyes. Saw something I'd never seen on any of his faces before. Indecision.

"I *know* I can make it happen," I took one last try. "But I need a way in to do it."

"Do it *for* her? Or *to* her?"

"That's yours; I already said that. You get me that one-on-one with her. Then it's all on me."

"You're that confident?"

"I've got one card to play," I told him,

sending out the truth, hoping he could pick it up. "That card is me — and I'm the only one who can play it."

"You know what happens if you're wrong."

"That doesn't change anything. *Can't* change anything. Like I said, I don't know what you're ready to bet, but I put down everything I had the minute I asked you to set up the meet with her, didn't I? And that was *my* choice. I could have just fan-danced my way through some 'investigation,' told you I struck out, and walked away."

"Then why *didn't* you just let it play itself out?" he asked, narrowing his eyes. "You already got paid. And not half in front, either — you've already collected it all. So what's in this for you?"

"You're not the one I have to answer that question for," I told him.

I worked hard the next few days. Supposedly to practice, get my timing right. Focus, concentration, one-strike finishers. I never left the dojo, except for meals with Max's family.

I might have fooled Flower, but Immaculata knew why I'd moved in. I saw it as she watched me say goodbye to her daughter, even though that word never passed my lips.

Flower gave me the same kiss she'd been

giving her uncle Burke since she hit her teens, standing on her toes and reaching her hand into my outside jacket pocket for the "secret" money she knew would be there.

Immaculata kissed me, too. Said something in that French-Vietnamese language I didn't have to translate to understand.

Max and I tried a formal bow. It didn't work for either of us.

"I must —"

"Only me, brother," I told Clarence, turning to our father for confirmation.

"Ain't none of us can be around when this one goes down," the old man agreed. "The boss even *smells* a cross, he's gonna nuke the whole juke." He looked at me carefully. "You skydiving on a real old parachute, son."

"At least this time I bought my own ticket," I told him.

The old man squeezed my forearm. "You ain't gonna miss the wedding, Schoolboy. Ain't no place you end up that I can't go and fetch you back."

"This is it?"

"You expected something more . . . elaborate?" the Mole answered.

"I guess I did," I told him, fingering a short length of inch-thick stuff that looked as if it came off a roll of insulating material. Only this wasn't rough fiberglass; it was putty-colored, and smooth as a top-class escort's legs.

"It has to withstand moisture for as long as several days. And it must remain in place, too," the Mole said, as if that explained anything.

"But it'll definitely — ?"

"Or more, depending on how close it can be placed," the man with the cottage-cheese complexion promised. His denim eyes were magnified by the Coke-bottle lenses, as unreadable as ever.

When we came upstairs, we told Michelle and Terry. Not everything, just enough. Despite what the Prof had said, once they found out the Mole was going to walk with me, I had to give them each some part to play.

There are places in this city where you can buy any uniform you might want. Not a copy, the real thing. Cop, firefighter, sanitation, you name it. Even federal: FBI, DEA, ATF, whatever. Badges and insignia, too. But I couldn't use any of those places —

they all have authentic telephones, too.

"This is just a generic jumpsuit," Michelle said, after examining the photos I showed her. "There has to be a better image I can work from."

"I don't need to leave the computer to do that," Terry said, going to work.

"You are *ruining* those shoes," she snapped at the Mole. He was meticulously replacing the steel shanks in her strappy spike heels with an exact match made of something else. Since his craftsmanship was far superior to the original, everyone in the room translated Michelle's bitching to: "You have to buy me another pair."

Mole smiled at that one. He knew his woman. Knew she was really saying, "You'll be back."

The subway is closer to the sidewalk, but we had to start down in the sewer system. And *stay* down there until we found the access point.

We plodded along, miner's lamps blazing on our yellow hardhats. Anyone we ran into down there wouldn't expect EPA workers to be moving around in the dark without them. The oxygen masks we wore over our faces wouldn't look out of place, either.

And nobody who saw us carrying orange

422

equipment packs with **TOXIC** stenciled across the back was going to try and start up a conversation.

We didn't run across any alligators. I don't know if those old urban legends ever had any truth in them, but it didn't matter. There isn't an alligator on earth who'd stand a chance against the mutated rats that owned this part of the city.

In fact, it was those same rats who showed me how we could pull this off. When that video of them invading a fast-food restaurant had aired on every TV station in town a while back, I'd filed away some vital information — rats don't have food preferences. This city is rotting from the bottom up, the barriers between the underground and the street getting weaker every day. That fast-food joint had just been sitting over a thin spot. Since the same restaurant had been given a passing grade by the "health inspector" the day before, the media went berserk.

The City Council immediately responded with the perfect solution — they shut down the restaurant. I guess they figured those rats had been strolling down the street like those hapless foodies whose idea of a "date" is checking sidewalk window restaurant menus. One rat says to the other, "This one looks interesting," and it's game on. Yeah, right.

The same tracks run beneath penthouses and slums. If you think your building's basement is rat-proof just because you pay a few grand a month for a one-bedroom, change your meds.

I kept my stride as unvarying as possible, checking the pedometer strapped to my ankle. The Mole had some kind of sonic probe with him, too, but we still followed the plastic-coated map I carried, brightly colored arrows marking our route.

We both stopped in the same spot. The Mole nodded his okay. His method of calculating distance was light-years ahead of mine, but he was a scientist in his soul, and he never ran an experiment without a control.

The subway station at Sixty-third and Lex had never actually opened for business, but the tunnels were still operational. So was the "Authorized Personnel Only" elevator.

I guess they thought the sign was security enough. Why bother locking the door to an abandoned house?

The elevator took us to just below the sidewalk, where we rechecked the maps. We'd ended up so close to our target point that finding the exact spot only took another minute.

I unfolded the collapsible aluminum ladder so that it formed a horizontal platform between the two sets of rungs. Standing, we each had plenty of room to reach up and work.

My watch glowed 12:09. Plenty of lunch-hour foot traffic would be right above us, perfect cover for Michelle. We had told her twelve-fifteen.

She was early. We couldn't hear the tap of her heels on the sidewalk above us, but the Mole's meter went from pale green to bright red, held for a second or two, then back to green.

When the meter repeated the message, he nodded and we unfurled the putty-colored stuff, carefully peeling off the self-stick backing. Then we patted it into place, neither of us being gentle about it.

Once satisfied it would hold, the Mole took what looked like four spikes from his kit, handed me two of them. We pulled the cork off the tips, then pushed them in deep. One went into each of the short sides of the rectangular blanket, the other two into the center.

We climbed down. The Mole used his flash to check one more time. Then I folded up the ladder and looped it over my shoulder. The Mole signaled "go back" with a gloved finger.

The only company we had along the way was the occasional rat. Some of them were ready to take on moving food, but we were too big, walking too steadily, and didn't smell like prey. The Mole never had to use the spray-hose connected to whatever he had loaded in that oxygen tank.

By the time we were halfway back, we'd negotiated a treaty with the rats. Everybody survives; nobody talks.

While the uniforms were being incinerated — including the gloves and boots and hooded bodysuits we'd worn under them — the Mole and I took a shower with military-grade disinfectant. The biggest danger lurking in prison today isn't AIDS, it's hep-C . . . and what we just walked through would probably kill diphtheria on contact.

"That's a lot of steel and concrete, brother," I said.

"The signal won't be traveling the same route."

"But it'll still set off the — ?"

"Yes," the underground man said. "And my son will be nowhere near."

"I didn't mean —"

"I know," he said, kindly.

A Mercedes S600 long-wheelbase sedan with diplomatic plates pulled up outside a *très*-elite salon. An alert man slid out of the back seat, followed by a slender woman in a simple blue dress and matching pumps. The man didn't offer her his hand, never made physical contact of any kind.

They waited on the sidewalk until a third man emerged, from the front passenger side. Same height as the first, but bulkier in build.

The black Benz pulled off immediately. Smart move. The woman's standing appointment was for three hours, so waiting at the curb was out of the question. Cops in that precinct hated limo drivers on general principles, and Arab diplomats already owed the city millions in unpaid parking fines.

The two men bracketed the woman as they walked her to the door. Not bodyguards; body-*guarders.*

The bulky one opened the door. The woman stepped inside. The second armed servant followed. We knew who they served.

"Princess Aabidah!" the exotic-looking ornament at the front desk trilled.

Within seconds, a straw-thin male wearing a burgundy smock and enough attitude to keep the Goodyear Blimp floating for weeks flounced in.

"Princess," he said, very formally. Then he made an imperiously ushering gesture toward a remote section of the salon that was behind a set of "Look how expensive I am!" Japanese paper screens.

The body-guarders took up positions on either side of the front door, watching the shadow-play of their charge being seated behind the screen.

A mirror fell to the floor, shattering on impact. "Oh, no!" an effeminate voice shrieked. Everyone's head swiveled at the noise as a river of burgundy smocks rushed between the guards and the screen. A few seconds passed before the smaller body-guard smoothly removed his right hand from inside his suit jacket.

As long as they kept their distance, the property-protectors would never realize that their charge was already behind another door. The woman whose shadow they were now watching was getting a bonus whoever she worked for hadn't offered in the hiring brochure.

We had no doubt they *would* keep their distance. To directly observe the Princess in the midst of such an intimate moment was forbidden; it had taken months to work out this special arrangement before their master had been satisfied.

The Princess had no time to even gasp before the thick door closed behind her with a hissing sound that announced it had been soundproofed. "Please sit," I said formally, indicating a chair opposite her. When she didn't move, I held up a large, blown-up photo of her missing baby. I remained seated, made no move of any kind.

"I demand to —"

Balance disruption, I reminded myself. "You are Aabidah Amatullah," I said aloud, my voice carrying the low-volume potency of the not-to-be-doubted. "Your baby was stolen. I know the truth of that. You believe *you* know that truth, but you do not. You are in no danger. You are not a prisoner. All this" — I pointed to the heavy padding that covered each inch of the room we were in — "is to *protect* you."

I waited three heartbeats, then said, "We understand you are under the scrutiny of the men who brought you here. At this very moment, your husband's servants are watching a woman behind the Japanese screens. They will never dare to come closer, as you know.

"You are safe here. Not just from them, from us as well. If you wish to leave, nobody will stop you. All I can do — all I *will* do — is to beg you to listen first to what I must tell you. I told you that you were in no danger, Aabidah Amatullah. That was the truth. But your son, Ghazi, *is* in danger. Mortal danger. If you will let me explain, I will prove this to you. And I will show you how to save him."

Her face showed no trace of inbred royalty; she had the profile of a desert hawk. And the eyes.

What those eyes saw was a man whose face was a road map of damage, hurt, and pain. His eyes were two different colors. The keloid dimple in his cheek was something she might have seen before, in her earlier life — a poorly repaired bullet wound.

Suddenly she sat down. Saying nothing with her mouth, and everything with the gesture.

"Those people your husband sent to guard you will know nothing of this meeting," I promised her. "When you emerge from behind the screen, your hair will be done, your skin treated, a manicure and pedicure if you wish. All I ask is that you not look at the person performing such services."

She said nothing.

I struck without warning: "Your son was

430

not kidnapped."

She had been trained since birth to keep emotion from her face, but she couldn't stop her eyes from telegraphing. She was fighting off shock, using her will as a sword.

"You arranged for him to be taken," I said. Still formal, still respectful. Not accusing, reciting a fact. "I know why you did this. I admire you enormously for the decision you made. No mother ever made a greater sacrifice."

Her body was stone, but her eyes had shaken off the paralysis, soundlessly screaming.

I went deep into myself, reaching out to sync her heartbeat with mine.

I knew I had locked on when she finally spoke: "Why would you say such things?"

"I say what I know."

"*How* could you know such a thing?"

"Because you did for your son what my mother did for me," I told her, sensing her heartbeat accelerate as I textured my voice. "My mother was in a burning building. She knew rescue for herself was impossible, so she threw her son out into the black night, with only her prayer that someone below would catch him."

Her hooded eyes narrowed as if against the desert sun, but she said nothing.

"My mother believed she was throwing me either to safety or to death," I went on, feeling her heart pulsate. "She knew her own life was already finished. She knew she would never live to raise me herself. All she could do was try to give me a chance. A chance at another life."

I felt her heartbeat slow as she accepted it all. Then I struck again:

"But what my mother never knew was that she threw me into a fire worse than the one that finally consumed her. That fire took her body, but the one she threw me into took my soul."

That hit too deep for her to maintain the stony silence. Heat lightning strobed her dark eyes. "My son's soul —"

"Is not where you believe it to be, Aabidah Amatullah," I interrupted. "May I tell you my story? My own story? Please? Then you will make a decision, as you did before. What*ever* decision you make will be respected. Respected *completely.* Do you understand? Even if you choose to leave your baby with al-Qaeda, your husband will never, ever know."

She took that body-shot without flinching, shielded by her frozen silence. But her eyes crackled, a fuse burning down.

"Please?" I asked again.

She made an untranslatable gesture with her hand.

I made a gesture of my own. Michelle stepped in behind her like a gentle breeze, a comb and scissors in her hands.

I took a deep breath in through my nose, letting it all come into me until I was full enough to overflow. I'd only get this one chance to tell my story, and I had to make it *become* the truth. I exhaled, felt my core, and lifted the curtain:

"My mother gave birth to me when she was fourteen years old," I told the Princess, my voice very measured, as if fighting for self-control. "Or perhaps even younger. I will never know, because I never saw my mother, not even for a second. I never tasted a drop of her milk.

"I was born in the emergency ward of a charity hospital. My mother used a false name when she came in, and she fled, still bleeding, before they even realized she was gone. This is the birth certificate they made for me," I said, reaching into my jacket and offering her a piece of paper.

She gave it a quick glance, said: "Anyone can —"

"Yes," I agreed. "Anyone can lie. I know. I *should* know. I have lied all my life. Especially to myself. That paper you hold says 'Unk' in the space for 'Father.' That means 'Unknown.' The made-up name my mother gave the hospital was Brenda Burke, so I am 'Baby Boy Burke' forever. A child without a name."

She blinked twice, steadied herself, then stepped back inside her silence.

"The State became my father," I told her. "In this world, some are born as powerful as gods, while some are born to be lower than dirt. This you already know. So, when my mother fled, I was placed in what you might call 'orphanages.' Institutions for unwanted children, where every person who touches you knows you are less than nothing, without even a family to avenge you should they cause you harm.

"My first memories are of screaming. I never stopped. Some children are adopted, but nobody wanted me. They put me in foster homes. Those are places where people are paid by the State to act as substitute families. Some of those families are sent from Heaven. And some would be barred from Hell."

Again she blinked rapidly, resettled herself, and maintained her silence.

"In one of those families, I was raped. Yes," I said, catching the faint snarl before she suppressed it. "I mean exactly what you are thinking: I was used as a woman. I was burned with cigarettes, made to do things I will not say in your presence.

"After they were done with me, I was sent to a prison for children. There I learned the ways of the Outcast. And I embraced them.

"That is where I was taught my religion, in prison. My religion is Revenge. That became my reason to live. And, later, my reason to take lives."

Any chance that she would get up and walk out was long gone. The air between us was vibrating with things I couldn't name, but always trusted.

"I have committed murder, Aabidah Amatullah," I said, an unrepentant confessor. "I have robbed, stolen, lied, and cheated. I have committed more crimes than I can count, sinned against every god. That is my life. A criminal is what I am, now and forever. Branded from birth."

A storm threatened to break in her eyes. Michelle kept right on with her work.

"And *this* is also true," I told the woman across from me. "I took a vow that I would never hurt a child, never commit a rape. And I have kept that vow. All I wanted from my life was to seek vengeance, again and again.

"Once, I went to war against a group who preyed upon little ones. I stopped them just as they were about to sacrifice a baby. Hate guided my hand. In the exchange of gunfire, the child himself died. Yes, he would have died anyway. Yes, his death was instant, not the slow one they had planned for him. But, no matter what lies I have told myself ever since, I know I am responsible. The child's death is on my soul, forever."

Her eyes never left mine, but I could feel the subtle shift from a princess who had refused to be intimidated by a criminal to a mother who would not hesitate to kill to save her own child.

"Only a short time ago, I finally accepted the truth," I went on. "I had always believed that my mother had been a prostitute, and my father had been some faceless customer. I believed that my mother *chose* to return to selling her body. I believed that she discarded me, not caring that I might be delivered to tormentors. My heart could not contain my hate for such a mother, a hatred beyond the power of words to express."

The woman across from me blinked rapidly again, but she stayed wordless. She hadn't learned patience the same way I had, but she knew its value.

"And now," I told her, "now, when it is

436

too late, I finally know the truth. My mother was no prostitute; she was a slave. She was not only my mother, she was also my sister. Do you understand?"

"Your father . . . !?"

"Yes. The . . . creature whose seed I carry, he began raping my mother when she herself was just a child. She was not his daughter; she was his property. Just as you are your husband's property.

"When my mother learned she was about to give birth, she ran. Not for *her* life, for *mine.* When she left me in that hospital, she believed she was giving me a chance. A chance she never had, and never would. And then she went back to the life she had been cursed to live. She stayed in that fire until it swallowed her alive."

The woman across from me nodded. Not saying, "I get it"; saying, "I would do the same."

"Maybe my mother dreamed of meeting me someday," I said, sadly. "Maybe reading about me in the newspapers, hearing about some wonderful thing I had done. And she would say to herself, 'That is my son. He will never know that I gave my life for him, but *I* know, and that is enough.' "

Her mask wanted to crack, but she held it in place by the same force that had guided the maybe-mythical mother I had been telling her about.

"I have spent my whole life as a criminal," I continued, now in a just-the-facts cadence. "What saved me from becoming a vile monster was not my mother, it was my family. Understand me, please. I speak not of a blood family; my blood is so diseased from my father's filth that I had surgery performed on myself to make certain I could never create a child."

The woman across from me made a sound without moving her lips.

"I *found* a family," I told her. "It took me a long time. The woman behind you, the one who is cutting your hair so expertly, she is my sister. She chose me; I chose her.

"Our family was created at the intersection of our paths. I found love then. But I never stopped believing that it wasn't the government who had sentenced me to a life of torture as a child — it was my own mother.

"In prison, alone at night, I used to wish I could meet her someday. So I could tell her what she had done to me . . . before I killed her."

A tear formed at the corner of the Princess's eye, but she still embraced her silence as if it was an amulet against evil itself.

"Your son was taken by an al-Qaeda cell," I told her, switching too quickly for her to throw up a shield. "A cell that has been planted here for years. Such men are much too valuable to be wasted on suicide missions."

My tone was without emotion, a tour guide pointing out exhibits.

I was back to pure truth. Pryce had delivered his little lecture about the banzai pilots sent to their certain deaths, as if those were the *only* planes the Japanese had. But the Imperial Navy also had a fleet of their infamous Zeros. Those sky-dominators were reserved for ace pilots, not human sacrifices. And *those* pilots weren't sent out to die; they were sent out to kill.

The no-choice robots who dive-bombed the Twin Towers were unskilled labor. For top-level work, you need Zero pilots. Such men are not bound by the same rules as the expendables. If one of them feels like having a few drinks to relax after a hard day's work serving Allah, so be it.

To a war commander, the higher the skill level, the higher the tolerance for off-duty conduct. Your best sniper has a preference for little girls, your top chopper-pilot's hobby is rape — so what? It's *your* men they're protecting; that's not just their job, it's yours, too. Your only one. Always been that way; always will be.

"You *paid* them to take him, Aabidah Amatullah," I said, careful not to call her by her title. "In your mind, in your *heart,* you were throwing your child from a burning building. Yes, he might later die in battle, but he would die a man. A *man,* not the hideous beast your husband was training him to be."

Her sharp intake of breath was like a blast of luminol on bloodstains.

"You knew all about *that* training, Aabidah Amatullah. And your mother's heart could never allow such filth to infect your son. Better a desert fighter than a prince, yes? Better honor than degeneracy.

"You knew Allah would never accept your husband. He chose his life; he will have to answer for that choice. But to bar your son from Allah's grace, this you, his true mother, could never allow. So, you see, I *do* understand."

She still held her silence tight against the hideous spirits my words had let loose in that room.

But she bowed her head. Saying nothing, confirming everything. "But *you* do not understand." I spoke very quietly, every word leaden with grief. "Mothers offer their

440

children for adoption every day. That is often an act of heroism. They want another life for their child than the one they are doomed to themselves. But they can never really know," I said, thinking of how a creature who would be despised by jackals had "adopted" Lisa Steinberg years ago. And how not one damn thing had changed since then.

"But there is no such mystery for your son, Aabidah Amatullah," I struck mercilessly. "He will never become a warrior! No, he will be raised in fear and torture, as I was. Those who took him, they will bring their prize back to the training camps, and present him to the Taliban. 'Here is the firstborn male child of Prince Fazid el Kandal.' What do *you* think will happen then?"

She tried to freeze her face against the intrusion, but I could see every terror-frisson as it burst in her eyes. I leaned forward, thick sinuous venom now coating my voice as I opened the cage to let each terrifying word slither toward her.

"What joy those who loathe everything your husband represents will feel as they castrate your son! His horrible screams when they shove a hot iron inside his body will be music to their hearts! And it will all be videotaped, so that those who dare oppose them can know the true meaning of terror."

She was shuddering with soundless sobs. I felt nothing. All I saw was an opponent. Against the ropes, bleeding. *Close the show!* I heard the Prof scream from ringside.

"Your child can *never* be one of them, Aabidah Amatullah. If he lives — and he probably will not — he will be used all his life by grinning perverts. His pain will be their ultimate thrill.

"And each time they torture him, he will be told that his mother sold him into slavery to buy herself another diamond necklace. That lie will make him hate you with every sobbing breath he takes. Allah may forgive you. Of this, I know nothing. But your son — and this I *do* know — your only son, he never will. This is inside me, this truth. Look for yourself," I challenged her.

She met my eyes. I watched as the unspeakable penetrated her heart. Her hands were soaking in some kind of lotion bowls Michelle had placed on the arms of her chair, but she wouldn't have moved anyway — her body was in rigor.

I was empty. Couldn't even raise my hands to punch again.

It was so quiet I could hear my heart.

"What other possible choice . . . ?" she finally whispered.

"Your son is still here," I whispered in return, knowing if I had been wrong about that she would have stopped listening a long time ago. "I don't know how you contacted the al-Qaeda cell, and I don't want to know. But I know they didn't come over here just to take your son; they had another mission, a mission yet to be completed. So they are still here. And they still have Ghazi. They would not dare to harm him themselves. Such pleasures belong only to masters, not servants.

"Your baby is worth a fortune to them if delivered untouched, Princess. He is *merchandise,* and the more pristine the condition, the higher the price," I said, watching the nightmare I was painting drain the blood from her face.

That gave me the strength I needed to strike again. "Their reward for allowing their leaders to mock the name that your husband gave his son will be great. To them, they will have performed a holy act . . . and will be well paid for it. But they cannot just ship your son out of this country. That takes planning, and planning takes time.

"Only one thing can change this, Aabidah Amatullah, mother of Ghazi," I said, as if taking an oath. "If you love your only son enough to tell me where they are keeping him now, he will be returned to you."

She raised her head, laser-lanced my eyes. "And those who . . . those who have him, they will die?"

"No. They will be paid. Money is their only true god. You already know this. Why try to block that truth? They took *your* money, didn't they?"

"A ransom? And my husband would return to his —"

"A ransom will be paid, yes. A fortune for those who took him, and *their* masters will never know what they did. But your husband will not pay this ransom."

As confusion glazed her eyes, I threw my finisher, putting everything I had left behind it: "I swear this to you on all that is sacred. If you save your baby now, your husband will never poison his soul again. Never."

"You are saying . . . ?"

"Yes," I said, not knowing if she would hear a threat or a promise in the word.

"How do I know any of what you say is true?"

"You threw your son out of a burning building, into the black night below. I have let you see into that night. I have told you things no man says aloud, especially to a woman. Your blood is burning now. That is your heart, telling you the truth. You know it *now.*

"I have shown you your son's future. That future sits across from you; it speaks through my mouth. Ask Allah if I lie. He will answer. Ask him *now.* If you truly want to save your child, you have been shown the way."

"You might be his . . . employee yourself."

"If I was, you have already said enough to guarantee that the only person on this earth who truly loves Ghazi will die. You know what your husband would do with you. It would be a thousand times worse than the Haya."

She closed her eyes.

As Michelle worked on the Princess's shoulders, I reached deeper, enveloping her silently in the truth of my hate.

It seemed as though hours passed before she decided. I don't know who or what she was listening to when she finally spoke.

Her voice never quavered. The power of a mother's love ripped through every word of the address she spat out.

"Police Operator 2193. Where is the emergency?"

"Right on the corner, just across from the —"

"What borough are you calling from?"

"Borough? This is the City. The fuck's wrong with you people?"

"Sir, it would help if you would stay calm, all right? We need as specific a location as you can provide. If you —"

"Corner of Seventy-first and Third. Motherfuckers rolled up on this guy and just blasted him. He down on the sidewalk, blood all over, *okay?*"

"Personnel are responding, sir. If I could please have your —"

The caller hung up. No surprise to the 911 operator; happens all the time.

By then, calls would be flooding in from a dozen different locations within the same sector. Central Command might get the joke, but they'd figure it for professionals at work: a jewel heist in progress, a bank drill-through . . . something like that. When all you need is misdirection, you don't care *which* wrong direction your opponent picks.

But way before anyone could even start to analyze the pattern, the Prince would have covered the ground from his set-back doorway all the way down the path to the front gate, surrounded by his bodyguards. All he had to do was step on the sidewalk and climb into the waiting limo.

He was on three different kinds of visual

as he strolled, every self-assured movement monitored.

Buttons were pushed.

One of them signaled Pryce.

The explosion blasted across the headlines. Seven lives lost. The Prince, five of his servants, and a jaywalking civilian.

But the papers were late with the news. Person or persons unknown had already sent a JPEG of the blast scene to Al Jazeera, with

בּוֹגֵד

plastered in see-through symbols across the face of the photo.

Whoever sent that JPEG was a champion cyber-slinger. The symbols had been embedded within the digitized image; any attempt to Photoshop them out would erase the whole thing.

Al Jazeera ran it as received. Maybe because they're actual journalists, not the propaganda tools some say they are. Maybe because their attempts to remove the embed failed, and they knew if they didn't run it someone else would.

Maybe they just wanted to be first.

Not my problem. Let the al-Qaeda hon-chos argue over why whoever blew up a Saudi sheikh and his whole entourage had written "traitor" across the photo of the carnage.

In Hebrew.

"There were only four of them there when we hit the place," Pryce told me three days later. "Two survived. We extracted the baby, then waited for the others to show up.

"That was a *major* cell, in place for years, well before the current administration took office. All kinds of expertise there; probably the very best they had."

"You're a patriot and a half," I said, know-ing Pryce was just talking to thicken the fog. Taking out a few terrorists meant as much to him as the citizen jaywalker who died in the same blast that had blown up the Prince. Cost of doing business.

"The Princess turned down our offer," he went on, as if I hadn't spoken. "We could have hidden her and her son so deep nobody could have found them. But she said she wanted to go home."

"You never know about some people," I said. "Those soldiers of Allah? when you searched their hideout, you happen to find any booze around?"

448

■ ■ ■ ■

Clarence was gone for a while. Trying out his new passport on a trip to Trinidad and Tobago. He had something important to say to Taralyn's mother.

We stayed low, but that was just out of habit. The "investigation" was a series of jurisdictional battles. Best way to prove it wasn't your fault was to be given the job of finding out whose fault it was.

It turned out like one of those nuclear-warfare child custody cases. You know, where the parents are bull elephants in mating season and the kid's the grass that gets trampled under them as they duke it out.

What *did* finally come to light was instantly spun so many times by so many different "reporters" in so many different ways that you'd get vertigo just from listening.

But why bother listening? Every Internet-twit knows there's only one place to find *ultimate* truth: they were waiting for the movie to come out.

Michelle told Clarence that only a red diamond would be acceptable. White was so totally yesterday. And nowhere near rare enough, either.

"But, my sister, this one would cost —"

The Prof sadly shook his head at Clarence's pitiful attempt to assert himself.

"Get used to it, boy," was all the backup he offered.

White wasn't totally yesterday to Taralyn, not when it came to her wedding dress.

And the marriage *was* going to be in a church.

Michelle was only placated by the promise that she could go along to shop for the gown. And that she wouldn't have to wear a bridesmaid's dress.

When the Prof walked Taralyn down the aisle on a fresh spring day, there were a lot of people in the church whose faces I didn't recognize. Taralyn's mother, some of her family members . . . and a man with webbed fingers.

The reverend wasn't in the Prof's class, but that didn't matter; nobody was there to listen to him.

Terry stood tall, bracketed by the Mole and Michelle. Flower glowed between Immaculata and Max. Mama had passed up Vera Wang for Susie Wong — her Mandarin-collar jade dress shimmered from neck to

450

ankles. And her eyes muted the whole outfit.

Rosie watched from Gateman's lap. Me and Gate wore matching suits. Only Clarence had been allowed to choose his own outfit, Michelle throwing him one last bone.

When the bronze limo pulled away with the new bride and groom inside, I knew none of us would be seeing Clarence for a while. And when we did, there wouldn't be a semi-auto under his jacket.

"It's all done, son," the Prof said, just before sunrise. But I knew he was only talking about one piece of it.

I don't know what's next. I can't hear the whistle yet, but I can feel the vibrations through the tracks.

A freight train's coming, and I'm going to hop it blind. I don't know what it's carrying, but I know it'll take me to where I need to go.

Another life.

ABOUT THE AUTHOR

Andrew Vachss has been a federal investigator in sexually transmitted diseases, a social-services caseworker, a labor organizer, and has directed a maximum-security prison for "aggressive-violent" youth. Now a lawyer in private practice, he represents children and youths exclusively. He is the author of numerous novels, including the Burke series, two collections of short stories, and a wide variety of other material including song lyrics, graphic novels, essays, and a "children's book for adults." His books have been translated into twenty languages, and his work has appeared in *Parade, Antaeus, Esquire, Playboy,* the *New York Times,* and many other forums. A native New Yorker, he now divides his time between the city of his birth and the Pacific Northwest.

The dedicated Web site for Vachss and his work is www.vachss.com.

The employees of Thorndike Press hope you have enjoyed this Large Print book. All our Thorndike, Wheeler, and Kennebec Large Print titles are designed for easy reading, and all our books are made to last. Other Thorndike Press Large Print books are available at your library, through selected bookstores, or directly from us.

For information about titles, please call:
(800) 223-1244

or visit our Web site at:
http://gale.cengage.com/thorndike

To share your comments, please write:
Publisher
Thorndike Press
295 Kennedy Memorial Drive
Waterville, ME 04901